Prize Stories 1972:
THE O. HENRY AWARDS

Prize Stories 1972:

THE O. HENRY AWARDS

Edited and with an Introduction by

WILLIAM ABRAHAMS

Doubleday & Company, Inc., Garden City, New York

1972

CONTENTS

PUBLISHER'S NOTE

This volume is the fifty-second in the O. Henry Memorial Award series.

In 1918, the Society of Arts and Sciences met to vote upon a monument to the master of the short story, O. Henry. They decided that this memorial should be in the form of two prizes for the best short stories published by American authors in American magazines during the year 1919. From this beginning, the memorial developed into an annual anthology of outstanding short stories by American authors published, with the exception of the years 1952 and 1953, by Doubleday & Company, Inc.

Blanche Colton Williams, one of the founders of the awards, was editor from 1919 to 1932; Harry Hansen from 1933 to 1940; Herschel Brickell from 1941 to 1951. The annual collection did not appear in 1952 and 1953, when the continuity of the series was interrupted by the death of Herschel Brickell, who had been the editor for ten years. Paul Engle was editor from 1954 to 1959 with Hanson Martin co-editor in the years 1954 to 1956; Mary Stegner in 1960; Richard Poirier from 1961 to 1966, with assistance from and co-editorship with William Abrahams from 1964 to 1966. William Abrahams became editor of the series in 1967.

Doubleday also publishes *First-Prize Stories from the O. Henry Memorial Awards* in editions which are brought up to date at intervals. In 1970 Doubleday also published under Mr. Abrahams' editorship, *Fifty Years of the American Short Story,* a collection of stories selected from the series.

The stories chosen for this volume were published in the period from the summer of 1970 to the summer of 1971. A list of the magazines consulted appears at the back of the book. The choice of stories and the selection of prize winners are exclusively the responsibility of the editor. Biographical material is based on information provided by the contributors.

INTRODUCTION

We are into the 1970s—but I suspect that even the most enthusiastic dispenser of labels would be forced to agree that it is too soon in the decade to speak of a "70s story," as it differs from a "60s story" or will differ from an "80s story," even assuming that one were inclined to do so and believed that styles in art are as subservient to the next page of the calendar as women's fashions. I will content myself here, introducing the 52nd collection in the series, with less "epochal" discriminations, and begin at the point where misunderstandings about the O. Henry Awards most often arise—with the ground rules and procedures governing the Awards themselves.

At the end of the present volume, as in each of its predecessors, there is a list of Magazines Consulted. From among the nine hundred and fifty-four stories that first appeared in their pages the choice of the prize-winning stories is made. The responsibility for that choice belongs to the Editor; but the list of Magazines Consulted reflects no prior editorial selection or prejudice. Any magazine publishing fiction that sends copies to the Editor of the O. Henry Awards is automatically included in the list of Magazines Consulted, and its stories are carefully read. This has been standard practice since the Awards were established in 1919. All magazines, the large and the small alike and regardless of their editorial bent or publishing auspices, are welcomed. But since, as a glance at the list of Magazines Consulted will suggest, the greater number of magazines published in America today are not in general circulation and not easily obtained, it is virtually impossible for the Editor to inform himself of their existence unaided. Accordingly, in the future as in the past, the initiative must come from the magazines themselves; and it is hoped that magazines newly born or about-to-be-born will not hesitate to make themselves known.

Once the magazines are in hand, the editorial process begins. Certain stories are automatically ruled out, for the choice is restricted, as it has been from the inception of the Awards, to stories written in English (no translations) by American authors that were published in magazines (usually American) during the preceding twelve-month period, from one summer to the next—in this volume the earliest of the stories included was published in July 1970, the latest in July 1971.

Logically, and by custom, the First, Second and Third Prize stories lead off the collection. Thereafter, however, the stories are arranged in an order that is meant to show them to best advantage—especially to that perhaps mythical reader who goes straight through from first page to last. Considerations of variety in subject matter, length and style, do enter into the arrangement, but there is no question of relative rank or merit: none is intended and none should be inferred from a story's place in the table of contents.

There are two further misapprehensions that I would like to clear up, if possible. The first has to do with a supposed editorial preference for stories from one or another group of magazines; the second with the notion that the stories have been chosen to fit a "theme" or to illustrate a "tendency" decided upon by the editor in advance. Neither has any basis in fact.

One chooses stories, not the magazines that publish them; and good stories are not so easily come by that one can afford to overlook any possible source, "little" or "large." In the present volume there are eighteen stories, eight from the "little" magazines, ten from the "large"; but it was purely chance that the stories should have divided in this fashion. (As regular readers of the collection will recall, however, in recent years the balance has consistently favored the "little" magazines; and so I think I should say, with a proper degree of caution, that it seems to me the quality of fiction in some of the magazines of very large circulation has noticeably improved. The so-called "slick" story, manufactured according to formula and once synonymous with those magazines, is no longer ubiquitous, perhaps because the readers who wanted it are happier now with the TV version—whatever the reason, it means that their editors can fill the limited space allotted to fiction with such remarkable stories as Margery Finn Brown's "In the Forests of Riga the Beasts Are Very Wild Indeed.")

As for the themes and tendencies that may be thought to emerge from the stories collected here, they were not settled upon as a predetermined requirement for entry into the collection, nor willed into being to give it an effect of unity that might otherwise be absent. I am not at all persuaded that such a "unity" is desirable, and even if it were, I am doubtful that it exists. Having said this, I must appear to contradict myself, for it is inevitable that there will be some quality or characteristic common to all these stories: at the least, what it is that makes them contemporary.

After all, we are not choosing from among the short fictions of a long period, when the spirit of the age in which they were written has become historic and in the light of hindsight is easily defined. The stories in this volume were written at the beginning of the 1970s, after a decade of war in Vietnam and all those other public pressures that bear down on the individual life in our time—violence, racial hatred . . . but even to begin to list them is to fall back upon stereotypes. What is unexpected—but also, upon reflection, understandable—is how insistently these stories have turned away from public and towards private concerns. Only Joyce Carol Oates in her coruscating "Saul Bird Says: Relate! Communicate! Liberate!" appears to be dealing with an explicitly public subject—the turmoil on campus that has become a standard feature of contemporary university life—but in fact, Saul Bird, her grotesque but all too believable protagonist, is a monster of egotism whose "politics," however *chic* and momentous-seeming, are dedicated to no more than the gratification and advancement of Saul Bird. So that ultimately Miss Oates's story, too, is private in its concerns: the terrible emptiness in the lives of Wanda Barnett and Erasmus Hubben that they, deluded souls, imagine Saul Bird will somehow magically fill.

I have said that the turning away from public concerns is unexpected, given their weight and omnipresentness, but it is also understandable. For the inescapable pressures that the public world, the world we live in, imposes upon each of us, have come to be taken for granted. They no longer need to be explicated or specifically responded to. Which is not to say that they are ignored: the contemporary story is not written in an ivory tower. But the background (the condition of modern life) beyond the background (the condition of one particular life) can be taken as a shared assumption of writer and reader: we know too well what is in the air we breathe.

In Donald Barthelme's fable of dehumanization, "Subpoena"; in Judith Rascoe's "Small Sounds and Tilting Shadows," with its plaintive, reiterated questions, "Who's there . . . who are you . . . who's there?"; in so many of these stories, one recognizes the determination to salvage as much of the individual life as is still possible in an age where individuality becomes a kind of eccentricity, and the self promises to be supplanted by the mass-self. (No wonder, then, that so many of the characters in these stories, merely by being themselves, seem "odd.")

The theme and the tendency are exemplified and most fully realised in the very beautiful story by John Batki, "Strange-Dreaming Charlie, Cow-Eyed Charlie," to which I have awarded First Prize. Since reading this story at the time of its publication in *The New Yorker,* I have read it numberless times, always with pleasure, and at each reading discovering further rewards, further subtleties. In the circumstances, I am reluctant to shrink it down to make a point, or to attach a label to it, and do so only tentatively and with the certainty that whoever reads and rereads this story will find in it more than I begin to suggest. Mr. Batki himself alludes to Fitzgerald, and the story reflects not so much Fitzgerald's *influence* (as would have been the case, say, twenty years ago) as his having been assimilated into the literary tradition— the tradition that Mr. Batki, with this story, promises to join. But Jay (surely the echo of Jay Gatsby is intentional?), the hero of this story of the 1970s, is pursuing a different dream than those that excited Fitzgerald and his characters: simply to "dream," to be free to dream, in opposition to the "daily rounds of scientific worship" in the great hospital whose corridors "hide a secret enemy, the omniscient White Sheep." There is a memorable encounter when "Jay, from the corner of his eye, catches a glimpse of the furtive villain he has been after. It is none other than the White Sheep, the wise old White Sheep, oppressor of dreams . . . 'Give me your dreams, my son,' says the White Sheep, who is expressionless and radiating doom." And earlier there has been his encounter with the sensible spokesman of the anti-dream real world:

'Jay,' said the Dean, 'we have been rather puzzled by your failure to live up to your potential. Is it a lack of interest or could it perhaps be some special problem with which we could help you?'

Jay understood. But asking for psychiatric help seemed absurd; he knew that Abnormal Psychology defined the norm as 'maximal personal and social adjustment in keeping with long-term social welfare.' He already had more than enough of that. Now was the time to paint your hair blue and drive a yellow wagon all the way to L.A. This was quite impossible to explain to the Dean . . .

Jay's allegiance is with the gypsies—"A gypsy woman nursed him, that is why he has wings"—and in a world of triumphant hussars, there is a conscious choice to be made. When, at the story's end, Jay spreads his wings and makes his marvelous dream-flight over Central Park, it is a gesture of escape, not escapism: he knows what he is giving up. And when he comes down to earth, it is not to pay heed to the rhetoric of the opinion-makers and politicians ("As we move into a generation of peace, as we blaze the trail toward the new prosperity, I say to every American . . ."), but the morning song of the sparrows. There is something cleansing and reassuring in those bird-syllables: "Chirple. Cheep. Christle. Creep. Pip. Chip. Wheep."

—WILLIAM ABRAHAMS

Prize Stories 1972:
THE O. HENRY AWARDS

JOHN BATKI was born in Hungary in 1942. He received his B.A. from Columbia College in 1964 and his M.A. from Syracuse University in 1969. His home is Syracuse, New York.

STRANGE-DREAMING CHARLIE, COW-EYED CHARLIE

JAY came back to Celeste, to New York City, and to the start of his first year in medical school. He came from a summer in Europe that was highlighted by the tame sparrows of St. James's Park, the stag beetles of the Boboli Gardens, and a hedgehog discovered at midnight on a street in Copenhagen. He told Celeste about all of these, not forgetting to mention the remaining parts of the memory clusters—Jane, Sylvia, and Ingrid. (Jane, standing on a bridge, feeding sparrows from her hand, exclaimed to Jay, nearby with a camera, "Oh, Mother will never believe this!" Sylvia, anxious to leave Florence, said to him, "Let's go to Burgenland." And Ingrid was Jay's roommate for a week.) But he still thought he loved Celeste alone. She, on her part, told him about her summer at a New England art camp, about the pot she smoked, the dances she danced, and the artists she met, although she did not say a word about one artist in particular, whose name was Larry. She invited Jay for a weekend at her parents' place on Long Island, and this set his mind at ease. He spent his first night at the medical-school dorm in a friendly discussion of titration curves with his new classmates, Shaffer and Carapella.

He had been uneasy in Europe, because he had received only two letters from Celeste all summer. The letters, which followed him through several countries, were shortish, with a detached kind of cheerfulness. ("I am glad the wooing pigeons of London can go on wooing undisturbed by you.") Jay thought a lot that summer about a gift for Celeste, and finally, in Florence, he found just the right bracelet for her, but on the way back, in Innsbruck or perhaps in Vienna, the bracelet disappeared from his suitcase—a souvenir too tempting for one of the chambermaids in a succession of cheap hotels and student residences. Jay felt ashamed for suspecting them without proof, he felt ashamed for having anything worth being stolen, and he felt ashamed for returning in September with a gift as practical and nondescript as a leather handbag.

That weekend in the country, in the middle of September, Jay was still full of the summer, Europe, and the paintings of Carel Fabritius. Although Celeste appeared to be somewhat aloof, it could still happen then, while everyone was resting or sprucing up for dinner, when the air was filled with lotions and notions. It could still happen then: he saw her small car as an exotic conch, before tasting, with surprise, the bitterish taste of seashells. Earlier on that warm afternoon, they had gone for a swim, the last outdoor swim of the season, after a game of mixed, intergenerational doubles, in which Celeste proved to be a sulking partner, apparently resenting a certain flashiness in Jay's play (at the net, he jumped for some volleys that could have been reached easily), and her parents ended up winning the set. But it could still happen then, upstairs in the big house with Louis XVI furniture, when late-summer scents and stillness hung in the air, and the thick, mossy carpets swished and muffled all footsteps. In the room next to his, she stood half dressed and making funny little faces while she tried on her mother's long evening gowns (mother bustier), very low cut, that left her back and shoulders bare, and he helped her put them on and take them off, the soft carpet muffling their footsteps. Her door had been left ajar, and a mirror's glint shimmered through the opening; somewhere down the hall, faucets were turned on and off, and the voices of other guests rose from a distance. Her door was left ajar, and he entered, and the door sighed, and the mirror sighed, and the carpet swished and sucked its breath, long and deep. It could still happen then.

In a corner of the shuttered room upstairs, there is a pair of giltwood armchairs with oval backs and padded arms and elegant, fluted legs. Jay sits down in one of them.

"They are signed by Jean-René Nadal the Elder," says Celeste.

The period's leading cabinetmaker, she goes on to explain, was Georges Jacob. He worked mostly in mahogany, although the small oval writing table is made of kingwood and pearwood. Celeste points out the three slim drawers and the breccia marble top. Could it be that Maître Georges was also a poet on the side? That is a matter of sheer conjecture; the fact is that he worked mostly in mahogany.

And what do we know about Carel Fabritius besides the fact that he died in the Delft explosion of 1654, at the age of thirty-two, and that less than a dozen of his paintings survive today? Well, we know that in his small self-portrait at the Boymans-van Beuningen Museum in Rotterdam Fabritius devotes seemingly more loving care to the rough, gritty surface of the well-lit wall behind him than to his own face, which is bathed in semi-darkness. And when asked what is the first rule of good composition, Carel Fabritius answered, "To select and organize the finest things in nature" (*"de edelste natuerlijkheden"*). Jay would like to provide Celeste with more details, but it is time for dinner.

The other guests that weekend were two actors, an art dealer and his wife, and a painter with a studio nearby. The actors by their sheer presence—Jay couldn't help but notice—somehow disqualified their performance. They seemed to vitiate their own existence by innumerable tiny exaggerations—a barely noticeable lilt of speech here, a slightly greater than expected tilt of the head there, or perhaps an ever so insignificantly heightened stress, or a somewhat teetering sway or shuffle. And that seemed to be catching. At dinner, Jay's right-hand neighbor, the art dealer's wife, turned to him with a sudden flash of her frosted blond hair and a challengingly engaging smile—her dark eyebrows knitted and her handsome steel-blue eyes narrowed into an ultra-intense glance that was at the same time not without an ambiguous tinge of irony—merely to pose a question about his field of study. Having found out that Jay was in his first year at medical school, she showed her apparent uninterest by resuming her conversation with her husband across the table, and discussing, with an air of burning urgency, the problem of whether their Christmas was to be spent in Switzerland or St. Croix. A few moments later, taking Jay by surprise, she shot in his direction a glance that appeared to be laden with significance and was perhaps even accompanied by a hint of a smile. Then, inexplicably, she performed an abrupt motion with her hips that, accidentally or not, hitched her short skirt even higher up on her nut-brown thighs.

Once, in his childhood, which was spent in a small country in Eastern Europe, Jay saw the single, smooth movement made by a gypsy woman as she opened her blouse and flipped out her breast to the child in her lap. Gypsies, he was told, wander in the night. Most of them live by begging, he was told. At times, they have been known to take children with them, and people say they can steal a chicken in the bat of an eyelash. Then, too, they are notorious for their hypnotic and magic powers, their rank sexuality, their crooked teeth. A gypsy woman hypnotizes a chicken by drawing a chalk line on the ground. Farm animals look on the gypsies with mistrust; they won't be marching with *them* on the winding road to Heaven, not with those gypsies. The winding road to Heaven is reserved for hussars—the handsome Blue Hussars, with their blue dolmans hanging from their shoulders in devil-may-care fashion, and the daring Red Hussars on their prancing steeds. They are on their way to Heaven, toward the high castle in the clouds. The farm animals also march with them in ranks of unbroken, devoted solidarity; some are even carrying banners. The chickens, the geese, the ducks, the pigs, the sheep, the cows, and the old faithful puli. Even the yellow canary marches along, carrying her cage. And none of these good domestic animals would dare to be caught marching with a gypsy. But then, gypsies don't march much. They just go on telling fortunes, flaunting their sexuality, and sharpening their teeth with files. However, their musicians are superb. And why does Nanny sing the song "A gypsy woman nursed him, that is why he has wings"?

Even though Jay is too busy at medical school to see Celeste often, he sees her face every day. The childishly long bangs of her smooth dark hair hang with a Cleopatra straightness across her eyebrows, and her pose has an archaic, Egyptian frontality. Her solemn dark eyes look straight back at him, perhaps with a touch of mistrust. Her lips are set in a subtle pout, a hint of a pout in the manner of Leonardo. She sits there, immersed within herself, sunk back in an old wood-and-canvas garden chair, in the summer sun and shadows, wearing a tiny one-piece bathing suit. Her knees are drawn up; her hands are clutching her ankles. The grainy black and gray shadows of leaves are fixed for all time on her smooth child's skin. Her shapely thighs are the thighs of a little girl. She looks at Jay in tones of silver, in soft gradations of gray and white, from the frame of the mirror on the dresser in his room; in the photograph, Celeste is five years old.

In medical school, Jay and his colleagues, neatly dressed in ties and white jackets, go through the daily rounds of scientific worship. They meditate on twentieth-century Western koans. The pentose phosphate shunt. Polyfunctional catalysis of mutarotation by alpha-hydroxypyridine. The Meerwein-Ponndorf-Verley Reaction. How do the thalamic projection systems control the activity of corticospinal neurons? In matutinal sessions, the students chant, "The terpenes are geraniol, limonene, borneol, pinene, camphene, farnesol, bisabolene, cedrene." They pronounce magic names: entropy, enthalpy. They ponder the mysteries of birdlike ornithine, deathly cadaverine, exotic shikimic acid. Jay's favorite amino acids are silvery arginine, asparagusy asparagine, hysterical histidine, proletarian proline, throbbing threonine, tyrannical tyrosine. His head bent over the physiology text, he hears his father's voice from the past: "What are you doing, my son? Drawing a diagram of the middle ear? Good, my son. Just keep working. . . ."

And the weight of his father's friendly hand remains on Jay's shoulder. He raises his head to recite the prayer of the senses: gustation, olfaction, vision, audition, taction, baresthesis, thalposis, algesis, kinesthesis, tickle sense, vibration sense, vertigo sense, sexual sense, fatigue sense, common sense. At lectures, additional cabalistic words and diagrams appear on the blackboard. The words are written out and they turn into observances, rituals; they fill lives, these signs and symbols written by the hand of a stranger who could be a maniac. The students sit and watch in silence, and learn their lesson. In the middle of the lecture, Jay writes on the margin of his notebook, *"Il pleut doucement sur la ville."* And, "Earwax tastes bitter."

A patient, a balding, flabby man in his forties, sits in front of the students. He is complaining of complete ptosis of the right eyelid, absent left corneal sensation, greatly impaired pain, thermal, and tactile sense over the left side of the face, weakness and atrophy of the left temporal and masseter muscles, deviation of the jaw to the left on opening the mouth, coarse intention tremor with accompanying coarse intentions, dysmetria, and difficulty in performing rapid successive movements of the left extremities. The students are asked, after the man is led away, to decide which section of the brain stem contains the irreversible lesions that account for the above symptoms. Irreversible, that is, by means known to medical science.

Yet Jay wants to know each little part of the human body by its name. Volumes of Sobotta's "Atlas of Human Anatomy" lie scattered over his bed. Celeste, covered only by Jay's robe, is examining the illustrations of the body's hidden parts. Then, for a study break, they go down to the swimming pool in the basement of the dormitory building. Sitting by the poolside, Peter Hodgkin winks at Jay and eyes Celeste with admiration. He tells Jay, "I'll take her any time." Under his breath, Jay answers, "I wish I had her to give away."

Late in October, Jay took Celeste to a little club in the East Fifties, where a devilishly soft and nonchalant trio was playing

"Smoke Gets in Your Eyes." The people in the club spoke in low tones, smoked, drank, acted confidential and intimate. Everyone, without exception, would every once in a while touch his or her own face. That was fun to watch; it was a Fitzgeraldian game, new to Celeste. But then Jay lost concentration; the thought overtook him that somewhere around the corner there was another place, another *boîte* with even dimmer lights and even softer music, where a husky-voiced chanteuse was perhaps singing, "Huggin' and a-kissin', oh, what we've been missin'. . . ." Thinking of this infinitely near, infinitely distant and twilit place, Jay asked Celeste if it was possible to have a true and sincere friendship between a man and a woman—yes or no, and if no why not? She was insulted, and withdrew into her shell—a shell whose harsh calcium reality had just dawned upon Jay.

Then, for days on end, Celeste was unreachable. She was off hunting for an apartment, she said, and she didn't need his help. Jay found it difficult to study and began to spend more time at night working in the hospital laboratory, while Celeste was presumably resting from the exhausting task of combing midtown Manhattan for a suitable apartment.

The time they went to Lincoln Center, to the film festival, could perhaps be called their last date. After the movie, they had a drink. He shouldn't have asked her to come up to his place, but he did. She said no—not angrily but with a sullen force that shook his defenses and opened undefendable breaches in his inner bastions, through which the invading Turks could pour in with ease by day or enter under cover of dark. He already saw those hours of lonely waiting in the dark. His next question was a feeble effort to hold his position: "Are you going to spend the weekend with your parents?"

"No," she said. "I am seeing someone else."

The cold satisfaction of her voice left him defenseless. There were no more walls to hide behind. A cold wind was blowing through everything. Her long dark hair was streaming in front of her face; she hid behind it and looked away. They had stopped walking—she stopped first—and he lit a cigarette for her with some trouble. "I'll take the bus from here," she said, and he was afraid to offer to take her home. He was afraid of another "No." Then the bus pulled up. She stepped inside, taking a last drag on her cigarette, which she then unexpectedly handed to him. There was a puzzling flicker at the corners of her mouth. And then he was alone in the wind on the corner of the avenue, with a half-smoked cigarette, which he smoked down to the butt. Its tiny glow of warmth explained nothing. What had happened to the light in her eyes? It was gone. Then it could be told by her eyes? Yes, you could tell by her eyes.

After that, there were a few barren telephone conversations, one of which resulted in an invitation to her new apartment. Jay was introduced to Larry, who sat on the sofa for a few minutes and then tactfully went out to buy a paper. Jay watched Celeste silently prepare a gin-and-tonic. She wore dungarees and a red jersey. He drank the gin-and-tonic in quick gulps, and acted insanely neutral, saying at first nothing, then making falsely cheerful comments about the new apartment.

"What do you do nowadays?" he asked.

"I meditate," she answered.

He left after a few minutes, not even waiting for Larry to come back. Then, on a street below, a relentless dry hand grabbed his chest from the inside, then formed a tightly clenched fist in his throat. In the darkness, he looked up at their window near the top of the building. He knew more about that window than any of the other passersby, he thought. But then, perhaps each one of them had his own lit-up window in the night.

Dr. Wargoff, whose eyelids were thick and semi-lunar, tapped his pipe on the lectern to begin his lecture on dreams. "We who speak of the psychophysiology of dreams know that salami, sodas, and stomach gases are the stuff dreams are made on, heh, heh. Contrary to what you might think, dreaming is not a random and fortuitous phenomenon. Why, today the very idea of non-dreamers is obsolete! In 1955, Aserinsky and Kleitman monitored a sleeping subject by placing electrodes on the lateral and medial canthi.

And what did they find? That dreaming occurs simultaneously with rapid eye movements—abbreviated REM. The able French neuroanatomist Jouvet has even localized the site essential for dreaming in the cat—the nucleus reticularis pontis caudalis! You see, sections of the brain stem above this locus are not needed for dreams. Thus you find that a decorticate or decerebrate cat can still retire into blissful dreams with tail thrashing and whiskers twitching. By the way, Jouvet used these synonyms for dreaming: paradoxical sleep, REM sleep, rhombencephalic sleep, and hindbrain sleep. What is more important, Jouvet in 1961 showed that the same neuroanatomical centers control dreaming in man as in the cat. Of course, there remains the difficulty of defining dreaming itself, or, for that matter, the concept of 'depth of sleep.' But we have learned much from studies of sleep deprivation and dream deprivation. For example, after nights of dream deprivation there is a progressive increase in the number of 'dream attempts,' as seen from studies of cats on a treadmill. We hope that additions to our knowledge of dreaming will perhaps cast light on the nature of psychosis. Many researchers have already pointed out the similarities between psychotic episodes and dream-deprivation symptoms—such as visual, auditory, and somatic hallucinations, intrusive thoughts, bizarre verbal constructions and neologisms, paranoid delusions, and a failure to discriminate between fantasy and reality. In fact, Fisher and Dement in 1961 demonstrated that there is a striking increase in the number of dreams in the case of acute psychosis." Thus saying, Dr. Wargoff relit his pipe.

Dean Herardt and Jay had a sobering interview. As the Dean talked, Jay's thoughts ranged from the summer dance of the gypsies to the calm of Carel Fabritius's paintings and back to the mad whirl of molecules with magic names.

"Jay," said the Dean, "we have been rather puzzled by your failure to live up to your potential. Is it a lack of interest, or could it perhaps be some special problem with which we could help you?"

Jay understood. But asking for psychiatric help seemed absurd;

he knew that Abnormal Psychology defined the norm as "maximal personal and social adjustment in keeping with long-term social welfare." He already had more than enough of that. Now was the time to paint your hair blue and drive a yellow wagon all the way to L.A. This was quite impossible to explain to the Dean. And it would be awkward to drag in Celeste at this point. What would old Deano say?

"Otherwise, Jay, I am afraid I'll have to warn you about your academic standing."

"I see, sir. I'll try my best." He saw the Dean's three-piece gray Edwardian herringbone tweed suit, his modest tiepin, and his superbly buffed black brogues. Were these things even worth noticing? But somehow they were already inerasable in his mind.

Late one spring afternoon, after a demonstration of Einthoven's triangle, students stream out of Physiology Lab. Carrying their notebooks, they walk in the light of the setting sun, like a procession of ancient scholars bearing the hoarded wisdom of the ages down to the river. Jay, near the end of the line, imagines them followed by various stragglers, eidetic gypsies all—entertainers, gardeners, wanderers, who are calling to him to join them, to take his place with them. Then Sam Wickersham steps in front of him, and behind Wickersham is a black Rolls-Royce, parked by the curbside. It belongs to Wickersham's father, who is a physician. Wickersham is piling people into the Rolls, which is driven by a chauffeur named Mel. Jay gets in. The first stop is a bar on upper Broadway. When Wickersham offers Mel a drink, the chauffeur says, "But Mr. Sam, you know you shouldn't." He winks, grins and drinks.

The Rolls sails up the West Side Highway to a girls' college on the outskirts of the city. On the way, they make one more stop, at Jay's request, to pick up his friend called the Duke, whose considerable bulk is squeezed into the back seat. And when they see the neatly landscaped little campus in the failing light, they are both impressed.

"Wouldn't you like to be a gardener here?" Jay asks. A year ago, the Duke cut himself loose from school, and he has been living in freedom ever since. If he wanted to become a gardener here, he would really be free to do so. To be a gardener, to plant, to plow, to cultivate the shoots and gather the buds. Jay points to a flower. Ahead of them, on the gravel walk, a girl with solemn dark eyes is eating a chocolate candy bar in the last light of the evening.

Jay wanted to see a van Gogh exhibition at the Guggenheim Museum and, on an impulse, called up Celeste to invite her. To his surprise, she agreed to go. He was eating an ice-cream cone when she walked up to him in front of the museum, and he shivered in the heat of her sudden, voluntary closeness. Swallowing the ice cream became an incongruous, almost impossibly difficult task. He offered her some, but she refused. She wore a white dress and had an out-of-town suntan—Mediterranean, she explained. He found out that she and Larry had a new apartment and that they were going to Vermont for the summer, to build a house with another couple. Halfway through the museum, Jay realized that he was talking too much and with too much enthusiasm about the paintings. They stopped in front of a small oil—a dark branch with pink and white blossoms against a robin's-egg sky. The petals were painted in such thick impasto that they were in effect three-dimensional. Jay looked at the blossoms, trying to memorize each feature. Then he looked at Celeste. She was silent, and her mouth was set in an awkward, almost friendly expression. They walked on. Before they parted, she asked Jay if he still had her photograph, because she wanted it back. He promised to return it.

Jay first met Amy in the medical-school bookstore. Pretending to be thumbing through a book, he kept eying her blond hair. As he walked around the stalls, he kept looking back at her. She was small and slim, and her eyes made him think of a wildcat. Finally he settled on a Rembrandt book to buy. She was one of those girls with terrific legs and small breasts. (She knew all along that he was watching her, and he knew that she knew.) She flashed a bright smile at him. "What a pretty smile," he thought—and surprised himself by saying it out loud, looking straight into her eyes, facing her animal smile, her fox smile, her narrowing blue eyes and flashing teeth.

"Have we met somewhere before?" she asked.

"Perhaps in a dream," he answered, and felt proud, because it was good to find a girl who liked to be looked at and who showed her appreciation of appreciation; it was good to feel like a smooth conversationalist in early spring. She wore a nurse's uniform.

The hospital lab where Jay worked at night was constantly filled by a hum that was attributable to the air-conditioning, but that also contained the subtle undertone of the machinery of death. Over the hum, the patient voice of the paging system droned, "Inhalation Therapy, Inhalation Therapy." Someone always on his last breath. Through the microscope, Jay was studying blood cells—red blood cells, monocytes, lymphocytes. He was whistling softly. When he raised his head, he saw Amy, her little cap atop her blond hair, her impeccable figure in impeccable white. She smiled, and handed him a test tube. "I'm down in the Emergency Room," she said, and smiled.

During the night, behind the tangled curtains of dreamwork, the hospital corridors hide a secret enemy, the omniscient White Sheep. Jay is determined to find him. He progresses through the hum and whir of sardonic sighs in endless corridors, under the gray glare of neon lights, through trapdoors and torture chambers with skeletal frame beds that support pulsing, slurping coils of transparent tubes, soft stirrings, and untraceable moans. The walls exude hallucinogenic droplets of a thick yellowish fluid, visions vibrate out of obscure recesses, elevators whine and snap to attention with a startling whoosh. Doors open and close, moved by unseen hands. Then Jay, from the corner of his eye, catches a glimpse of the furtive villain he has been after. It is none other than the White Sheep, the wise old White Sheep, oppressor of dreams. With characteristic deceptiveness, the White Sheep pretends to be running from Jay, who is compelled to follow, although he knows this is a ruse. Then the doors close one by one: Jay is locked in, trapped face to face with the benevolent, calm, fatherly visage of the White Sheep. "Give me your dreams, my son," says the White Sheep, who is expressionless and radiating doom.

Toward five one morning, Jay visits the Emergency Room, where things are slow, and Amy is knitting a sweater. She welcomes him with fresh coffee, and asks about his plans for the coming day, which happens to be her day off. At six, her hand touches his, not accidentally. At seven-thirty, they leave the hospital, having decided to have breakfast in her nearby apartment instead of at the hospital cafeteria. At nine in the morning, Amy smiles at him through a few tears; her record-player is on, her clothes mostly off. Disarray and early sighs.

Jay wakes toward midafternoon. List of classes missed: Anatomy, Histology, Biochemistry, Embryology. It is almost too late to show up for Anatomy Lab.

In Anatomy Lab, Melchior Sweatham, who has not been to a single class in weeks, shuffles up to Jay and blinks at him. His face is unshaven; his scaly lips seem to mutter dark prayers. Then Sweatham invites him to a party. All around, people are bent over their dissecting tables, unwrapping dank cadavers from plastic bags for an afternoon's perusal of the prolapsed uteri of old age. The heavy smell of preservatives in the air. Jay looks at Melchior. Melchior nods his head of wild hair. Jay takes off his lab apron. He looks around. At the next table, Shaffer is patiently peeling fascia with scalpel and forceps. His four dissecting partners are completely engrossed in his work. Jay closes his dissecting manual with a snap: it is a goodbye.

The party that night was on Riverside Drive. It was still early, so Jay, Amy, and Melchior strolled on Broadway, past grocery stores and vegetable stands offering cabbages, hyacinths, and young tomatoes. "Hiya, hiya, hyacinths!" said Jay, and Amy laughed. It was that time of the day when the darkened silhouettes of rooftops swim against the western sky, which shades from apricot rose to a pale plum green, the color of green-gage. The first lights blazed stark lemon yellow in the black bulks of buildings on 110th Street between Broadway and Riverside. When they got to the corner building, they found they had to climb eleven flights to the apartment—elevator out of order. Inside, people in every corner, and smoke, smoke, smoke. The Duke was there, swaying, with a Swedish girl on one arm and a Norwegian girl on the other. A girl's voice sang a song that was new to Jay: "Strange-dreaming Charlie, cow-eyed Charlie, don't go chasing those girls. . . ." Then the smoke took over.

Through the smoke, Jay saw that he and Celeste were at some kind of outdoor performance, sitting high up in an amphitheatre. A rock group was making music down below—music that held the audience in absolute command. Most of the people there were high, smoking pot and freely passing around the joints. Jay wasn't; he had the sensation that he was only an onlooker, the only onlooker. Then the singers sang about a wild wandering gypsy, and as they neared the end of the song they began to strip; the lead guitarist was already completely naked. The audience, under a blazing sun, ecstatically followed their example. All around, people were jumping up, throwing off their clothes, and running down to the stage. Celeste, showing unusual energy, jumped up, too, and her clothes were off in a second. She cast a brief glance at Jay, who remained motionless, and then she vanished into the throng. The violence of loss vibrated in Jay's chest with the resonance of a painful twang on an electric guitar. He looked around in the smoke, and saw Amy embraced by someone. He did not care. He was far away.

Somewhere in the Park, he paused near a fence—the high wire fence behind the home plate of a baseball diamond—and suddenly found himself rising toward its top. He was flying! He looked down: a small group of people had already gathered below. They were pointing at him with agitated, outraged gestures, and he could hear a dark-uniformed official say, "There's another one of 'em!" They ran after him, having noticed that his flying ability was beginning to sag; he was dangerously close to the ground. But luckily

his descent was only momentary, and just when a burly man in
dark uniform was about to grab Jay's heel and bring him down to
earth, he took off with a powerful kick and soared high, out of
his reach. He flew by the museum, and, to his inexplicable delight, saw Dr. Wargoff walking on the Avenue. Jay, in the midst
of his flight, greeted Dr. Wargoff, but not with words and not
with silence. He inscribed circles of joyous flight in the sky over
the Park, over the city. As he flew, chaos subsided; order appeared. In his wake, poems and paintings dropped from the sky,
but no sculptures; he still remembered the weight of gravity. As
he soared higher and higher, summer blossomed out and exposed
the heated heart of the city and tired people flocking to its cool
extremities—to brooks, fields, lakes, beaches. High up there, Jay
knew he was free to send back to Celeste her photograph. He
floated above people's lives.

Jay landed unnoticed in a quiet corner of the Park, early in the
morning, when the shadows were still very long. Pigeons and squir-
rels began their daily rounds near his feet. He was drunk with
dawn, scared and alone. In a rumpled shirt and a crumpled jacket.
His shoes full of dust. What's needed is a morning song. At six
in the morning, each tree, each shrub, each blade of grass has
such a long shadow. An inverted twilight. And what do the sparrows say? Chirple. Cheep. Christle. Creep. Pip. Chip. Wheep.

JOYCE CAROL OATES has written many short stories, poems, and several novels, her most recent of which is *Wonderland*. In 1970 she won the National Book Award for Fiction with her novel *them*. Miss Oates was born near Lockport, New York; she received her B.A. from Syracuse University and her M.A. from the University of Wisconsin. She is an Associate Professor of English at the University of Windsor in Windsor, Ontario.

SAUL BIRD SAYS: RELATE!
COMMUNICATE! LIBERATE!

WANDA BARNETT, born in 1945, received her bachelor's degree at Manhattanville College of the Sacred Heart in 1965, as class valedictorian, received a fellowship from the University of Michigan for graduate studies in English in the fall of that year and, in the spring of 1969, accepted a temporary lectureship at Hilberry University, a school in southern Ontario with an enrollment of about 5000 students. On September 9, 1969, she met Saul Bird; someone appeared in the doorway of her office at the university, rapping his knuckles loudly against the door. Wanda had been carrying a heavy box of books, which she set down at once.

"How do you do, my name is Saul Bird," he said. He shook hands briskly with her. His voice was wonderfully energetic; it filled the narrow room and bounced off the empty walls, surrounding her. Wanda introduced herself, still out of breath from carrying the books; she smiled shyly. She leaned forward attentively, listening to Saul Bird, trying to understand what he was saying. He talked theatrically, elegantly. His voice wound about her like fine ribbon. She found herself stooping slightly so that she might seem less obviously taller than he.

"What are your values? Your standards? Everything in you will be questioned, eroded here, every gesture of spontaneity—if you love teaching, if you love working with young people, you've certainly come to the wrong university. Are you a Canadian? Where are you from? Have you found an apartment? I can help you find one if you haven't."

"I have to look for an apartment today——"

"The economy is maniacal here. Are you a Canadian?"

"No, I'm from New York."

"Oh. New York." His voice went flat. He took time to light a cigarette and Wanda stared at him, bewildered. He had blond hair that was bunched and kinky about his face, like a cap; his face had looked young at first—the eyebrows that rose and fell dramatically, the expressive little mouth, the nose that twitched slightly with enthusiasm—but, really, it was the face of a 40-year-old, with fine, straight lines on the forehead and around the mouth. His complexion was both dark and pale—darkish pale, an olive hue, difficult to describe. He had a hot, busy, charming face. "I'm from New York, too. I don't actually approve—I want to state this clearly—of this university's persistent policy of hiring Americans to fill positions that could be filled by Canadians, though I myself am an American, but I hope not contaminated by that country's madness. I am going to form a committee, incidentally, to investigate the depth of the Americanization of this university. Do you have a Ph.D.?"

"I'm writing my dissertation now," Wanda said quickly.

"On what?"

"Landor."

"Landor," he said flatly. The set of his face was now negative. He did not approve. Wanda nervously wiped her hands on her skirt. With one foot, Saul Bird turned a box of books around to read their titles. "All this is dead. Dried crap."

She stared at him in dismay.

His eyes darted quickly about her office. His profile was stern, prompt, oddly morose; the lines deepened about the small mouth. "These books. This office. The desk you've innocently inherited— from Jerry Renling, whom you will never meet, since they fired him last spring for taking too much interest in his students. All this is dead, finished. Where is your telephone?"

He turned back abruptly to her, as if impatient with her slowness. She came awake and said, "Here, it's here, let me move all this. . . ." She tried to pick up another box of books, but the box gave way and some books fell onto the floor. She was very embarrassed. She cleared a space for him. He sat on the edge of her desk and dialed a number.

Wanda waited awkwardly. Should she leave her office while he telephoned? But he seemed to take no notice of her. His blond hair appeared to vibrate with electricity. On the bony ridge of his nose, his black-rimmed glasses were balanced as if by an act of fierce will. . . . Why was her heart pounding so absurdly? It was the abrasive charge of his voice—that demanding, investigative air—it put her in mind of men she had admired, public men she had known only from a distance, a meek participant in a crowd. Saul Bird had a delicate frame, but there was something powerful in the set of his shoulders and the precise, impatient way he dialed the telephone.

"Any messages there?" he said, without introducing himself. "What? Who? When will he call back?" He paused for a moment. Wanda brushed her short hair back nervously from her face. Was he talking to his wife? "We have four more signatures on the petition. Yes. I *told* you to forget about that. It's twelve-ten now; can you get down here at one and pick me up? Why not? There's someone here looking for an apartment——"

Wanda stared at him. At that moment, Saul Bird turned and smiled—fond, friendly, an intimate smile—or was she imagining it? He looked like a child in his dark turtleneck sweater and brown trousers. He wore sandals; the grimy straps looked gnawed. Wanda, in her stockings and new shoes, in her shapeless dress of dark cotton, felt foolishly tall in his sight: *Why* had she grown so tall?

When he hung up, he said, "My wife's coming. We'll find you an apartment."

"But I really don't——"

Someone appeared in the doorway, leaning in. "Saul?" He was a young man in a soiled trench coat.

"Come in, I've been waiting for you," Saul Bird said. He introduced Wanda to the young man. "Wanda, this is Morris Kaye in psychology, my friend 'K.' This is Wanda Barnett. Susannah and I are going to find her an apartment this afternoon."

"Something has come up. Can I talk to you?"

"Talk."

"But it's about—I mean——" The young man glanced nervously at Wanda. He was about 23, very tall, wearing a white T-shirt and shorts under his trench coat. His knees were pale beneath tufts of black hair. His face, dotted with small blemishes that were like cracked veins, had a strange glow, an almost luminous pallor. Wanda could feel his nervousness and shied away from meeting his eyes.

"We may as well introduce Wanda to the high style of this place," Saul Bird said. "I was given notice of nonrenewal for next year. Which is to say, I've been fired. Why do you look so surprised?"

Wanda had not known she looked surprised—but now her face twitched as if eager to show these men that she was surprised, yes. "But what? Why?"

"Because they're terrified of me," Saul Bird said with a cold smile.

Susannah Mayer Bird, born in 1929, earned doctoral degrees in both history and French from Columbia University. In the fall of 1958, she met and married Saul Bird. Their child, Philip, and Susannah's formidable book on Proust both appeared in 1959. The next year, Susannah taught at Brandeis, while Saul Bird taught at a small experimental college in California; the following year, they moved to Baton Rouge, where Susannah worked on her second book. When Saul Bird was dismissed from Louisiana State University, Susannah accepted an appointment at Smith College. The following year, however, she received a Frazer Foundation grant to complete her second book—*The Radical Politics of Absurd Theater*—and decided to take a year's leave from teaching. Saul Bird had been offered a last-minute appointment from a small Canadian university on the American border. The two of them flew up to Hilberry University to look it over: They noted the ordinary, soot-specked buildings, the torn-up campus, the two or three "modern" buildings under construction, the amiable, innocuous student faces. They noted the grayness of the sky, which was the same sky that arched over Buffalo, New York, and which was fragrant with gaseous odors and ominous, as if the particles of soot were somehow charged with energy, with electricity; not speaking, not needing to speak, the Birds felt a certain promise in the very dismalness of the setting, as if it were not yet in existence, hardly yet imagined.

They could bring it into existence.

On September ninth, after Saul Bird called, Susannah changed her clothes, taking off her pajama bottoms and putting on a pair of blue jeans. The pajama top looked like a shirt—it was striped green and white—so she did not bother to change it. "Get dressed, your father wants us to pick him up at the university," she said to the boy, Philip. "I'm not leaving you here alone."

"Why not?" the boy said cheerfully. "Think I'd kill myself or something?"

"To spite your father and me."

The boy snickered.

She drove to the university. Saul was standing with a small group—K and a few students, Doris and David and Homer, and a young woman whom Susannah did not recognize. Saul introduced them: "This is Wanda Barnett, who is anxious to get an apartment." Everyone piled into the car. Wanda, demure and homely, seemed not to know what to do with her hands. She squeezed in next to Susannah. She smiled shyly; Susannah did not smile at all.

That was at one o'clock. By five that afternoon, they had located an apartment—not exactly within walking distance of the university—but a fairly good apartment, just the same, though quite expensive. "Someone will have to wash these walls," Saul Bird declared to the manager. "You don't expect this young woman to sign a lease for such filth, do you? This city is still in the Nineteenth Century! Well, Wanda, are you pleased with this?"

He turned to face her. She was exhausted, her stomach upset from the day's activity. Anxious not to disappoint Saul Bird, she could only nod mutely. She felt how the others in the room—everyone except the child had come up—were waiting for her reaction, watching her keenly.

"Yes," she said shakily, "yes, it's perfect."

Saul Bird smiled. "I'm on my way to a private conference with Hubben, I must leave, but we want you to have dinner with us tonight. I might be stopping at T. W.'s apartment to see what they've heard. Wanda, you're not busy tonight?"

"I really can't——"

"Why not?" Saul Bird frowned. He put out his arms and a cigarette burned eloquently in his fingers. Wanda felt the others watching her, waiting. Susannah Bird stood with her arms folded over the striped, sporty shirt she wore.

"I have work to do of my own, and I can't intrude upon you," Wanda said miserably.

"Relax. You take yourself too seriously," Saul Bird said. "You must reassess yourself. You may be on the verge of a new life. You are in Canada, a country not free of bourgeois prostitution but relatively innocent, free, at any rate, of a foreign policy, a country that is a *possibility*. You grant me Canada's a possibility?"

Wanda glanced at the others. Saul Bird's wife had a thin, ravaged, shrewd face; it was set like stone, with patches of black hair like moss about it. A blank. K was staring at Wanda's shoes, as if waiting painfully for her response. The students—Homer McCrea and David Rose—eyed her suspiciously. Their young nostrils widened with the rapidity of their breathing. Clearly, they did not trust her. Both were very thin. Their faces were eaglelike and intense; in imitation of Saul Bird, perhaps, they wore turtleneck sweaters that emphasized their thinness, and blue jeans and sandals. Their feet were grimy. Their toes were in perpetual movement, wiggling, appearing to signal the unbearable tension of the moment. David Rose wore a floppy orange-felt hat that was pulled down upon his head; his untidy hair stuck out around it. Homer McCrea, hatless, had a head of black curly hair and wore several rings on his fingers.

Wanda thought: *I must get away from these people.*

But Saul Bird said swiftly, as if he had heard her thoughts, "Why are you so nervous, Wanda? You look very tired. You look a little sick. Your problem is obvious to me—you do not relax. Always your mind is working and always you're thinking, planning, you're on guard, you're about to put up your hands to shield your private parts from us—why must you be so private? Why are you so terrified?"

"I—I don't know what you——"

"Come, we must leave. Susannah will make us all stuffed breast of veal."

A wave of nausea rose in Wanda.

Erasmus Hubben, born in Toronto in 1930, completed his doctoral work in 1955 with an 800-page study called "The Classical Epistemological Relativism of Ernst Cassirer." Every summer, Hubben traveled in Europe and northern Africa; friends back in Canada received postcards scribbled over with his fine, enigmatic prose—sprinkled with exclamation points and generally self-critical, as if Hubben were embarrassed for himself. He was conscious of himself, always: Students could not quite understand his nervous jokes, the facial tics and twitches that were meant to undercut the gravity of his pronouncements, the kind of baggy shuffling dance he did when lecturing. His face, seen in repose, was rather sorrowful, the eyebrows scanty, accenting the hard bone of his brow, the nose long and pale as wax, the lips thin and colorless; in company, his face seemed to flesh out, to become muscular with the drama of conversation, the pupils of the eyes blackening, the lips moving rapidly, so that tiny flecks of saliva gathered in the corners of his mouth. He was a good, generous man, and the somewhat clownish look of his clothes (seedy, baggy trousers with fallen seats; coats with elbows worn thin; shoes splotched with old mud) was half deliberate, perhaps—while Hubben suggested to his colleagues, evasively and shyly, that they must play Monopoly with him sometime (he had invented a more complicated game of Monopoly), at the same time he waved away their pity for his loneliness by the jokes, the puns, the difficult allusions, the jolly cast of his face and dress alike . . . and he carried in his wallet the snapshot of a smiling, beefy young woman, which he took out often to show people as if to assure them that he had someone, yes, there was someone back in Toronto, someone existed somewhere who cared for Erasmus Hubben.

He came to Hilberry University in 1967, having resigned from another university for reasons of health. He taught logic, but his real love was poetry, and he had arranged for a private printing of a book of his poems. They were always short, often ending with queries.

Actual adversaries
are not as prominent as quivering
speculations

When you think of me, my dear,
do you think of
anything?

He took teaching very seriously. He liked students, though he did not understand them; he liked their energy, their youth, their *foreignness*. During his first year at Hilberry, he prepared for as many as 20 hours for a single lecture. But his teaching was not successful. He could not understand why. So he worked harder on his lectures, taking notes by hand so as not to disturb the family he lived with. (He boarded with a colleague and his family.) Late in the winter of 1968, a student named David Rose came to see him. This student did not attend class very often and he was receiving a failing grade, but when he sat in class with his arms folded, his face taut and contemptuous beneath a floppy orange-felt hat, he impressed Hubben as a superior young man. Wasn't that probably a sign of superiority, his contempt? Erasmus Hubben shook hands with him, delighted that a student should seek him out, and made a joke about not seeing him very often. David Rose smiled slowly, as if not getting the joke. He was very thin and intense. "Dr. Hubben," he said, "I have been designated to approach you with this question—would you like your class liberated?" Hubben was leaning forward with an attentive smile—*liberated?* "Yes. Your course is obviously a failure. Your subject is not entirely hopeless, but you are unable to make it relevant. Your teaching methods are dead, dried up, finished. Of course, as a human being, you have potential," the boy said. Hubben blinked. He could not believe what he was hearing. The boy went on to explain that a certain professor in English, Saul Bird, was conducting experimental classes and that the other Hilberry professors would do well to learn from him before it was too late. Saul—everyone called him Saul—did not teach classes formally at all; he had "liberated" his students; he met with them at his apartment or in the coffee shop or elsewhere, usually at night; his students read and did anything they wanted, and some skipped all sessions, since in any case, they were going to be allowed to grade themselves at the end of the year. "The old-fashioned grading system," David Rose said angrily, "is only imperialistic sadism!"

Hubben stared at the boy. He had been hearing about Saul Bird for a long time, and he had seen the man at a distance—hurrying across campus, usually dressed badly, with a few students running along with him—but he had never spoken to him. Something about Saul Bird's intense, urbane, theatrical manner had frightened Hubben off. And then there was the matter of his being a Jew, his being from New York. . . . Hubben's family was a little prejudiced, and though Hubben himself was free of such nonsense, he did not exactly seek out people like Saul Bird. So he told David Rose, with a gracious smile, that he would be delighted to talk with "Saul" sometime. He hoped he wasn't too old to learn how to teach! David Rose did not catch this joke but gravely and politely nodded. "Yes, the whole university better learn. It better learn from Saul or go under," he said.

Soon, Hubben began to hear of little else except Saul Bird. Bird had been fired and would fulfill only the next year's contract. His department—English—and the dean of arts and sciences had voted to dismiss him. Now, it seemed that many of Hubben's students were also "Saul's" students. They sat together in the classroom, when they came to class, their arms folded, their eyes beady and undefeated, though Hubben's finely wrought lectures obviously bored them. David Rose had enrolled for another course, still wearing his orange hat; a girl named Doris had joined him, perhaps his girlfriend—Doris, all angles and jutting lines, very thin, with stringy blonde hair and sweaters pulled down to her bony hips as if they were men's sweaters, her voice sometimes rising in a sarcastic whine that startled the other students, "Professor Hubben, doesn't this entirely contra*dict* what you said the other day?" Another boy, Homer McCrea, had black curly hair and a dramatic manner that put Hubben in mind of Saul Bird. Sometimes he took notes all period long (were these lecture notes going to be used against him?—Hubben wondered), sometimes he sat with his arms folded, his expression distant and critical. Hubben began to talk faster and faster, he spiced up his lectures with ironic little jokes of the sort that superior students would appreciate, but nothing worked—nothing worked.

Saul Bird came to see him the first week in September, striding into his office. "I'm Saul Bird. I would like your signature on a petition," he said. Hubben spent many minutes reading the petition, examining its syntax, to give himself time to think. Saul Bird's presence in this small room upset him. The man was very close, physically close to Hubben—and Hubben could not stand to be touched—and he was very *real*. He kept leaning over Hubben's shoulder to point out things in the petition. "*That* is the central issue. *That* will break someone's back," Saul Bird said.

Hubben, rattled, could not make much sense of the petition except that it seemed to support excellence in teaching and the need for dedication to students and for experimentation to pre-

vent "the death of the humanities." Hubben could not see that it
had much to do with the case of Saul Bird at all. But he said, not
meeting Saul Bird's stare, "I really must decline. I'm afraid I don't
sign things."

"You what?"

"I'm afraid I don't——"

"You refuse to involve yourself?" Saul Bird said sharply.

Hubben sat staring at the petition. He read it over again. Would
this awful man not go away?

"I think you'll reconsider if you study my case," Saul Bird said.
"Most of the faculty is going to support me, once the injustice of
the case is aired. Here is my own file—read it tonight and tell me
what your response is." And he gave Hubben a manila folder of
Xeroxed memos, outlines, programs, personal letters from students in praise of Saul Bird, dating back to March of the year
that Saul Bird had signed a contract with Hilberry. Hubben sat
dizzily looking through these things. He had his own work to
do. . . . What sense could he make of all this?

On September ninth, he was to meet with Saul Bird at four in
the afternoon, but the hour came and went. He was immensely
relieved. He prepared to go home, thinking of how much better
it was to stay away from people, really. No close relationships.
No intimate ties. Of course, he liked to "chat" with people—
particularly about intellectual subjects—and he enjoyed the simple-
minded family dinners in the Kramer household, where he boarded.
He liked students at a distance. Women made him extremely nervous. His female students were as colorful as partridges and as un-
predictable—so many sudden flutterings, the darting of eyes and
hands! The young men in his classes were fine human beings, but,
up close, the heat of their breath was disturbing. Better to keep
people at a distance. . . . And as Hubben thought this clearly
to himself, the telephone rang and Doris Marsdell announced
that Saul Bird was on his way. "But he's an hour late and I'm
going home," Hubben protested.

"You hadn't better go home," the girl said.

"What?" said Hubben. "What did you say, Miss Marsdell?"

"This is a matter of extreme importance, more to you than to Saul. You *hadn't better go home.*" Shaken, Hubben looked around his dingy, cluttered office as if seeking help—but he was alone. The girl went on quickly, "Saul is a genius, a saint. You people all know that! You're jealous of him! You want to destroy him, because you're jealous, you're terrified of a real genius in your midst!"

"Miss Marsdell," Hubben said, "are you joking? You must be joking."

"I don't joke," the girl said and hung up.

When Saul Bird arrived 15 minutes later, he was in an excellent mood. He shook hands briskly, lit a cigarette and sat on the edge of Hubben's desk. "Did you read my file? Are you convinced of the injustice of this university?"

Hubben was extremely warm. "I'm not sure——"

"Most of your colleagues in philosophy are going to sign in my behalf," Saul Bird said. "What is your decision?"

"I wasn't aware that most of them were——"

"Of course not. People are afraid to talk openly of these matters."

"I still don't think——"

"My wife wants you to have dinner with us tonight. We'll talk about this quietly, sanely. Intelligent discourse between humanists is the only means of bringing about a revolution—until the need for violence is more obvious, I mean," Saul Bird said with a smile.

"Violence?" Hubben stared. He felt something in his blood warming, opening, coming to life in arrogant protestation against himself, his own demands. He was very warm. Saul Bird, perched on the edge of his desk, eyed him through glasses that looked as if they might slightly magnify the images that came through them.

"People like you," Saul Bird said softly, "have been allowed to live through books for too long. That's been your salvation—dust and the droppings of tradition—but all that is ending, as you know. You'll change. You'll be changed. My wife would like you to come to dinner. You're rooming with the Kramers, aren't you? Old Harold Kramer and his 'ethics of Christianity' seminar?"

Hubben wanted to protest that Kramer was only 46.

"People like Kramer, according to the students, are hopeless. They must go under. People like *you*—and a very few others— are possibilities. The students do admit certain possibilities. They are very wise, these twenty-year-olds, extraordinarily wise. The future belongs to them, of course. You are not anti-student, are you?"

"Of course not, but——"

"Telephone Kramer's wife and tell her you're eating out tonight," Saul Bird said.

Hubben hesitated. Then something in him surrendered: Really, it would not harm him to have dinner with the Birds. He was curious about them, after all. And then, it could not be denied that Saul Bird was a fascinating man. His face was shrewd, peaked, oddly appealing. He was obviously very intelligent—his students had not exaggerated. Hubben had heard, of course, that Saul Bird had been fired for incompetence and "gross misconduct." He did not teach his classes, evidently. He did not assign any examinations or papers and his students were allowed to grade themselves. But in the man's presence, these charges faded, they did not seem quite *relevant*. . . . Hubben made up his mind. He would spend the evening with the Birds. Wasn't it a part of the rich recklessness of life, to explore all possibilities?

And so it all began.

The group met informally at Saul Bird's apartment, at first two or three times a week, then every evening. Wanda went as often as she could—she had to work hard on her class preparations and on her dissertation, she was often exhausted, a little sick to her stomach and doubtful of her subject (*Landor,* Saul Bird had said flatly)—but still she showed up, shy and clumsy about this new part of her life. Saul Bird and his group were so passionate! They were so wise! They asked her bluntly how she could devote her intelligence to the analysis of a *medieval* writer when the world about her was so rotten. It was based on hypocrisy and exploitation, couldn't she see? The world was a nightmarish joke, unfunny. Nothing was funny. It was a fact of this life, Saul Bird lectured to his circle, that *nothing was funny*.

And he would stare openly at Erasmus Hubben, whose nervous jokes had annoyed the circle at first.

Hubben was transformed gradually. How had he been blind for so long? His students told him that half the faculty was going to be fired, hounded out, shamed out of existence, if Saul Bird was not rehired. When Saul Bird was rehired, however, he would not be gratefully silent but would head a committee of activist faculty and students to expose the hypocrisy of the rest of the faculty. Their findings would be published. Would he, Erasmus, like to contribute anything to help with printing costs? As the fall semester went on, Hubben turned up at Saul Bird's more and more often, he stayed later, he became quite dependent upon these nightly meetings. How was it possible that he had known so little about himself? about his own stultifying life? He began to speak wildly, parodying his own professorial manner, and the saliva flew from his lips. He believed that Saul Bird listened closely to him. The very air of Saul Bird's crowded little apartment was exhilarating to Hubben; he and the two other faculty members who showed up regularly began to feel younger, to dress in an untidy, zestful, youthful manner. Hubben gained a new respect for Morris Kaye, whom he had never taken seriously. And a new lecturer, a young woman named Wanda, attracted Hubben's eye: Vague in her speech, flat-chested, her eyes watery with emotion or shyness, she did not upset Hubben at all and she seemed to admire his speeches.

On the walls of the apartment there were many posters and photographs, and those that caught Hubben's eye most often were of blazing human beings—Buddhist monks and nuns, and a Czechoslovakian university student. A human being in flames! Maniacal flames leaping up from an oddly rigid, erect human being, sitting cross-legged in a street! It was unimaginable. But it had happened, it had been photographed. Hubben had the idea as the weeks passed that only so dramatic an act, so irreparable an act, would impress Saul Bird.

When Wanda could not go to the apartment, she thought about the group and could not concentrate on her work. What were they talking about? They usually talked for hours—sometimes quietly, sometimes noisily. The air would be heavy with smoke. Everyone except Wanda smoked; even Saul Bird's little boy showed up, smoking. (The Birds did not exactly live together. Susannah had an apartment on the top floor of a building and Saul had a smaller apartment on the second floor, in the rear.) The little boy, Philip, would come down to visit and stand behind his father's chair, watching everyone. He was a fascinating child, Wanda thought. She feared children, usually, but Philip did not seem to be a child; he was dwarfish rather than small, wise and almost wooden, with thick kinky hair a little darker than his father's and his father's cool, intelligent face. He would not attend public schools and the Birds supported him. (Some kind of legal case was going on over this.) He said little, unlike other children Wanda had known, and she was very pleased one day when the Birds asked her to take Philip out to get a pair of shoes. She took him on the bus. He was silent except for one remark: "Don't fall in love with my father, please."

Wanda laughed hysterically.

She began to lie awake at night, thinking about Saul Bird. He often looked directly at her, pointedly at her. He often nodded in support of her remarks. If only they could talk alone!—but the apartment was always crowded with students who were staying overnight, some of them even bringing their sleeping bags along. The young man with the orange hat, David Rose, had moved out of his parents' house and Saul Bird had gladly agreed to house him, for nothing. The telephone was always ringing. Susannah sometimes showed up around midnight, silent and dark. She reminded Wanda of a crow. But the woman was brilliant, her book on Proust was brilliant. Wanda despaired of such brilliance herself. Susannah had a deft, witchlike, whimsical style, her small face sometimes breaking into a darting, razorish smile that was really charming. And her wit frightened everyone—"If my husband could function normally, he would function normally," she said once, winking. And Hubben was always there. He sent out for pizzas and chop suey and hamburgers. K—"I am a character out of Kafka, pure essence," he declared—was always there. And the students, always the students. They seemed to live on air, disdaining Hubben's offers of food. They did not need food. They lived on the hours of intense, intoxicating dialog:

SAUL BIRD: What conclusions have you come to?

DORIS: That I was an infant. I was enslaved.

SAUL BIRD: And what now?

DORIS: Now I am totally free.

SAUL BIRD: You're exaggerating to gain our respect.

DORIS: No, I'm free. I'm free. I detest my parents and everything they stand for—I'm free of them—I am my own woman, entirely!

During the day, Hubben began to notice that his colleagues at the university were jealous of him. They were probably curious about the renewed interest in his notoriously difficult subject, logic. How strange that young people should begin to hang around Erasmus Hubben's office! Hubben spent hours "chatting" with them. *I must get closer. I must wake up to reality,* he thought. His colleagues were not only jealous of his popularity but fearful of it. He began closing his office door and opening it only to Saul Bird's circle. He took around Saul Bird's petition and tried to argue people into signing it. When Kramer would not sign it, Hubben became extremely angry and moved out of the Kramer home and into a cheap riverfront hotel. He told the Kramers that their attitude toward Saul Bird was disgusting. They were sick people, he could not live under the same roof with such sick, selfish people! Kramer, a professor of ethics, an old-fashioned Catholic layman, was brought to tears by Hubben's accusations. But Hubben would not move back. He would not compromise with his new ideals.

I have friends now. I have real friends, he thought 50 times a day, in amazement. He doodled little poems, smiling at their cryptic ingenuity—

One savage kiss is worth
a thousand savage syllogisms—

and showed them to Saul Bird, who shrugged his shoulders. Though he was a professor of English, Saul had not much interest in poetry. He argued that the meaning of life was *action,* involvement with other *human beings;* the trappings of the past were finished—books, lectures, classrooms, buildings, academic status! He, Saul Bird, was being fired only because he represented the future. The establishment feared the future. In a proclamation sent to the local newspaper, calling for an investigation of the financial holdings of the university's board of governors, he stated: "Because it is my duty to liberate the students of this university, I am being fired. Because people like myself—and we are numerous in Canada and the United States—are loyal to our students and not to the establishment, we are being persecuted. But we are going to fight back."

"We certainly are going to fight back!" Hubben cried.

He hurried about the university with a wild, happy look. He felt so much younger! Though living in the White Hawk Hotel did not agree with him, he felt much younger these days; it was mysterious. He and the young lecturer Wanda Barnett often sought each other out at the university to discuss the change in their lives. At first, they were shy; then, guessing at their common experiences, they began to talk quite openly. "I was always lonely. I was always left out. I was always the tallest girl in my class," Wanda said, gulping for breath.

Hubben, feeling a kind of confused, sparkling gratitude for this woman's honesty, admitted that he, too, had been lonely, isolated, overly intelligent, a kind of freak. "And I was selfish, so selfish! I inherited from my father—a pious old fraud!—an absolute indifference to moral and political commitment. I skipped a stage in the natural evolution of mankind! But thanks to Saul——"

"Yes, thanks to Saul——" Wanda said at once.

Just before the break at Christmas, the university's Appeals Committee turned down the Saul Bird case.

"And now we must get serious," Saul Bird said to the circle.

They began to talk of tactics. They talked of faculty resignations, of the denunciation of the university by its student population; guardedly, at first, they talked of demonstrations and breakage and bombings. They would certainly occupy the humanities building and only violent police action could get them out—maybe not even that, if they were armed. They could stay in the building for weeks and force the university's administration to rehire Saul Bird. As they spoke, they became more excited, more certain of themselves. The blazing suicides on Saul Bird's walls were luminous, as if in sympathy with their cause.

How could one live in such a rotten society? Why not destroy it with violence?

The telephone was always ringing. Sometimes Wanda answered, sometimes one of the girl students; if Saul Bird nodded, they handed the receiver to him; if he shook his head, they made excuses for him. He was not always available to everyone. This pleased them immensely, his belonging to *them*. When they did not talk directly of forcing the administration to rehire him, they talked about him, about his effect on their lives. They were frank and solemn. A first-year arts student, a girl, clasped her hands before her and said breathlessly, "Saul has changed me. No cell in me is the same."

K, enormously moved, sat on the floor and confessed, "He revolutionized my concept of reality. It's like that corny *Gestalt* of George Washington's face—once it's pointed out to you, you can't see anything else. Not lines and squiggles but only Washington's face. That is fate."

But sometimes, very late at night, the discussions became more intimate. It was in January that Saul Bird turned to Hubben, who had been unusually noisy that evening, and said, "You assure us you've been transformed. But I doubt it. I doubt that you are ready yet to face the truth about yourself."

"The truth?"

"The truth. Will you tell us?"

It was so late—around four in the morning—that only about 12 students remained, as well as Wanda, K and a recent convert, a peppy, bearded sociology lecturer. The air was suddenly quite tense. Everyone looked at Hubben, who tugged at the collar of his rumpled shirt.

"I don't know what you mean, Saul," he said.

"Of course you know what I mean."

"That I'm prejudiced? Against certain races . . . or creeds . . . ?"

Saul Bird was silent.

"I admit to a slight primitive fear . . . an entirely irrational fear of people different from myself. It's Toronto instinct! Good old Anglo-Saxon stock!" Hubben laughed.

"We know all that," David Rose said coldly.

"How do you know that? Did you—did you know that?" Hubben said. He looked around the room. Wanda Barnett was watching him, her face drawn with the late hour. K's look was slightly glazed. "But I like all human beings personally, as—as human beings. Today I was chatting in the lounge with Franklin Ambrose, and it never occurred to me, not once, that he was a—that he was a Negro——"

Hubben looked miserably at Saul Bird.

"Franklin Ambrose is not a Negro," said Saul Bird shrewdly.

Everyone barked with laughter. It was true: Frank Ambrose, a black man of 30, whose Ph.D. was from Harvard, who dressed expensively and whose clipped high style was much appreciated by his female students, was not really a "Negro" at all.

"What about Jews, Erasmus?" Doris Marsdell said suddenly.

"Jews? I don't think about Jews. I have no feelings one way or another. I do not think about people as Jews—or non-Jews——"

"Tell us more," another student said with a snicker.

"Yes, tell us."

"Tell us about your most intimate instinct," Saul Bird said. He leaned forward to stare down at Hubben, who was sitting on the floor. "What is the truth about your feeling for me?"

"Extreme admiration——"

"Come, come. I think we all know. You might as well admit it."

"Admit what?"

"Your inclinations."

"But what—what are my inclinations?"

"Your obsession."

Hubben stared. "What do you mean?"

"Tell us."

"But what—what do you mean?"

"Your desire for me," Saul Bird said.

"I don't——"

"Your homosexual desire for me," Saul Bird said flatly.

Hubben sat without moving.

"Well?" said Saul Bird. "Why are you so silent?"

"I don't—I don't——" Hubben wiped his forehead with both hands. He could not bear the gaze of Saul Bird, but there was nowhere else to look. And then, suddenly, he heard his own voice saying, "Yes, I admit it. It's true."

Saul Bird lifted his hands in a gesture that matched the lifting of his eyebrows. "Of course it's true," he said.

The discussion leaped at once to another topic: tactics for the occupation of the humanities building. Hubben took part vociferously in this discussion. He stayed very late, until only he and a few students remained, and Saul Bird said curtly, "I forgot to tell you that Susannah and I are flying to New York this morning. Will you all go home, so that I can get some sleep?"

"You're going away?" everyone said.

A weekend without Saul Bird was a lonely weekend. Hubben did not leave the White Hawk Hotel; Wanda, staying up in Susannah's apartment in order to take care of Philip, hoped for a telephone call. While the child read books on mathematical puzzles, or stared for long periods of time out the window, Wanda tried to prepare her Chaucer lectures. But she could not concentrate: She kept thinking of Saul Bird.

Who could resist Saul Bird?

The White Hawk Hotel was very noisy and its odors were of festivity and rot. Hubben, unable to sleep, telephoned members of the Saul Bird circle during the night, chatting and joking with them, his words tumbling out, saliva forming in the corners of his mouth. Sometimes he himself did not know what he was saying. After talking an hour and a half with K about the proper wording of their letters of resignation, he caught himself up short and asked, startled, "Why did you call me? Has anything happened?"

The next Monday, on his way to class, he overheard two students laughing behind him. He whirled around; the boys stared at him, their faces hardening. No students of his. He did not know them.

But perhaps they knew him?

Getting his mail in the departmental office, he noticed that the secretary—a young woman with stacked blonde hair—was eying him strangely. He glanced down at himself—frayed trouser cuffs, unbuckled overshoes. She was so absurdly overdressed that she must sneer at an intellectual like him, in self-defense. She must.

And yet, perhaps she had heard . . . ?

He went over to the English department to see Wanda, but she stammered an apology: "A student is coming to see me right now. About the special edition of the paper."

"The special edition? Can't I stay and listen?"

"Not right now," Wanda said, confused.

Hubben had donated $500 for a special edition of the student newspaper, which was going to feature an interview with "Saul Bird: Teacher Extraordinary."

He walked quickly back to his office and closed the door. His head pounded. He covered his face with his hands and wept.

Saul Bird. . . .

Saul Bird returned in three days and the activities of the circle were resumed. It was necessary to begin plans for the occupation of the humanities building in earnest. They must be prepared for violence. Now the telephone was ringing more than ever: The local newspaper wanted an interview to run alongside an interview with the president of the university; a professor in civil engineering, of all fields, wanted Saul Bird to come to dinner, because it was "time we all communicated"; the head of Saul's department wanted an explanation of all this intrigue; David Rose's father called to demand angrily what was happening to his son; long-distance calls came in from Toronto, in response to a full-page advertisement Hubben had paid for in the Toronto *Globe and Mail,* headlined "WHY IS HILBERRY UNIVERSITY PERSECUTING A MAN NAMED SAUL BIRD?"

Wanda walked through a cold sleeting rain to watch a television interview show at the home of the Episcopal chaplain, Father Mott, a young, balding man who was Saul Bird's newest disciple. The show was a local production, rather amateurish, but Saul Bird spoke clearly and strongly and made an excellent impression. Wanda stared, transfixed, at his image on the screen. It was impossible to tell how short he was! He talked for 15 minutes in his urbane, imploring voice: "It must be smashed so that it can live! Those of us who are prepared to smash it are feared, especially by our own generation; but this fear is hopeless, it will stop nothing—the future will come, it will be heard! We may have to destroy higher education in both Canada and the United States in order to save our young people!"

"Dr. Bird," said the interviewer, "may I ask a more personal question? We've been hearing about a possible occupation of one of the university's buildings. Is there any basis to this threat?"

"Absolutely not," said Saul Bird.

The occupation had been planned for the following Tuesday, the second week in February. Wanda, who had been staying up almost every night, got so nervous that she could not sit still. She could not even stay in her office for long. She imagined that people were staring at her. The older faculty members, unsympathetic to Saul Bird, in some cases hating Saul Bird, began to look at her in a most unpleasant way. In the faculty lounge, Wanda believed that they laughed at her because she came in so rushed, her short hair untidy about her face, her books clumsily cradled in her arms. She blushed miserably.

February was dim and cold and few students showed up at her morning classes. Inspired by Saul Bird, she had announced that all students enrolled in her sections would be allowed to grade themselves at the end of the year. Saul Bird had predicted a renewed enthusiasm on the students' part, but in fact, the students were disappearing; what had gone wrong? Didn't they understand her devotion to them? She was so nervous that she had to hurry to the women's rest room before classes, fearing nausea. Sometimes she did throw up. And then, shaken, pale, distraught, she hurried across the windy quadrangle to her classroom, arriving five minutes late, her glasses steamed over.

As the date of the occupation approached, she became even more nervous. She could not sleep. If she telephoned Saul Bird, it often happened that someone else answered—it sounded like Doris Marsdell—and said loftily, "Saul is not available at the moment!" If she telephoned Susannah, the phone went unanswered. Erasmus Hubben, at his hotel, would snatch up his telephone receiver and say hello in so panicked a voice that Wanda could not identify herself. So the two of them would sit, listening to each other's frightened breathing, until they both hung up.

She kept thinking and rethinking about the past several months. Her mind raced and would not let her sleep. For some reason, she kept glancing at her wrist watch. What was wrong? What was happening? She caught a bad cold waiting for a bus to take her to Saul Bird's apartment and could not get rid of it. When she met other faculty members in the halls, she stammered and looked away. She could not concentrate on her dissertation. That could wait; it had nothing to do with real life. But people were looking at her oddly. When she hurried into the coffee shop to sit with K and a few students, it seemed that even these people glanced oddly at her. But it was Erasmus Hubben they were analyzing. "People just want to discredit his ad in the Toronto *Globe and Mail!*" Doris Marsdell said sourly. She had a very thin, grainy face, rubbed too raw and drawn with exhaustion; her blonde hair hung in strands. When she waved her arms excitedly, she did not smell good. "Sanity and insanity, Saul says, are bourgeois distinctions we don't need to observe. It's all crap! If society tries to say that Erasmus is unbalanced, that is *their* distinction and not ours. Society wants to categorize us in order to get power over us! Sheer primitive imperialist power!"

The occupation began on February tenth, at 10:30 P.M. Saul Bird's supporters—about 40 students and 8 faculty members and the wiry little Episcopal chaplain—approached the humanities building with their sleeping bags, helmets, goggles and food, but the campus police must have been tipped off, because they were waiting. These police—about five of them—blocked the entrance to the building and asked for identification cards.

Erasmus Hubben pushed his way through the shivering little group. "Are you the Gestapo?" he cried. "The thought police? What is *your* identification?" A few of the students began shoving forward. They broke past the campus police—who were middle-aged, portly men in uniforms that looked like costumes—and ran into the building. "Fascists! Gestapo!" Hubben cried. His long dark overcoat was unbuttoned and swung open. Wanda, whose throat was very sore, wondered if she should not try to calm Erasmus. But something about the rigidity of his neck and head frightened her. "I dare you to arrest me! I dare you to use your guns on me! I am an associate professor employed by this university, I am a Canadian citizen, I will use all the powers of my station and my intellect to expose you!" he cried. The students inside the building were now holding the doors shut against the police, but this prevented the other students from getting in. The policemen moved slowly, like men in a dream. Erasmus was pulling at one of them, a plump, catfaced, frightened man in his mid-50s, and was shouting, "Are we threatened with being fired, indeed? Are these loyal students threatened with expulsion? Indeed, indeed? And who will fire us and who will expel us when this university is burned to the ground and its corrupt administration put to public shame?"

"Somebody put a gag on him!" one of the students muttered.

Then something happened that Wanda did not see. Did Eras-

mus shove the policeman or did the policeman shove Erasmus?
Did Erasmus truly spit in the man's face, as some claimed gleefully, or did the policeman just slip accidentally on the steps?
People began to shout. The policeman had fallen and Erasmus
was trying to kick him. Someone pulled at his arm. Hubben
screamed, "Let me at him! They are trying to castrate us! All my
life, they have tried to castrate me!" He took off his overcoat and
threw it behind him and it caught poor Father Mott in the face.
Before anyone could stop him, Erasmus tore off his shirt and began undoing his trousers. Wanda could not believe her eyes—she
saw Erasmus Hubben pull down his trousers and step out of them!
And then, eluding everyone, he ran along the side of the building,
through the bushes, in his underclothes.

"Get him, get him!" people cried. A few students tried to head
him off, but he turned suddenly and charged right into them. He
was screaming. Wanda, confused, stood on the steps and could
not think what to do—then two young girls ran right into her, uttering high, shrill, giggling little screams. They were from her
Chaucer class. They ran right into her and she slipped on the icy
steps and fell. She could not get up. Someone's foot crashed onto
her hand. About her head were feet and knees; everyone was
shouting. Someone stumbled backward and fell onto Wanda,
knocking her face down against the step, and she felt a violent
pain in her mouth.

She began to weep helplessly.

Saul Bird, who had thought it best to stay away from the occupation, telephoned Wanda at three o'clock in the morning. He
spoke rapidly and angrily. "Come over here at once, please. Susannah and I are driving to Chicago in an hour and we need you to
sit with Philip. I know all about what happened—spare me the
details, please."

"But poor Erasmus——"

"How soon can you get here?"

"Right away," Wanda said. Her mouth was swollen—one of her
teeth was loose and would probably have to be pulled. But she

got dressed and called a taxi and ran up the steps into Saul Bird's apartment building. In the foyer, a few students were waiting. Doris Marsdell cried, "What are you doing? Is he letting you come up to see him?" Her eyes were pink and her voice hysterical. "Did anything happen? Is he still alive? He didn't attempt suicide, did he?"

"He asked me to take care of Philip for a few days," Wanda said.

"*You?* He asked *you?*" Doris cried in dismay.

Susannah answered the door. She was wearing a yellow-tweed pants suit and hoop earrings; her mouth was a dark, heavy pink. "Come in, come in!" she said cheerfully. The telephone was ringing. Saul Bird, knotting a necktie, appeared on the run. "Don't answer that telephone!" he said to Susannah. The boy, Philip, stood in his pajamas at a window, his back to the room. Everywhere there were suitcases and clothes. Wanda tried to cover her swollen mouth with her hand, ashamed of looking so ugly. But Saul Bird did not seem to look at her. He was rummaging through some clothes. "Wanda, we'll contact you in a few days. We're on our way out of this hellhole," he said curtly.

She helped them carry their suitcases down to the car.

Then, for three days, she stayed in the apartment and "watched" Philip. She fingered her loose tooth, which was very painful; she wept, knotting a handkerchief in her fingers. She could not shake loose her cold. "Do you think—do you think your father will ever recover from this?" she asked, staring at the little boy.

He spent most of his time reading and doodling mathematical puzzles. When he laughed, it was without humor, a short, breathy bark.

Saul Bird did not telephone until the following Saturday, and then he had little to say. "Put Philip on the Chicago flight at noon. Give him the keys to both apartments."

"But aren't you coming back?"

"Never," said Saul Bird.

"But what about your teaching? Your students?" Wanda cried.

"I've had it at Hilberry University," Saul Bird said.

She was paralyzed.

Preparing Philip for the trip, she walked about in a kind of daze. She kept saying, "But your father must return. He must fight them. He must insist upon justice." Philip did not pay much attention to her. A cigarette in the center of his pursed lips, he combed his thick hair carefully, preening in the mirror. He was a squat, stocky and yet attractive child—like his father, his face wooden and theatrical at once, a sickly olive hue. Wanda stared at him. He was all she had now, her last link with Saul Bird. "Do you think he's desperate? Will he be hospitalized like poor Erasmus Hubben? What will happen?"

"Nothing," said Philip.

"What do you mean?"

"He has found another job, probably."

"What? How do you know?" Wanda cried.

"This has happened before," said Philip.

In the taxi to the airport, she began to weep desperately. She kept touching the child's hands, his arms. "But what will happen to us . . . to me . . . ? The year is almost gone. I have nothing to show for it. I resigned from the university and I cannot, I absolutely cannot ask to be rehired like the others. . . . I cannot degrade myself! And my dissertation, all that is dead, dried up, all that belongs to the past! What will happen to me? Will your father never come back, will I never see him again?"

"My father," said Philip coldly, "has no particular interest in women."

Wanda hiccuped with laughter. "I didn't mean——"

"He makes no secret of it. I've heard him talk about it dozens of times," Philip said. "He was present at my birth. Both he and my mother wanted this. He watched me born . . . me being born . . . he watched all that blood, my mother's insides coming out . . . all that blood. . . ." The child was dreamy now, no longer abrasive and haughty; he stared past Wanda's face as if he were staring into a mystery. His voice took on a softened, almost bell-

like tone. "Oh, my father is very articulate about that experience.
. . . Seeing that mess, he said, made him impotent forever. Ask
him. He'd love to tell you about it."

"I don't believe it," Wanda whispered.

"Then don't believe it."

She waited until his flight was called and walked with him to
the gate. She kept touching his hands, his arms, even his bushy
dark-blond hair. He pulled away from her, scowling; then, taking
pity on her, staring with sudden interest at her bluish, swollen
lip, he reached out to shake hands. It was a formal handshake,
a farewell.

"But what will I do with the rest of my life?" Wanda cried.

The child shook his head. "You are such an obvious woman,"
he said flatly.

JUDITH RASCOE was born in San Francisco in 1941, and grew up there and in Boise, Idaho. She studied at Stanford and at Harvard, and in 1969–70 she returned to Stanford as a Creative Writing Fellow. She is now living in London, working as a free-lance journalist and finishing a screenplay.

SMALL SOUNDS AND TILTING SHADOWS

WHEN I was twenty-one I was half-crazy—I spent myself on that, as if madness were entailed on my maturity. Perhaps it was: I am the youngest child of an elderly family, and when I came along they had already been confined in middle age, convalescing from the strenuous regime of pills, drink, and lawsuits that had cured them of youth.

When I was half-crazy I went to Paris, intending to be old. "Why do you have all these dark dresses?" my boyfriend said. "Look at them: dark green, dark blue, brown. Gray. Black." They lay folded on the bed, with black stockings, black leather shoes, black leather gloves, and handbags fitted with brass and secret locks. I had a diary bound in oilcloth and a letter folder that made a desk of one's lap and dispensed paper, envelopes, and stamps. I had a Swiss knife.

"I'll be with you in a month," my boyfriend said.

I thought he was lying, but now I think perhaps he meant to come, although I didn't want him to. I had a return passage on a ship and no companion; my family didn't even consider the hazards of my traveling alone—they had met no temptations in twenty years. They worried more about sickness and insisted I have all my teeth fixed before I left.

A week after I arrived in Paris I was sick and lay abed while the woman who managed my small hotel brought me broth and tea. I said *Merci,* echoing her voice that was lower and rustier than mine. The bellboy was a little Yugoslav who thought love would cure me. He came late at night and kissed me and brought magazines the guests had left in their rooms; he turned off the lamp and tried to get under the covers. "Ai ahm note ofraid," he said. At last the manageress called a doctor. He listened to my lungs and felt my pulse. *"Mademoiselle,"* he said, *"vous avez la grippe,"* and he ordered a vial of charcoal flavored with licorice.

When I could get out of the hotel again, I came to hate Paris. Although I wore a wrinkled coat, my hair was limp, and my face was spotty, I was followed in the streets and cafés by rat-faced men who usually claimed they had jobs with foreign consulates. When I yelled at them, *Allez!,* I humiliated myself more than them. I fixed on the idea of going to London, where people spoke English, for sometimes my head swam from listening too hard to French and finding words for my replies. *"J'irai, Madame, je voyage en Londres,"* I said to the manageress. *"L'addition, s'il vous plaît."*

In London I looked up all the names in my address book and went to "events." From a bed-and-breakfast hotel near Regent's Park I wrote letters home in my new italic handwriting to say that I was having a wonderful time. Air letters swiftly responded: why wasn't I in Italy? My aunts liked to talk about going to Italy: they took extension courses in the language and subscribed to travel magazines; but Wenona's husband hates airplanes and Vivian's husband, a diabetic, is convinced that there is no adequate medical care in Europe. "I hope you go to Rome," Wenona said in every letter.

But I was contentedly growing older: I bought walking shoes, mackintoshes, and tweed skirts, and with guidebooks and mystery magazines I went to Brighton and Horsham, Canterbury and Ely. The autumn came in languidly, filling the countryside with mists.

One evening in London I was walking out of Regent's Park when I realized that my stomach hurt and my face was hot. Mr.

Wing at the hotel sent me to Doctor Evans, who asked me a good
many questions—I had only one: was this *la grippe* again?—and
touched me gently here and there and then prodded me until I
squeaked. It was appendicitis—he suggested it had always been
appendicitis—and the next morning my appendix was gone. Two
or three of my new friends came to the hospital and seemed full
of concern.

"I can't travel," I said. "They want to send me to a convalescent
home."

Then by lucky chance somebody knew somebody else who knew
of a flat.

"I can't afford a flat," I said.

"It's rent-free. You'd be caretaker. But you must be prepared
to leave on a moment's notice."

"Well, that's no good," I said.

"It'll be weeks before you have to go."

"Then I'll take it," I said.

There are hundreds of squares in London that are indistin-
guishable from Canon Square, a meanly fenced little park surrounded by Georgian houses, each with its below-stairs rooms
made into a "garden flat," with a flight of steps up from the street
and staring big windows that the tenants must cover with heavy
curtains to keep out the cold. Some of the houses on Canon Square
were bed-and-breakfast places. One was a tenement full of Pakis-
tani immigrants. Another (they said at the pub) was a brothel.
"Which one?" I asked. Nobody was certain. On the side streets that
did not command a view of the park there were cheap cafés and
butcher shops, greengrocers, ironmongers. When I first moved
to Canon Square, I hobbled, still bent double from my stitches,
from shop to shop and satisfied the British taste for grotesquerie.
"This is the lass what lost her appendix!" the greengrocer said to
his other customers when I came into his shop. "When are you
going to show us the stitches, love?"

"Here, look at this!" the butcher's wife said. She kicked off her
shoe to show us a webbed toe. Everybody laughed but me.

Despite the discomforts of walking bent over, I stayed out much of the day. Partly it was the sheer inconvenience of the place, for the flat was at the very top of the house and there was no elevator, only steep, uncarpeted stairs. The rooms were low and had whitewashed walls and dark gray fitted carpeting. A tiny window in the kitchen looked down on Canon Square and the treetops that were losing their leaves by handfuls. Larger windows in the back rooms looked down into a wasted garden, across to other rooftops and chimneys. I bought flowers, several bunches at a time, but their color was lost in the dim white light of the rooms.

"Come back with me," I begged friends and acquaintances. "Let me fix you a meal. Let me fix you dinner." I turned on all the electric fires and kept the record player going all the time.

"It's a grim sort of place, isn't it," everybody said, sooner or later.

For a week I had an English boyfriend. "Don't mind my stitches," I said. "It doesn't hurt. Stay. Please stay." But as we lay side by side under cold sheets and rough blankets, the eye of the electric fire upon us, we were too much alone; the loneliness sifted between us, like falling snow. Silences blew into drifts and froze solid. At the end of the week he had to go up to Manchester, to see his family. His dad was ill.

The next week I went to a party where I met a big aggressive man who produced programs for the BBC. He sweated as he drank, and he wore a lot of rings. "What will you do with yourself, darling?" he asked, when he'd got my story out of me. "Will you go back to university? Or will you be an air host*ess?* Who are you, tell me that, will you, who are you?" I burst into angry tears. "Why do you want to know?" I said. "You don't care who I am."

"Come on," he said, aiming for a taxi, his flat, his bed. "Come on, darling, it's late."

"No," I said, though I wanted to go with him. It would be cozy in his flat: I imagined lots of magazines and whiskey. But I'll never know: he didn't find it worthwhile to argue with me.

I got into a taxi alone and said, "Canon Square, please," but then I pictured what the flat would look like when I got there.

The light from any lamp I switched on would fall in a crisply drawn figure on the carpet; the bedroom had curtains of dark gray velvet, from the floor to the ceiling, and if I did not open them, I could not tell whether it was day or night. Sometimes I went into that room at noon and found myself staring at the shadow of the bed, the unchanging shadows in the curtains. I rapped on the taxi's partition. "Gloucester Terrace," I said. "I'm sorry. I've changed my mind."

A nice boy named Michael lived in Gloucester Terrace—a socialist who ran an office somewhere helping somebody. When I rang the bell, he came to the front door in robe and pajamas. "I'm sorry," I said, "but I couldn't stand to go home. Can I stay here tonight?" He looked at me as if he wanted to say no with all his heart, but he let me in anyway and gave me pajamas and tucked me into a far corner of his bed.

The moon came through the window and shone on the corner of the high-headed bed. It was silent and cold; Michael slept inaudibly, but I lay awake for a long time because I felt safe.

The next day, when I got back to Canon Square, I was obsessed by the big man who wore so many rings. He had asked who I was. I knew who I was, all right—so I said to myself: I am . . . and listening, I heard only water in the pipes, wind rapping on a window, my own sigh.

"Who lives here?" I said out loud.

The flat's leaseholder, the man with his name on the bell, was a Canadian journalist, I'd been told. The flat had come to me from a friend of his, who had been charged with its safekeeping and who had decided to go to Italy instead. I was to keep it clean, dusted, have the window washer in, and keep the cupboards stocked with tinned food. When I was given the key, I had asked: "Where is he? When will he be back?"

"I think—but you mustn't tell anybody—I think he's in China," said the departing buddy.

"Then what should I do with the mail?"

"Keep it. Unless there's something that looks very urgent; you can send that to this address; let me write it down."

Finally a letter came that looked urgent. I telephoned the address I'd been given. "There's a letter here," I said, "that looks urgent. Can you . . . should I send it on to you? Where is he?"

"I suppose," said a woman who didn't sound as if she thought it urgent at all. "I don't know where he is, honestly I don't."

"I don't mean to pry," I said.

"It's no secret," she said. "He's in Cuba."

Because I read mystery novels I began to wonder if my so-to-speak landlord was a genuine journalist, but when I looked up his name in a library, I found, to my disappointment, that every month or two he appeared in one magazine or another. He had been to Cuba before and had written three accounts of his visit, for *Maclean's,* the *Spectator,* and *Queen.* There were pieces on the theater in Prague, rural socialism in Yugoslavia, an academic dispute at the University of Toronto, and lots of reviews for English weeklies of books by Canadian writers. His style was distinguished for its impersonality, touched with a suggestion of "I would . . . if I could" and things unsaid but understood among friends: it was impossible to learn from his articles whether he was leftward or rightward in politics; whether he thought Canadian writing was comparable with contemporary stuff from France or America, or whether he thought it was a provincial disaster.

After reading his writings, I began to mention his name (these were the weeks of the boyfriend and the party), and everybody professed to know it, even to know him. "Oh, yes, Willie," was the typical response. "So that's where you're living, in Willie's flat."

One night I met a man who worked in a publishing house. Willie, he assured me, was in the American South, where he was writing about the civil rights movement.

A little more than three weeks after I had moved to Canon Square, I woke up late one morning and lay in bed, watching the sky for a bird or a change of hue upon the gray. Sometimes I dozed and the small noises of the house, pipes and drafts, filled my head so that I sank into sleep like a floating bottle that a wave

tilts, and with a sigh is filled and sunk. And then I rose again. The
clock said eleven, but it had stopped. I got out of bed and turned
on the electric fire. I thought I heard footsteps.

"Who's there?" I said. "I'm coming."

The door of the flat opened upon a landing and a cascade of
stairs, through darkness to the mat of light from the fanlight, three
floors below. Walking downstairs, I saw that everybody's door was
shut. In the mailbox there were two magazines for Willie Ferland
and an advertising circular. I went upstairs again but hesitated on
the threshold. "Is somebody there?" I said.

When there was no answer, I made myself go in and walk
around the flat, from room to room. "Hello?" I said. "Hello,
there?" Nobody was there.

Had there been somebody to ask me: "Do you think somebody got in the flat?" I would have said, No, I don't think so, because I did not think so in the ordinary way one thinks that, say,
the telephone has rung or there's a strange noise from the garage.
Rather it was as if a passing thought—"What if somebody darted
into the flat while I went down for the mail?"—had lodged in my
mind so tenaciously that it claimed a reality of its own and began
to feed upon every sound and tilt of light. Or like a thought which,
on the verge of sleep, becomes a dream.

I opened the closets. One held brooms and overshoes. Another
held towels and a cigar box filled with prescription bottles. A third
contained the immersion water heater and some stiff towels, left
there to dry and forgotten. The closet in the bedroom was a big
one with a rod at least six feet long. At one end hung my dresses
and coats, with my suitcase open on the floor beneath them, spill-
ing stockings, and at the other end of the rod were a few things
that must have belonged to Willie: a green Irish sweater, a couple
of jackets—one tweed and one corduroy—a Hudson's Bay wool
shirt, and a dark blue woolen robe. I put on the robe and learned
that Willie was a small man, for the robe almost fit me. In one
pocket I found an expensive American ball-point pen, in the other
a key on a piece of string. The warmth of the robe picked up my
spirits; I went to the kitchen to make tea and then dialed the tele-

phone to find out the time. It was almost three in the afternoon.

It began to rain. Straining over the sink, I could see the pavement round Canon Square darken, the only mother and child in the park hurry out of it, latching the iron gate behind them. I put Bach on the record player, ate toast with my tea, and chose one of Willie's books—he had stacks of them in the room that he used as a study, mostly Canadian novels. I read about a brave couple living alone in Saskatchewan. It grew dark. I switched on the lights and had sardines on toast for supper. The Bach record played over and over again until it began to sound comical, like a mechanical rainstorm. With Willie's ball-point pen I wrote a shopping list as an excuse to study my handwriting. It was nothing like Willie's. In the back of his books he had made notes for his reviews: his handwriting was small and upright, without ornament. I tried to copy it.

Willie Ferland, I wrote. My capitals were larger than his, my letters more florid.

Inaccuracies description p. 36 repeated later, I wrote, getting the knack of it: if I held the pen close to the tip, if I squeezed it tight and pressed each letter into the paper with a few hard strokes, I had the look of his writing. Yet only the look: the original was too small for me, done with an impulse of control I could not imitate. I essayed an independent sample:

Dear Mike: Sorry but my French isn't up to this. Who ever told you we were all bilingual? All my best, Willie.

Comparing it with a paragraph penciled in the back of a guidebook to Quebec I thought my forgery looked convincing at first glance. But forgery didn't interest me; the spirit of the writing did. I found a sheet of paper in the drawer of his desk and wrote the word *description* several times; then I decided to look for more examples. The desk had two drawers, one with stationery and the other full of manila envelopes marked Yugo Co., Chichester etc., Anthlgy, and *Blue Over and Under.* Peeping inside the envelopes I found typescripts, and put them back.

The only other objects in the study, besides desk and chair and

stacks of books without shelves, were two pasteboard boxes. I
opened one and found it full of letters addressed to Willie, all of
them put back into their torn envelopes; the other box was full of
manila folders holding typewritten manuscripts. I could imagine
what would happen if I were to go through the letters and the
manuscripts and then turn to find that somebody had been watching me.

I turned, saying, "Yes?"

There was nobody there.

I lifted out one manila folder and closed the box. There were
no curtains on the window in the study: from the window I saw
the raincloud lit up by the sodium lights and dabs of light on the
curtained back windows of houses behind Number 12. I made
myself a drink from the single bottle of whiskey that Willie had
left behind and wrote *Scotch, Teacher's* in his handwriting on the
back of an envelope addressed to me.

The next morning Michael called me. "Who's this?" he asked
when I answered the phone.

"It's me," I said.

"I thought it was someone else for a minute. So you're still
there in your gloomy great flat, are you? Do you ever leave it?"

"Most of the time," I said.

"Would you leave it for an excursion to the cinema?"

"Yes," I said. "Anytime."

I dusted and threw out dead flowers and changed the sheets.
I wore Willie's robe because it kept me warm, and I carried on
imaginary conversations with Willie because they kept me occupied. *Have you been in this country long?* I asked him.

Ten years, he said. *Five years.*

You don't want me to know.

I'm secretive, he said. *Why do you want to know?*

Do you like it here? Will you stay?

What do you think?

I don't know, I said.

In the cabinet in the living room I found a set of highball
glasses wrapped in store tissue, a windup tin train engine, orna-

mental matchboxes, a spring device for exercising the arms, and a half-dozen big enlarged photographs of a handsome woman with windblown dark hair. She looked everywhere but at the camera, she favored her right side.

Michael came and said, "Christ, this is dreary."

When we left Canon Square and got to a main thoroughfare, I was surprised to find that London was full of people. They hurried along the pavements with their heads down and umbrellas up; the women's boots smashed through the puddles; their shopping bags bumped and swayed. The butcher was almost hidden by a crowd of heads in scarves; his wife wrestled with the goods in the window, elbowing hanging sides of beef out of her way as she went for the tray of kidneys. We had to wait in line for our fish and chips; we were pushed against the wall as we ate. The pub was noisy and steamy; not an empty table in the lounge, the dart board busy. There was even a queue for the movie. We bought chocolates and tickets for the middle stalls, and afterwards I said I'd had a super evening.

"Me too," Michael said.

We went to another pub, and in the closing-time uproar Michael said he was going to Bristol at the week's end: a job in social work had appeared; he didn't want to run the London office any longer.

"Why don't you come with me?" he said.

"Why?" I said.

"What's keeping you here?"

I was offended: "I have things to do."

"Oh, what?"

"I want to get a job teaching. I like London. I've been writing to the LCC—they might need somebody in the middle of the year. I expect I'll hear soon." It was a lie, but he had no reason to think so; instead he looked hurt and changed the subject.

The manuscript in the manila folder was a short story about a man who tries to get his wife into a lunatic asylum: he has taken a long train ride to the asylum so that he can talk to the doctors. They say that they have too many patients already, that they're understaffed. One doctor, a young Welshman, wants to talk only about what he could earn if he went into private practice. On the lawns of the asylum the patients take aimless walks or sit in the sun. An old man is lost and found again: the nurse comes to the psychiatrist's office to ask if he wants to see the old man. "Why shouldn't he try to escape?" the psychiatrist says. "It's the first sensible thing he's done. I don't want to see him." At last the visitor says he has to go back to London; the doctors advise him to care for his wife at home as long as he can manage it. The man leaves, and during the train ride back to the city, we learn he is not married.

"Who's there?" I said, when I finished it. I thought I'd heard a doorstep. I called the number of the woman who thought Willie was in Cuba. To a housekeeper I said, "It's about Willie Ferland." Then a man came to the telephone.

"Willie," he said. "Is that you?"

I hung up without answering.

That evening the telephone rang, and a man said, "Hello, Willie? I heard you were back."

I didn't answer that time, but when the telephone rang again within a minute I was scared he might call the police, and so I said, "Hello? Who is this?"

"Who's this? Is Willie there?"

"I'm afraid you have the wrong number."

"Is this EDGeware 4494?"

"This is EDGeware 3494."

"I'm sorry," he said.

He rang a couple of times but I didn't pick up the receiver. For the rest of the night, for the rest of the next day, I waited for the police, but nobody came. The telephone rang occasionally, but I would not answer it. Instead I went shopping for fresh flowers and Scotch, and I bought paper and envelopes—heavy, large cream sheets and large, stiff envelopes—to write to the London County Council.

"Dear Sirs," I wrote. "I am an American, just graduated from university, and having settled in London, I think I would like to teach.

"I have a B.A. degree in music and five credits of work in elementary education." But I hadn't. I had a B.A. in English and five or ten or fifteen credits in drama. I had signed for two courses in education and dropped them both; I could teach German expressionist drama, but that did not seem suitable for a London primary school. In the *New Statesman* I read of appointments vacant: librarians, scientists, lecturers in Anglo-African history at the University of Ibadan.

I twisted the heavy cream paper into spills and threw them into the basket. On a fresh sheet of paper I wrote in Willie's hand:

Dear Mike. No bloody luck with the jobs. I refuse to go to Malawi. Anything opening up at the magazine? Let me know soonest. Willie.

The mail brought a book from Jonathan Cape, Ltd., a collection of Canadian verse. I skipped about in it and thought it wasn't very good. On another piece of paper I composed a note to Willie: "This came October 2 and I opened it because I was curious. I look forward to your review." As I wrote I found myself trying to forge my own handwriting, but the letters were too carefully drawn, and some of Willie's mannerisms had crept in. So I copied the note again on the typewriter and put it in the book.

The telephone rang. "Willie, listen." I'd never heard the voice before. "I've got her in trouble, God help me. Do you understand? Do you know a doctor?"

"Willie's not here just now," I said.

"Who is this?"

"I'm just visiting."

"Leave a message for him, will you? Tell him to call John Webb. I don't suppose you know a doctor, do you?"

"No," I said. "Leave a number, and he'll call you."

"Tell him it's urgent."

"I will."

I called the fat man who worked for the BBC. "Listen," I said.

"I'm sure you don't remember me, but I'm in an awful fix. I'm pregnant, and I'm really stuck."

"I don't see what I can do," he said. "Sorry, darling."

"Listen, I have nobody else to ask."

"Wait a mo'."

The receiver smashed against something, and there were voices in the distance, a woman's voice sounding querulous.

"You *might* . . ." he said. "You might give this girl a ring. Explain everything to her. Be absolutely frank. Do you understand me?"

"Thank you, oh, I can't thank you enough," I said.

"That's all right," he said. "I'm sorry to hear it."

I called the number, and when a girl answered, I was absolutely frank: my boyfriend was an American airman in Germany, I said, and I'd got knocked up by this man in London, a married man, and my boyfriend was coming and I was desperate.

"Love, that's terrible," the girl said. She had a nice alert voice. "Love, I can't help you much, I can only give you the number of this doctor in Maida Vale. Ring him and see if he can help. Otherwise, I dunno. It's been a couple of years."

"You've been a great help," I said.

"If he's not there, ring me again," she said. "I'll ask my girlfriend."

Then I called John Webb. "Willie had to go out again," I said. "But he asked me to give you this number. It's a doctor in Maida Vale. He doesn't know if it's still any good or not."

"Kiss him for me, love," John Webb said.

That same day a woman called who said that she had just arrived from Vancouver and that she loved his articles, she had read every one.

"He'll be happy to hear that," I said. "I'm sorry he's not in just now."

"I'll be in London for the rest of the week."

"Try later," I said. "I just can't say when he'll be back. But I'm glad you called. Lots of people don't realize that a writer doesn't get many compliments about his work. People think of writing to him and then they're shy. So I'll be sure to tell him you called."

"Thank you very much, Mrs. Ferland," she said.

I typed a note for Willie: "November 10, woman called to say she liked your articles, will call back."

The telephone didn't ring again that day, and I didn't leave the house. Wearing Willie's bathrobe I lay on the couch in the living room, reading Canadian verse and listening to Mozart. The clock stopped again and the rain started again. When my stomach ached I convinced myself I hadn't recovered from appendicitis. I went to bed early and drew the curtains in the bedroom and fell asleep with the light on. Sometime, I don't know when, I sat up in bed with my heart pounding.

"Who is it?" I said. "Hello?"

The rain trickled against the window, and I didn't know if it was day or night: I got up and opened the closet and looked at Willie's jackets. They were so frightening: what if I had to get up and put on Willie's clothes? Was that what I had to do? Then why was I frightened? That meaningless fancy seemed peculiarly horrible to me: what if I had to get up and dress in his clothes and do what he had to do? There was a smell of self-hatred in the flat. He kept no mirrors, no photographs of himself, no souvenirs to remind himself of who he was. He put his letters back in their envelopes, ready to be returned. On some days no letters came at all. If he held his breath, he would disappear. But when I held my breath I could hear voices chattering on in my head, like a dozen radios from neighboring houses: "The bears. You will. Don't. Can in glory, here give Gladys. Exactly. That's exactly right. Do you have any of the other? Shelves. I can g. it for you! Don't lie!" They were not real voices, I knew; they were words caught in my head, scooped up like lint as I had been this place and that place; then they settled on certain rhythms of my mind. Hearing but not listening I had collected these voices. Now I listened. A voice called my name.

"Who is it?" I said. Perhaps it had been a real one.

Nobody answered. I looked at the bedroom door and tried to

get myself to open it, but I couldn't. I had to sit down on the
bed, and then I had to lie down, and at last I fell asleep. Sometime
later I woke up because the doorbell was ringing. I put on Willie's robe and went as quietly as I could through the apartment
until I could hear their voices:

"Ella said he was back."

"Did you ring up?"

"No, but I expect he's here, that is, if he's here."

"I thought I heard someone inside."

"I don't hear anything. Push the bell again."

"Let's go."

"He might not want company."

Their footsteps dwindled away down the stairs.

That night I went to an Italian restaurant on the next block.
I was the only customer. When the manager-waiter finished cutting ravioli on a table in the back of the room, he sat down with
me.

"Very good food," I said.

"Where you from? I don't see you round this place."

"I live on Canon Square."

"No you don'. I never see you there. Where you live?"

"Number twelve."

"Then why don' I never see you? I live just across."

He went back into the kitchen. Now and then a passerby put
his face to the window and stared at me.

"Business is slow," the manager said, when I paid him. "Winter
comes now."

He turned the lights out when I left.

The streets were full of water: it soaked through the seams of
my shoes and chilled my feet, soaked my stockings. In the lamp-
light I saw black spots on my legs where drops had flown up as I
walked. The light was confusing: black shot with bright lights and
reflections, cracks from drawn curtains, the oddly unilluminating
brilliance of the streetlights. A taxi crashed past, only its parking
lights on. When I got to the newsagent's shop he was pulling

down the shutter. "Wait," I said. "I'm closed, Miss," he said. "Sorry, I'm quarter of an hour late as it is. Sorry, Miss." So I went into a pub, where the drinkers stared as I entered the lounge. Then they started talking to each other again. A small table was free in the corner. "Whiskey, please," I said to the waiter; he brought whiskey and paper napkins and a dish of peanuts. I thought I heard somebody say "Whiskey" behind me, but when I turned my head, two middle-aged women were absorbed in a conversation. The sporting section of the *Telegraph* lay on the chair next to me, and so I read it and drank my whiskey and left. "Sorry," a man said, as we bumped at the door.

When I got to Canon Square I rang the doorbell, then ran up the stairs and knocked on the door. I found the key, unlocked the door. "Hello," I said. "It's me. I'm here." In the bedroom I took off my clothes and put on Willie's blue robe. In the living room I put on the Bach record and made myself a drink. "Yoo-hoo, it's just me," I said. I went to the closet with the towels and the box of pills and I studied each little bottle in turn. "Just looking," I said; then I remembered the story in the manila folder, and hurriedly I returned it to its place in the study.

"Yes?" I said. "Yes."

A wind moved a door.

"I'm just in here," I said.

I thought of a voice saying, Why don't you like her? Well, she's, *you* know. I just don't. Don't ask me why. Who is she, after all? Who's he?

"I'm in here," I said.

The telephone rang. "Is that you?" I said, and finally I picked it up. "Hello, who is this?"

"Who are you?"

"Who's this?" I said.

"Is Willie there?"

"Yes," I said. "Just a moment. Who shall I say is calling?"

"Tell him Joe Dolly."

"Can you hang on just a moment? Please?" I put the receiver gently on its side and walked from that room to the next and the

next, calling, "Willie? Willie? It's Joe Dolly on the phone. Can
you take it?" Then I went back to the phone and said to hold on,
please.

"Willie?" I called. "Where are you? It's Joe Dolly."

"Oh, I'm awfully sorry," I said, at last. "He must have just
stepped out. I don't know where. Down to the newsagent's, I
guess. Is there a number he can call back?"

"Tomorrow'll do," he said. "Just remind him, would you? Tell
him it's urgent."

"Right-o," I said.

By then I was convinced that he was coming back that night.
I packed my suitcase, leaving only my raincoat on the rack, and
I went over the bathroom looking for cosmetics and stray hairs.
When the floor creaked, I said, "Yes? Hello?" On the bed I laid
out a wool dress and undergarments and a pair of jade earrings;
then, out of curiosity, I picked up the clothes and threw them
across the room. They hit the velvet curtains almost soundlessly
and dropped to the floor. Next I drew a bath and got in but got
out soon because the shapes under the water were strange, my
legs looked too long, my back hurt. "I'm in the bathroom," I said,
putting on Willie's robe again. "I'm almost ready."

The question was, where should I go? And so I waited in the
living room, listening and looking for an answer; and after a while
I learned I had to go to the bedroom. "I don't want to," I said
out loud, but I went anyway; I opened the door and stepped into
the room and closed the door again. There were six things in the
room, as far as I could make out: the velvet curtains, the bed,
a black night table, a lamp, a clock, and the closet. Some clothes
lay on the floor in front of the curtain, so I put them out of sight
on a shelf in the closet. After listening a while longer I learned
I had to sit down on the bed. "I don't want to," I said again. I
imagined Willie saying, *But I want to meet you. I'm sorry,* I said.
Something wicked was going to speak to me, and I trembled, waiting for its voice. If you sat in the room as I did, and as he did,
the voice would speak after a while, when it was quiet.

Then the voice began to speak. I didn't hear its words—that is to say, the words were as usual: confused, entangled in other words: "Interest of, now, let's, my goodness! here you hand me, she's going. Give it up. That's. An elephant, isn't it? You don't, careful, if you don't follow, how can you?" But I understood now.

"No," I said, as each temptation came to me in turn, as bright in my mind's eye as Christmas cards: the window over Canon Square—open, a fresh cold vowel of air spoken to me; then the shady gas oven; the pills—medicinal allsorts; and at last the razor blades—they were thin and new: a matter of brightness, colors galore.

"No," I said. "Please don't. Oh, please don't. I beg of you."

I hung onto the blankets; I caught the belt of Willie's robe and then pushed it away as if it were a snake, or a rope.

"Wait," I said. "Not yet."

Somebody called my name.

"Who's there?" I said. "Who said that?"

Nobody, nobody, nobody.

I ran out of the bedroom and opened the front door and looked down the stairwell; there was nothing to be seen, nothing to be heard. When I went back to the bedroom, I took off the robe and put on my wool dress and my coat and picked up my suitcase. I dialed the time: it was almost two in the morning. So I opened all the curtains, made a jug of coffee, and sat up the rest of the night in the living room with my suitcase at my feet. It was not until dawn that I could make myself write a note:

"Thank you for letting me use your flat. Everything is as I found it. I hope you had a good trip. Here is the key I was given."

A little after six in the morning I left the building and found a taxi and went to Victoria Station. The Southern commuter trains were already disgorging men with bowler hats and umbrellas; moving against their tide, I caught the first train to Paris, and from Paris I went on to Florence.

"Having a wonderful time," I wrote, in any old handwriting at all. It was a lie, anyway. The beautiful *things* pierced my heart like hatpins, but there wasn't a drop of blood left. I bought one notebook and then another to solicit the expression of my new-

made heart, but there was nothing to say. From my reflection in
the wardrobe's mirror I photographed my face and learned what
pinched meant. My eyes were too pale. In the evenings, after
going round the churches and museums, I ate enormous sup-
pers and drank lots of wine. Nobody seemed to see me; the Italians did not notice me. In the mornings, with cappuccino, I ate
up American papers, but I might as well have been the charlady's
daughter. So one morning I threw away all my clothes. It was
hard to do, but quick, like a painful inoculation. I took the dark
dresses, the walking shoes and tweed skirts, and made a bundle
of them and tied them with string and left them in a public lava-
tory. From my spy-hole across the street, the window of a pastry
shop, I saw the toilet-paper lady go in, come out, the bundle in
her hands. She turned it around and around, as if it were a bomb.

The salesgirls fell on me like pigeons on breadcrumbs. They
had lipsticks that tasted like icing; their boyfriends had magical
scissors, and my hair fell to the floor in a pale brown wreath around
the barber chair. "I was robbed," I said in Italian, and to please
them I added that the thief was a German tourist.

Sometimes, at night, I looked in the wardrobe mirror at the un-
familiar head and caught a *familiar* look, a knowing glance. "Are
you there?" I asked. The girl in the mirror ran her tongue over
her icing-pink lips and lifted her curls with her fingers: she was
terrible, worse than anybody I could imagine. In the daytime
she wore tight skirts and stockings that hissed as she walked. She
took to smoking cigarettes, left ashes all over the table, left behind air-mail editions of the London *Times,* but at last I decided
she would not leave me, that nothing I could do would keep her
away. She liked movies, after all, good food, strangers: at night,
when I could feel the silence dissolve inside me like a pill in a
glass of water, she got me out of the hotel, out to a café or a movie.

At Christmastime I went back to England. A girl I'd known
at university had invited me to her house for Christmas, and she
met me at Victoria.

"Gosh, look at you!" she said. Her look wasn't altogether happy.

"Do you have any shopping to do before we go? I thought we'd take the six-forty train from Paddington."

"That's wonderful," I said. I began distributing money to porters, and my baskets and cases went into a taxi to Paddington; then from there I went in another taxi to Canon Square. A mean snowfall had left white streaks in the fenced park, and the lights were on in all the houses. At the top of Number 12 I seemed to see a light. The mailbox was empty, and I went up the stairs without ringing the bell downstairs. Only the bell beside the door. I could hear a new record on the Gramophone. Then it stopped. The door opened. Willie stood there in his blue bathrobe. His face was deathly white.

"I took care of the flat," I explained. "I wanted to thank you."

He looked me all over, but mildly, as if he didn't understand me. After a while he said, "Yes, you left a note. Do you want to come in?"

"I brought you something," I said.

It had not changed at all, except that there was a newspaper spread on the carpet in the front room and a tray of drinks on the record cabinet.

"This is it," I said. He opened the box and took out a bathrobe: it was white Italian wool, edged with cream-colored silk.

"This is a very expensive present," he said. "I thank you." Then he gave me a drink. "Who are you?" he said. "You're American, aren't you?"

"Yes," I said. "I'm American."

"You should lose your passport," he said, and laughed. Then he told me he had been in Quebec looking for a story about the Nationalists there. "I'm a Canuck," he said. "Didn't you know?"

"I thought of it," I said.

"I bet you did. But it's nothing. One wants to be something, but what is there to be? Now I wish I were an American, now that's something to be! Without a passport. Yes? Don't you feel it? It's worth traveling for, to *become* an American. Isn't that what's happened to you? How long have you been here? You were wrong to go to Italy, you should have stayed in London. Was everything all right here? What happened?"

"I just wanted to go to Italy," I said.

"Look at you," he said. "And this *present*. Do you understand what you've done?"

"What?" I said.

"I got the idea something had happened," he said.

"So did I," I said, and looked straight at him.

"Let me show you something," he said. He stood up and put his hands around my throat: they were as cold as glass.

"You'd better go," he said.

"Yes," I said. "I have to go. I have a lot to do."

"That's rich," he said. "Christ, you've become a crazy woman. You should try to control yourself." But he had the white bathrobe in his hands, and even as he spoke his hands explored the material; I could feel his interest fading like a breath on a cold window.

"You'll be back," he said.

But I never went back. That night Renata and I met at Paddington and got on the train stinking of perfume. We lighted cigarettes from my pack and drank gin from her picnic flask, and our laps and our coats were covered with fashion magazines. London disappeared into the dark; when we arrived at our destination, two boys were there to meet us. "Honey child," one of them said to me; and when he kissed me full on the mouth, I could taste fresh whiskey. "Who are you?" he said, after the kiss.

MARY CLEARMAN was born and grew up on a small ranch in central Montana, where her family has lived since 1882. The home she knows best was her great-grandfather's homestead. Mrs. Clearman received the B.A. and M.A. degrees from the University of Montana, and the Ph.D. from the University of Missouri at Columbia, where she taught English five years. At the present time she teaches English and directs the drama program at Northern Montana College. She has written short stories, poems, and critical articles, and has a novel in progress. She is married and has two children.

LAMBING OUT

THE WEATHER forecast had predicted that the snow would come in scattered flurries, but instead it began to fall steadily in a deepening blanket over the hills and fences and last year's dead grass. There was no wind, and the snow fell straight down without letting up or increasing all through the day. It fell in a dull rhythm as though no power could make it alter, and what it touched it silenced. By three o'clock it had so darkened the world that the fence posts and telephone poles and occasional cattle drifting ahead of the storm were dim shapes through the white falling curtain, and lights from the scattered ranches were beginning to wink between the shrouded hills and the snow-filled sky. The snow flakes glistened in the reflection of the lights, and kept falling.

The snow was still falling when Nettie Evan got off the school bus at the gate by the barn. She stood out of the way while the bus groaned and spun in the snow and finally lurched back down the road. Its tail lights shone briefly through the snow and were gone. Nettie turned to the gate. The milk cows were waiting to get

into the barn, their shaggy winter hair crusted with snow that had
melted from their body warmth and frozen again. Nettie pushed
a deep swath through the soft snow with the poles of the gate,
and let the cows lumber ahead of her with their eyes bulging at
the snow and their heavy udders swaying. The snow was capping
the corral poles and banking against the barn.

By the time Nettie had reached the house, her scarf and wool
coat were crusted with snow, and it was so dark that she could
not see the hills that rose up around the huddle of buildings. The
willows in the yard were snow-draped and ghostly, and a yellow
light beyond them marked the lambing shed. Nettie stopped and
looked at the falling snow for a minute before she went inside. It
had a monotony that deadened the senses just as it muffled the
hills and ranches and even the moving creatures in white. The
same flakes seemed to be falling over and over into the growing
depth. Nettie thought of the weather forecast they had heard on
the radio that morning, and how her father had silently eaten his
breakfast and then gone out to look at the ewes that were waiting
in the lambing shed. This snowfall was so steady that it might go
on for days. Already the snow was six inches deep. There had
been no wind today, but if the wind should rise in the night, the
snow would drift and the roads would be blocked. Nettie looked
down at the schoolbooks in her arms, the senior lit text and the
geometry book with the assignment marked. She would probably
not get to school in the morning, and the class would be ahead of
her again. Holding her books in one arm, she brushed the caked
snow off her coat and scarf with the other, and opened the kitchen
door.

The heat from the coal range hit her face as she kicked the
door shut behind her, and with it came a stench that she could not
identify. The kitchen was dark, even with an electric light burning
in the ceiling. Nettie's mother was hunched at the kitchen table with
an empty coffee mug in front of her, staring out at the snow, and
her little sister was squatting down in front of an apple box in the
corner by the stove. Nettie set her books down on the oilcloth,
and untied her scarf. Her hair was limp and damp under it.

"Look what we got, Nettie," said her little sister. Her eyes were dark blue above her chapped cheeks. Nettie hung her coat and scarf on a nail by the door, and went around the roaring stove so that she could see into the box.

"So that's what smells!"

There were two lambs in the box, limply splayed against one another. Their minute hoofs were yellow and rubbery, and their eyes were closed. At first Nettie thought they were not breathing, but when she looked closely she saw the rise and fall of the woolly sides.

"So the lambing's started," she said. "Fine time to pick."

At the table, her mother stirred for the first time. "Damn good thing he got coal yesterday," she remarked, and fell silent again. Nettie looked around at the unswept kitchen, at the egg-smeared dishes stacked in the sink, and at her mother's heavy back stretching through her soiled housedress. It was the snow, Nettie thought. Through the kitchen window, the flakes seemed to be spinning. She looked down at the sleeping lambs. The flour sack on which they lay was stained with yellow mucus.

"They're scoured," she said.

"What's scoured?" asked her sister.

"Their milk doesn't agree with them. Makes their bowels run. What kind of milk did they have?"

"Just milk."

"It'll have to be boiled, or they'll die."

The little girl sat on the edge of the box, looking down. Her matted, fair hair was almost white in the light. "They're bums," she said. "Twins. We're going to feed them with a bottle. And I can play with them."

"If they live," said her mother from the table.

"Where's Dad?" Nettie asked. Her mother sat staring out over the coffee cup as though she had not heard. The falling snow spun in the light from the kitchen window.

"Out at the shed," said the little girl. "He went to water the sheep and see if more lambs come."

"Guess I better go help."

The child got up. "Can I come?"

Nettie looked down at her. Her denim overalls were torn, and a thin knee protruded. "You'll have to put on some different clothes," Nettie told her.

"Told you to change your pants this morning, Sylvie," said her mother without turning away from the table. "You've worn 'em for a week."

"Come on," Nettie said. "I'll help you. But hurry up. Poor Dad's carrying water all by himself."

Her mother threw her chair back from the table, making Sylvie jump, and stood up. Carrying her coffee cup with her, she crossed to the stove and filled the cup from the pot. Her hand was shaking, and the coffee spattered and skittered in drops across the top of the range. "I knew those goddamn sheep were a mistake. Too old, for one thing. And he don't take care of 'em right. But you can't tell him—" Returning to the table, she sat down heavily and slopped more coffee on the oilcloth.

Nettie took her sister by the hand and led her up the kitchen stairs to the room under the eaves that they shared. She found an intact pair of overalls for Sylvie, and helped her change. Then she hung her own school clothes behind the curtain that served as a closet, and took down her blue jeans and a darned sweater. As she pulled the sweater over her head and straightened it around her hips, she caught sight of herself in the cloudy mirror that hung over the bureau. The girl peering out at her was anxious-eyed and muscular, with strong legs and thighs under the blue jeans. Her hair was limp. Nettie touched it, thought of taking time to comb it, and changed her mind.

"Come on, Sylvie, get your jacket."

By the time Nettie had bundled up her sister and started her out the back door, her own tracks that she had made coming home from school were nearly filled with snow. The flakes were still falling in rhythm, but now that it was completely dark, they seemed more erratic. Nettie could feel them on her face and see them whirl in the square of light that fell from the kitchen window. Sylvie stepped high and spraddle-legged, for the snow was nearly

to her knees. She put out a hand and caught a few flakes on her
mitten; put them to her tongue and tasted.

"Ugh."

"That's your mitten you taste. Wet wool, silly."

Sylvie ran ahead toward the lambing shed, kicking up the snow
as she went, then turned and ran back to her sister. The snow
had frosted her scarf and sparkled as she turned up her face.

"I like the snow!"

"That's because you haven't been out in it long." Nettie stopped
at the water trough outside the shed and filled the pail that she
found there. The water dissolved the snow that had collected in
the bucket, and splashed on the ice around the trough as Nettie
lifted it out and let her left arm swing out to balance. Sylvia frisked
ahead of her, glad to be out of the house.

"Sing!" she called back to Nettie.

"Sylvie say she love me, but I believe she lie—"

Nettie pulled the shed door open, maneuvered through with
her pail of water, and blinked for a moment in the light. The
shed was a little warmer than it was outside, but the chinking
was falling from between the old logs, and the snow was seeping
through into the straw bedding. A dirty light bulb burned in the
ceiling, where more wisps of straw hung from the reinforcing lath
and chicken wire. Straight ahead of her was an aisle between the
pens, and at the far end her father was leaning over and watching
a ewe, his foot cocked on the bottom board of a panel. He looked
up and saw Nettie.

"I got all that side watered. You might start down the other
side."

Nettie turned to the first pen. The ewes were separated by rough
board panels that could be wired together in different arrangements, depending upon the need. Now they were joined to make
individual cubicles for the waiting ewes. Nettie lifted her bucket
into the first pen and poured water into the trough. The ewe in
the pen backed away and stamped her foot, yellow eyes looking
through Nettie, wool caked with filth. Nettie half-emptied her
bucket and went on to the next pen.

Her father was still watching the ewe in the end pen when Nettie had filled all the remaining troughs and had hung up the bucket. He shot a look at her as she came to stand beside him, his eyes blue pinpoints in a grizzled face. He rubbed his bristles and turned back to the ewe.

"She going to lamb?" Nettie asked, to give him an opening.

He spat tobacco juice into the straw. "When she gets damn good and ready."

The ewe stopped pacing in her pen and backed into the far corner. She stamped, fidgeted, and stamped again. Her water was untouched. Nettie leaned on the panel, looking at the white-ringed yellow eyes that were fixed on a point far beyond her. The pupils were oblong and dilated, giving the ewe a wild, malevolent look. Nettie wondered why a sheep's eye seemed to hold so much concentrated and scheming evil, when the truth was that the sheep was the stupidest of animals, too stupid to scheme anything.

Her father shot her a look. "How's your mother?"

"She's not saying anything."

He leaned heavily on the panel and pulled down the brim of his felt hat. "Snow gets to her."

"Nobody likes it much."

"Well—" he spat again into the straw. "You got to be raised to it. Somebody raised in town like your mother, it gets to them."

Nettie watched the ewe. Behind the sheep, where the log walls rose up out of the straw bedding, the bank of fine snow was growing. There was a sifting, then a trickle, and then a gust. Nettie's hand closed on the rough grain of the panel. Far outside the shed and the limits of the bare light bulb, a sound was gathering momentum, howling in the pines high up the ridges and swooping over the crests of the hills until, as though at its climax, it hit the north wall of the lambing shed. The old logs creaked, and more snow gusted in. The ewes were edgy, heads high and eyes wild.

"I should of got up to the haystack today," said Nettie's father.

Nettie stared at him. "How much have we got?"

"Enough for tomorrow."

"Can't you get up to the stack with the tractor?"

"Hope so."

The shed door opened, and Sylvie shot in on the crest of a wave of snow and cold air. The sheep jumped at the disturbance, lurching in their cubicles. Sylvie's nose and cheeks were red, and her dark blue eyes gleamed. "The wind!" she cried. "It blew me over in the snow!"

"Easy!" said her father. "You've scared the ewes."

Sylvie paid no attention to his caution, but ran panting to them. Her scarf had slipped back, and her fair hair rose up over it. Snow was sticking to her eyelashes and melting in her hair, and more snow was crusted up and down her leg and shoulder where she had fallen. She was hopping in excitement.

"You look like a snowman," Nettie told her. "A snow girl."

"She ought to learn to mind," said her father. He hunched his thick shoulders under his coat, and darted a look at Nettie. "No school for you tomorrow?"

"I don't suppose. Not with this wind."

His eyes roved over the nervous ewes. "Guess there'll be nothing doing till after supper. May as well go in."

"Sure."

"Just as well you'll be home a few days, the way your mother feels. Damn weather gets her down."

With Sylvie prancing ahead of them, Nettie and her father walked between the rows of sheep to the door. The wind whipped snow into their faces as they went out, and Nettie saw that there was already a drift running parallel with the lambing shed. More snow lifted across it like white smoke; then her father switched off the shed light, and there was only the wind driving them through the darkness toward the yellow patch that was the kitchen window. It howled and sprayed them with hard grains of snow, and then slammed into their backs with all the force it had gathered in its career over the faraway ridges and empty plains, and only by walking stiff-legged with their backs braced could Nettie and her father, with the child between them, keep from being driven into the snow.

Nettie cooked supper on the coal range, and washed the dishes afterward while she boiled milk for the lambs. Her father went out once to check the ewes again, and came back in with a gust of snow and the news that there were no new lambs. The wind did not let up, but banged and rattled around the eaves of the house. Its high whining note was far away, an undertone of the true noise of the storm, but Nettie found herself listening to it with her teeth biting hard together.

Sylvie listened to the wind with her eyes gleaming. The storm seemed to excite her. Nettie was pouring milk into a clean beer bottle when the little girl began whirling around and around in one spot, her head thrown back and a high squeal like the wind's coming from between her teeth.

"Stop it!" cried Nettie. She spilled milk over the lip of the full bottle, and reached for the dish cloth. Sylvie stopped and stared at her sister.

"Bad enough to hear it outside without her screeching in here," remarked their mother. She went on through the kitchen and into her bedroom with her bathrobe hunched around her.

Nettie looked at Sylvie's face. "Come on. You can help me feed the lambs," she offered.

Armed with the beer bottle of boiled milk, Nettie sat down on the edge of the apple box and got the biggest lamb under her arm. It did not resist having the nipple shoved into its mouth, but let its eyes roll back while the thick milk dribbled from between its gums and over Nettie's arm.

"Why isn't he hungry?" asked Sylvie, squatting by the box.

"Hasn't got sense enough, I guess." Nettie clamped the limp body between her leg and elbow, and used the fingers thus freed to massage its throat. The lamb gulped and choked, and Nettie took the nipple away. "Guess maybe he swallowed some that time," she said, and forced the nipple into the lamb's mouth again. Working the bottle back and forth, she tried to tease the lamb into taking an interest in the milk.

"Let me hold the bottle," begged Sylvie.

"Guess you may as well." Nettie gave it to the child, but Sylvie could not keep the nipple in the lamb's mouth. Its head lolled on Nettie's leg, and the milk soaked into her blue jeans.

"Maybe he drank a little," said Nettie at last. "Let's try the other one." She let the first lamb sag back into the apple box, and got her fingers under the second, but it was cold.

"It's dead," she said, and set down the bottle.

Sylvie peered with interest into the box. "Why?"

"Oh, it just *is!*" Nettie tried to keep from snapping, but she felt tired. Her father got up and came over from his chair in the corner. He looked down at the two lambs, then bent and picked up the dead one by its middle. It dangled from his hand, four thin legs and a ropy tail. He crossed the kitchen unhurriedly, and went out the door. Presently he returned without the lamb, and went back to his chair.

The wind was still blowing when Nettie took Sylvie up to bed. Up under the eaves, the storm seemed closer. The girls shivered as snow drove against the shingles and rattled on the loose panes. A curtain moved up and down, sank, and rose again with the blast. Nettie put Sylvie in bed, and undressed herself in front of the mirror. Her hair hung lank on her neck, and even though she knew that there would be no school tomorrow, she found her comb and bobby pins and began winding up the loose strands.

Somebody should do something about Sylvie's hair, she thought, and glanced at the bed, but the little girl was already asleep. Nettie jacked open the last bobby pin on her teeth, shoved it into her hair, and got into bed beside her sister. Her arms and shoulders ached from carrying buckets of water, and the quilts smelled musty. Sylvie turned in her sleep and rolled against Nettie, who turned to let the child settle into the curve of her body. Her sides rose and fell gently with the movement of the curtain. The wind whipped against the house. Nettie thought about Sylvie's hair. It should be cut, or at least kept combed. When Nettie had been Sylvie's age, her mother had fussed with her hair, and kept it curled. But her mother was different now. Nettie stretched, and let her eyes close.

The bang of the kitchen door woke her in the morning. She

sat up in bed, shivering in the cold air and remembering the ewes.
The bedroom window was frosted over, and everything was still.
It took her a minute to realize that the wind had died in the night.
Then, tucking the quilts around the still sleeping Sylvie, Nettie got
out of bed and crossed the floor with her bare toes curling. Snow
had sifted through the loose window pane in the night, and she
could see her breath. She found her sweater and blue jeans, and
dressed as fast as she could.

In the kitchen the range was roaring hot, and Nettie held her
hands over it for a minute. Through her parents' door, she could
see her mother's bulk under the bedclothes. Nettie started a fresh
pot of coffee, and went to the kitchen window. It was frosted over
in a glittering forest of ice crystals, and she had to scrape a hole
before she could see. Even when she had a spot the size of her
palm cleared, there was only whiteness, and she blinked.

"Oh lord!" she said aloud. Between the house and the fence
was a nearly level expanse of snow, but the wind had made a drift
against the fence, or where the fence had been—Nettie was not
certain, for the fence was invisible under the great flowing dune
of snow, six feet high and running as far as Nettie could see.

"It still snowing?" her mother called.

"No. Guess it quit in the night. But you never saw such a drift."

Her mother did not answer, but Nettie heard the springs creak
as she turned over in bed. The coffee pot boiled over, and she went
to move it to the back of the stove. When she did, she saw the
lambs in the boxes, two in one box and one in another. One of the
lambs might be the one she had tried to feed the night before, but
even so there must be at least one more dead ewe and maybe two.
Otherwise her father would have left the lambs with their mothers
in the lambing shed. Nettie wondered whether they had been fed,
or if she should boil more milk.

The kitchen door opened, and her father came in, stamping the
snow off his feet. There was more snow on his coat and collected
on the brim of his hat. "Had to shovel my way out to the shed," he
told her. "Let me have some of that coffee."

As Nettie poured him a cup, she saw that he had another lamb under his coat. He laid it in the second box, and came over to the table to sit.

"You up many times in the night?" she asked.

"Two-three."

"Should have called me."

"Almost did, that last trip. Christ, you ought to see it out there."

Nettie wondered about the hay and the dead ewes. "Many lambs out there?"

"Four. That last one's a twin. The old bitch wouldn't claim him, so I brought him in." He drained his cup and leaned over so that he could see through the bedroom door. "You going to get breakfast?"

"Sure."

"I'll take another look and be back in." He got up slowly and went out.

Nettie went to the door before she started breakfast, and looked out. For a minute she had to squint, protecting her eyes against the glare of light on the snow. Then her pupils contracted, and she saw that the whole world was sculptured white, broken only by the winding foxhole that her father had shoveled from the kitchen door to the lambing shed. He was just disappearing, shoulders brushing the top of his path on both sides. By standing on tiptoe, Nettie could see back toward the barn and corrals and the road. The wind had swept down from the hills across the whole expanse, driving the snow into elongated waves and drifts that skimmed up to the tops of the corral poles on one side and dropped off suddenly on the other. There was not a sign of life. Nothing moved. Even the leafless chokecherries below the barn were muffled in snow so that they could hardly be seen against the sweeping whiteness. Nettie shivered, and went quickly back into the kitchen.

She made breakfast, fed her father and Sylvie, who came stumbling downstairs in her underpants with icy hands and feet, and boiled more milk for the lambs. By the middle of the morning, her father had brought in three more, but two of the first ones had died, and he carried them out to join the pile of frozen corpses on the south side of the shed. Her mother finally got up and sat in her bathrobe at the kitchen window, drinking cup after cup of thick coffee.

Sylvie moped about, resisting Nettie's attempt to comb her hair, and taking an interest only in the lambs. She tried to play with them, but they were too young or too despondent.

"What's the matter with them?" she asked Nettie.

"I don't know. They're always like that. Guess they don't care if they live or die."

"I thought they'd be fun to play with."

"They are, when they get bigger."

"They're cute," Sylvie said, and petted a head. She did not seem to mind the sour odor of milk and slime. Nettie herself was getting used to it, but she still thought that the lambs were repulsive, with their flaccid bodies and slack eyes.

Before it was time to start dinner, Nettie scrubbed the boiled milk off her arms and tidied the kitchen and the cold front room. She straightened the chairs and dusted the bric-a-brac and the photographs of the two little sisters who had died of polio before Sylvie was born, and then she sat down at the kitchen table to do her geometry assignment. She was very good at mathematics, even considering how much school she missed every year, but this morning she could not concentrate on the problems. At last she closed the book and got up to get dinner. Her mind kept wandering from the geometry teacher who said that she should go to college, to Sylvie's hair and whether she could cut it to look like anything.

In the late afternoon she helped her father feed and water the ewes again. There were several lambs in the cubicles now, and some of them were nursing and seemed to be all right. And there were some empty pens.

"How's the hay?" she asked.

"Enough for morning." Her father's eyes were bloodshot from the glare of the snow. When they came out of the shed, it was snowing again.

The next morning her father tunneled his way to the tractor

and made an attempt to reach the haystack a half-mile away, but he ran into snow above the fenders before he was beyond the barn and had to abandon the tractor in a waste of churned snow.

"If we caught one of the horses, maybe we could get up there that way," Nettie suggested.

"Not with the hayrack."

"I mean, maybe we could drag down a few bales. Enough to get by on."

"Could be." He rubbed his bristles, considering, and spat tobacco juice in the snow. "Think you could catch old Pete?"

Nettie looked at him, at his bent shoulders and the grizzled folds about his mouth. "Probably. If I take some grain. You keep Sylvie with you?"

"All right," he said, and tramped off. Nettie went back to the house to get her boots and gloves. There was a trail shoveled to the barn, where she collected a bridle and a lariat and a handful of grain. Then she struck off for the ridge where the horses would be hunting for exposed grass.

At first the snow was knee-deep, and she made fair progress, stepping high and breaking the crust only when she had to. Her breath steamed out in front of her, and she stopped twice to pant. Below her the drifts rippled down to the meadows and across the barnyard. She could see the shingles of the house where the heat had melted off the snow, and her father's square figure, shrunken by the distance, coming out of the shed door. From where she stood, the buildings and the tiny human figure were specks in a frozen sea. It was very quiet. She shivered and went on.

Near the top of the hill, she fell into a deep drift to her thighs and had to spread out on her belly to push herself out. Snow went down her neck and into her boots, and she thrashed until she found herself in knee-deep snow again. Ahead of her was bare ground where the wind had swept the snow from the crest of the ridge. She looked back at the churned snow. "Looks like a walrus went through there," she said aloud, to hear her own voice.

Once on bare ground, her legs felt light and unencumbered. She walked north, swinging the wet bridle and stamping her feet.

Across the gully on the upper meadow, she could see the haystack, a white-capped knob rising from the snow.

"Pete!" she called. "Pete!"

At last she felt something watching her, and turned. Three horses were standing on a bare knob, eyes almost hidden under their winter fur, ears pricked toward her.

"Here, Pete!"

They did not budge, and Nettie swore. To reach them, she would have to wade through more snow. Holding the bridle and rope behind her, she swung off the ridge toward the horses. She would have to get by the two yearlings to reach Pete, and if the colts decided to run, he might follow. And she would never catch him.

"Pete!" she called, and held out her grain. To her relief, he stuck out his nose and came toward her, with the two colts snorting behind him.

"That's a good Pete." He lipped at the grain in her gloved hand. Nettie fastened a bridle rein around his neck for insurance, then waited until he had eaten the grain. A few wet kernels fell on the snow as she slipped the bit in his mouth, and he nosed after them while she fastened the headstall.

"Hold still, now." She got a double handful of mane and jumped until she had her belly over his back, then swung her leg over. His fur was warm under her thighs, and she could feel his ribs under the long hair. She nudged him with her boot heel, and he moved off obediently toward the stack.

By picking her way, Nettie managed to get across the gully without floundering the old gelding. Once he broke through the crust to his belly, and thrashed before getting back out, but they found shallower snow the next minute. At the stack, Nettie slid down and kicked the snow from a post before she tied Pete to it. She looked around. Last summer there had been a piece of corrugated tin along the haystack fence somewhere, if it hadn't rusted away. She walked along the fence, casting through the snow with her feet until she kicked the tin. Then she had to kick the snow away before she could get it out. She picked up the ten foot length and pushed it up against the stack. It would hold about four bales, she thought.

She pushed two of the heavy, snow-weighted bales off the stack and then sat down to pant. The snow was seeping through the seat of her blue jeans, but she ignored it. Her hands hurt from hauling at the twine on the bales. All around her was snow.

Ten miles to the south, invisible now, would be the town and the school. She wondered if they were having classes, or whether the storm had closed the schools. A picture of the warm study hall came to her, and she saw the bent heads of the students, the clutter of books, and the whispers from the seniors as they talked about graduation and their applications for college. Nettie got up, dusted the snow off her rear, and tackled the next bale.

Once she had the bales on the strip of tin and anchored with the lariat, she felt more hopeful. She tied the other end of the rope in a bowline knot around Pete's neck, and stood back to study her outfit. It looked all right. She climbed back on Pete and took up the reins.

"Okay, let's see what happens." Eyes on the hay, she nudged Pete into motion.

While they were on level ground, the hayload moved well, gliding over the crusted snow and making Pete snort and roll his eyes at it. The first trouble came when they started down off the hill, for the tin moved faster than Pete did and skidded into his hind legs, making him jump and shy. The tin sailed on by, and came to a stop at the end of the rope. Pete's neck stretched forward, but he held fast.

Nettie urged him forward a step at a time. The hay edged downward for several feet, then overturned against a drift. Nettie slid down off the horse and waded through the snow to right it. Then they started down again.

They worked down by stages, while the afternoon darkened and the air grew colder. Nettie's fingers were numb on the reins by the time she finally reached the shed with her load. Her father came to meet her with his eyes on the hay. He untied the rope and pulled off the first bale.

"This'll get us through tonight," he said, then added, "There's a ewe down—think you could keep an eye on her?"

"Okay." Nettie unbridled Pete and let him go to stand under the shelter of the end of the shed. She wobbled, and stamped her feet to bring the feeling back. Then she entered the shed.

Sylvie was sitting on the top of a panel with her nose running, looking down at the ewe that lay panting on the dirty straw. The little girl turned at her sister's steps. Her eyes were knowing.

"She's having a baby," she told Nettie.

Nettie leaned on the panel. Bedding was short, and the straw was wet. Below it was the frozen ground, and frozen sheep dung. The ewe strained, and saliva dribbled from her mouth. Nettie watched, hoping that things were going right, because she didn't know what to do if they weren't. Sylvie's eyes were solemn.

At the end of the shed came the familiar drive of the wind, and a skiff of snow. Nettie's arms ached, and her back ached. If the wind picked up again, if they got more snow, she didn't know if she could reach the haystack again. And there was only enough hay for the night. At her feet the ewe bleated, mouth against the straw, and heaved. Her sides worked. Slime ran from her, and then the rubbery front hoofs emerged with the lamb's wet head between them.

She heard her father banging a door somewhere, and wondered if she should call him. It seemed all right, but she didn't know. The ewe's feet jerked twice, a bleat rattled from her throat, and she heaved again, hard. The lamb's body slid out on the ground.

"She had it," observed Sylvie.

The ewe raised her head, then put it down again. The lamb moved a little, but the ewe paid no attention.

"She ought to be mothering it," said Nettie. She took a gunny sack from the stack by the aisle, and stepped into the cubicle. Using the sack, she rubbed the slime and membranes from the lamb, and cleared its nose of mucus. It squeaked and breathed.

"Watch out, Nettie!"

The ewe was on her feet, focusing her eyes on Nettie. Her head lowered. Nettie stepped aside, and as the ewe staggered up to butt her, kicked her on the side of the head. The ewe shook herself, trying to find another target.

"You old bitch, take care of your kid!" Nettie caught her by the ears and forced her nose against the lamb. "He's your lamb, you old fool!"

The ewe sniffed at the lamb. Nettie held her nose against it, wondering what she was doing wrong. Some ewes just never claimed their lambs. She scooped up the lamb and propped it against the ewe's hind legs, working the teat into its mouth. Then suddenly it was sucking milk, and the ewe was turning to smell it. Nettie let go cautiously, and backed out of the pen.

Her father appeared behind her. "Listen to that wind!"

Nettie turned. To her amazement, her father was smiling, cracked lips stretched away from his teeth.

"It's from the west. It's chinooking!"

Nettie and Sylvie followed him outside, and around the shed. The wind streamed against their faces, and across the snow. Water was dripping from the eaves of the shed, and the great snow fields around the cluster of buildings seemed damp and shrunken.

"It must be twenty degrees warmer," said Nettie.

"That's that chinook wind for you," said her father. "We'll be knee-deep in water by tomorrow."

"We won't be able to get hay for mud."

"That's about right." Her father straightened. "We'd better get what lambs we can in the kitchen, or they'll die of pneumonia."

Sylvie followed them back and forth. The warm wind brought a more natural color into her cheeks and made her frisk. "What's a chinook?" she asked, and Nettie told her about the warm wind from the Pacific coast that dropped over the mountains and thawed the prairie states. Her father listened.

"Good thing for her you're graduating this spring."

That night Nettie went to sleep listening to water run off the eaves of the house, and in the morning the kitchen was full of damp and bleating lambs. Her father dragged more hay from the stack on the piece of tin, snaking it through soggy grass and mud, and they kept the ewes fed. The next day Nettie's mother got out of bed and dressed, and washed a load of sheets. Some of the lambs died of pneumonia, but some lived, and frisked in the back lot where the snow had melted away from the rotted corpses of dead sheep. Sylvie caught an orphan lamb and sat in her swing with it dangling over her arm.

"I know where you came from," she told it, and sang the song that she liked Nettie to sing to her.

"Sylvie say she love me, but I believe she lie—hasn't been to see me since the last day of July!" Nettie sang when she drove the little band of sheep up to the spring pasture. She road bareback on Pete, swinging the tin dogs ahead of her and making the sheep scurry away from the rattling cans. Sylvie, with her hair matted in snarls and more willful than ever, was playing with the bum lambs back at the house. Looking over her shoulder, Nettie could see green grass cropping through the dead undergrowth and the last dirty patches of snow. The chokecherries were budding, and magpies were nesting. Nettie had heard them squabbling over the carcasses of the dead sheep. Below her, her mother's wash flapped, and ahead of her the lambs ran and jumped straight into the air, careening against their mothers and butting at one another. Some of them were the ones that she had forced to swallow boiled milk.

The wind stirred in the underbrush and ruffled Pete's winter hair that was shedding in handfuls over Nettie's legs. It penetrated her shirt, and she shivered, remembering.

STARKEY FLYTHE, Jr., was born in Augusta, Georgia, and has had stories published under the names F. X. O'Connor and Sam Walton. He is at work on a novel.

POINT OF CONVERSION

MRS. CLEMENTSON had had pregnant girls before. Father Sheehan sent them mainly, but they'd come from the welfare agency too. Even from the WACs. The girls came, swelled for their months, weeping copiously about the men who'd done them wrong, laid their egg, then painted their faces to go out and do it all over again. But left. That was the point. They left. Verna hadn't. After Verna's baby was born, and Mrs. Clementson, or Clemmie as everybody called her—the social tongue never saw fit to title her—stood masked in the delivery room and saw a bungling nurse carry the baby out the wrong door for adoption so that Verna, alert, insistent on natural childbirth, the exercises, the breathing, saw the baby, saw *her* baby and Godknowswhoelse's baby, saw it was a *boy* baby, saw that she would never see him again, and in sobs stayed with Mrs. Clementson.

Clemmie was glad at first. In this garden that she as an ex-public health nurse ran, where girls blew up and never grew up, Verna seemed to learn. Was hurt. Would do better. Clemmie was retired now. Sixty-five, on a pension, living in her grandmother's house, dead now, the grandmother and the house, a victorian draft with a roof like a salt shaker. But rooms. Rooms gone to bed. So that was how Father Sheehan got her into this. And they paid her for it, too. They, the church, the county, the state, the government. "Did you know that?" she said to Mary Murphy, her oldest

friend, her roommate, her sounding box. "Did you know that
the government—you and I—pay for the girl to have her baby?
Then give her six weeks of post natal care? The WACs. Did you
know that?" Mrs. Murphy, oldest and dearest, yawned. She had
become a crank. Was not retired. Completely taken up with her
job at the Veteran's Hospital. Smoked. Wore her hair in a tumble.

When time finally shrank Verna, Clemmie got her a job at a
friend's office. Typing out statements. The Madonna Shop. Bills.
Orders. The shop sold greeting cards, penny pictures of vapid
Jesuses made in Italy, to women who stuck them in books and
forgot about them. Verna was not a Catholic. And that was the
wonder. After all, it was to Father Sheehan she talked in the
months of agony when she wondered why the boy she loved
wouldn't marry her and be happy with the child she was going to
give him. "You wouldn't want to marry him if he doesn't love
you now, would you?" Father asked the girl in the back room
while Clemmie washed supper dishes, and wondered why he didn't
close the door, though knowing that he could never forget—and
how could *she*—that she was a convert, hence some different sort
of clay, clay that had to have it explained by open doors and commonplace chats over commonplace cups of coffee, that there were
no secrets in the Church, no mysteries that she herself couldn't
partake of. "I could tell you what they're like. *Men*. Use you like
Kleenex, then toss you in the garbage." Her own experience was
brief. Husband who drank. Divorce that didn't leak.

Verna went on weeping. But she wouldn't be Baptized.
Wouldn't. Went to mass with Clemmie, Sunday, twice a week,
sometimes more. Sat there in the pew. Knelt. Recited. But
wouldn't come in. "Why in heaven's name?" asked Mary Murphy.
"She only talks to Father Sheehan. Thinks he's wonderful, goes
with you fifty times a week to mass. Why?" she yawned. Verna
said sometimes "I know everybody thinks I'll get over this. But
I won't. You don't know. I'll never, never get over it." Clemmie
looked in a blue horse notebook she kept and read the names of
fourteen girls she'd kept who had had illegitimate babies. "And

you won't get over it," she thought. So Verna kept on with the greeting cards and penny pictures and helped out at the house which didn't make Clemmie mad since she'd taken in two old ladies who couldn't stand a rest home, and whose two nieces said, "Will you take them? Clemmie?" and Clemmie, seeing the nieces' chops water in anticipation of the estate, smiled and said, "Yes. Two hundred apiece." Anyone else she would have done free. She liked to take care of people, wait on them. "You should've been a waitress," Mary Murphy said. "I was," Clemmie came back. "A waitress with bed pans and enemas and specimens. A white winged waitress." "Talk yourself into paradise if you can," cranked Mrs. Murphy.

Verna was young. Never answered back. Ran errands. To the grocery. To the parish hall. To wherever in the world Clemmie wanted her to go. Lickety split. Clemmie was deep into the Catholic family parish life. Nuns from Sacred Heart School came to supper. She had, almost, a brogue, from Father Sheehan, from Mrs. Murphy, from the brothers, the sisters, the fathers. An occasional monsignor. People even said—people who knew her when she was Scotch, when she was Presbyterian, when her father played the pipe organ at the First Presbyterian Church and her mother taught Sunday school, people who knew her before the conversion—the conversion of St. Clemmie, Mrs. Murphy called it, and after half a bottle of sherry had drawn it on the table cloth; Clemmie struck by light, Clemmie on her knees, stigmata spiking her hands, her tennis shoed feet, Father Sheehan holding the reins of her bike—people said, at parties, or any other place where Clemmie, on her bike, in her Nash Metropolitan, went, said, "Now, look at her. If she isn't the epitome of Irish Catholic potato famine, the *epitome*." And Clemmie didn't mind because her potato famine Irish friends were jolly and common-to-the-core and who, she herself included, wasn't? And being ostracized—Greek for pottery shard said Mary who knew everything unimportant— "Broken pieces of pottery and you wrote the name of some crook politico on it and if he got enough—out, and I could think of a few, the mayor included, I'd like to break pottery on"—being ostracized from the *non*-Irish didn't mean anything but being taken in by the Irish. Besides it was 1970 and nobody was anybody but out of the pot. "Everybody else her age has a pot. Except her. She's always pedaling off her pot on her bike. Other ladies peddle insurance but fair Clemmie pedals pot." (Mrs. Murphy on the subject.) And Verna didn't feel so alone if someone else was ostracized. Verna. A mother without a mother's child. But wouldn't she come in? If the haves threw you out, shouldn't you go in with the have nots? Anyway, not all of them were so have not. The O'Shaughnessys owned a liquor store—a chain of them and if the haves didn't think that made mon, and fun . . . Mrs. O'What's-her-name shot Mr. O'What's-his-name's lover—and him with eight children . . . as the lover descended the bus at the corner of Amiens and Roule Street in full view of Tabby O'Something else who clerked in Mr. O's booze store number 6, but who refused to testify at the trial saying he was under the counter when it happened though as everybody who's ever had so much a sip of Italian Swiss Colony knows, store number 6 is a glass box with no counter to speak of and that inside you can see everything that takes place in this world including the mating of an insect which Tabby had also noticed, Mr. O' and his lady love having rented a room in the building opposite number 6. And every Christmas, Easter and All Saints' Day, having been acquitted, Mr. O' sent his lawyer, and Tabby, a case of Dewar's scotch and if that wasn't mon and fun, what was?

Why Verna wouldn't come in, in to that cozy, chatty, warm-your-bones-by-the-fire-with-a-little-whisky Irish life, God only knew. But she wouldn't.

She was from a little town in east Tennessee, a teeny eenie iny town of 150 with a high school that graduated two. (Verna was voted most likely, the other girl most beautiful.) Well, naturally, she was suspicious, but not old enough to have prejudices, especially old prejudices. Ate her breakfast eggs any kind of way.

Thursday, Clemmie pedaled to the Madonna Shop. Verna was out to lunch and her boss, Clemmie's old friend, said, "I'm going.

Closing up shop and going. Pilgrimage. The holy land or Rome. Can't decide. Or maybe even Dublin." This with a wink and a slap on the rear, a conscious Irish manner which all of a sudden Clemmie found not quite so cutie pie as she had pictured it to Verna who was on the outside looking in.

Verna was out of a job. It was all right when she was working and bringing in something for her room and board and going out on errands and helping around the house that really needed help. Now she wasn't part of the hive—the economic part—she'd never picked up with the social part. "Maybe I use her," thought Clemmie. "Maybe she uses me. The uses of uses. Anyway, she ought to have something, something to do."

Verna's unemployed status made her sulk, made her consider any employment—going to the grocery store, the parish—a drudge. Clemmie sent her to the green grocer and Verna banged the cabbage and squash down on the kitchen table with the change. "Here, here, this won't do," Clemmie school-teachered. And Verna female logiced right back, "Won't do? Well, count the change. It's all there. Look at the ticket if you think I took any of your money," and stormed out of the room.

Thursday a week, Clemmie heard the front door slam. Tears— she heard tears—Verna going through the living room, the parlor, the dining room, then into her own room. Another slam. More tears. Clemmie went to the front door. "Now why wouldn't she go straight down the hall to her room instead of zigzagging through every chamber in this heavenly mansion?" Following Verna's steps —her tears, she thought, but actually it was raining—she found a letter moireed with the water from Verna's eyes or the sky's—she picked it up and read—none of her business but after all she had examined penises in the public health service and if that wasn't business what was:

My dearest darling V. My thoughts—and prayers have been with you this last month. I praid your baby—(your baby! bracketed Clemmie) *was safely delivered. You would have been a wonderful and devoted mother.* (You.) *Since*

*leaving you and the Army, I have tried to build a new life
for myself. Dad is happy with the progress I am making in
college and thinks I can easily assume a position in his business when I graduate. But I am not kidding myself. I know
it will be hard work. The whole thing has been very painful
for me.* (Painful. Oh I wish men could lay eggs.) *But I believe everything has worked out for the better. Dad has given
me a new car and this afternoon, I have been out driving
around with a friend. We stopped by a hillside and just
walked around for hours, doing nothing, just staring off into
space. Perhaps you and I can go for a ride some day. Seattle
is a long way for you to come, though, but who knows?*

*May the Lord help you as he has helped me. I know you
will soon forget me and if sometime in the far distant future
our paths should cross, you would say, Who was that, I don't
remember. But I will never forget.*

Yours very truly,
R. B. H., Jr.

When Mary Murphy came home from work, Clemmie said,
"Verna is in her room crying." "Well, I'll be in mine crying if I
don't get these shoes off." "Well, what's wrong with you?"
"Cement."

At supper, her feet reposing in red bunny slippers, Mrs. Murphy read the letter. Verna would not come out of her room. The
old ladies—two hundred dollars—ate in theirs. "Why would she cry
over that?" "I can't guess," Clemmie said. Sarcasm.

"Well, I'll tell you one thing. Every country has its type. In La
Belle it's the aging French bébé, England's got the moustache, and
we have the Dear John." "Her name's Verna." "Don't smart it.
Just pour the sherry," Mary said. "All right."

Verna wept for R. B. H., Jr., her job, her baby. "Well, can you
get her another job?" Clemmie asked. "Yes, if we don't get flooded
out the front door."

The next day, Mary Murphy paddled down the hall to the
source of Verna's tears and told the girl she had a job for her—

temporary replacement in a doctor's office. Verna stopped weeping long enough to go to work. A week went by and she liked it. Breezed in and out. Clemmie mopped up the hall.

Before, Verna had walked to work. Or ridden Clemmie's bike. The Madonna Shop was only four blocks away. Now she had to drive. Clemmie lent her the Nash. Mary: "Is she careful?" Clemmie: "Is she timely? I've got to go to mass five minutes before she gets back."

A month she was on time. Then she wasn't. Clemmie, in hat and coat, temporally and spiritually prepared for the mass, was in flame. "Where have you been? Where! You know I'm late to mass already when you get here. Now it's too late, and here I am lending you *my* car." "*That* car!" Verna said. "Well, you can walk tomorrow, then." Clemmie took off her hat and coat, her armor of light. Verna went to her room. Clemmie put on her apron and started peeling potatoes. "Verna!" She called, "You get in here and peel these!" Verna came out and peeled them, her large clumsy fingers leaving in the eyes and gouging out most everything else.

Next day she walked to work, came home with two friends, two pregnant friends. "This is Louanne and Becky. They were in the WACs with me. Now the same thing's happened to them." She giggled. They went to Verna's room. Shut the door. Giggles. Clouds of smoke.

When Mary got there, they came out and were introduced. They were leaving anyway. They giggled. Rested their arms on their stomachs. "What's so funny? You think a pin'll make that go down? Do you?" They giggled harder, went out the front door, up the street, laughing to cry.

At 8:15, Mrs. Tonley, the regular nurse in the office where Verna worked, called. Mary knew her. They were chummy. "I've asked her," Mrs. Tonley said. "She won't give me an answer. August is my vacation, I can't leave the doctor with nobody. I want to know if Verna's going to stay. Or what." "We thought she loved the job." "I think she does. I just want to know. About August."

In the doctor's office next day Mrs. Tonley said to Verna, "What I want to know is are you going to be here August? Or aren't you? All of it." "See, I really do like it here. You and Dr. Blake are real good to me. I put in for this government job at the Fort. Teaching. That's what I did in the WACs. I don't know if I'll get it. Then you know I get the G.I. Bill. But I'm saving that." "That's fine. Are you going to be here August? Else I've got to get somebody who will." "Well, see, teaching—like I was doing in the Army— it's all I really know how to do. I know what to teach them." "I bet you do," said Mrs. Tonley, and the doctor rang. Some patient couldn't get back into his clothes. Geriatrics.

Next day, Mrs. Tonley said, "Which, Verna? *Now*. Decide." "Oh, Mrs. Tonley . . . If they accept my application at the Fort, I'd have to go right out. They have a lot of girls in line for the job. . . ." "Which, Verna. Now!" "If they don't take me out there, I won't have a job." "Verna. I want somebody here for August." "I don't know."

Mrs. Tonley called Mary that night. "Tell her not to come in tomorrow. I got somebody else. I never saw anything like that girl. Wouldn't *say*." "Don't blame me. She's none of mine. It's Clemmie brings home the strays around here." "How is Clemmie, anyway?" "She's all right. This'll give her something to do. Finding Verna a job." "Something *else*."

When informed, Verna cried. Clemmie said, "Dear God," rising to the occasion by breaking out in hives. She couldn't lie on her bed. Couldn't wear clothes. Wouldn't give in. "I've got something better to do." In a hospital gown—all she could wear—hives and all, her hands pinching the flaps together over her naked behind, Clemmie went out to the hospital. "Don't you have some course out here in Practical Nursing?" "Yes ma'am. But you're too old." "Well now, sonny, how old do you have to be?" "Eighteen and a high school graduate. September 5th." "Well, she's that." On the spot, hives stinging like so many wasps, Clemmie enrolled Verna, at least as far as she could, she not having Verna's thumb prints, birth certificate, high school diploma and a spare notary public.

Verna said No, she wouldn't go, wouldn't use her G.I. Bill, wouldn't. Said Clemmie could go herself if she wanted to go so bad. But, September 5th, she got her history together, got it notarized publicly, and went. Two weeks later, a boy brought her home. She was wearing a starched uniform, pink and white stripes. Smiling. "You look fairly pretty," Mary Murphy said.

The boy turned out to be a male nurse. Clemmie disapproved. "He hasn't got bat brains. And he's three years younger than she is." "Oh, what do you know about love?" snided Mary. Clemmie had given Verna back the car. Verna was later and later. Clemmie gave up mass. Sundays Verna worked part time in a nursing home. With him. "She could do that around here," Mary said. "I'm worried," Clemmie said. "What you need is some more pg girls. To distract you. . . . What's the moon doing tonight?" "Gibbous waning." "Nothing there."

One afternoon, Clemmie and Verna were out shopping. They rode by the First Baptist Church, biggest church in town. "That's where I'm going to be married." "It's a lovely church," Clemmie said vaguely, wistfully. Vague because she couldn't think what Verna meant, or if she meant anything; wistful, because her own church took up two hundred dollars every other Sunday while this Goliath raked in a national debt.

He came to supper that night. During dessert—floating island— Verna said to him, him who never identified himself on the phone, said Is Verna there? nothing else, ran through amber lights—Him, seventeen and a male nurse—"Tell her." As easily as asking for more dessert—which he did—he told them.

Clemmie gritted her teeth: "I'm not going to break out in hives. *Not*." After he left, she went to Verna's room. "Is that what you want? Really want?" "We love each other," Verna said. "You've been through one junk-bunk already. This probably won't be any better, will it?" "This is going to make everything in my life all right. Everything I went through. We're going to have our own apartment, our own job, our own friends, our own baby, our own *car*."

Clemmie went with her to the First Baptist where the preacher said it was fifty dollars for non-members to be married in his church which squelched that. And to the Key Wholesalers where they bought dishes and stainless steel, and sheets. . . . And what else does a man need to live by? Clemmie tried to remember.

Verna found another Baptist church—it was called either the Third Baptist Church or the Fourth Baptist Church. Mrs. Murphy didn't bother to say, "What about Father Sheehan?" Verna and her boy wondered whether to wait till their year course was up. Clemmie said, "Yes. Do. You'd better." They decided not to.

"What is it?" Clemmie demanded of Mary Murphy. "What don't we do right? I tried. I did for her . . . she can't deny that. Her parents wouldn't let her in the house. I let her. Maybe it's the generation gap." "Generation gap? I should hope so. One of those 'youths' tries to get familiar with me, I'll break its. . . ." "No, I meant, maybe *we* can't talk to *them*." "It's them can't talk to us. Mouths all stuffed up with bubble gum." "Oh, Mary. Sometimes you're a comfort," Clemmie changed gear to a snicker, "and sometimes you're not." "Has she told him?" Mary asked. "What?" "About the baby, the po' lil' unwanted baby. 'It was just a *little* baby, your honor.'" "Oh, dear God, Mary. It's not so funny. No. She hasn't told him." "Well, don't you think she oughter?" "She says he won't marry her if he knows." "Won't he find out? On the wedding night?" "She's going to a gynecologist." "A gynecologist!" "Yes, she says he can make her like she was before. . . . Like a virgin." "You get the name of that doctor, I'll have one of those."

When the male nurse kissed Verna good night in the hall, Clemmie, sitting up late with the Annals of Good St. Anne de Beaupré, saw them, thought, "What a pretty thing. Their kiss. Teeth hidden. Muted lips. Breathless wonder." He left her, lips first; last, the hands. As he left, Verna said, curiously, Clemmie thought, "Immersion?" "Total immersion," he said. Clemmie imagined, "Love. Totally immersed in love."

It was baptism they were speaking of, though. The following morning Rev. Reold called. "We are happy to have a new soul." "Who wouldn't be, brother?" thought Clemmie, fundamentalist emerging. "Happy with a new soul for our body, the church. Please tell the applicant to bring a large towel and a change of dry underwear." "She wouldn't bring wet, now would she," said Clemmie, the receiver safely down, Mary's personality drenching her.

Clemmie got it all together and at six she and Mary stood behind the altar in the Fourth Baptist Church and watched Verna in a white robe walk down into the water. Then in the robing room they dried her and saw her without makeup, naked, saw how plain she was, how young, how forlorn.

The next day they were married. Clemmie and Mary stood on the steps of the church, the prefabricated church, stark and new. ("Thank God for all our *papier maché*," confided Mary, hatted and respectable for the occasion) as Verna and her male nurse dashed for the Nash in a thin shower of rice given up by the two pregnant friends and Clemmie and Mary as far as their bursitised arms allowed. Clemmie thought of them driving—that was her wedding present, the car—driving, driving God knows where, God knows to what motel, driving, the insects, drawn by the lights, splattering against the windshield, and she felt a terrible sense of failure, terrible.

BRENDAN GILL was born in Hartford, Connecticut, and received his A.B. from Yale. He has been a contributor to *The New Yorker* since 1936; was film critic for that magazine during 1960–67 and has been drama critic since 1968. He is the author of *The Trouble of One House,* and *The Day the Money Stopped,* an adapted play with Maxwell Anderson. His home is Bronxville, New York; also Norfolk, Connecticut.

FAT GIRL

JEANNE was a big, soft bolster of a girl, with no sharp edges anywhere. She had sky-blue eyes that would suddenly go blank and, after a few seconds, as suddenly come back into focus, and if this was strange what was stranger still was the fact that she seemed to be unaware that it was happening. There was also something odd about her pouting mouthful of pearly teeth—either they were exceptionally small and fine or, young as she was, they were false. Her feet were broad and flat-soled, and from a long way off she could be heard marching slump-slump over the linoleum-covered floors of the office corridors. She had a pretty face, with a well-modelled nose and a high, smooth forehead, from which her hair was drawn back in fine, light-gold threads to a bun behind. Men fell in love with her readily, and she was not surprised.

Two years ago, at eighteen, Jeanne got her first full-time job, with a firm of engineers in a building in the East Forties. The firm is a large one, occupying several floors in the tower of the building; from the office windows you look far out over Long Island, whose distant reaches seem an unpeopled low green wilderness against the sky. Until early this summer, when a number of substantial aircraft contracts were cancelled, the firm had enjoyed many years of unbroken prosperity. At the first hint of hard times, it started cutting down on its office staff, and Jeanne was certain to be among those who would be dismissed, more because her dismissal would serve as a warning to other girls on Jeanne's secretarial level that they must henceforth work harder than they were used to than because the firm was in serious financial difficulties. "We are taking advantage of this opportunity of putting our house in order," the president of the firm noted, not without relish, in a memorandum circulated among his board of directors. "A little bad news can be a healthy thing."

A week or so later, on the very day that Jeanne was given notice, she was battered to death by a young photographer with whom she had been living. (Though the newspapers didn't mention it, an executive of the firm was with her at the time. Roused by her screams, he ran to get help from neighbors, and so may have escaped being murdered himself.) Jeanne's death was shocking for many reasons, not the least of which was the discovery that she had, or appeared to have, no family. The data she had given the personnel office on applying for a job—place of birth, parents, schooling, and the like—had all been made up, perhaps on the spur of the moment. In any event, the body was never claimed by relatives, and after the police were finished with it it was buried, without a funeral ceremony, in the plot of a family named Archer, in a small cemetery in Connecticut.

People in the office found it incomprehensible that good-natured, slow-moving, slovenly Jeanne could be implicated in a deed so violent and bloody—the weapon the young man used in smashing her skull was a camera tripod, and it did its work badly —but the fact is that her fate was in every way characteristic of her; she died as she did because, up to the very last moment of her life, she was kind, lazy, and accommodating: a fat girl content with her lot, who pleased herself and pleased others.

The two most extraordinary things about Jeanne were her size and her skin, which didn't resemble ordinary human skin at all; it was as if she had been upholstered in yard upon yard of some marvellous translucent fabric, very thin and strong, which had been drawn taut over her abundant flesh and blood and which effortlessly kept in place the clutter of her internal organs. When that silky pinkness was touched anywhere, it went white, then red, and the mark of fingers remained on the spot for a long while afterward. A stranger taking hold of her nakedness with his eyes closed might have supposed that he had come into possession of a bundle of some ancient, sumptuous Venetian bedding, and he would have been every bit as astonished when, from time to time, the bedding stirred of its own accord or gave up a sleepy sigh, as when, at the very start of lovemaking, a small, pointed tongue emerged from the pale, little-girl lips and set conscientiously to work.

What puzzled everyone at first was not only her size but also her attitude toward her size, which was one of unquestioning approval. She was totally unlike most fat girls, who suffer openly or secretly from their condition; they rarely choose, as Jeanne did, to ignore the problem. More accurately, not "ignore," since for her the problem didn't exist; her body satisfied her just as it was, and if, undressing her in your mind, your lust was given a momentary check by the thought of the thickness of the great thighs guarding the portal of her trunk, or by the thought of the loop of flesh that would surely hang from her waist as she knelt swaying above you in bed, it was, Jeanne seemed to imply, your loss, not hers—let your goggle-eyed adolescent mind busy itself undressing other girls, the skinnier the better. She managed to convey without the least taint of vanity the impression that she believed herself to be a remarkable physical specimen. It was as if she had gathered up every scrap of available information about herself and had fed it into a computer and had then learned, without surprise, that the reading provided by the computer was the single word "Perfect."

Jeanne took exceptional pleasure in eating and drinking. They were activities that she engaged in aggressively, as other people climbed mountains or competed in games. The sight of food and liquor made her eyes shine. Her first meal of the day was a hasty one—so hasty that she often had no recollection of having eaten it and would say later to girls in the office that it was no wonder she felt starved, having had to go without breakfast that morning. It was her own fault that the meal had to be gobbled on the run. She set her alarm clock to go off too late to allow time for all the tasks she knew she ought to perform in the apartment; moreover, when the alarm rang, she frequently turned it off without so much as opening her eyes and, hugging a pillow in her big bare arms, dozed until the second warning system, a clock-radio on a bureau well beyond her reach, filled the room with its clangor. Jeanne would then plunge groaning up out of bed, a cloud of pink skin that smelled of a childish intensity of sleep and, ever so faintly, of the previous evening's cigarettes and whiskey, and stumble through washing and dressing. In that morning rush, it was impossible for her to leave her room as tidy as she hoped to find it on her return. She acted as if she believed in a magic by which inanimate objects would be able to perform their own housekeeping, and the bed that she left unmade in the morning was always a disappointment to her when she came home at night and found it still unmade. As she clumped heavily down the stairs of the apartment house, the taste of breakfast, which consisted of whatever she had managed to find in her closet-sized kitchen—an open Coca-Cola and a couple of brick-hard brownies, say, or, with luck, a leftover hamburger flecked with white grease and all the more delicious for being cold —mingled not unpleasantly in her mouth with the taste of tooth- paste and fresh lipstick.

Jeanne was expected to reach the office by nine, but she was always late, in part because she allowed herself too little time to walk the ten or twelve blocks between her apartment house on First Avenue in the Fifties and the office, and in part because she stopped at a delicatessen along the way to pick up a Danish pastry ring and a plastic container of coffee. ("Heavy on the cream," she would say, in her sweet, rather infantile voice.) Reaching the office, she lifted the coffee and pastry out of their brown paper bag and set them on her desk, on a blotter that bore the stain marks of innumerable other coffee containers of precisely the same circumference. With a concentration that turned the simple, necessary acts into a ceremony, she prized the lid off the container of coffee, unwrapped the waxed paper from around the Danish, and sat motionless for a few seconds, enjoying the look of the steam that rose from the coffee and the crisp fragrance of the pastry. She picked up the ring in both hands, the plump little fingers held at a sharp angle to the rest, and bit off the ring in large chunks, working them as steadily into her mouth as if she were stoking a furnace. Now and again, she would stop to wipe flakes of pastry from her smeared lips and chin, not with the paper napkin provided by the delicatessen but with her fingertips, which she would afterward lick carefully, one by one. When the Danish was finished and her fingers thoroughly licked, she ran the palms of her hands along the sides of her chair, which was covered with a stout brown furze and which, in the course of her two years in the office, took on a hard, yellowish patina. She ended by brushing any remaining crumbs of Danish from her lap onto the floor and uttering a long-drawn-out sigh of satisfaction. She fed and cleaned herself with the raptness of some outsize domestic animal, staring straight ahead of her and seeing nothing; she didn't like to be spoken to on such occasions, and despite her good nature she would generally refuse to answer any questions that were put to her, affecting as a form of politeness not to hear them.

This was the first of several between-meal snacks that Jeanne treated herself to in the course of the day. The second came shortly after ten, when Amos Archer, for whom she worked as secretary, arrived at the office. Archer would be as breathless as if he had just raced in on foot from Riverdale, though in fact he lived in a single room in a cheap hotel across the street. Sometimes it happened that smoke would be curling up out of the righthand pocket of his tweed jacket when he arrived. Archer had old-fashioned good manners and believed that nobody should smoke in elevators; on entering one he would thrust his lighted pipe into his pocket and, as often as not, would forget its presence there until somebody happened to notice the smoke, or until the jacket itself, after smoldering away for a time (his jackets were famously

old and threadbare and as dry as tinder), would suddenly burst
into flames, which Archer would beat out with his bare hands,
shouting "Damn! Damn! Damn!" in a high voice that sounded not
altogether displeased with his adventure.

Archer was a good-looking, gray-haired man who, in his fifties,
gave an impression of benign senility. He let his glasses ride well
down over the bridge of his nose, and he would fix his attention
on you over the tops of them, perhaps thinking that this would
serve to increase the seeming sharpness of his appraisal of you.
What it did, on the contrary, was to make him look dimmer and
more elderly than ever—a foxy grandpa who had somehow pre-
maturely mislaid his foxiness. Trained as an engineer, he had long
since been eased out of any responsibility for design in the firm;
though he was listed as one of the vice-presidents, he had been
reduced to serving as a sort of office manager, whose duties were
supposed to consist of keeping the place in order. It was he who
parcelled out the chronically insufficient office space and purchased
necessary equipment and supplies, and the high-strung ineffective-
ness with which he performed these tasks was, for as long as the
office remained prosperous, a cherished office scandal—Archer was
the example always cited when the senior partners wished to reas-
sure themselves that, big and rich as the firm had grown, it had
not lost the common, cranky touch.

Archer and Jeanne suited each other to perfection. They were
alike in geniality and incompetence, and from the start their days
passed without friction and without accomplishment. As soon as
Archer had seated himself at his desk, Jeanne would hurry down
to the short-order restaurant in the lobby of the building and ask
for tea and a buttered raisin bran muffin for Archer and a blue-
berry muffin and coffee for herself. ("Heavy on the cream," she
would say again, not for the last time that day.) Scattering crumbs
of muffin along his desk and occasionally, with too violent a gesture, overturning his tea—"God damn these silly containers! Why
don't they make the bottoms broader than the tops? Why don't
they *engineer* them? My underdrawers are soaking!"—he would
harangue her passionately from his inner office about the problems

heaped on his shoulders by his unconscionable superiors, while Jeanne in the glass-walled outer office would sit munching her muffin and sipping coffee, hearing nothing and saying nothing.

Once they had finished their snack, Archer would summon her to his desk and set about dictating memoranda, in extended reply to memoranda received by him from other executives of the company. Jeanne had claimed, applying for the job, to be capable of taking shorthand, but this was no doubt as untrue as everything else she had set down on that occasion; she wrote out laboriously, in a round, childish longhand, the messages that Archer intended to have strike like thunderbolts his innumerable adversaries up and down the hall. He spoke rapidly, in bursts of intricately cluttered phrases, and Jeanne would have been unable to set down six consecutive words as he had uttered them, but her incompetence scarcely mattered; no sooner had he tossed off a sentence than it turned out that he was merely testing the sound of it. "No, no, change that, change that!" he would exclaim, with mounting excitement, for the power of veto, even though it was being exercised only against himself, invariably went to his head. "Make it 'In answer to your inquiry'—no, make it 'In answer to your impertinent inquiry'—no, let's save 'impertinent' for later—make it just 'inquiry'—'inquiry of the seventeenth, let me refresh your recollection concerning the disposition of the . . . ah, the desk and chairs that you have the impertinence to imply'—yes, 'impertinence' is excellent there—'the impertinence to imply were promised you as of the first of the month. Nothing could be farther—further? —farther from the truth. Indeed . . .' "

By one, the usual time at which Jeanne went to lunch, she was again, so she claimed, starved. If she was having lunch with some of the girls in the office, they went to the nearest Schrafft's or Stouffer's, but if, as was more likely, she was being taken to lunch by some man in the office, or by some client of the firm whom she had met, this guaranteed a substantial meal at one or another of the three or four middle-priced French restaurants in the neighborhood. In any event, lunch was always preceded by her first drink of the day: a vodka Martini on the rocks. *"Oh,* but that's *good!*" she would protest, in a tone of astonishment, as if she had never tasted alcohol before and had heard nothing but bad about it. Three or four long swigs and her glass would be empty. Most of the other girls, whose masters were sterner than Jeanne's, would limit themselves to a single drink, but Jeanne had no fear of Archer, and the speed with which she gulped the first Martini allowed her ample time for a second before the usual fruit salad or grilled-cheese sandwiches arrived.

When Jeanne was with a man and he asked her if she would like a second drink (his attention having perhaps been called to this possibility by Jeanne's habit of spinning ice cubes about in the empty glass with her forefinger), she would roll her sky-blue eyes and say, "I know I shouldn't, but, oh, Lord . . ." Later, if the man asked whether she would like a glass of wine with her meal, she would roll her eyes again and in the same voice say, "I know I shouldn't, but . . ." And if the man proposed a bottle of wine instead of a glass, Jeanne's spirits would rise in proportion. "That would be *lovely,*" she would say, reaching her hand out over the red-checked tablecloth and giving her companion's hand a warm, prolonged squeeze. The palm of her hand would be moist; by this time her smooth, high forehead would be covered with innumerable tiny beads of sweat. "Mr. Archer will be furious."

"Nonsense. He's dotty over you."

"No. Yes. That's true. He's a lamb."

"Who happens to bark like a dog. Yap, yap, yap."

"No, no, no!"

"Yap!"

"Nope!"

Delighted with their wit, they filled the restaurant with a shout of laughter. Heads turned, regarding them.

When she had lunch with the girls, she was back at the office by two-thirty; when she had lunch with a man she rarely got back before three-thirty and sometimes as late as four. On these exceptionally tardy occasions, Archer would greet her by not greeting her, silence serving him as a sign of wounded feelings, and

Jeanne would spend much of the rest of the short afternoon making up to him and forcing him to forgive her. She was, of course, drunk, but less conspicuously so than one might have expected, and, while it was impossible for her to work at anything that required precision (the typewriter keys swam before her eyes in a blur of %'s and @'s), she found a dozen harmless errands to perform between their offices. She would think of questions to ask that required her to seat herself, dishevelled and pinkly incandescent, beside his desk, or she would carry in papers to sign that permitted her to hover beside him, her damp bosom grazing his head, and the bizarrely mingled smells of her body—Johnson's baby powder, Arpège, garlic, cigarette tobacco, and the odor of skin and hair—would steadily, relentlessly encircle him. Soon he would be sputtering away on the subject of the intolerable burden he bore on behalf of the company night and day without a word of complaint to anyone, and Jeanne would perceive that she had been forgiven, not for the first time, not for the last.

Sometime between four and five, depending on the hour of her return from lunch, she would pay a second visit to the restaurant in the lobby, picking up two orders of tea, toast, and strawberry jam, with perhaps a couple of slices of pound cake on the side, or a piece of lemon meringue pie—dishes that she described every day to Archer as "your special surprises." Archer never tasted them; half a piece of toast without jam, dipped into milky tea, was as much as his stomach dared to encounter at that hour. Jeanne would consume the surprises to the last morsel, saying with the coquettish smile that she used only when she spoke of food, "Waste not, want not." She had a large stock of such sayings, which she squandered continuously throughout the day: "A stitch in time saves nine." "Let sleeping dogs lie." "Least said, soonest mended." She used them like stage money, in lieu of the real thing; they let her hold up her end in conversations without the bother of taking thought, and the pleasure she derived from not thinking became a part of her companion's pleasure, as palpable as the touch of her hand or mouth.

Tea over, it was a matter of scarcely an hour before it was time to stop work for the day. Jeanne's mind would have begun to clear by then, which meant that an energetic befuddlement was replaced by torpor. She enjoyed this lull between periods of drinking; as the first waves of a delectable lassitude stole up her legs and into the stronghold of her body, she would march along the hall to the ladies' room and, kicking off her broad, ugly pumps, stretch herself out on the couch that occupied a third of the little, mirrored anteroom. Provided that she had remembered that morning, in the hurried hurly-burly of dressing, to furnish herself with a handkerchief, she would arrange it daintily over as much of her face as it could be made to cover; otherwise, and more commonly, she would cover her face with a couple of pieces of Kleenex, or, failing that, with a few lengths of the cheap speckled white toilet paper that Archer had ordered no telling how many thousands of rolls of over the years. She held the paper in place with her left arm, which she kept crooked over her eyes to shut out the harsh, naked fluorescent light above her in the ceiling, and to any of the girls who happened in before she fell asleep she explained that she was taking forty winks. That was one of her usual sayings— "forty winks." She had never been known to say that she was going to take a nap. As the girls went to and from the toilets and sinks, or stopped in front of the mirror to comb their hair and restore their makeup, they chattered together without regard for the bulky object on the chintz-covered couch behind them. They knew that once Jeanne had fallen asleep, no ordinary sound would waken her. From time to time, she would speak a word aloud, or utter a faint moan, in response to some remembered or perhaps only dreamed-of pleasure; then her enormous thighs would part, her legs separating into the upright strokes of an A and her plump feet, pink toes packed together inside gauzy nylon, pointing stiffly left and right, like the feet of dolls.

The alarm that served to rouse her from her forty winks was the hubbub of closing time, when the door of the ladies' room was in constant, clattering motion. Jeanne uncrooked her arm, removed the handkerchief or paper covering her eyes, and peered at the ceiling unseeing, as, slowly and with difficulty, she came back into the world. She got up, thrusting her feet reluctantly into her pumps, and made her way into the bathroom proper, where she splashed cold water onto her closed eyelids, dried her face and hands with half a dozen paper towels, and returned to the anteroom. She stared fixedly at herself in the mirrored wall, repeating softly, "Oh, God, oh, God." Then she borrowed lipstick and eyeshadow from one or another of the girls, made up her face in slapdash fashion, and walked slump-slump to the office, where Archer, unmindful of the hour, was sure to be hammering away on his ancient typewriter, the room blue with smoke.

Teetering in the doorway: "Time to stop, Mr. Archer."

"Stop now? Stop *now?*" A fusillade on the keys, struck at great speed with two fingers. "Just getting started."

"Tomorrow is another day."

"I like working late, after the rabble has gone. Gives me a chance to use my head."

If she happened to have no date that evening, or if the date was a late one: "Come buy me a drink instead."

"You've already drunk too much today."

"You're not my father."

"Old enough to be. Your grandfather, if I'd got into trouble early enough. You were practically falling down when you got back from lunch. Which of my lecherous, aging colleagues was trying to seduce you, God damn the whole mindless lot of them?"

"Nobody."

"Ha! No kneesies, no invitations to a midtown matinée?"

"Just one drink. Then you can send me home."

"Never. Not a drop.

In the end, they would go across the street to a small bar in the hotel where Archer lived, and he would buy her the one drink that she had exacted from him and in return would try to learn from her something about her relationships not only with the men in the office (this as possible ammunition for his running battle with them) but also with the college boys who were, so he instructed Jeanne, her only suitable beaux. Archer had been married twice and divorced twice and had no children. His idea of how a good father ought to behave toward a daughter like Jeanne—and he never for a moment risked assuming any other role—was based on recollections of how his father had behaved toward him and his sisters forty years earlier. He gave her advice, but he had no confidence in it, and he was grateful that she did not laugh at him. He was also grateful that she spared him, surely as much from boredom as discretion, particulars of her relationships with men. When she spoke about sexual matters, it was in general terms, and with unself-conscious candor. One gathered that she felt about sexual activity much as she did about her body: that it was a good in itself and had, and needed to have, no connection with any emotion of love. She spoke of other people's sexual practices with an ease that astonished men of Archer's age. She seemed to assume that anyone who had the ability to go to bed would do so as often as possible and that the choice of a partner was by no means the crucial aspect of the performance; which was to say that it was, after all, only a performance and could be judged accordingly. Sometimes, when she was having lunch with girls from the office and they happened to be seated near a window giving them a view of the street, she would offer comments on one or another of the male passersby. "That one there, in plaid," she would say. "He'd be great in bed."

"Jeanne, what a faker you are," one of the girls would say, egging her on. "Nobody can tell by looking."

And Jeanne would smile her pearly smile and say, "*I* can."

Four or five evenings a week, Jeanne went out on dates. Her escorts ranged in age from twenty to sixty. The very young men were unmarried, but nearly all of the rest had wives or, at the least, ex-wives. Most of them were commuters, with houses in Westchester or Connecticut, and no doubt their wives were used to eating dinner alone or with the children. Married men in their thirties who took Jeanne out were inclined to be still somewhat uneasy over not catching their habitual trains; to keep their wives from worrying about them, they felt obliged to telephone home that they had been held up in town on business, but they hated to have

Jeanne overhear the falsehoods that made it possible for them to be with her—perhaps to be sprawled with her, telephone in hand, on her rumpled couch, with their loafers off and their mouths a smear of lipstick. Sometimes she found the evidence of their discomfiture touching, as when a young man would wait until she went to the bathroom before picking up the phone and, in a low voice, telling his wife in the suburbs the squalid, necessary lie.

Jeanne wondered why the young men took everything so hard. Their bad consciences were a matter of indifference to her, except to the extent that she was puzzled by their having them. What possible injury could be done to anyone, directly or indirectly, by a man's taking her to dinner and, in some cases, to bed? Even if some of them fell in love with her, what harm? She would never try to take them away from their wives; she was neither ambitious enough nor conspiratorial enough to find such an undertaking attractive. She was lazy and she disliked secrets. The guilty feelings of the young men were tiresome, which was one of the many reasons that she preferred going out with older men; they would have solved any problems in respect to the structure of their private lives long before. They liked feeling desire for her, whether they acted on it or not, and they liked having a companion for whom other men obviously felt desire. Finally, they liked her because she made no demands. She was warm and soft and slovenly and cheerful, and these are qualities that young men do not put a sufficient value on.

The youngest of her regular escorts was a black messenger boy in the office, who invariably took her to a mock-Irish pub in the same block as her apartment house and stared at her over bacon-burgers and beer for a couple of hours, scarcely speaking a word (the jukebox, which he fed continuously, took his place as the object she was expected to listen to, and Jeanne was well satisfied with this arrangement), and the oldest was the senior vice-president of the firm, a celebrated engineer and no less celebrated womanizer, who had had a heart attack a year or so earlier and who was terrified of dying of a second attack. No longer willing to risk making love, he was as eager as ever to be in the presence of desirable girls, and more eager than ever to be *seen* to be in their presence; he would take Jeanne to "21" or Quo Vadis and sit staring at her with something like the same immobile, silent longing as the young black, while Jeanne ate and drank with gusto and from time to time brushed his cheek with her open mouth.

Jeanne lived on the fourth floor of her apartment house. Since it was a walkup, the vice-president was forced, for his heart's sake, to meet and say good night to her in the tiny ground-floor lobby. Most of the other men in the office felt that they owed it to their manhood to make the climb to her door at the beginning and end of the evening, hoping for much or little according to their natures. It was a stiff climb, and when they rang her bell at the top of the third long flight of stairs they would be breathing hard. Some of them, aiming to give an impression of youthful vitality, would wait a minute or two outside her door to catch their breath, but, if Jeanne had ever troubled herself with such trifles, the ruse would not have deceived her at all—they had to press the button beside her name in the vestibule of the lobby in order for her to release the lock of the front door, and she could have calculated to the second how long it would take them to reach her floor. In fact, she had no thoughts about them between the time they pressed the button downstairs and the time they pressed the button outside her door. When she opened the door, they began to exist, and when she closed it they stopped existing: it was as simple as that. If they were visibly winded, she took pity on them, and this was never, as they feared, because she assumed that their momentary fatigue was a sign of diminished sexual power. Her imagination was exceptionally economical; she could entertain a single concern for a long time without feeling obliged to let it lead her into a second or third one. Sometimes, greeting them at her door and, for a wonder, being ready to go out, she would say, "Poor thing, you look exhausted! Don't you want to come in and rest?" And her middle-aged escort, wanting nothing so much as a few minutes' respite in her blowsy living room, would reply pantingly, "Nonsense! Never . . . felt . . . better in my life! Away we go!"

Equally contrary to what Jeanne's admirers supposed was how

little she speculated about their bodies. In her presence, the older men fretted to themselves about their approaching or actual baldness, about their jowls and thickening waists, about the bellies that could no longer be sucked in and rendered comparatively invisible. They would hold their heads unnaturally erect to strengthen the line of the jaw, and, seated, they would keep a picture magazine spread on their knees to conceal the flagrant thrust of their pots. At the moment of undressing, they would become as skittish as maidens, turning off lights and taking advantage of half-opened closet doors to hide behind, then making a rush, phantoms of white, rippled, ungainly flesh, for her ill-made bed. Jeanne, who undressed at leisure in the bathroom, would return to find her bedroom in darkness, the man tucked away under the covers and dimly smiling, like a child in a nursery waiting for Nanny's good-night kiss. "But I can't *see* anything!" Jeanne would complain, turning on the light beside the bed and throwing herself down naked beside the man, with only the thickness of the covers left between them. Propping herself up on one elbow, her big body running the length of the bed like an Appalachian range of translucent pinky-white alabaster, she would say, "Let me look at you," and throw back the covers, exposing him. She would contemplate him without haste, reaching out from time to time to touch his body at one point or another and saying, to his astonishment and pleasure, "Nice. Oh, that's nice."

Jeanne's agreeable promiscuity, centered for so many months on the office, was brought to an end when a young man named Ross Fisher fell in love with her. He was a graduate student at Columbia, getting a Ph.D. there for his parents' sake but planning, for his own sake, to become the greatest photographer in the world. They met at a cocktail party one weekend, somewhere in the gusty upper reaches of Riverside Drive, and that was the first thing he ever said to her: "I'm going to be the greatest photographer in the world."

"Do you always say that to people when you first meet them?"

"To girls I do."

"And are they always very impressed?"

"They always say I ought to be analyzed and I always say I've tried that, so then we take it from there. Or we don't take it from there, you know?"

Afterward, neither of them could remember the name of their host, or even why they had happened to go to the party, and Ross considered these facts proof that they had been ordained to meet. Promptly at five the following Monday, Ross was at the office to pick up Jeanne and take her to dinner. He was there on Tuesday as well, and on Wednesday; by then, everyone in the office was aware that an intense courtship was under way—indeed, Ross had announced it to the girl at the reception desk. "I'm courting Jeanne," he said. "I'm going to take her by storm, you'll see. Once I make up my mind to do a thing, nothing can stop me."

Even Archer, who seemed to observe so little, soon became aware of Ross. By the end of the first week, he was in the habit of nodding to Ross, and by the end of the second week he occasionally went so far as to utter a muffled "Hi" to him. Working his pipe up and down in his strong yellow teeth, Archer said one morning to Jeanne, "Not much to look at, but at least he's the right age."

"I hate the babies you want me to like."

"Give him a chance."

"He won't let me not. I wonder what makes him so sure I won't get sick of him. I always do, his type."

"That young man seems pretty sure of everything."

Archer had been wrong to say that Ross was not much to look at. He was a slender, small-boned boy, with features that had the look of having been almost too carefully chosen. Because he was the same height as Jeanne, beside her he seemed smaller than he was. It was true, moreover, that he weighed less than she did, which led to a good deal of ribald speculation in the office about the ways and means of their making love. In fact, there was nothing particularly novel about it. Ross had known but two or three girls, and they had been as inexperienced and tentatively exploratory as he. He was enchanted by the speed and ease with which

Jeanne engulfed him. It was as if the boundaries of their bodies had been abrogated; there was no beginning or end to him or to her. In whatever fashion, or sequence of fashions, she led their flesh to become entangled, the feeling on his part was always that of being plunged—weightless, his heart bursting—into an abyss. Making love with Jeanne was by far the most extraordinary physical experience of his life, and sitting beside her afterward at a bar, or across from her at some rickety restaurant table, he marvelled at the composure with which, having returned to the world, she faced the world. The tranquil impassivity of that big body had no connection with the fierce engine that had wracked him and wrung him and left him a breathless eunuch, curled in its shadow.

For Jeanne, Ross was a lover like any other. With time, she knew, he would learn to give her greater satisfaction, but what he already gave her was enough for her needs. It was the surprising modesty of these needs that made it easy for her to say that she would try to be faithful to him. At first, it had not occurred to her that this would be a matter of concern to Ross; she was amused and touched by how shocked he was to discover, in the early stages of their affair, that she was continuing to see and go to bed with other men. It turned out that he had not supposed, from what he had read and heard about affairs, that such conduct was permissible. He was still more shocked when, having accused her of behaving unnaturally, she laughed at him. "Unnatural would be *not* going to bed with people I like to go to bed with," Jeanne said.

"I don't want to make love to anyone but you."

"Then you don't have to."

"And I don't want you to make love to anyone but me."

"That's being piggy."

"People who love each other—"

"Oh, Christ! Who said anything about that?"

"You have, in bed."

"Those times don't count. You always beg me to say something then, so I do."

He said furiously, again a six-year-old, "I'll kill you if you go
to bed with anyone else."

"Sticks and stones can break my bones, but words will never
hurt me."

He burst into tears, and she held him in her arms on the edge
of the bed. When he could speak again, he said, "I *am* going to
be the greatest photographer in the world, you wait and see. You'll
be terribly proud of me."

"If you don't stop that kind of baby talk, I'll never be proud
of you."

He curled his fingers into her bare thigh; the skin went white.
"That hurt?"

"Yes."

"Now?"

"Yes."

"Want me to stop?"

"I don't give a damn what you do."

"Tell me to stop. Tell me to stop. Tell me to stop."

But she would say nothing. Eventually, he took his hand away,
and the red and white mark of his fingers was on her thigh for
days.

She had intended not to see him anymore, but she could never
stay angry with anyone for long. She not only went on seeing
Ross but agreed to make the experiment of remaining faithful to
him. The only condition that she exacted for what he solemnly
called her "fidelity" was that he never ask whether she was having
sex with someone else. There was no way for him to be sure that
her fidelity was absolute, but after a few weeks she allowed him
to move into her apartment, and this was assurance of a kind:
if she was ever with another man, at least it was no longer in the
bed that she shared with Ross.

His presence in the apartment proved a convenience to her, as
well as a guarantee to him that he enjoyed privileges in respect
to her time and body greater than anyone else enjoyed. For it
turned out that Ross had a natural bent for housework. He was as
tidy in his domestic habits as Jeanne was sloppy in hers. In the

morning, it was he who insisted on their making the rumpled bed
that Jeanne would have left unmade until evening, and sometimes
when, despite his repeated warnings, she was late for work he
would hurry her out of the apartment and make the bed himself,
then carefully wash and dry the breakfast dishes before setting out
on the long crabwise uptown journey to Columbia.

Jeanne had no interest in his graduate studies. Her education,
such as it was, had sunk in her without a trace; she could read
and write and (though not easily) multiply and divide, but she
never mentioned a book that she had liked or disliked and her
knowledge of history embraced only such figures as Washington
and Lincoln. Once, when Archer asked her to name the fifty states
of the Union, with a bottle of Scotch for a prize if she could name
them all, she was able to name only twenty-seven, and one of
these turned out to be Omaha. Ross was often furious with her
for being ignorant. "How can you stand knowing so little when
you ought to know so much?" he would ask her, looking up from
his reading. "I'd hate to have my mind as empty as yours is."

"You can be bright for both of us, baby."

Even his photography didn't interest her. He fashioned a make-
shift darkroom out of a closet between the bedroom and bathroom
and spent at least two hours of every day taking and developing
pictures, and the most that she would say of the results was "That's
very pretty," or "That's ugly. What do you see in such ugly
things?" He took scores of pictures of her—a languorous oda-
lisque, always fully clothed, for though she offered to pose for him
in the nude, he rejected the offer with a taunt: "You're too fat."

"You never thought so before."

"You're not. Of course you're not. But I want your body to be
mine. I don't want anyone to see it except me."

"Lots of people have seen it."

"Never any more."

"Then go back to taking pictures of chimneys and dead trees."

"What a bitchy thing to say. You don't care whether I become
a good photographer or not."

She smiled and held out her arms. "Come to Mama."

Trembling with contempt and anger, he went to her.

The day of her death began like any other. She was, of course, behind schedule, and Ross shouted to her as she padded down the apartment-house stairs that he had a seminar that evening and wouldn't be back from Columbia until late. She stopped at the delicatessen and ordered a Danish and coffee ("Heavy on the cream"), which she savored slowly at her desk. Archer came in ahead of his usual time. The cutting down of the office staff had made him uneasy for Jeanne's sake, and he was determined that he and she should be seen to be getting a great deal of hard work accomplished. "I've already had my tea downstairs," he said.

"What a rotten liar you are."

"Listen, you know as well as I do what a panic my witless colleagues are in. They've lost two cents and they whimper like bankrupts."

"I'm not worrying. I'll go down and get us a special surprise. Something gooey."

"No, God damn it, you'll stay here and work." Archer's glasses slid to the very tip of his nose and hung there, and he was too distracted to push them back. "Please, Jeannie," said Foxy Grandpa, and because he had never said "please" and because he had never called her "Jeannie," she sat down beside him with pencil and paper and let him churn up the contents of his "in" and "out" baskets and fire off savage memos to his enemies until, to their astonishment, it was one o'clock.

"Watch the time," he said. "Be back by two."

"Time and tide wait for no man."

"I warn you, they'll throw you out."

"Let's cross that bridge when we come to it."

With a couple of girls from the office, she had lunch at Schrafft's, and perversely she took care to have her usual two vodka Martinis, followed by a glass of wine. When the other girls returned to the office, Jeanne drifted through midtown, window-shopping and enjoying the heat of the sun on her damp face and throat. She got back to the office to find an envelope waiting for her on the desk. It was her notice. Plainly, it had been prepared a day or two earlier, so plainly she had done well to dawdle over lunch. Coupled with her slight drunkenness, the sensation of having been fired—of having had something harsh and irrevocable happen—exhilarated her. She went into Archer's office to share this unexpected pleasure with him. "I feel—" she began, intending to tell him that she felt like a child let out of school, like a child at a circus, like a child with a red balloon, but seeing his face she guessed instantly what had befallen him, and in the same breath but in a different voice she ended, "Oh, Christ. I'm sorry."

No pipe, no glasses—why had he taken off his glasses? Had it been to keep them from being broken while they stripped him of his badge of office? He said, "They're making me put in for early retirement. I said I'd fight it, but of course I won't. I haven't anything to fight it with."

"Buy me a drink."

"You're already drunk. You ought to be ashamed."

"Now, Daddy-o."

"One drink, then, just to spit in their eye."

In the little bar of his hotel, they sat drinking until after dark. Archer found his glasses in one pocket, his pipe in another. He never stopped talking, having thirty years of grievances to explore. He grew cheerful as he drank, and the worse the grievance the more uproarious it began to seem to them. Once or twice, he interrupted himself to say, "You don't have to stay and listen to all this dreary vomit, you know," and she smiled and patted his hand on the bar and, shaping the words with care, said, "Jeannie is a very, very, *very* good lis'ner." Around nine, they set out to find a place to eat. Holding tight to each other and tacking with brave abandon from one side of the pavement to the other, they made their way toward a restaurant that Jeanne remembered liking, a block or so from her apartment house. When they reached Jeanne's doorway without having located the restaurant, she suggested that he come up and let her cook supper for them. She worried a key out of her purse and between them they found the keyhole and unlocked the door. As they started up the stairs, Jeanne warned Archer that it would be a long climb and that he must stop talking in order to save his breath. The stairs proved even more treacherous than the sidewalk. Archer fell to his knees on almost every landing, when the counted-on next step failed to materialize. Occasionally, he took to his backside, bumping his way upward from tread to tread. Jeanne reached the fourth-floor landing ahead of him, and the door of the apartment was already open when, puffing with exertion, Archer arrived. He stumbled past Jeanne into the living room. "Welcome!" he said to her as she followed him in, and then, "Bathroom?"

Leaving the bathroom, Archer took a wrong turn, wheeled into the dark bedroom, tripped over a camera tripod, and crashed to the floor, carrying the tripod and a small table with him. Jeanne hurried to him from the kitchen, switching on lights as she went. Archer was moaning and Jeanne was laughing as she gathered him up off the floor and propped him, a crumpled tweed sack, on the edge of the bed. She peeled off his jacket, trousers, and shoes, and pushed and rolled him onto the far side of the bed. "Take forty winks while I get supper," she said. Archer made no answer. Curled with his face to the wall and holding his bony, bruised knees in his hands, he was already asleep.

Jeanne went to the bathroom to sprinkle cold water on her face. She felt very drunk and very cheerful and only a little sick as yet. Rocking from foot to foot, she stared at her bathrobe hanging in its accustomed place on a hook on the back of the bathroom door. Even sober, she had room in her mind for but one thought at a time; the bathrobe before her, she no longer remembered her plan for making supper. She washed her hands and brushed her teeth, fumblingly undressed herself, and returned to the bedroom. With a sigh of pleasure, she lay down naked upon the bed and crooked her arm over her eyes to ward off the light. As she fell asleep, she turned on her side and drew up against the soft warmth of her breasts Archer's wiry little body. And there they lay when Ross came back at midnight and walked into the apartment ablaze with lights and called her name.

ANNE TYLER was born in Minneapolis in 1941, but has spent most of her life in North Carolina. She went to Duke University and Columbia, majoring in Russian, and has published three novels, most recently *A Slipping Down Life* (1970), and short stories in various magazines. A new novel will be published this spring. She now lives in Baltimore with her husband, a psychiatrist, and two small daughters, Tezh and Mitra.

WITH ALL FLAGS FLYING

WEAKNESS was what got him in the end. He had been expecting something more definite—chest pains, a stroke, arthritis—but it was only weakness that put a finish to his living alone. A numbness in his head, an airy feeling when he walked. A wateriness in his bones that made it an effort to pick up his coffee cup in the morning. He waited some days for it to go away, but it never did. And meanwhile the dust piled up in corners; the refrigerator wheezed and creaked for want of defrosting. Weeds grew around his rose-bushes.

He was awake and dressed at six o'clock on a Saturday morning, with the patchwork quilt pulled up neatly over the mattress. From the kitchen cabinet he took a hunk of bread and two Fig Newtons, which he dropped into a paper bag. He was wearing a brown suit that he had bought on sale in 1944, a white T shirt and copper-toed work boots. These and his other set of underwear, which he put in the paper bag along with a razor, were all the clothes he took with him. Then he rolled down the top of the bag and stuck it under his arm, and stood in the middle of the kitchen staring around him for a moment.

The house had only two rooms, but he owned it—the last scrap of the farm that he had sold off years ago. It stood in a hollow of dying trees beside a superhighway in Baltimore County. All it held was a few sticks of furniture, a change of clothes, a skillet and a set of dishes. Also odds and ends, which disturbed him. If his inventory were complete, he would have to include six clothespins, a salt and a pepper shaker, a broken-toothed comb, a cheap ball-point pen—oh, on and on, past logical numbers. Why should he be so cluttered? He was eighty-two years old. He had grown from an infant owning nothing to a family man with a wife, five children, everyday and Sunday china and a thousand appurtenances, down at last to solitary old age and the bare essentials again, but not bare enough to suit him. Only what he needed surrounded him. Was it possible he needed so much?

Now he had the brown paper bag; that was all. It was the one satisfaction in a day he had been dreading for years.

He left the house without another glance, heading up the steep bank toward the superhighway. The bank was covered with small, crawling weeds planted especially by young men with scientific training in how to prevent soil erosion. Twice his knees buckled. He had to sit and rest, bracing himself against the slope of the bank. The scientific weeds, seen from close up, looked straggly and gnarled. He sifted dry earth through his fingers without think-ing, concentrating only on steadying his breath and calming the twitching muscles in his legs.

Once on the superhighway, which was fairly level, he could walk for longer stretches of time. He kept his head down and his fingers clenched tight upon the paper bag, which was growing limp and damp now. Sweat rolled down the back of his neck, fell in drops from his temples. When he had been walking maybe half an hour he had to sit down again for a rest. A black motorcycle buzzed up from behind and stopped a few feet away from him. The driver was young and shabby, with hair so long that it drizzled out beneath the back of his helmet.

"Give you a lift, if you like," he said. "You going somewhere?"

"Just into Baltimore."

"Hop on."

He shifted the paper bag to the space beneath his arm, put on the white helmet he was handed and climbed on behind the driver. For safety he took a clutch of the boy's shirt, tightly at first and then more loosely when he saw there was no danger. Except for the helmet, he was perfectly comfortable. He felt his face cooling and stiffening in the wind, his body learning to lean gracefully with the tilt of the motorcycle as it swooped from lane to lane. It was a fine way to spend his last free day.

Half an hour later they were on the outskirts of Baltimore, stopped at the first traffic light. The boy turned his head and shouted, "Whereabouts did you plan on going?"

"I'm visiting my daughter, on Belvedere near Charles Street."

"I'll drop you off, then," the boy said. "I'm passing right by there."

The light changed, the motor roared. Now that they were in traffic, he felt more conspicuous, but not in a bad way. People in their automobiles seemed sealed in, overprotected; men in large trucks must envy the way the motorcycle looped in and out, hornet-like, stripped to the bare essentials of a motor and two wheels. By tugs at the boy's shirt and single words shouted into the wind he directed him to his daughter's house, but he was sorry to have the ride over so quickly.

His daughter had married a salesman and lived in a plain, square stone house that the old man approved of. There were sneakers and a football in the front yard, signs of a large, happy family. A bicycle lay in the driveway. The motorcycle stopped just inches from it. "Here we are," the boy said.

"Well, I surely do thank you."

He climbed off, fearing for one second that his legs would give way beneath him and spoil everything that had gone before. But no, they held steady. He took off the helmet and handed it to the boy, who waved and roared off. It was a really magnificent roar, ear-dazzling. He turned toward the house, beaming in spite of himself, with his head feeling cool and light now that the helmet was gone. And there was his daughter on the front porch, laughing. "Daddy, what on *earth?*" she said. "Have you turned into a teeny-bopper?" Whatever that was. She came rushing down the steps to hug him—a plump, happy-looking woman in an apron. She was getting on toward fifty now. Her hands were like her mother's, swollen and veined. Gray had started dusting her hair.

"You never *told* us," she said. "Did you ride all this way on a motorcycle? Oh, why didn't you find a telephone and call? I would have come. How long can you stay for?"

"Now . . ." he said, starting toward the house. He was thinking of the best way to put it. "I came to a decision. I won't be living alone any more. I want to go to an old folks' home. That's what I *want,*" he said, stopping on the grass so she would be sure to get it clear. "I don't want to live with you—I want an old folks' home." Then he was afraid he had worded it too strongly. "It's nice *visiting* you, of course," he said.

"Why, Daddy, you know we always asked you to come and live with us."

"I know that, but I decided on an old folks' home."

"We couldn't do that. We won't even talk about it."

"Clara, my mind is made up."

Then in the doorway a new thought hit her, and she suddenly turned around. "Are you sick?" she said. "You always said you would live alone as long as health allowed."

"I'm not up to that any more," he said.

"What is it? Are you having some kind of pain?"

"I just decided, that's all," he said. "What I *will* rely on you for is the arrangements with the home. I know it's a trouble."

"We'll talk about that later," Clara said. And she firmed the corners of her mouth exactly the way her mother used to do when she hadn't won an argument but wasn't planning to lose it yet either.

In the kitchen he had a glass of milk, good and cold, and the hunk of bread and the two Fig Newtons from his paper bag. Clara wanted to make him a big breakfast, but there was no sense wasting what he had brought. He munched on the dry bread and washed it down with milk, meanwhile staring at the Fig Newtons, which lay on the smoothed-out bag. They were the worse for their ride—squashed and pathetic-looking, the edges worn down and crumbling. They seemed to have come from somewhere long ago and far away. "Here, now, we've got cookies I baked only yesterday," Clara said; but he said, "No, no," and ate the Fig Newtons, whose warmth on his tongue filled him with a vague, sad feeling deeper than homesickness. "In my house," he said, "I left things a little messy. I hate to ask it of you, but I didn't manage to straighten up any."

"Don't even think about it," Clara said. "I'll take out a suitcase tomorrow and clean everything up. I'll bring it all back."

"I don't want it. Take it to the colored people."

"Don't want any of it? But, Daddy——"

He didn't try explaining it to her. He finished his lunch in silence and then let her lead him upstairs to the guest room.

Clara had five boys and a girl, the oldest twenty. During the morning as they passed one by one through the house on their way to other places, they heard of his arrival and trooped up to see him. They were fine children, all of them, but it was the girl he enjoyed the most. Francie. She was only thirteen, too young yet to know how to hide what she felt. And what she felt was always about love, it seemed: whom she just loved, who she hoped loved her back. Who was just a darling. Had thirteen-year-olds been so aware of love in the old days? He didn't know and didn't care; all he had to do with Francie was sit smiling in an armchair and listen. There was a new boy in the neighborhood who walked his English sheepdog past her yard every morning, looking toward her house. Was it because of her, or did the dog just like to go that way? When he telephoned her brother Donnie, was he hoping for her to answer? And when she did answer, did he want her to talk a minute or to hand the receiver straight to Donnie? But what would she say to him, anyway? Oh, all her questions had to do with where she might find love, and everything she said made the old man wince and love her more. She left in the middle of a sentence, knocking against a doorknob as she flew from the room, an unlovable-looking tangle of blond hair and braces and scrapes and Band-Aids. After she was gone the room seemed too empty, as if she had accidentally torn part of it away in her flight.

Getting into an old folks' home was hard. Not only because of lack of good homes, high expenses, waiting lists; it was harder yet to talk his family into letting him go. His son-in-law argued with him every evening, his round, kind face anxious and questioning across the supper table. "Is it that you think you're not welcome here? You are, you know. You were one of the reasons we bought this big house." His grandchildren when they talked to him had a kind of urgency in their voices, as if they were trying to impress him with their acceptance of him. His other daughters called long distance from all across the country and begged him to come to them if he wouldn't stay with Clara. They had room, or they would make room; he had no idea what homes for the aged were like these days. To all of them he gave the same answer: "I've made my decision." He was proud of them for asking, though. All his children had turned out so well, every last one of them. They were good, strong women with happy families, and they had never given him a moment's worry. He was luckier than he had a right to be. He had felt lucky all his life, dangerously lucky, cursed by luck; it had seemed some disaster must be waiting to even things up. But the luck had held. When his wife died it was at a late age, sparing her the pain she would have had to face, and his life had continued in its steady, reasonable pattern with no more sorrow than any other man's. His final lot was to weaken, to crumble and to die—only a secret disaster, not the one he had been expecting.

He walked two blocks daily, fighting off the weakness. He shelled peas for Clara and mended little household articles, which gave him an excuse to sit. Nobody noticed how he arranged to climb the stairs only once a day, at bedtime. When he had empty time he chose a chair without rockers, one that would not be a symbol of age and weariness and lack of work. He rose every morning at six and stayed in his room a full hour, giving his legs enough warning to face the day ahead. Never once did he disgrace himself by falling down in front of people. He dropped nothing more important than a spoon or a fork.

Meanwhile the wheels were turning; his name was on a waiting list. Not that that meant anything, Clara said. "When it comes right down to driving you out there, I just won't let you go," she told him. "But I'm hoping you won't carry things that far. Daddy, won't you put a stop to this foolishness?"

He hardly listened. He had chosen long ago what kind of old age he would have; everyone does. Most, he thought, were weak, and chose to be loved at any cost. He had seen women turn soft and sad, anxious to please, and had watched with pity and impatience their losing battles. And he had once known a schoolteacher, no weakling at all, who said straight out that when she grew old she would finally eat all she wanted and grow fat without worry. He admired that—a simple plan, dependent upon no one. "I'll sit in an armchair," she had said, "with a lady's magazine in my lap and a box of homemade fudge on the lampstand. I'll get as fat as I like and nobody will give a hang." The schoolteacher was thin and pale, with a kind of stooped, sloping figure that was popular at the time. He had lost track of her long ago, but he liked to think that she had kept her word. He imagined her fifty years later, cozy and fat in a puffy chair, with one hand moving constantly between her mouth and the candy plate. If she had died young or changed her mind or put off her eating till another decade, he didn't want to hear about it.

He had chosen independence. Nothing else had even occurred to him. He had lived to himself, existed on less money than his family would ever guess, raised his own vegetables and refused all gifts but an occasional tin of coffee. And now he would sign himself into the old folks' home and enter on his own two feet, relying only on the impersonal care of nurses and cleaning women.

He could have chosen to die alone of neglect, but for his daughters that would have been a burden too—a different kind of burden, much worse. He was sensible enough to see that.

Meanwhile, all he had to do was to look as busy as possible in a chair without rockers and hold fast against his family. Oh, they gave him no peace. Some of their attacks were obvious—the arguments with his son-in-law over the supper table—and some were subtle; you had to be on your guard every minute for those. Francie, for instance, asking him questions about what she called the "olden days." Inviting him to sink unnoticing into doddering reminiscence. "Did I see Granny ever? I don't remember her. Did she like me? What kind of person was she?" He stood his ground, gave monosyllabic answers. It was easier than he had expected. For him, middle age tempted up more memories. Nowadays events had telescoped. The separate agonies and worries—the long, hard births of each of his children, the youngest daughter's chronic childhood earaches, his wife's last illness—were smoothed now into a single, summing-up sentence: He was a widowed farmer with five daughters, all married, twenty grandchildren and three great-grandchildren. "Your grandmother was a fine woman," he told Francie; "just fine." Then he shut up.

Francie, not knowing that she had been spared, sulked and peeled a strip of sunburned skin fron her nose.

Clara cried all the way to the home. She was the one who was driving; it made him nervous. One of her hands on the steering wheel held a balled-up tissue, which she had stopped using. She let tears run unchecked down her face and drove jerkily with a great deal of brake-slamming and gear-gnashing.

"Clara, I wish you wouldn't take on so," he told her. "There's no need to be sad over *me*."

"I'm not sad so much as mad," Clara said. "I feel like this is something you're doing *to* me, just throwing away what I give. Oh, why do you have to be so stubborn? It's still not too late to change your mind."

The old man kept silent. On his right sat Francie, chewing a thumbnail and scowling out the window, her usual self except for the unexplainable presence of her other hand in his, tight as wire. Periodically she muttered a number; she was counting red convertibles, and had been for days. When she reached a hundred, the next boy she saw would be her true love.

He figured that was probably the reason she had come on this trip—a greater exposure to red convertibles.

Whatever happened to DeSotos? Didn't there used to be a car called a roadster?

They parked in the U-shaped driveway in front of the home, under the shade of a poplar tree. If he had had his way, he would have arrived by motorcycle, but he made the best of it—picked up his underwear sack from between his feet, climbed the front steps ramrod-straight. They were met by a smiling woman in blue who had to check his name on a file and ask more questions. He made sure to give all the answers himself, overriding Clara when necessary. Meanwhile Francie spun on one squeaky sneaker heel and examined the hall, a cavernous, polished square with old-fashioned parlors on either side of it. A few old people were on the plush couches, and a nurse sat idle beside a lady in a wheel chair.

They went up a creaking elevator to the second floor and down a long, dark corridor deadened by carpeting. The lady in blue, still carrying a sheaf of files, knocked at number 213. Then she flung the door open on a narrow green room flooded with sunlight.

"Mr. Pond," she said, "this is Mr. Carpenter. I hope you'll get on well together."

Mr. Pond was one of those men who run to fat and baldness in old age. He sat in a rocking chair with a gilt-edged Bible on his knees.

"How-do," he said. "Mighty nice to meet you."

They shook hands cautiously, with the women ringing them like mothers asking their children to play nicely with each other. "Ordinarily I sleep in the bed by the window," said Mr. Pond, "but I don't hold it in much importance. You can take your pick."

"Anything will do," the old man said.

Clara was dry-eyed now. She looked frightened.

"You'd best be getting on back now," he told her. "Don't you worry about me. I'll let you know," he said, suddenly generous now that he had won, "if there is anything I need."

Clara nodded and kissed his cheek. Francie kept her face turned away, but she hugged him tightly, and then she looked up at him as she stepped back. Her eyebrows were tilted as if she were about to ask him one of her questions. Was it her the boy with the sheepdog came for? Did he care when she answered the telephone?

They left, shutting the door with a gentle click. The old man made a great business out of settling his underwear and razor in a bureau drawer, smoothing out the paper bag and folding it, placing it in the next drawer down.

"Didn't bring much," said Mr. Pond, one thumb marking his page in the Bible.

"I don't need much."

"Go on—take the bed by the window. You'll feel better after awhile."

"I *wanted* to come," the old man said.

"That there window is a front one. If you look out, you can see your folks leave."

He slid between the bed and the window and looked out. No reason not to. Clara and Francie were just climbing into the car, the sun lacquering the tops of their heads. Clara was blowing her nose with a dot of tissue.

"*Now* they cry," said Mr. Pond, although he had not risen to look out himself. "Later they'll buy themselves a milk shake to celebrate."

"I wanted to come. I made them bring me."

"And so they did. *I* didn't want to come. My son wanted to put me here—his wife was expecting. And so he did. It all works out the same in the end."

"Well, I could have stayed with one of my daughters," the old man said. "But I'm not like some I have known. Hanging around making burdens of themselves, hoping to be loved. Not me."

"If you don't care about being loved," said Mr. Pond, "how come it would bother you to be a burden?"

Then he opened the Bible again, at the place where his thumb had been all the time and went back to reading.

The old man sat on the edge of the bed, watching the tail of Clara's car flash as sharp and hard as a jewel around the bend of the road. Then, with nobody to watch that mattered, he let his shoulders slump and eased himself out of his suit coat, which he folded over the foot of the bed. He slid his suspenders down and let them dangle at his waist. He took off his copper-toed work boots and set them on the floor neatly side by side. And although it was only noon, he lay down full-length on top of the bedspread. Whiskery lines ran across the plaster of the ceiling high above him. There was a cracking sound in the mattress when he moved; it must be covered with something waterproof.

The tiredness in his head was as vague and restless as anger; the weakness in his knees made him feel as if he had just finished some exhausting exercise. He lay watching the plaster cracks settle themselves into pictures, listening to the silent, neuter voice in his mind form the words he had grown accustomed to hearing now: Let me not give in at the end. Let me continue gracefully till the moment of my defeat. Let Lollie Simpson be alive somewhere even as I lie on my bed; let her be eating homemade fudge in an overstuffed armchair and growing fatter and fatter and fatter.

JAMES SALTER appeared in the O. Henry collection once before, in 1970. His stories are published in *The Paris Review*. His best-known novel is *A Sport and a Pastime*.

THE DESTRUCTION OF THE GOETHEANUM

IN THE GARDEN, standing alone, he found the young woman who was a friend of the writer William Hedges, then unknown but even Kafka had lived in obscurity, she said, and so moreover had Mendel, perhaps she meant Mendeleyev. They were staying in a little hotel across the Rhine. No one could seem to find it, she said.

The river there flowed swiftly, the surface was alive. It carried things away, broken wood and branches. They turned, went under, emerged. Sometimes pieces of furniture passed, ladders, windows. Once, in the rain, a chair.

They were living in the same room, but it was completely platonic. Her hand bore no ring, no jewelry of any kind. Her wrists were bare.

"He doesn't like to be alone," she said. "He's struggling with his work." It was a novel, still far from finished though parts were extraordinary. A fragment had been published in Rome. "It's called *The Goetheanum*," she said. "Do you know what that is?"

He tried to remember the curious word already dissolving in his mind. The lights inside the house had begun to appear in the blue evening.

"It's the one great act of his life."

The hotel she had spoken of was small with small rooms and letters in yellow across the facade. There were many buildings like

First appeared in issue no. 51, Winter 1971, of *The Paris Review*.

it. From the cool flank of the cathedral it was visible among them, below and a little downstream. Also through the windows of antique shops and alleys.

Two days later he saw her from a distance. She was unmistakable. She moved with a kind of spent grace, like a dancer whose career is ended. The crowd ignored her.

"Oh," she said, "yes, hello."

Her voice seemed vague. He was sure she did not recognize him. He didn't know exactly what to say,

"I was thinking about some of the things you told me . . ." he began.

She stood with people pushing past her, her arms filled with packages. The street was hot. She did not understand who he was, he was certain of it. She was performing simple errands, those of a remote and saintly couple.

"Forgive me," she said, "I'm really not myself."

"We met at Sarren's," he explained.

"Yes, I know."

A silence followed. He wanted to say something quite simple to her but she was preventing it.

She had been to the museum. When Hedges worked he had to be alone, sometimes she would find him asleep on the floor.

"He's crazy," she said. "Now he's sure there'll be a war. Everything's going to be destroyed."

Her own words seemed to disinterest her. The crowd was pulling her away.

"Can I walk with you for a minute?" he asked. "Are you going towards the bridge?"

She looked both ways.

"Yes," she decided.

They went down the narrow streets. She said nothing. She glanced in shop windows. She had a mouth which curved downwards, a serving girl's mouth, a girl from small towns.

"Are you interested in painting?" he heard her ask.

In the museum there were Holbein's and Hodler's, El Greco's,

Max Ernst. The silence of long salons. In them one understood what it meant to be great.

"Do you want to go tomorrow?" she said. "No, tomorrow we're going somewhere. What about the day after?"

Thursday. He woke early, he was already nervous. The room seemed empty. The sky was yellow with light. The surface of the river, between stone banks, was incandescent. The water rushed in fragments white as fire, at their center one could not even look.

By nine the sky had faded, the river was broken into silver. At ten it was brown, the color of soup. Barges and old-fashioned steamers were working slowly upstream or going swiftly down. The piers of the bridges trailed small wakes.

A river is the soul of a city, only water and air can purify. At Basel, the Rhine lies between well-established, stone banks. The trees are carefully trimmed, the old houses hidden behind them.

He looked for her everywhere. He crossed the Rheinbrucke and, watching faces, went to the open market through the crowds. He searched among the stalls. Women were buying flowers, they boarded streetcars and sat with the bunches in their laps. In the Borse restaurant fat men were eating, their ears were close to their heads.

She was nowhere to be found. He even entered the cathedral, expecting for a moment to find her waiting in the great, holy coolness. There was no one. The city was turning to stone. The pure hour of sunlight had passed, there was nothing left now but a raging afternoon that burned his feet. The clocks struck three. He gave up and returned to the hotel. There was an edge of white paper in his box. It was a note, she would meet him at four.

In excitement he lay down to think. She had not forgotten. He read it again. Were they really meeting in secret? He was not certain what that meant. Hedges was forty, he had almost no friends, his wife was somewhere back in Connecticut, he had left her, he had renounced the past. If he was not great, he was following the path of greatness which is the same as disaster, and he

had the power to make one devote oneself to his life. She was with
him constantly. I'm never out of his sight, she complained. Nadine:
it was a name she had chosen herself.

She was late. They ended up going to tea at five o'clock; Hedges
was busy reading English newspapers. They sat at a table over-
looking the river, the menus in their hands long and slim as air-
line tickets. She seemed very calm. He wanted to keep looking at
her, he couldn't. *Hummersalat,* he was reading somehow, *rump-
steak.* She was very hungry, she announced. She had been at the
museum, the paintings made her ravenous.

"Where were you?" she said.

Suddenly he realized she had expected him. There were young
couples strolling the galleries, their legs washed in sunlight. She
had wandered among them. She knew quite well what they were
doing: they were preparing for love. His eyes slipped.

"I'm starving," she said.

She ate asparagus, then a goulash soup, and after that a cake
she did not finish. The thought crossed his mind that perhaps they
had no money, she and Hedges, that it was her only meal of the
day.

"No," she said. "William has a sister who's married to a very
rich man. He can get money there."

It seemed she had the faintest accent. Was it English?

"I was born in Genoa," she told him.

She quoted a few lines of Valery which he later found out
were incorrect. *Afternoons torn by wind, the stinging sea . . .* She
adored Valery. An anti-Semite, she said.

She described a trip to Dornach, it was forty minutes away by
streetcar, then a long walk from the station where she had stood
arguing with Hedges about which way to go, it always annoyed
her that he had no sense of direction. It was uphill, he was soon
out of breath.

Dornach had been chosen by the teacher Rudolf Steiner to be
the center of his realm. There, not far from Basel, beyond the
calm suburbs, he had dreamed of establishing a community with

a great, central building to be named after Goethe, whose ideas
had inspired it, and in 1913 the cornerstone for it was finally
laid. The design was Steiner's own, as were all the details, techniques, the paintings, the specially engraved glass. He invented its
construction just as he had its shape.

It was to be built entirely of wood, two enormous domes which
intersected, the plot of that curve itself was a mathematical event.
Steiner believed only in curves, there were no right angles anywhere. Small, tributary domes like helmets contained the windows
and doors. Everything was wood, everything except the gleaming Norwegian slates that covered the roof. The earliest photographs showed it surrounded by scaffolding like some huge
monument, in the foreground were groves of apples trees. The
construction was carried on by people from all over the world,
many of them abandoned professions and careers. By the spring
of 1914 the roof timbers were in position, and while they were
still laboring the war broke out. From the nearby provinces of
France they could actually hear the rumble of cannon. It was the
hottest month of summer.

She showed him a photograph of a vast, brooding structure.

"The Goetheanum," she said.

He was silent. The darkness of the picture, the resonance of
the domes had begun to invade him. He submitted to it as to
the mirror of a hypnotist. He could feel himself slipping from
reality. He did not struggle. He longed to kiss the fingers which
held the postcard, the lean arms, the skin which smelled like lem-
ons. He felt himself trembling, he knew she could see it. They
sat like that, her gaze was calm. He was entering the grey, the
Wagnerian scene before him which she might close at any moment
like a matchbox and replace in her bag. The windows resembled
an old hotel somewhere in middle Europe. In Prague. The shapes
sang to him. It was a fortification, a terminal, an observatory from
which one could look into the soul.

"Who is Rudolf Steiner?" he said.

He hardly heard her explanation. He was beginning to have
ecstasies. Steiner was a great teacher, a savant who believed deep

insights could be revealed in art. He believed in movements and mystery plays, rhythms, creation, the stars. Of course. And somehow from this she had learned a scenario. She had become the illusionist of Hedges' life.

It was Hedges, the convict Joyce scholar, the rumpled ghost at literary parties, who had found her. He was distant at first, he barely spoke a word to her the night they met. She had not been in New York long then. She was living on Twelfth Street in a room with no furniture. The next day the phone rang. It was Hedges. He asked her to lunch. He had known from the first exactly who she was, he said. He was calling from a phone booth, the traffic was roaring past.

"Can you meet me at Haroot's?" he said.

His hair was uncombed, his fingers stained. He was sitting by the wall, too nervous to look at anything except his hands. She became his companion.

They spent long days together wandering in the city. He wore shirts the color of blue ink, he bought her clothes. He was wildly generous, he seemed to care nothing for money, it was crumpled in his pockets like waste paper, when he paid for things it would fall on the floor. He made her come to restaurants where he was dining with his wife and sit at the bar so he could watch her while they ate.

Slowly he began her introduction to another world, a world which scorned exposure, a world more rich than the one she knew, certain occult books, philosophies, even music. She discovered she had a talent for it, an instinct. She achieved a kind of power over herself. There were periods of deep affection, serenity. They sat in a friend's house and listened to Scriabin. They ate at the Russian Tea Room, the waiters knew his name. Hedges was performing an extraordinary act, he was fusing her life. He, too, had found a new existence: he was a criminal at last. At the end of a year they came to Europe.

"He's intelligent," she said. "You feel it immediately. He has a mind that touches everything."

"How long have you been with him?"

"Forever," she said.

They walked back towards her hotel in that one, dying hour which ends the day. The trees by the river were black as stone. *Wozzeck* was playing at the theater to be followed by *The Magic Flute*. In the print shops were maps of the city and drawings of the famous bridge as it looked in Napoleon's time. The banks were filled with newly minted coins. She was strangely silent. They stopped once, before a restaurant with a tank of fish, great speckled trout larger than a shoe lazing in green water, their mouths working slowly. Her face was visible in the glass like a woman's on a train, indifferent, alone. Her beauty was directed towards no one. She seemed not to see him, she was lost in her thoughts. Then, coldly, without a word, her eyes met his. They did not waver. In that moment he realized she was worth everything.

They had not had an easy time. Reason is unequal to man's problems, Hedges said. His wife had somehow gotten hold of his bank account, not that it was much, but she had a nose like a ferret, she found other earnings that might have come his way. Further, he was sure his letters to his children were not being delivered. He had to write them at school and in care of friends.

The question above all and always, however, was money. It was crushing them. He wrote articles but they were hard to sell, he was no good at anything topical. He did a piece about Giacometti with many haunting quotations which were entirely invented. He tried everything. Meanwhile, on every side it seemed, young men were writing filmscripts or selling things for enormous sums.

Hedges was alone. The men his age had made their reputations, everything was passing him by. Anyway he often felt it. He knew the lives of Cervantes, Stendhal, Italo Svevo but none of them were as improbable as his own. And wherever they went there were his notebooks and papers to carry. Nothing is heavier than paper.

In Grasse he had trouble with his teeth, something went bad in the roots of old repairs. He was in misery, they had to pay a French dentist almost every penny they had. In Venice he was bitten by a cat. A terrible infection developed, his arm swelled to twice its size, it seemed the skin would burst. The *cameriera* told them cats had venom in their mouth like snakes, the same thing had happened to her son. Hedges was in agony, he could not sleep. The bites were always deep, she said, the poison entered the blood. It would have been much worse fifty years ago, the doctor told them. He touched a point up near his shoulder. Hedges was too weak to ask what it meant. Twice a day a woman came with a hypodermic in a battered tin box and gave him shots. He was growing more feverish. He could no longer read. He wanted to dictate some final things, Nadine took them down. He insisted on being buried with her photograph over his heart, he had made her promise to tear it from her passport.

"How will I get home?" she asked.

Beneath them in the sunlight the great river flowed, almost without a sound. The lives of artists seem beautiful at last, even the terrible arguments about money, the nights there is nothing to do. Besides, through it all, Hedges was never helpless. He lived one life and imagined ten others, he could always find refuge in one of them.

"But I'm tired of it," she said. "He's selfish. He's a child."

She did not look like a woman who had suffered. She drove very fast. Her teeth were white. On the far pathways couples were having lunch, the girls with their shoes off, their feet slanting down the bank. They were throwing bits of bread in the water.

The development of the individual had reached its apogee, Hedges believed, that was the essence of our time. A new direction must be found. He did not believe in collectivism, however. That was a blind road. He wasn't certain yet of what the path would be. His writing would reveal it, but he was working against time, against a tide of events, he was in exile, like Trotsky. Unfortunately, there was no one to kill him. It doesn't matter, my teeth will do it in the end, he said.

Nadine was staring into the water.

"There are nothing but eels down there," she said.

He followed her gaze. The surface was impenetrable. He tried to find a single, black shadow betrayed by its grace.

"When the time comes to mate," she told him, "they go to the sea."

She watched the water. When the time came they heard somehow, they slithered across meadows in the morning, shining like dew. She was fourteen years old, she told him, when her mother took her favorite doll down to the river and threw it in, the days of being a young girl were over.

"What shall I throw in?" he asked.

She seemed not to hear.

"Do you mean that?" she finally said.

It was arranged, they would all have dinner together, would Hedges sense something or not? He tried not to think about it or allow himself to be alarmed. There were scenes in every literature of this moment, but still he could not imagine what it would be like. A great writer might say, I know I cannot keep her, but would he dare give her up? Hedges, his teeth filled with cavities and all the years lying on top of his unwritten works?

"I owe him so much," she had said.

Still, it was difficult to face the evening calmly. By five o'clock he was in a state of nerves, playing solitaire in his room, re-reading articles in the paper. It seemed that he had forgotten how to speak about things, he was conscious of his facial expressions, nothing he did seemed natural. The person he had been had somehow vanished, it was impossible to create another. Everything was impossible, he imagined a dinner at which he would be humiliated, deceived.

At seven o'clock, afraid the telephone would ring at any moment, he went down in the elevator. The glimpse of himself in the mirror reassured him, he seemed ordinary, he seemed calm. He touched his hair. His heart was thundering. He looked at himself again. The door slid open. He stepped out, half expecting to find them there. There was no one. He turned the pages of the Zurich paper while keeping an eye on the door. Finally he managed to sit in one of the chairs. It was awkward. He moved. It was seventen. Twenty minutes later an old Citroën backed straight into the grill of a Mercedes parked in the street with a great smashing of glass. The concierge and desk clerk went running out. There were pieces everywhere. The driver of the Citroën was opening his door.

"Oh, Christ," he murmured, looking around.

It was William Hedges.

They all began to talk at once. The owner of the Mercedes, which was blinded, fortunately was not present. A policeman was making his way along the street.

"Well, it's not too serious," Hedges said. He was inspecting his own car. The stoplights were shattered. There was a dent in the trunk.

After much discussion he was finally allowed to enter the hotel. He was wearing a striped cotton jacket and a shirt the color of ink. He had a white face, damp with sweat, the face of an unpopular schoolboy, high forehead, thinning hair, a soft beard touched with grey, the beard of an explorer, a man who washed his socks in the Amazon. He was alone.

"Nadine will be along a little later," he said.

When he reached for a drink, his hand was trembling.

"My foot slipped off the brake," he explained. He quickly lit a cigarette. "The insurance pays that, don't they? Probably not."

He seemed to have reached a stop, the first of many long, of enormous pauses during which he looked in his lap. Then, as if it were the thing he had been struggling to think of, he inquired painfully, "What do you . . . think of Basel?"

The headwaiter had placed them on opposite sides of the table, the empty chair between them. Its presence seemed to weigh on Hedges. He asked for another drink. Turning, he knocked over a glass. That act, somehow, relieved him. The waiter dabbed at the wet tablecloth with a napkin. Hedges spoke around him.

"I don't know exactly what Nadine has told you," he said softly. A long pause. "She sometimes tells . . . fantastic lies."

"Oh, yes?"

"She's from a little town in Pennsylvania," Hedges muttered. "Julesburg. She's never been . . . she was just a . . . an ordinary girl when we met."

They had come to Basel to visit certain institutions, he explained. It was an . . . interesting city. History has certain sites upon which whole epochs turn, and the village of Dornach gave evidence of a very . . . The sentence was never finished. Rudolf Steiner had been a student of Goethe . . .

"Yes, I know."

"Of course. Nadine's been telling you, hasn't she?"

"No."

"I see."

He finally began again, about Goethe. The range of that intellect, he said, had been so extraordinary that he was able, like Leonardo before him, to encompass all of what was then human knowledge.

"All of knowledge," he said distractedly.

That, in itself, implied an overall . . . coherence, and the fact that no man had been capable of it since could easily mean the coherence no longer existed, it was dissolved . . . The ocean of things known had burst its shores.

"We are on the verge," Hedges said, "of radical departures in the destiny of man. Those who reveal them . . ."

The words, coming with agonized slowness, seemed to take forever. They were a ruse, a feint. It was difficult to hear them out.

". . . will be torn to pieces like Galileo."

"Is that what you think?"

A long pause again,

"Oh, yes."

They had another drink.

"We are a little strange, I suppose, Nadine and I," Hedges said, as if to himself.

It was finally the time.

"I don't think she's a very happy woman."

There was a moment of silence, of indecision.

"Happy?" Hedges said. "No, she isn't happy. She isn't capable of being happy. Ecstasies. She is ecstatic. She tells me so every day," he said. He put his hand to his forehead, half covering his eyes. "You see, you don't know her at all."

She was not coming, suddenly that was clear. There was going to be no dinner.

Something should have been said, it ended too obscurely. Ten minutes after Hedges had gone, leaving behind an embarrassing expanse of white and three places set, the thought came of what he should have demanded: I want to talk to her.

All doors had closed. He was miserable, he could not imagine someone with weaknesses, incapacities like his own. He had intended to mutilate a man and it turned into monologue—probably they were laughing about it at that very moment. It had all been humiliating. The river was moving beneath his window, even in darkness the current showed. He stood looking down upon it. He walked about trying to calm himself. He lay on the bed, it seemed his limbs were trembling. He detested himself. Finally he was still.

He had just closed his eyes when the telephone rang in the emptiness of the room. It rang again. A third time. Of course! He had expected it. His heart was jumping as he picked it up. He attempted to say hello quite calmly. A man's voice answered. It was Hedges. He was humble.

"Is Nadine there?" he managed to say.

"Nadine?"

"Please, may I speak to her," Hedges said.

"She's not here."

There was a silence. He could hear Hedges' helpless breathing. It seemed to go on and on.

"Look," Hedges began, his voice was less brave, "I just want to talk to her for a moment, that's all . . . I beg you . . ."

She was somewhere in the town then, he hurried to find her. He didn't bother to decide where she might be. Somehow the night had turned in his direction, everything was changing. He walked, he ran through the streets, afraid to be late.

It was nearly midnight, people were coming out of the theaters, the café at the Casino was roaring. A sea of hidden and half-hidden faces with the waiters always standing so someone could be hidden behind them, he combed it slowly. Surely she was there. She was sitting at a table by herself, his eyes would find her in a second.

The same cars were turning through the streets, he stepped among them. People walked slowly, stopping at lighted windows. She would be looking at a display of expensive shoes, antique jewelry perhaps, gold necklaces, old watches with faces white as biscuits. At the corners he had a feeling of loss. He passed down interior arcades. He was leaving the more familiar section. The newsstands were locked, the cinemas dark.

Suddenly, like the first truth of illness, the certainty left him. Had she gone back to her hotel? Perhaps she was even at his, or had been there and gone. He knew she was capable of aimless, original acts. Instead of drifting in the darkness of the city, her somewhat languid footsteps existing only to be devoured by his, instead of choosing a place in which to be found as cleverly as she had drawn him to follow, she might have become discouraged and returned to Hedges to say only, I felt like a walk.

There is always one moment, he thought, it never comes again. He began going back, as if lost, along streets he had already seen. The excitement was gone, he was searching, he was no longer sure of his instincts but wondering instead what she might have decided to do.

On the stairway near the Heuwaage, he stopped. The square was empty. He was suddenly cold. A lone man was passing below. It was Hedges. He was wearing no tie, the collar of his jacket was turned up. He walked without direction, he was in search of his dreams. His pockets had blue bank notes crumpled in them, cigarettes bent in half. The whiteness of his skin was visible from afar. His hair was uncombed. He did not pretend to be young, he was past that, into the heart of his life, his failed work, a man who took commuter trains, who drank tea, hoping for something, some proof in the end that his talents had been as great as the others'.

This world is giving birth to another, he said. We are nearing the galaxy's core. He was writing that, he was inventing it. His poems would become our history.

The streets were deserted, the restaurants had turned out their lights. Alone in a café in the repetition of empty tables, the chairs placed upon them upside down, his dark shirt, his doctor's beard, Hedges sat. He would never find her. He was like a man out of work, an invalid, there was no place to go. The cities of Europe were silent. He coughed a little in the chill.

The Goetheanum of the photograph, the one she had shown him, did not exist. It had burned on the night of December 31, 1922. There had been an evening lecture, the audience had gone home. The night watchman discovered smoke and soon afterwards the fire became visible. It spread with astonishing rapidity and the fireman battled without effect. At last the situation seemed beyond hope. An inferno was rising within the great windows. Steiner called everyone out of the building. Exactly at midnight the main dome was breached, the flames burst through and roared upwards. The windows with their special glass were glowing, they began to explode from the heat. A huge crowd had come from the nearby villages and even from Basel itself where, miles away, the fire was visible. Finally the dome collapsed, green and blue flames soaring from the metal organ pipes. The Goetheanum disappeared, its master, its priest, its lone creator walking slowly in the ashes at dawn.

A new structure made of concrete rose in its place. Of the old, only photos remained.

PATRICIA ZELVER was born in Long Beach, California, but her home town is really Medford, Oregon, where she grew up. She received her A.B. and M.A. from Stanford. She has sold many short stories to both popular and literary magazines, most recently *Atlantic Monthly* and *Virginia Quarterly*. Her first novel, *The Honey Bunch*, was published in 1970, and a second novel, *The Happy Family*, has just been published. She is married to an urban planner and has two sons.

ON THE DESERT

EARL C BENNET had integrity. He knew his luck would change one day; it had to on account of the Law of Averages; therefore, compromises weren't necessary. But even if he hadn't believed in the Law of Averages, he wouldn't have given in. That was the kind of man he was.

Earl C was forty-nine years old. The "C" in his name didn't stand for anything, but was just part of his Christian name given to him by his mother and daddy. He was six feet tall, almost, if he stood up straight. But for a long time now he had slumped. The slump had solidified into a little hump between his skinny shoulder blades; Earl C accepted the hump as matter-of-factly as folks accept a proper part of their body. His face was long and bony; his skin and hair were the color of the Mojave in late summer. He wore khaki pants and a white T-shirt. The only color to him was his eyes, which were the translucent blue of the bottles he collected out on the desert and kept on the windowsill, and which had a neutral expression as if, like the bottles, they had been put there just for decoration.

Earl C lived in his place of business, which was called Earl's Place. It was a three-room wooden shack with a tin roof, right next to the Highway, seventy-six miles from Vegas and twenty miles from "The Heart of America's Favorite Recreation Land."

The front room was the Café, where he served sandwiches and soft drinks and sold thunder rocks and other souvenirs; next to the Café was the storage room, where he kept his freezer and supplies. The other small room, beneath the sloping tin roof, was his bedroom. He used the outdoor public Gents for his toilet.

Five years ago the Highway had been busy, but now, owing to the new Freeway, it had turned into a frontage road, and only local traffic went by. Darlene, Earl C's wife for twenty years, had seen the Freeway coming and had tried to persuade Earl C to sell the Place and buy a motor court on the Freeway. Earl C had refused.

It wasn't because he didn't think Darlene was right; she was usually right about things like that. It was just that he didn't intend to be pushed around by Big Shots in Government. He had voted against the Big Shots all his life. His favorite candidates for President of the United States had been William Lemke, Roger Babson, and Claude A. Watson.

"You slay me, Earl C," Darlene had said, her soft, fat body shaking with silent laughter.

Earl C thought he remembered she had been pretty once. But, imperceptibly, throughout the years, she had put on flesh; the flesh had smoothed out her features and other distinguishing parts of her body, so that it sometimes seemed every part of her looked the same.

"You really slay me," she wheezed helplessly, wiping tears of amusement out of her little piggy eyes.

Then she had took off. With the money she had inherited from her first husband and had hoarded in the bank all the years of their marriage, she had bought the Cactus Motor Court. The Cactus Court had Beautyrest mattresses, air conditioning, wall-to-wall carpets, and a plaster burro out in front. Darlene had her own little unit, where folks registered. She had equipped it cozily, with a new sofa and two overstuffed chairs, plastic potted shrubs that looked real, and a color TV. During the season, her No Vacancy sign was on most of the time.

She had also got herself a divorce for what she called "business reasons." But this didn't stop her from dropping in every Saturday night during off season to play casino and heckle Earl C about his lack of business sense.

"How's your smelly old zoo?" she would say, as she deftly shuffled the cards.

"Flourishing," said Earl C.

"That zoo just costs you time and money. You ought to go out there with your deer rifle and shoot them all."

"I like my zoo," said Earl C firmly.

"How many thunder eggs you sold this month?"

"Didn't keep track."

"You ought to get rid of this place and come over to the Cactus, Earl C. I'd put you up in the trailer. I could use somebody to do the night shift and work as handyman. You never were much good fixing things, but at least you don't drink. I fired that drunken Mexican last week."

"I like it here," said Earl C.

When Darlene was amused, which was most of the time, her eyes screwed up so tight they vanished inside the folds of her flesh. They did that now. "There's no fool like an old fool, Earl C," she said. "You ain't going nowhere. I was just out at your Ladies Rest Room. It's a filthy mess."

"I got a new idea," Earl C said slowly. "I got it in a place in Las Vegas." He showed her a verse he had copied down on the back of an envelope. "I was thinking of putting this up in the rest rooms."

Darlene read it.

Let no one say to your shame,
There was cleanliness here 'til you came.

Darlene rocked with soundless laughter. "You slay me, Earl C," she said.

Since business was slow, Earl C spent a lot of time sitting on his

tiny front porch, next to the frontage road. On the other side of the
road the desert stretched out until it reached the row of rocky hills
in the distance. In the daytime, the hills were lavender; at night,
black, craggy silhouettes. Somewhere up there, it was said, was a
hidden uranium mine. In his younger days, Earl C used to go into
these hills with a horse and search around in the dry gullies between the barren cliffs. He had not discovered the mine, but he
had brought back many bleached bones of animals—skulls, pel-
vises, rib cages, and femurs of cows, horses, and coyotes. He arranged these bones artistically out in front of his place and
planted cacti in and among them for a pretty effect. But he always
examined them carefully first. He had heard that dinosaurs, in all
sizes, from that of a chicken to eighty-foot-long giants, had once
roamed these parts; it was necessary to keep your eyes open; you
never could tell when you might come upon a find. He also picked
up interesting specimens of rocks and minerals, which he polished
and labeled and placed on a bench beneath the bottle window.

Now he had arthritis, and horseback riding shook up his spine.
But he liked to stare across the road to the mysterious hills. "I'm
not getting any younger," he would say to himself. "I'm not getting
any richer, either. But someday, something will happen. It's got to,
on account of the Law of Averages."

Out in back of his place, Earl C kept his zoo. He had had, from
time to time, a horned toad, two rattlers, a gila monster, a de-
odorized spotted skunk, a sidewinder, a ring-tailed cat, a kangaroo
rat, an iguana, a prairie dog, and two alligators (not indigenous)
which he had ordered, against Darlene's wishes, from a shop in
Florida. Most of the zoo had now passed away. The Mexican
family down the road had stolen and eaten the iguana; Earl C
could never prove this, but he knew it in his bones. The gila monster had caught a chill during the rainy season, and passed, too; it
was his favorite, and he had taken it to Kingman and had it stuffed,
and then returned it to its cage. But folks complained he had advertised a *Live* Zoo, and they weren't getting their fifty cents'
worth, so he put the gila monster on the back of the counter, next
to the live Black Widow in a mason jar. The Zoo now consisted

of one rattler, one sidewinder, the kangaroo rat, which never came out of its nest in the daytime, and the ring-tailed cat, which was mangy and turning mean.

Earl C had advertised his Place for ten miles in each direction with signs he had painted himself, and nailed to telephone poles. Each sign pointed out a different attraction.

10 miles to Earl's—Cool Drinks

7 miles to Earl's—Eats

5 miles to Earl's—Live Family Zoo

2 miles to Earl's—Clean Rest Rooms

When you got to Earl's Place there were many other signs, including a big one he had added after the Freeway went in. It said, "If you can't Stop, Wave."

Recently, Earl C had had bad luck about the signs. A young man with a crew cut and wearing a jacket and tie, who was from the County Planning Department, had stopped by and told Earl C the signs had to go; they didn't comply, were his words, with the county's new sign ordinance. Earl C felt gravely put upon by this government man, but what could he do? Nothing! That was the way it was with those Big Shots. They made laws that suited only them. One day, about a month later, the signs vanished.

"I see your signs are gone," said Darlene, on the following Saturday night. She kept up with things; nothing escaped her notice.

Earl C explained the situation to her.

"You're a dope, Earl C," Darlene said. "That county man just wanted his palms greased, that's all."

Earl C would never offer a bribe, on account of his integrity. Just the same he was curious about how you went about it. He asked Darlene how much money the county man would have expected. Darlene's fat body quivered and quaked with amusement. He asked her how you gave it to him; did you just hand it straight out, mail it in a letter, or leave it lying on top of the counter for him to pick up?

"There ain't no rules," she chortled. "You just have to have a business head."

There was one thing Darlene never could get through *her* head, business-like though it was, and that was Earl C's conviction, based on scientific evidence, that things would change for the better. A taciturn man, he had a mind filled with images he could not express. They took the form of flickering, incandescent shapes, much resembling the neon splendor of Las Vegas, where he occasionally went to play keno.

El Dorado
Golden Nugget
Four Queens
The Mint

"Twenty-Four Hour Excitement" was what they promised, and Twenty-Four Hour Excitement was what he dreamed about. One day, he knew, it would come about.

Earl C could recall the exact moment when it did. It was ten-twenty-two A.M., November 15, 1967, at the Buy-N-Save Market in Kingman, where he went once a week to buy supplies. Darlene dropped in that evening, and right away she sensed the new look about him. It was the Twenty-Four Hour Excitement look, which, though he tried, he could not suppress.

"How's business?" she said, as they sat at one of the tables in the Café, where they played cards. Her voice wasn't smug this time; it was sharp and suspicious, and her eyes remained wide open.

"Middling," said Earl C.

"How's that ornery bobcat?" she went on, fishing.

"Ring-tailed. Same as ever."

Still eyeing him, cannily, she said, "Gin rummy or casino?"

"Don't know as I have time for either. I got to think."

"Think?" she said scornfully, but he detected an anxiety in her voice. "When did you ever think last, Earl C?"

"I have to find a good lawyer, not in Kingman, but in Vegas."

She put down the deck. "You're in trouble?" she said gleefully.

"Nope. Some Big Shots are, though. Some Big Shots back in Chicago."

"Earl C, you slay me." He could tell her heart was not in her words. "Now just what do you want a lawyer for?"

"I found something today," he said with dignity.

Her eyes were bulging out of her face, reminding Earl C of the gila monster.

"Or maybe it kind of found me. The Law of Averages has come about."

"What is it, Earl C?" Her voice was threatening.

"Don't know as I better tell anyone until I see the attorney."

"If you need an attorney, you better tell me first. You don't have a drop of business sense in your head."

"I'll tell you if you can guess!" He thought for a moment. Then he put it another way. "I'll give you a hint, though. I found it in a cube of Vi-Rite Oleomargarine."

"I reckon you found a thousand-dollar bill," she said sarcastically.

"Might turn into more." He hummed under his breath.

"All right. Animal, vegetable, or mineral?"

His lips twitched. "Animal."

"What are you getting at, Earl C?" She appeared to have stopped breathing; her flesh barely rippled. He recognized the symptoms; she was in a real pucker.

"Animal," he said. "Maybe a mouse."

"For your Live Family Zoo, I reckon."

He hummed again, softly.

"I didn't come here to play kids' games, Earl C," she said, between her teeth. "You tell me, or I hightail it out of here."

Earl C knew his teasing had gone far enough, because he had to tell Darlene; it was part of his Twenty-Four Hour Excitement. He said, "Just a minute, you wait here." He went into the back room, where he kept his freezer, and returned with a small plastic tackle box. Slowly and elaborately he opened the box and removed a small package, wrapped in aluminum foil. Slowly, even grandly, he undid the foil, then the Vi-Rite wrapping, and held its contents up under the lamp for her to gaze upon.

She stood up and hung over his hand and stared.

"I see a cube of oleomargarine, Earl C. What's so special about that?"

"Look close." He pointed to a particular part.

She bent down to study it. There, smoothly encased in the pale yellow mold, was a darkish section; on close scrutiny it appeared to be made of a hairy organic matter.

"Well?" said Earl C proudly.

"Look here, Earl C, you've got something there all right, and you know it." Darlene was breathing heavily. "Yes, sir, you got a find."

"I'm pretty sure it's half a mouse. I'm fixing to get it scientifically analyzed, for sure."

"It's a something that doesn't belong there, no matter what it is," Darlene said. "Listen, Earl C, you better let me handle it. They'll make you a nice settlement if we go about it correct."

Earl C carefully wrapped up the oleo, fitted it back into its plastic box, and returned it to the freezer. He came back and sat down opposite Darlene.

"You got a lock on that freezer?"

"Yes, ma'am!"

"We could get a real good settlement if you don't bungle things."

"I ain't taking no settlement," Earl C said. His voice took on a kind of rapturous quality. "Those Big Shots in Chicago are going to fix me up with a place in Palm Springs, maybe, or I just might get me a Mobile Home and tour the world. I've always wanted to see the Yellowstone National Park, and New York City. They're going to arrange things for Earl C Bennet nice. I'll take it all the way to the Supreme Court if need be. This time the law's on my side."

"The Supreme Court takes money, Earl C, and you don't have none. But I know something about business. Those folks back in Chicago would make you a decent payment just to get that thing back."

"I don't settle," Earl C said again. "That ain't my way."

The attorney in Las Vegas, a young chap in a fancy office, wearing a bolo tie and expensive boots, said right away that Earl C had a case. "A case," he said, emphasizing the "a" part. "We'll take some photographs of that cube, then I'll get a letter right off, and we'll see what transpires. In this kind of action, they usually oblige by settling out of court. My fee will be a percentage of the settlement." He looked Earl C over. "Twenty percent," he said.

Earl C, holding the traveling styrofoam icebox, with his find in it, on his lap, shook his head. "I ain't going to settle for nothing less than ten grand."

"You may have set your sights a bit too high," the lawyer chap said easily. "But I think we could manage to get a few hundred for you."

Earl C hugged the icebox more closely.

"Those Big Shots sold me an inferior product," he said. "I got this here inferior product on my lap. I'm fixing to get ten grand, you can tell them that."

Two years went by in which Earl C made many trips into Vegas. He had turned down three offers from Chicago, the highest and last one being $300. He had changed attorneys four times. The last attorney had a new letter in the mail right now.

Other things had happened, too. Busy with his case, Earl C had neglected what was left of his business, and he was in trouble about his taxes. He had scarcely enough money left to keep him going for a month. The ring-tailed cat had passed, and the kangaroo rat had eaten his way out of his cage and run off. Thick dust had collected on his rock and mineral collection, and the bottles were so dirty they were no longer translucent. People drove by and stopped to use the rest rooms, without patronizing the Café; Earl C was forced to padlock the doors.

But his spirits stayed high; he was still experiencing the Twenty-Four Hour Excitement. Even Darlene's disgust at his turning down the offers did not dampen his dream. He sat in the evenings on his porch and looked out at the hills. "I'm not getting any younger," he said to himself, "but I'm getting richer, slow but sure." He was betting hard on the most recent letter, which the lawyer had made severe.

When the answer came it was a repeat of the last one, with an addition. The addition said this was a final offer; after that they would terminate the correspondence. The lawyer urged Earl C to accept it. Politely, but firmly, he declined. The fifth lawyer he went to see that same afternoon had already heard about the case and said he couldn't do anything more. Earl C packed up his find and headed home. "Right is right," he said to himself. "The law doesn't always serve justice."

That night Darlene stopped by. "What's that up in front of your place, Earl C?" she said. She was referring to the new sign he had made that afternoon in large letters:

ASK TO SEE WHAT I FOUND IN A
CUBE OF VI-RITE OLEOMARGARINE

"I've decided to handle the case myself," he told Darlene.

She sniffed, scornfully. "I just fired that Indian handyman," she said. "He was a no-good Indian. You're a no-good white man, Earl C, but if you accept that last offer, and give me half, you can still have the trailer in return for taking my night shift and some work around the motel. If you don't, the law's going to get you for your taxes."

"When word about my sign gets around, there'll be some activity," said Earl C calmly.

The sign did attract curiosity. Folks stopped by and asked to see what he had found; when he showed them, they looked and marveled. Earl C explained his position to them in detail. "I've been offered four settlements," he said. "I've got all the correspondence locked up in a drawer. But I'm holding out for ten grand. Those Big Shots ain't going to get away with it."

He could tell by their comments they approved of his stand. "That's right, that's the spirit, keep it up," they would say. Then they would drive on.

In late June, badgered by the tax man, Earl C put his Place up for sale. His only prospect, a car-wrecking-lot man, claimed the building was worth nothing and would have to be demolished.

Earl C sold out for peanuts. Then he released the rattler and the sidewinder and the Black Widow out on the Mojave, dropped his rock and mineral and bottle collection off at the Desert Museum in Kingman, took his stuffed gila monster and the tackle box which contained his fortune, and went to live at the Cactus Court. The gila monster decorated the small plastic-top table in the trailer; he put the tackle box in Darlene's freezer and added a lock. His agreement with Darlene was the night shift and doing cleanup and repairs. He didn't tell Darlene that he was just biding his time; he had a new secret plan concerning his litigation.

His new plan involved a lawyer in Phoenix who, he had been told, had special experience in personal injury cases. Earl C liked the sound of that; if there was anybody who had been personally injured, he had. The first chance he had to sneak away from Darlene he drove there with the tackle box. Though the lawyer asked for a higher percentage of the fee, on account of his specialty, he said he felt sure he could do something for him. He would let him know what transpired.

For this reason Earl C had difficulty putting his mind to the work Darlene demanded. He fell asleep on the night shift, while Darlene snored in the back room; folks rang the bell, then drove off when they got no answer. The "No" on the No Vacancy sign stayed unlit more than usual when Earl C took over the desk. Darlene's temper took a turn for the worse.

She put him to whitewashing the rocks which bordered the parking lot; Earl C spilled the whitewash on the pavement and had to endure her wrath. While she puttered around in bedroom slippers and a muumuu and screeched at him to do this, do that, he just smiled to himself, knowing he would soon be rid of her. He had decided on the Mobile Home for sure. But, now, rather than New York City, he favored Southern California. He had never seen the ocean, except in movies and on TV, but he had heard it was much like the desert—shifting shapes, changing colors, and unexpected finds washed up on the shore. When Darlene popped her eyes at him, he blinked and looked right through her. Instead of seeing that massive blob of flesh, he saw the pretty California sea.

One day Darlene brought him a letter from Phoenix which she had already taken the liberty of opening. She threw it down on the table and said, "There you are, Earl C. Take it or leave it."

The Phoenix lawyer had arranged for Earl C to be awarded $1000, minus his fee. If Earl C didn't accept this, the lawyer wrote, it was all that anyone could do. Earl C read the letter several times over, then he put it down.

"Well?" said Darlene.

"I guess I'll have to get me another lawyer," he said.

Darlene began to control her breathing.

"I ain't going to compromise on a Once-in-a-Lifetime Opportunity."

Darlene began to yell. "You're more worthless than a Mexican or Indian, Earl C. You'd be better off if you drank yourself silly instead of having found that hunk of mouse! You take that offer, and you start paying me rent until you get down to business. You take that offer, Earl C, or you'll wish you had!"

Earl C said, "It ain't right, so I can't take it," and shut up.

Earl C knew Darlene was crooked, but he never realized how far her crookedness could go. Late that afternoon, purposely, and with malice aforethought, she took the tackle box out of her freezer, unwrapped the oleo, and set it on top of the plaster burro in the full sun in front of the Cactus Court. When she called it to Earl C's attention, it had already thawed. The oleo had slid down the burro's rump, leaving the bits and pieces of the hairy organic matter sticking to the plaster back.

Darlene stood there in her muumuu, watching Earl C. Then her eyes screwed up and her body began to quiver; soon her shaking grew epic like a mighty earthquake. Her laughter wasn't silent this time; little snorts of amusement escaped from her compressed lips. She took the garden hose and sprayed the burro off.

Earl C walked slowly to the trailer and got his deer rifle and loaded it and came back and shot Darlene through her heart. Darlene slid softly to the ground, clutching the garden hose. She looked funny dead. She seemed to have deflated, all at once, like a balloon. Her heart's blood mingled with the water and was changing from dark red to pale pink.

Some people, who had heard the shot, came out of their units, but Earl C paid them no mind. He turned off the hose, then walked slowly back to his trailer. When he got there, he sat down. From his window he could see the desert shimmering in the distance; in the background were the hills. The light was such you couldn't be sure just where they were every moment; they changed their position like phantoms. Sometimes they looked real close up, sometimes faraway.

If luck was on your side, you could come on finds in those hills. But he had had his luck and used it up; it was too late now for him. Just the same, he enjoyed knowing the finds were there. He waited, with quiet integrity, for the sheriff's men to come and hand him over to the law.

ELAINE GOTTLIEB was born in New York City and has lived most of her life there. She holds a B.S. in Journalism from New York University and an M.A. in Creative Writing from Ohio University. She was married to the late Cecil Hemley, writer and editor and founder of Noonday Press, where she was for a time Fiction Editor. She has worked for years on translations of the works of Isaac Bashevis Singer. Her first novel, *The Darkling,* was published in 1947; a textbook, an essay and several new stories will be published this year. Miss Gottlieb teaches Creative Writing at Stephens College, and lives in Columbia, Missouri. She has three children.

THE LIZARD

(for ROBIN H.)

. . . A HABIT of observing, surmising, decorating the sky. A look under things. No, it is not a sickness in itself, though the doctors assume this need to write is an indication of abnormality. Perhaps. But not in the way they imagine. I started writing long before I could use the typewriter. It was my grandmother's typewriter that started me, her crippled portable for which she showed an unreasonable affection, an affection she granted numerous inanimate objects. I started writing in my head, and my hearing began to fade soon afterwards. The doctors try to find a correlation. I do not believe them, but I make an attempt to remember. I see myself beside my grandmother's pool in Miami. Twenty years ago?

Perhaps I was thinking: I am a leaf, a drop of water, an instinct. I knew words like *instinct,* knew all kinds of words: tetragrammaton, analgesic, inconsiderate. My mother thought it ridiculous that an eleven-year-old took the dictionary to bed with him. I would hear her laughing about it with Nat (who never read anything).

Late at night when they went out and left me alone (suspecting babysitters' intentions) I heard house sounds and outside sounds. As if the house were full of voices that started in the walls, trying to intrigue me with stories or plays, episodes about other people elsewhere, in which I was asked to play a leading role, though generally I declined, watching instead their hasty shadows on the ceiling. And sometimes, after they had finished their performance, I would hear a night bird sing my name, or call out: Glorious . . . glorious . . . or palm fronds would rattle against my window like the low clapping of a polite audience.

When I sat alone beside my grandmother's pool I heard little things buzz about me, and other things made timid advances through the grass or in the bushes. At first, everything was green plants, water, sky, a fence, the house, what I knew, what everyone knew. Then it began to open up . . . the world within the world.

The brown one was the first. It was almost the color of the coconut palm, and it seemed to trickle down and lie in a pool of itself on a stone at the base of the tree; then it was the hue of the stone and I would not have seen it if it hadn't snapped at a grasshopper. Then, slipping through the grass, a yellow one, smaller, faintly green, almost transparent; its spine nearly visible. An orange tinge near the throat, and as if trapped by my gaze, transfixed beneath the cactus bush.

I lay with my cheek to the flagstones of the pool, alternately watching the immobilized lizards and the lacing of light through the water. I became aware of a small blue lizard, almost purple, resting near the fence. At least I supposed it rested; I couldn't see it breathe. Sometimes my mother lay as still as that on her bed, with pads over her eyes. She rested a great deal, when she was not at her receptionist job or out somewhere with Nat or having a party in our dim unfinished-looking house. The chairs were always in the middle of the floor; I don't remember anymore where they should have been. The couch was soiled and slightly worn;

my mother occasionally mentioned doing something about it, but always forgot. Blinds shut us in; light seemed to disturb her. On the wall in the foyer there was a painting of a black girl lying down, doing something I could not understand at the time, though in retrospect it appalls me. Yet even then I wondered about it. I did not want to, yet could not help looking at it. My mother had coaxed my father into leaving it there when they separated. She always told people how much it cost . . . as if she had won a bet.

In front of me the lizards seemed sunstruck, or stunned (by some exceptional news?). I touched one; it burned. But was its mind cool? Were the fluctuations of the day absorbed in its spiney shield? I went to sleep and when I awoke all the lizards had gone except one I didn't remember having seen before. It was larger than the others, green as Florida, and with muscular looking legs. I couldn't see any ears and its eyes were lost in the mottled pattern of its skin. But as I was about to touch it the eyes flicked open, opaque, defensive. I turned over on my stomach and squinted.

I thought, had the impression, wanted to believe, was all ready to believe that I saw the lizard doing an exercise. But it wasn't like the floor-touching and jogging and belt-shaking of my grandmother. It seemed more like a pose or a dance to me. I looked back because I knew that if my grandmother saw me, if she called out in her bottom-of-the-bottle voice (did all women speak to their children like that?): What are you doing there? What are you watching? . . . always suspecting something that might please me and not herself . . . I might have to show it to her. And then she would say: Why, it's just a dirty old lizard dying!

Nevertheless the lizard wasn't dying. Its legs were in the air, but that meant something else. Nor would it want to be turned right side up: it had the privilege of being on whatever side it pleased! The lizard's eyes shone golden.

Half its body was in the air; it seemed to be bringing its tail down over its head as it lay on its back, the two forelegs implanted on the ground. I tried to think where I had seen something like it; my mother's only exercises were swimming, tennis, golf. Then I remembered my aunt Sylvia, my father's sister who came to see me and take me out now and then. She was much younger than my father, still at college, studying philosophy, I adored her laugh. She told fantastic stories.

I recollected having seen her stand on her head. And turn herself into a pretzel. She had started to teach me a few things. Oga? I thought. No . . . yoga. A lizard doing yoga.

I laughed and turned on my back. Then I brought my legs over my head, too. But my stomach was full of the peanut butter and jelly sandwiches that were all, my grandmother insisted, I ever wanted to eat. It wasn't true. She just never cooked anything good.

My grandmother came out to the pool. She didn't look like a grandmother. I wondered if she ever would. She had curly blond hair and a wig just like it. Sometimes I couldn't tell which was which.

Pretending to be asleep, I could see my grandmother pussyfooting at the edge of the pool, a kerchief on her hair . . . it must have been her hair, she wouldn't have worn it over a wig. She was in her favorite tiger-striped shorts and a yellow sweater with a high neck and little sleeves. I wondered whether her neck sweated while her arms cooled.

She had pulled a deck chair out of the house and was setting it up with a frown and little impatient gestures and a look of disgust. Once, she kicked it. I was glad she thought me asleep, because she always asked me to do things before doing them herself. After settling in the chair (with a: Darn!) she went back to the house and returned with her baby-blue telephone which had an extremely long wire that she could plug in anywhere. She seemed to be doing a dance with the wire; it coiled around her bare feet and she stepped in and out of it and twirled it around and shook it out like a lasso. Then she fell into the chair and perched the phone on her shoulder and spoke into it and typed at the same time. My grandmother wrote fashion news, edited a fashion paper. Many people knew her: they were always embracing her in stores and restaurants. Flattering her, and I knew why. So she would write something nice about them or their clothes or their restaurants. For some reason, probably because it meant free meals, she also wrote gourmet news. I couldn't bear the way she looked at those people who came out from workrooms or behind cash registers or kitchens or dressing rooms and exclaimed: Francie, you look gorgeous today! Or: Francie, you get younger every minute. . . . Because I could see that it wasn't true, though at the same time a tremor of pleasure would pass through my grandmother's body as she smiled her smile of absolutely young-looking, astringent and perfectly modelled teeth. (No wonder. She was always jumping into the bathroom to brush them.)

Sometimes she would ask my opinion on the clothes she wore, as if I were the authority's authority. Or a man. Because, as she explained to me, a man's reaction to clothes was more significant than all the fashion predictions put together.

Women want to know what men think of them, she would say, as if she had worked years at this conclusion.

I liked to see her dressed up. She smiled more then, and sometimes even took me on dates. Occasionally a nightclub act might feature acrobats or animals. I loved animals.

But I tried not to notice the expression on her face when a man was with us. Because though she smiled, her eyes looked funny, as if she had caught something in them. She would glance up and down at the same time, fluttering her lashes and speaking rapidly and confusing me as to whether she was a friend or an enemy. Whatever her intention, there was a tone, a look about her that disturbed me; I preferred not to watch, or if watching were necessary, to make my mind go elsewhere. I practiced sitting still, smiling and nodding, while my thoughts reviewed something I had read the day before, or made up improbable stories. Occasionally, she caught me. Hoagy, are you there? . . . Yes (but I wished I weren't). On the other hand, my mother was worse than my grandmother. Always punishing me. For not listening, not cleaning the house, not knowing what the teacher had assigned. Yet my grandmother seemed suspicious of every breath I took. I tried to be quiet and get in no one's way.

On the phone again, her voice rose. I didn't know which of her friends she was scolding, but suddenly I realized she wasn't scolding, though she spoke angrily, her throat tensed like a bow. I closed my eyes, pretending to be a lizard. Not the kind that did yoga, but still, silent, dreaming, a sun-filled lizard on a stone, dreaming it was the stone.

She spoke of a sweater, the way she only spoke of her clothes . . . When women grew older, I thought, and didn't have husbands, maybe they fell in love with their clothes. Yet, how I hated the yesterday-smell of the closet, all those dresses pressed together in a conspiracy of stale talc and sweat. Why did she keep them? In her own room the closet was full of new clothes with the same body scent and perfume, though more potent, yearning.

. . . The blue sweater, she hissed, the darling Caribbean blue that matched my eyes, made me think of all the nice things that were ever said to me. . . . How I loved that color! And she takes it. Rosabel. My own daughter. Always stealing!

I winced at my mother's name, even though I saw that hunter's gleam in her eyes every time she visited my grandmother. Even so. And despite the fact that nothing pleased Rosabel. She was my mother; I felt responsible for her. I wished I could unplug the phone. Slowly, so as not to distract, I let my head roll to a side. Then, slowly again, my body. The lizard, a dappled green, blinked metallic eyes. And I blinked back.

Now it pressed against the ground. Raising its head slightly, looking to one side, then the other. I thought of Sylvia doing the same. I thought I heard her tell me: Clear your mind of all but the lizard.

. . . It will free your spirit, she said to me.

I turned on my stomach, but too rapidly. My grandmother noticed me at once.

Hoagy! she said. Didn't I tell you to do your arithmetic? Where is your math book?

I ran through the chilly house. Looking for my math book, I passed her inflatable furniture. The previous year she had become incensed at a moving van that charged too much to deliver a small piano, had then proceeded to sell everything in the living room and substitute the inflatable, disposable, or foldable. I thought of sticking pins in the plastic or luring the dog in to try a few bites. But she only allowed the dog on the sun porch.

I found my book under the big double bed that had been my mother's when she lived there, as a girl. She was still a girl when she married. A child of sixteen, my grandmother had reminded me. Eloped, but fortunately, Francie added, with a wealthy man. Later she could not understand why anyone would give up a wealthy man (who was wild about her!).

Though it was obvious, Francie liked to add, Rosabel didn't know how to make herself interesting to men. All she ever spoke of was her job, how everyone tried to rape her. Why didn't she learn something about politics or dianoetics or cybernetics?

I didn't like the bedroom. At night I would open the venetian blinds all the way so the moon and the palm trees and the smell of jasmine and oranges could enter. Then, with all forms hushed, I could forget the intrusion of the tank-shaped sauna with the radio on top . . . that made me think of robots; and facing it, the vanity with its tiny drawers in which everything from snapshots the color of tea stains to lost beads and dried up raisins had been stuffed. Or next to the bed, catty-cornered (she loved catty corners) the tall dresser in which she kept a medical encyclopedia (to diagnose herself), a roll of absorbent cotton, a muddy pink toy poodle, the color of syringes, and blue satin sheets. In the bookcase built into the headrest of the bed I found children's books so old they must have been her own. All over the house there were peanut butter jars of darkening pennies that she never turned into any bank, but kept as reminders of the days when pennies were useful. As each jar filled she would tell me: It's important. It will add up someday. They'll make lots of dollars for me . . . I was afraid to touch those jars. They threatened a nasty dollar-sized jangle.

And how I dreaded that dark closet where clothes at night seemed about to dislodge the door, the way a vampire, I imagined, might rise from a sewer. The door had a way of opening by itself, with a: pop! . . . revealing weary dresses, boxes, dirty towels and shoes on the floor, folded snack tables, whatnot. I trembled at the vulnerability of my own small trousers and shirts hanging with them. Was it the odor . . . like an armpit . . . that stifled me?

Walking circuitously to the pool, I carried my math book, notebook, and pencil. Briefly, over the telephone and above her glasses, Francie looked up; then she subsided into her work and dialed someone else.

The lizard was still there. It was actually balancing on its paws, perpendicular, tail in air. The math book fell from my hands.

Hoagy! my grandmother warned. Get that book before you kick it into the pool!

I retrieved it absently, lay on my stomach, propped the book before me, opened the notebook, and tried to start my work. But my glance kept wandering to the lizard, sill balancing. It came down soporifically in the sunshine. I lifted the pencil and began a letter:

Dear Sylvia, I am looking at a lizard who I think has magic powers. . . .

—I can't get your son to do a single solitary thing he's supposed to do for school, Francie complained when my mother and her friend Nat came for me after dinner.

Oh, he's a brat, Rosabel said without altering her expression or tone of voice, while her fat white leg hung over and clung to the arm of the inflatable chair.

Nat sat on the other chair, looking as if he had driven himself through his last game of tennis. His hair fringed his forehead, and his sport shirt met his chest with a stain of geographical shape. Black hairs springing from behind the opening of his shirt shone dewily. Some of the hairs were grey. He was older than Rosabel. It seemed to me that he would have suited Francie better, despite my mother's pretty face. Actually, he had known Francie first.

Rosabel always looked cool. Even when her voice changed

(like when she scolded me), her face remained serene. My grand-mother, on the other hand, seemed constantly suffused by some hidden source of heat. She wriggled, grimaced, coughed, smiled aborted, nervous smiles, and had, at the same time, an expression in her eyes that made me wonder what could console her.

Nat brought to mind a Christmas ornament still hanging from a chandelier, shining its last dull shine, and about to fall down. Both Francie and Rosabel thought him handsome, despite the pneu-matic waist, the oily skin, indifferent eyes.

I don't know why she doesn't let her hair down, Francie said to Nat. She has such beautiful hair. Thick, curly. Mine was never like that. All my life I've tried to make it grow; it just won't. Rosa-bel, why don't you let your hair down? You look forty years old.

I'm not eighteen.

She doesn't take advantage of her natural endowments. If I had hair like that, and skin, and features. . . . Think of the people I meet. Millionaires. But what difference does it make?

You still look pretty good, Nat grunted.

Francie thanked him without enthusiasm, adding: Forty years old . . . as Rosabel got up. I looked at her hard to see what Francie meant.

Hair wouldn't make much difference, I thought, if Rosabel didn't have such a big ass. I had noticed that older women usually had big asses. Francie too, though the rest of her was slender. Slacks didn't suit either of them. My mother always wore some-thing to half-cover her ass. This time she wore a blue sweater with silky hairs swaying.

Why don't you take off your sweater? Francie asked.

Because it's mine and I don't want you to claim it, Rosabel said from inside the refrigerator door.

Hers like heck, Francie commented to Nat. She never used the real curse words with which my mother shrank the atmosphere at home.

You two girls ought to stop fighting about that sweater, Nat said in his soft, exasperated voice.

Francie, sidling up to Nat, twisted her body a little as she held her hands out with the fingers spread, and batted her eyes: Now Nat, you know you love both of us. Why don't you get Rosabel a sweater so she'll give mine back to me?

The refrigerator door banged shut and my mother came listing back to the room, a cold lamb chop in her hand. —I'm on a diet, so I get hungry, she said to the chop, turning it around daintily.

And by the way, she added, her small mouth gleaming with fat, the sweater is mine, Dad bought it.

For me! Francie exclaimed. —He promised it to me the last time I went to his office. What I really wanted was a car because I heard he bought his wife one. He never bought me a car. But I couldn't bring myself to say it. I only talked about the clothes I'd seen that day. Especially the imported sweater. He just looked out the window. Finally, I cried. He never could stand me crying. So he said: O.K. The sweater.

You go to his office? Nat asked.

Why not? He invites me out sometimes for a drink or dinner. We're friendly; I still get money from him. Any time he feels like it he can come back to me. He knows that. He's the only man I ever really . . . . But he played around.

Yeah, said Nat. I know.

Dad delivered it to me, Rosabel asserted. You were off to Jamaica. He said I could keep it.

You're lying. Just like him.

Listen girls, said Nat, I'll buy you another.

Oh, in that case, Rosabel told Francie, you can have this thing. And she pulled it off as if she loathed it.

Francie clasped the sweater to her, adding: It has your perfume!

Rosabel went back to the refrigerator. I watched her butt swing like a buoy in a storm.

I told my grandmother the sweater looked great on her.

You're a doll! Francie grabbed me awkwardly; I didn't feel embraced. Her body seemed to have no substance. But I smiled, embarrassed. My mother saw the smile when she returned from the kitchen, with another chop. And though her voice was moderate, she frowned, which made me feel guilty. But it was Francie she accused:

Why are you always sneaking Hoagy away from me?

You're glad to get rid of him.

I was out of the house. You always come when I'm out, when you know I'll be out. Like a thief. In the afternoon.

Well, who was there to ask? Am I his grandmother or not? What about the time in St. Thomas when you kidnapped him from the hotel playground? I was frantic. You could have asked.

Me ask? I'm his mother.

I had the police out. . . . Francie appealed to Nat. He shrugged as usual.

Francie let out a sigh and stood up to view herself in the mirror, caressing the hairs on her sweater. Then she asked if anyone wanted coffee.

You'll make it? Nat asked. I thought you only ate in restaurants. Where'd you take lucky Hoagy tonight?

The Italian restaurant up the street. He had spaghetti. In every gourmet place it's either spaghetti or hamburger. I don't know why I bother. Except that I can't take the time to cook anymore. Even though I was a housewife for ten years.

Come to think of it, Rosabel said.

It broke your heart to live alone with me, didn't it? Francie asked, moving toward the kitchen.

While they were drinking coffee I went outside to look at the pool in the moonlight. I told them I had left some little boats out there. But I didn't think of boats when the warm air came twining over my arms and all the sweetness of invisible blossoms approached me. I wanted to get down on my belly and scurry beneath some bush.

Where are you? I thought.

Suddenly I heard the two women shriek at each other, and at the window their shadows reached out and seemed to merge. But I knew it only seemed that way.

Mine! I heard.

Mine!

The moon, fragmented over the pool, reminded me of Sylvia's hair, how it fell on her shoulders the day we took a glass-bottomed boat. We saw the miraculous fishes then, quick as impulse, curved and flowing, in all the illusory colors of their flight.

I said to her: I'll be a sea horse.

She said to me: We'll ride the sea together.

And her laughter sounded down the fluttering depths, and up to the silver-blue, white-birded sky.

Near the cactus bush a transparent shape. I lifted it and in the moonlight saw the emptied husk of the lizard. I thought: I shall slip inside and burrow into the night.

Then I hid it behind a stone.

. . . I have no one, no one, Francie moaned as I returned to the house. . . . Nobody cares what becomes of me. Except maybe Hoagy. . . . And she rushed to lay her wet, flaky face against mine, while my mother, indissoluble, linked her arm in Nat's.

They ushered me out with the smell of Francie's tears upon me, and at my neck the urgent: I'll leave it all to you, Hoagy, everything I've got. . . .

. . . I'm not sure I want it, I answered silently, looking up at the night sky, pretending not to hear, as the door closed and my mother and Nat walked ahead to the car, and I halted once, looking upward again, at miracles yet to come.

JACK MATTHEWS was born in Columbus, Ohio, and now lives in Athens, Ohio, where he teaches at Ohio University. His latest novel is *The Charisma Campaigns,* published by Harcourt Brace Jovanovich.

ON THE SHORE OF CHAD CREEK

MELVIN COMBS, his wife she died. Turned her head to the wall, her arms crossed. She was 81 year old.

Melvin he was 83.

The 2 of them live alone up there. You walk a footbridge across Chad Creek, and climb a footpath about 18 rod up there to the house. You cain't see the house from the road, but you can see it oncet you get across Chad Creek.

Melvin sit down and stare at his old woman for a long time. Her name was Maude. Everybody know them 2 for a long time, Melvin and Maude Combs.

Melvin sat there and sighed. He know in his heart it got to happen. She been waking up ever night since the middle of winter, saying, I am cold, I cain't seem to git warm.

Now it was spring time, and they was a dozen blackbirds out in back of the house, 3 or 4 of them on the roof of the shed. The trees was flowering. Maude loved to see the trees flower in the spring, but now she had turned to the wall with her arms crossed over her breast and died.

Melvin was a lone. He sat there in his rocking chair without rocking none at all, and stared at the dead woman's back. He could see from the slope of the covers that her 2 feet was curled around behind, like she was only a little baby sleeping.

Copyright © 1971 The Virginia Quarterly Review, The University of Virginia. First appeared in *The Virginia Quarterly Review.*

Outside, the birds was chirping and a fresh breeze was pushing against the window near her head. But she didn't feel nothing, and neither did Melvin, because the window was closed and the door was closed.

Melvin went over and open the door. When he did, he heard a car driving somewhere down on the road, but he couldn't see the car. You couldn't see the house from the road, and you couldn't see the road from the house. But you could hear the cars go past, and the trucks go past.

Melvin went out on the front porch and looked down the steep and crooked path, past the pine trees that grew on this slope but hardly anywhere else in the valley. Melvin stared down at the edge of the foot bridge, and he said to hisself, I am going to have to carry the body down there. Ain't nobody coming up here to git the body. Hit will be for me to carry the body down and across the foot bridge.

When he talked, he rub his wrinkled old hand on the porch banister, which he put up fifty year ago, and sanded down smooth and fine.

She ain't all that heavy, he said. Hit won't be nothing at all to carry the body down there and across the bridge.

He went back inside the house and said to his wife, I am going to have me a little sip. Then he recited, Early in the morning or late at night, a sip of corn will go just right.

She didn't like him to speak that poem. Melvin didn't drink very much, but he sure like to take his sip. He take a sip most any time he feel like it, but he didn't get cross-eye drunk like a lot of men do.

Now he walk into the little kitchen and stared out through the checkered muslin curtains she had bought only 5 or 10 year ago. The sun was out for a minute, and then it turn dark from the April clouds a drifting by overhead in the sky.

Melvin sighed and pulled out a jug from underneath the sink. Then he poured a couple fingers in a jelly glass and sat down in a chair. Then he change his mind and got up and open the back door, so's he could hear the blackbirds that was busy out in back.

The breeze come in through the door and made the little flowery dish towel on the rack by the counter flap around.

Hit's a right nice spring breeze, Melvin said.

He took hisself a little sip of the corn whiskey and smack his lips. Sweet tit, he said.

After a bit, he lean around the corner and look at the dead body, but it was still right there in the same place, the feet curled around like a baby's and the head half buried in the pillow.

She was a good wife, Melvin said out loud.

Then he sat and sip some more of the corn whiskey, and after a little bit, he got up out of his chair and walk outside onto the old splintered wood porch and down the cement block they use for a step and onto the bare ground. The grass was a growing high for April.

He walk out a little, took 2 or 3 steps in the sun and then a cloud pass overhead and he was walking 2 or 3 steps in cool dark shade. Then it was sunny again, and the blackbirds was flying here and there.

Melvin stood still and he sip the last of his whiskey. Then he turn around and look at the little house where he and Maude had lived for 50 years and more.

Maybe I better go down and get me some hep, Melvin said out loud. Maybe I better stop me a car and get some body to come up here and hep me with the body.

He stood and took a long breath and studied the back of the house. Then he said, No, she didn't like no body coming up here, unless they was invited. Unless she knowed they was a coming.

He walk back to the back door, step up on the cement block and stood on the tiny porch again.

Hit won't be no trouble, he said.

He went inside the house and put on his hat. Then he went over to the bed and look at the body.

I am strong, he said, and hit won't be no trouble for me to carry that body down to the foot bridge.

But it was heavier than he thought. He wrap it in a blanket and pick it up and was surprised to find out it was already getting to be a little bit stiff. No telling what time she had died in the night.

But he got her through the front door, and part way down the path. It was steep, but Melvin he knowed ever step, ever little turn, down through the dark pine trees.

He got the body halfway down, so's he could see parts of the road, and his feet slip out from under him, and both of them went just a sprawling. The body bounced a couple times and half rolled out of the blanket, and Melvin he skin his elbow and jarred his shoulder so's he could hardly move for a minute.

He decided he need some hep, so he wrapped the body up comfortable and went back up to the house. Then he went into the kitchen and poured hisself another 2 fingers of whiskey. He sat there in the chair. He could feel the numb feeling in his shoulder and he was a wondering if he should go down to the road for hep.

No, he said, I will do hit myself.

So after he finish the whiskey, he was feeling better. When he walk down the path, he said out loud, Ain't many 83 year old men can carry a dead body down a mountain path.

Maude was laying right there where he had dropped her, and he got downhill from her on the path, and then he pick her up pretty good and start walking once again. His old legs was a shaking, though, and it look pretty bad for about 50 or 60 feet, but then he made it to the foot bridge, and by God went all the ways across that foot bridge, without stopping once, and the foot bridge kind of jump and wiggle the way it does, but Melvin, he knowed it like the wobble in his own 2 knees and didn't stumble or fall down once.

When he got to the other side, he tried to set the body down gentle, but dropped it, and again it roll about half way out of the blanket. Poor Maude's face was pale and dead, and her arms was still crossed on her breast, the way she'd died. Her jaw was fixed open, and her eyes showed a little crack, like she was a taking a peek at him now and then to see how he was making out.

Melvin he sat there and breathed hard and tried to catch his breath, which took a pretty long time in coming back.

Then he got up and got the body in his car, which was parked there. He didn't drive it much, and ever now and then the battery was run down, but Melvin he always park it right there on the hill with the brake on, so's all he had to do if the battery was run down was let go the brake and the old car started a rolling down the hill, and before long, he just let out the clutch and the engine catch and start a running as smooth as ever.

This is what he done this time, too. Maude's body was laying half on the floor and half on the back seat, with its arms still crossed, like it was cold and was trying to keep warm.

Melvin drove all the way to town that way, a couple times moving over after cars had come up fast behind and honk for a while, because they want to pass.

When he got to town, he went to the undertaker who also had new and used furniture for sale in front of his store. The undertaker was Wilkie Thomas.

Melvin said, Wilkie, hit's Maude. She is outside there in the car.

What's the matter with her? Wilkie ask him.

She is dead, Melvin said.

Wilkie just raise up his eyebrows and stared long and hard at Melvin. You mean, your wife has died and you done brought her all this way by your *self*?

Who you think would bring her? Melvin said.

Then Wilkie said, Melvin, you been drinking?

Never mind about my drinking, Melvin said. Are you going to come out and get my dead wife's body or not?

Wilkie just raise his eyebrows once more, and stuck a toothpick in his mouth and said, Come on, then. Let's go take us a look.

When he saw the body lying in the back seat, all wrapped up like an Indian in a blanket, and with its arms crossed and its mouth open, Wilkie said, Well, lookee there!

How much for you to take care of it? Melvin said.

Well, Wilkie said. Well.

I said, how much will it cost to bury her? I ain't got much money, Wilkie.

Well, Wilkie said. How long she been dead?

She died last night, Melvin said. She told me she felt funny before she went to sleep. Didn't say she felt bad, just funny.

They say that a lot before they go, Wilkie said. Yes sir, they say they feel funny, and brother that's *it!* Know what I say when I hear that?

What? Melvin ask, rubbing his right shoulder with his hand.

I say that's a funny sense of humor, to think it's funny when you're about ready to die!

Wilkie give a little laugh then, but didn't keep it up when Melvin didn't join in.

When they went back inside, Wilkie got behind his desk and just sat there a few minutes, chewing on his toothpick. Finally, he said, Well, Melvin, I guess we better git started. Are you ready?

That's why I come here, Melvin said.

Wilkie nodded and then he yell out, Hey, Paul!

A voice answered from a room in back.

Come in here, Wilkie said.

A big young fellow wearing dark-rim glasses opened the door and asked Wilkie what he wanted.

Mr. Combs here, Wilkie said, has recently suffered the hardest blow of all. His wife of many years has passed away.

50 years, Melvin said. 52 years, to be exact. We was married 52 years ago. She was going on 30. She was a widow. I had been too busy a whoring around and a gaming and a traveling and a carousing and a drinking to settle down before that. I was 31.

While Melvin was talking, Wilkie and Paul was both a watching him, like what he was saying was the most important thing they had ever heard. They was paying so much attention that Melvin finally stopped, because he was not used to having other people listen very close to what he was saying.

When Melvin stop talking, Wilkie he just sat there nodding. He even pulled the toothpick out of his mouth and dropped it on the floor. He look like he was studying Melvin's words.

Then he started talking again, explaining to Paul what had happened. Paul, he said, this here's Mr. Combs, in case you haven't had the pleasure of meeting him yet. Mr. Melvin Combs and his wife, Rachel. . . .

Her name's Maude, Melvin said.

. . . which is what I meant to say, but I suffered a little slip of the tongue, momentarily; his dear wife, Maude, of 52 years went to a better realm in her sleep last night.

Died with her arms crossed, Melvin said.

Died with her arms crossed, Wilkie said, nodding.

You want me to go pick her up in the hearse? Paul said.

That won't be necessary, Wilkie said. Mr. Combs his self has brought his dear departed wife to us, saving us the trouble.

And gas, Melvin said.

And gas, Wilkie said.

Where is she? Paul asked.

Out in Mr. Combs' automobile, Wilkie said, passing his hand slowly through the air in the direction of the door.

I'll go out and get it, Paul said, and he walk out the door.

Smart fellow, Wilkie said. He goes away to college, and works for me part time.

Then Wilkie started a smacking his lips and shaking his head back and forth. Melvin, he said, do you have a death certificate?

No, Melvin said. You are the first person that seen her. Except for me.

Wilkie sighed and slapped both of his hands on the top of his desk. Well, he said, there are forms that have to be filled out and things that have to be done. I'll call Doc Wilson and see if he can come over and make out the death certificate. Meanwhile, you better fill out this form here.

Wilkie pulled a sheet of paper out of the desk drawer and shoved it toward Melvin. But Melvin he was just standing there a shaking his head no.

What's the matter, Wilkie said. You can write, cain't you?

Yes, I can write, Melvin said, but I cain't lift my arm. I done hurt my shoulder.

Hmmm, Wilkie said. If I lift your hand up onto the paper, do you think you can sign your name?

I can try, Melvin said.

It worked. Melvin he signed his name, and Wilkie filled out the form, explaining what was on it.

When they had finished with it, Wilkie said, Melvin, would you like to take a couple aspirin for that there sore shoulder of yours?

No, Melvin said, hit's all right.

Must not be all right, or you could write with it, Wilkie said.

No, Melvin said, the writing is over and done with, so I don't need my shoulder no more.

Maybe you broke something, Wilkie said.

No, Melvin said, it don't feel like anything is broke.

Wilkie took his watch out and look at it. I thought so, he said.

What did you think? Melvin asked.

I thought it was getting close to lunch time, Wilkie said. Would you like something to eat?

Melvin thought a second, and said, Yes, I could maybe eat a little something.

So could I, Wilkie said.

Then Paul he come back in, and Wilkie said, She was stiff, wasn't she?

Paul took a quick look at Melvin and then nodded, and said, Yes, she was getting pretty far along that way.

I thought so, Wilkie said. You get so's you can tell by just a looking.

I put her in the back room, Paul said.

You done right, Wilkie said. And wait here a minute, because we are going to have a little bite to eat.

Good idea, Paul said. I'm hungry.

Wilkie reached over and picked up the telephone. He dialed it, and said, Hazel, this is Wilkie. How about cooking six hamburgers with everything for us. I'll send Paul over in a couple minutes. Also a bag of potato chips. Also a six pack of ice cold Rolling Rock beer, and a can of 7 Up for Paul.

When he hung up, he looked at Melvin and said, Paul here don't drink, do you, Paul?

No sir, Paul said.

How much you weigh, Paul? Wilkie asked.

Oh about 230, Paul said.

If you drank beer, you would probably weigh more than that, Wilkie said.

230 is enough, Paul said.

Melvin said, I knowed her long before that. Long before she was married, even.

What? Wilkie said.

We was in school together, Melvin said. Just little shavers. I pushed her in the creek one time.

He's speaking of his wife, Wilkie explained to Paul in a low voice.

I figured, Paul said.

Then we growed up and went our own separate ways, Melvin said. Maude was married to a man named Chambers. He was killed in a mine accident about sixty years ago. And then I come back and there she was, a waiting for me.

Things certainly do work out funny, Wilkie said. Yes sir, they work out funny. You put that in a story book, and no body in the whole blessed world would believe it.

Chad Creek, Melvin said.

What? Paul said.

That's the creek he pushed his future wife in, Wilkie said. When she was a little girl. Then he said, Paul, you better go git on over and pick up our lunch, because it will be ready before long.

Yes sir, Paul said, and he went on out the door.

Where we been a living all these years, Melvin said. Right on Chad Creek.

Things certainly work out funny, Wilkie said.

When Paul come back with the hamburgers and things, all 3 of them sat down and started eating, right there in the office. Paul sat in a chair near the door, and read a book while he was eating.

He is studying his lessons, Wilkie said to Melvin.

Melvin drank 2 Rolling Rock beers, and Wilkie drank 4.

Paul went into the back room and went to work.

Doc Wilson came a little after 1 and pronounced Maude Combs dead.

Who crossed her arms? he asked.

She died that way, Melvin said.

Wilkie nodded and said, She told Melvin she felt funny before she died.

Doc Wilson just stood there and kind of looked at the 2 men, and then left.

Is that all there is to hit? Melvin asked after a little bit.

For right now, Wilkie said. Except for the funeral arrangements. However, you can come back later today and take care of them if you just want a simple service.

Melvin he didn't say any thing for a minute, and then he said, Hit just don't seem like enough, some how.

Oh it's enough, all right, Wilkie said.

But hit don't *seem* like it, Melvin said.

But it is, Wilkie said. Then he said, Melvin, did you carry the deceased's body all the way down that footpath and across the foot bridge?

Melvin nodded. Hit wasn't much, he said. Only thing was, I fell down like a blame fool and hurt my shoulder.

Can you move your arm now? Wilkie asked.

Melvin he move his arm a little bit and said, Looks like maybe I can.

You think you can get back to your place all right?

Why sure I can, Melvin said.

Well, just so's you can manage, Wilkie said.

A few minutes later, Melvin said good-by, and went out to his car.

He got in and drove back to the foot bridge.

He parked the car right on the rim and set the hand brake hard. He also put it in reverse gear. Then he got out of the car and walked across the foot bridge and went up the hill to the house. Then he turn around and look back at the road, but you couldn't see the road from his house. Only the pine trees a standing there thick and dark on the hillside.

Melvin stood there for a few minutes and listen to a car go past. Then he was sleepy, so he went inside the house and laid himself down on the bed, next to where she had died with her arms crossed.

For a while he didn't think of nothing very much, and then he remember that he hadn't even told them that he could remember when she had worn pigtails. This was even before he had pushed her into Chad Creek.

75 years ago.

His shoulder still hurt, but he knew he would go to sleep before long. He had always been a powerful sleeper.

He thought of her head sunk in the pillow, her legs curled up and her feet tucked back, her eyes not quite closed, so's she looked like she might be taking a peek at him, seeing how he was bearing up under it.

Stiff as a side of beef.

The whiskey and the beer was working on him, though. And he was drowsy.

He thought of her pigtails, and how he had pulled them until she give out with a yell that was so loud, ever body heard. The teacher had punished him then. Made him stand in the corner by his self.

It had all started way back then. Maybe even before.

ALICE ADAMS grew up in Chapel Hill, North Carolina, graduated from Radcliffe, and since then has lived mainly in San Francisco. She has published one novel, *The Fall of Daisy Duke,* and stories in *The New Yorker, Partisan Review, McCall's,* and other magazines. Her story "Gift of Grass" was awarded third prize in *Prize Stories 1971.* She is at work on a new novel.

RIPPED OFF

THE GENTLE, leafy day made Deborah high; she came home from her morning job light in her head and heart. When she saw that the small drawer from her desk had been pulled out and taken over to the bed and left there, its contents spilled out over the tousled blue sheets, she first thought, Wow, Philip, what are you trying to tell me? Philip lived with her in the Russian Hill flat, and what was—or had been—in the drawer was notes from him, notes or bits of paper that for one reason or another he had put his name on or drawn some small picture on. A couple of the messages said "Gone for walk. Later." But on one, a torn-off match cover, he had written "I love you," and passed it to her across a table in a restaurant. There was even a cancelled check made out to and endorsed by him, from a couple of months ago when Deborah had lent him some money.

Her second reaction was one of surprise; Philip was not nosy or jealous. Once she had known a boy, Juan, from Panama, who was both—violently so. She had had to burn her old letters and diaries so that he would not find them. In fact, he had finally left her because (he said) she was so friendly with other men. (She did not see herself as especially friendly to anyone.) It was not

like Philip to search through her desk. She thought he must have
been looking for a stamp or something. Still, why bring the drawer
over to the bed? What was he trying to tell her?

Deborah was a tall, rather oddly shaped girl. Her breasts were
large but her body was otherwise skimpy, and with her long, thin
legs she had somewhat the look of a bird that might topple over
but never quite did. Big front teeth made her appear shy, which
she was. Her wide, dark-brown eyes could show a great deal of
pain or love. She wore her brown hair long and straight in the hippie style, but for her Kelly Girl job—taken for two reasons: to
give herself freedom of movement (she only took morning work)
and to embarrass her mother, who expected her to have some
kind of career—she dressed in short non-mini skirts and straight
shirts. She tended to look for clothes that would hide her—hide
her identity as well as her breasts. Her mother and some of the
neighbors in that expensive San Francisco block—she and Philip
lived in a building owned by Deborah's stepfather, who charged
a ritualistic fifty a month for a high, wide studio room with an
overwhelming view of the bay and the ocean—described her as a
hippie. Deborah felt that that was not quite right, although she
could not have said what she was. She read a lot, and thought.
Now she was mainly thinking about what to make for dinner for
Philip, in case he came home for dinner.

As she picked up the bits of paper (nothing missing) and replaced the drawer and made the bed—bending awkwardly, tug-
ging at the recalcitrant sheets—her discovery seemed less funny
all the time. It was painful for Philip to know she was so senti-
mental. She blushed and pressed her fingers over her mouth. Nobody but a thirteen-year-old or a middle-aged woman (her mother,
with all her dead father's Navy things, and pressed dead gardenias
in a book of poems by Dorothy Parker) would keep stuff around
like that. What would Philip think? Nothing between them was at
all explicitly stated or defined. He had moved into the room shortly
after they had met (at the Renaissance Fair, in Marin County—
beautiful!) without much comment or any real plan, and he could
presumably leave the same way. No one said anything about how

long. Deborah sometimes thought he was there simply because of the coincidence in time between meeting her and the disbanding of his Mendocino commune and the start of a new term at the Art Institute. He was a little younger than she was—twenty-one to her twenty-three. His presence was kindly and peaceful, but he talked little, and it was not possible to tell what was in his mind. Sometimes he sang a line or two, like "It ain't me, babe, it ain't me you're looking for, babe." (Did he mean her?) Or "Lay lady, lay, lay across my big brass bed." (Had he met a new girl?)

As she straightened up from her own bed (the headboard of linen, not brass), she noticed what it was incredible that she had not seen before. Philip had taken his zebra-skin rug. Loss hit her hard—so hard that she sat down on the bed and stared at the dusty space where the skins had been. He's used that silly drawer as an excuse to go, she thought. Of course. That was why he emptied it onto the bed. He was telling her that she was a terrible, possessive woman, hoarding souvenirs (like her mother), trying to hang on to him. The rug was the first thing he had brought over, by way of moving in, and despite their ambivalence about it (they disapproved of hunting, and, too, the skins had a suggestion of decorator chic), it had picked up the look of the room, enhancing Deborah's wicker and white linen and the black leather chairs—leavings from her mother's tasteful (the taste of five years back) country house.

Deborah was given to moments of total panic such as this, when the world seemed to lurch beneath her like the funhouse floor at Playland-at-the-Beach, when she gasped for air and found it hard to breathe. A psychiatrist had explained this tidily to her as a syndrome: She feared abandonment. Her father had gone off to war and been killed ("At three, you would have viewed this as a desertion—a deliberate one"), and it seemed (to the psychiatrist) that she tried to repeat that situation. She readily felt abandoned, and picked people who would abandon her, like Panamanian Juan. But now, she thought, she was at least able to make an effort to think things through in a reasonable way. She controlled her breathing (with yoga breaths) and remembered that Philip had been talking about having the rug repaired. There was a rip in it

that could get larger, or could trip one of them. It made sense—
Philip finally took the rug off to be sewn. He had mentioned some
people on Union Street who did things with hides and who had
the right machines for skins.

Having decided so rationally on what had happened, Deborah
felt better, but not very much better. Some cobweb of fear or anxiety clung to her mind, and she could not brush it off. She knew
that she would not feel entirely well and reassured until she spoke
to Philip. She concentrated on his phone call, which always came
early in the afternoon, though by no stated arrangement. They
would say whatever had happened in the day so far, and make
some plan for the evening. Or Philip would say that he would see
her later—meaning ten or eleven that night.

Naturally, since she was eager for Philip to call, several other
people did instead, and each time her heart jumped as she answered, "Hello?"

Her mother said, "Darling, how are you? I was wondering if
you and Philip are possibly free to come to dinner tomorrow? A
couple of my professors from State are coming—you know, the
ones who were out on strike—and I thought you might have fun
with them."

Meaning: Her mother thought the professors, who must have
been quite young, would have a better time (and think better of
her) if they met her hippie daughter with her long-haired, bearded
boyfriend.

"Sure. I'll check with Philip," Deborah said, and then listened
to her mother's continuing voice, which was grateful and full of
love.

Once, when she was stoned, Deborah had said to Philip, "My
mother's love comes on at me like jelly, or some kind of glue. I
have to be careful to stay back from it, you know? All that total
approval I get poured over me. She doesn't even know who I
am."

Philip's mother, in Cincinnati ("She pronounces it with a broad
'a'—can you imagine? Cincin*nah*ti." He, too, was a person dis-
placed from the upper middle class), did not approve of him at

all—his beard and long hair, his Goodwill or Army-surplus clothes. Dropping out of Princeton to come to an art school in San Francisco. She had not been told about the commune in Mendocino; nor, presumably, about Deborah. "I don't mind her," he said. "She's sort of abrasive, bracing, like good sandpaper. She does her own thing, and it's very clear where we're both at."

Philip talked that hip way somewhat ironically, hiding behind it. "I think I'm what those idiot behavioral scientists call a post-hippie," he once said. "Sounds sort of like a wooden Indian doesn't it?" But he had indeed put various things behind him, including drugs, except for an occasional cigarette. For him, Deborah had thrown out all her posters, and with him she had moved from Hesse and Alan Watts to Mann and Kierkegaard. "Let's face it, babe, they've got more to say. I mean, they've really got it all together."

After her mother's call, two friends called (about nothing), and finally there was the call from Philip.

She said, "Wow, Philip, what are you trying to tell me?," as she had planned to, but she felt no conviction.

"What?"

"The desk drawer on the bed."

"What drawer?"

"Did you take the zebra rug to be sewn?"

"No. Deb, are you trying to tell me we've been ripped off, as they say?"

Crazily enough, this was a possibility she had not considered, but now she thought, Of course, it happens all the time.

"Debby," he was saying, "would you please look around and see what else is gone?"

As best she could she did look around; she found her shoebox full of inherited jewelry—the ugly diamonds that she never wore—intact under her sweaters, and the stereo safely in its corner. The books, the records. His pictures. She came back to the phone and told him that.

"But aside from the stereo what else could they have taken?" she asked. "We don't have TV and appliances, stuff like that. Who wants our books." She felt herself babbling, then said, "I'm really sorry about your rug."

"Oh, well. Maybe I wasn't supposed to have it."

"Should I call the cops?"

"I guess. I'll be home for dinner, O.K.?"

Relief made Deborah efficient. Philip had not moved out, and he was coming home for dinner. She began to put together a rather elaborate lamb stew. (She always bought meat on the chance that he would come home, even though sometimes after several days of his absences she would have to throw it out.) She shaved fresh ginger into the lamb, and then she called the police.

The two officers who arrived perhaps twenty minutes later were something of a surprise. They were young—about her age. (Who of her generation would want to be a cop, she wondered.) One of them was blond and looked a little like a short-haired, clean-shaven Philip. They were quite sympathetic and soft-spoken; they gave sensible advice. "Use the double lock when you go out," the blond one said. "This one could be picked in a minute. And fix the bolt on the kitchen door."

"Do it soon," said the other. "They could be back for more."

"It's sort of funny they didn't take the stereo, too," Deborah said, conversationally.

"Hippies love those fur rugs," they told her, unaware that they were not talking to a nice right-side-of-Russian Hill girl, and that for her they had just joined the enemy.

"More likely junkies than hippies, don't you think?" she coldly said.

For Deborah, the preparation and serving of food were acts of love. She liked to serve Philip; she brought in plates and placed them gently before him, like presents, though her offhand manner denied this. "It's that Indian stuff," she said of the stew. Then, so that he would not be forced to comment on her cooking, she said, "It's funny, their moving that drawer from my desk."

"Probably thought you kept valuables there—bonds and bank

notes and stuff." He was eating as though starved, which was how he always ate; he barely paused to look up and speak.

She felt herself inwardly crying, "I do! You are infinitely valuable to me. Anything connected with you is valuable—please stay with me!" She managed not to say any of this; instead, she blinked. He had been known to read her eyes.

"This stew is really nice," he told her. "And the wine—cool! Like wow!"

They both laughed a little, their eyes briefly meeting.

She asked, "How's school? How's the graphics class?"

"Pretty good."

Philip was thin, with knobby bones at his wrists, protuberant neck bones, and tense tendons. He had dark-blue, thoughtful eyes. His fine hair flew about when he moved. He looked frail, as though a strong wind (or a new idea) could carry him off bodily. "I tend to get into head trips" is how he half ironically put it, not saying what kind of trips they were. He seemed to be mainly concerned with his work—drawing, etching, watercolors. Other things (people, weather, days) passed by his cool, untroubled, but observant gaze—as someday, Deborah felt, she, too, might pass by.

At the moment, however, she was experiencing a total, warm contentment. There was Philip, eating and liking the stew she had made, and they had been robbed—ripped off—and nothing of value was gone.

"What was in the drawer?" he asked.

"Oh, nothing. Just some stuff I kept."

Again their quick glances met, and they smiled; then both ducked away from prolonged contact. Deborah had to look aside because she had suddenly thought how marvellous it would be if they could have a child, a straw-blond baby that she would nurse (she had heard that breast-feeding made big breasts smaller) and whom Philip would always love. The intensity of this wish made her dizzy. For concealment, she asked, "You really won't miss those skins?"

"Really not. You know I always hated them as much as I liked them. Good luck to whoever took them is how I feel."

After dinner, Deborah cleared and cleaned the kitchen, while Philip read in the living room. Early on in their life together, he had helped, or at least offered to, but gradually they both realized that cleaning up was something Deborah did not mind doing. She liked that simple interval alone, with nothing demanded of her that she could not accomplish. Her mother said of her that she was a throwback—"my quaint hippie daughter." Deborah supposed there was something to that. She liked to polish the wineglasses and to shine the chrome and porcelain on the stove and sink. She did all that tonight, and then went into the living room where Philip was and sat near him with a book of her own. With evening, the fog had begun to roll in. Outside, the distant foghorns announced a cold, moist, black night. Wind shuddered against the windows, beyond which nothing was visible. The surrounding dark and cold made an island of their room—to Deborah, an enchanted island. She thought, We could live like this forever; this peace is better than any high. She thought, Do I want to get married, is that what I mean that I want? And then, No, I only mean to stay like this, with no change. But someday a baby.

They read for several hours. Absorbed in his book ("Dr. Faustus," for the second time), Philip fought off sleep until he and then Deborah went into fits of yawns, and they gave up and went to bed.

While they were undressing, Deborah opened the drawer where she kept her scarves.

It was gone—her largest, most beautiful, pale striped silk scarf, all lavenders and mauves and pinks, the only present from her mother that she had ever liked. Wearing any dress at all, she could wrap herself in that scarf and be instantly elegant. Soon after she and Philip had met, she wore it to a party at the Institute, and he thought it was a wonderful scarf. The enormity of its absence had surely summoned her and made her for no reason open that drawer.

She felt hurt enough to cry, which, with a conscious effort, she did not do. Her second decision was not to tell Philip. This was less rational, and even as she slipped into bed beside him she was not sure why. Obviously, someday he would ask why she never wore it anymore. But at the moment she only knew that she felt diminished, as though without that scarf Philip would love her less, as though their best times together were over.

Philip turned on his side; having kissed her good night, he quickly fell asleep. She lay there in the dark, listening to the erratic mourning noise of the foghorns. She was thinking that even if she had a child he would grow up and go away. Finally, she couldn't stand it; all her thoughts were unbearable, and she turned and pressed her body against the length of Philip's slender warm back, holding him tightly with her arms, as though she could keep him there.

ROSELLEN BROWN was born in 1939; she attended Barnard. Her poems have appeared in many magazines, including *Atlantic, Poetry,* and *Nation.* Her book of poems *Some Deaths in the Delta* was a National Council on the Arts Selection for 1970. She has had stories in the *New American Review, Tri Quarterly, Hudson Review, Quarterly Review of Literature,* and other magazines. "A Letter to Ismael in the Grave" was written in Brooklyn, but she now lives with her husband and two young daughters in Orford, New Hampshire.

A LETTER TO ISMAEL IN THE GRAVE

SOMEBODY once told me I didn't have welfare mothers' eyes.

I. I. I. I. I. Like white is supposed to be made up of all the colors, I is made up of all the words you can possibly say all running together in a circle very fast. It is red and shiny and purple and sweet. A mouthful of I-berries. Here, have some. I want to put it on the mailbox. Use it for my signature. Frame it and hang it on the wall all gold. Put it between my legs in bed at night. Sing it out in church. Show it around like a fat new baby. It's the best baby we never had, the one I made myself, after the children had gone to bed, just before you died.

You know what your sister said to me, don't you. She says it with her pointy finger. Back to the ashes, Cinderella. Now be a dead man's wife the way you were a lost man's widow.

When I was a kid I once walked across the river on the third rail, right next to the BMT. While I was at it in those days making my mama and grandmama jump like fleas, I married you. But I couldn't do that once, like walking the rail, I had to do it and keep doing it for thirteen years. So I fell in the river, my feet in flames.

Does someone always have to get blamed in this world?

The headline was 2 MORE ADDICT DEATHS IN CITY THIS WEEKEND.

What I read was WIFE SAYS SHE DIDN'T KNOW; SAYS SHE STOPPED KNOWING ANYTHING A LONG TIME AGO. And who gets blamed for that?

You know my friend Nilda. Her husband takes a shot every single day of his life for diabetes, very carefully, so he won't go blind or something, or go crazy. How can it be that another man could use his veins for filthy highways—for alleys, that's what, dark dirty alleys. So they could find you collapsed in the thick black of one of your own ruined veins.

Merciful, merciful. That you died before you had to hock your children's eyes and little toes. Before your pig of a liver killed you instead. Before I sold myself out from under you and cheap, to get money for passage. I am not beautiful, no sir, I know that, but I do not have welfare mothers' eyes. In spite of you.

All right, I said to him. But you know I've got tattoos. Those shadows, those stripes of the El laying over me all these years since you (he, Ismael, my husband!) moved me here. I swear we've got the taste of all that darkness in our soup. You have to look pretty hard even in Brooklyn to find an El that they haven't taken down for scrap-iron and firewood but you worked hard on it and found us one. You couldn't get sunstroke over here if they gave you a million for trying. One time I saw the slats across my friend Rita's shoulders when she was standing down there on the stoop. They looked like those fox furs I used to stare at when I was a kid, the whole fox with the flat shiny eyes I always thought were real, and the long dark stringy tails. Didn't you used to wonder if it hurt them, and look in those live eyes, to be dragged around on some rich old lady's back?

He was looking at me the other day when I thought I was alone, sitting in the kitchen trying to think. And he said he never saw a woman who kept right on existing when her man wasn't with her. I guess I've had a lot of practice from you, with me and never with me all the same time. But Jesus, to be that way! What are we, frogs who need a swamp to croak about?

The kind of thing I've been so busy thinking is,
Whose fault were you?   But
Whose fault was the you whose fault you were? There's
a girl on the front of the Sun-Maid raisin box holding
a box of raisins with a girl on it, holding a box of
raisins with a girl on it holding

Something new, I heard them talking on TV about what's called crimes without victims? Do you think there could be something like victims without crimes? That's what we all could be, even the kids—victims' victims. Don't laugh.

It had nothing to do with heroes or heroines. But two people live in a room small enough so their shoulders touch when they pass —picture it—and don't know each other's names. One day one of them asks "What's your name?" and it turns out they have the same name. By accident. "Well," one of them says, "maybe we have something in common. What do you like best in the world?" She looks at him coyly and says, "You." She smiles because she thinks that's the right answer. "And what do you like best?" He thinks for a minute and says, "Me." So they fall together. It's a tight circle they can both fit into if they get down on all fours and crawl.

Poor Ismael. When you closed your gorgeous eyes that I envied, there must have been nothing behind them to look at. Just dark: your own closed eyes reflected and reflected.

You said I made the children a wall between us, you even made it seem that was all I had them for. But a wall is something to lean on when you have to lean, and anyway, what holds up a house, a roof overhead, if it isn't walls.

I asked you to leave. I threw you out. I left you. But I've heard about a kind of snake—this is a moreno belief, I think—that kills you and when it thinks you're dead it sticks its tail up in your nostrils to make sure you aren't breathing. If you are, it kills you again. What you used for a tail and where you went looking to see if I was still alive—I shouldn't have lay down dead for you so often.

If I ever loved you, even for a minute, then you were my fault too. I put a check-mark next to you and it wouldn't rub off. I said sure. I laughed. I said I'm behind you here, give me your footprints—even for a minute. I said we fit.

What did you say to me?

So it's going on. I think of myself, I shine up the me with powder and pink lips and what do I see but a roach climbing like a little trooper up from the baseboard, and what do I think of? Me is like a genie that goes in and out of my toilet water bottle but you are always somewhere around without being called. I paid money I didn't even have to get you a better place in the ground than you ever got me up here, and a woman to say the rosary a full three days, and you're still smoke around my shoulders. I looked at this fat roach that never got sick eating the paint off the walls because there's better things to pick at, and thought how that was you lying next to me in bed—that bed the man from welfare used to say was too big for one and leer at me—and that is still you lying in darker dark and a roach might be taking away your fingers right now for all I know. For all you know.

I know something you don't know.

The priest keeps saying, spreading out his big sweaty hands to calm me down, Now Ismael knows the last great secret, he is luckier than we are. Then he goes and names all the saints whose faces you're getting to see whether you want to or not. But I saw you dying and it was like watching you do something very very private when you didn't see me looking.

It wasn't merciful, I lied, something just got sucked away out of your eyes and when it was gone your cheeks began to collapse fast. But it was more of you than you ever showed me, dressed or naked, cold or hot, sick or sober. It was more.

Now how do I get out from under you. That's what I mean, I'm like one of those women a man died while he was inside of. Had a heart attack or something, you've heard about that. No matter where they take his body, she must always see his shoulders hunkering over her with his eyes wide on her face. I know it. And she thinks it's her fault too, a little bit, somehow a shadow of the fault, a sniff, a turn, an ooze of the fault.

The night he came home with me the first time and the last, Rosa who is your daughter no matter who's in my bed, came running into the bedroom crying Daddy is a ghost and he's scaring me. He tried to comfort her but she didn't even know who he was sitting there wrapped up in a sheet, and it took me an hour to get her back to bed. Then all he wanted to do was forget we ever saw each other, and he got dressed and went home. And I was glad. If you didn't get Rosa up out of her bed to come running in there on me just in the nick of time, then I think I did, with some strong part of my brain that I can't see.

I was planning another getaway when you escaped. Rosa was at my mother's and Chico was in his first week of sleep-away camp, and I was going out and get a job, I thought something on a boat going somewhere out of Brooklyn, I don't know, but I was standing right at the threshold, in a way. Singing, singing the whole day

how you weren't going to lock me up from myself the way you
locked me up from you. Then they came and told me they found
you and these little sunbursts of color kept popping in front of my
eyes just like when I drink, dark with rainbow colors. They had
to lead me. They told me as though it was no secret how you'd
been robbing me and telling me stories and laughing at me and
shooting your children's groceries up in your arm and my breasts
turned to clean round skulls that you had kissed in the morning.
Somebody, Julio, said he was surprised I cared so much, I looked
so weak choking on my own blood, and he took me to the hospital to breathe in the dead air you breathed out, and I said I don't
like to be made a damn fool of, that's all. And there you were
turned inside out in your skin like one of your own empty pockets
and who was the damn fool then? Julio, the last time I saw him
maybe a month ago, ran his hand down my behind with his finger
pointing like an arrow, and I thought for a second that I might be
free of you. I will tell you without shame I'd like to have made a
bow bent for your dear friend Julio's arrow. But after he took me
to your sweaty bed and showed you to me stretched out hot with
your brain dissolving right before my eyes, I told him to go away.
He shames me with myself.

They took you to the morgue and I had to go and check you out
like some lost package. I was right there when you died and the
doctor knew who I was and you didn't have to die in the street
but maybe I do have welfare mothers' eyes. So I traded them down
at that place, the morgue: They gave me what was left of you and
I gave them my feet and they locked them in a vault.

Now you see   a widow is a dry well. You always hear
the opposite. But I'll have them too, won't I? Heart's
beetles. Six fat maggots feasting on my tongue that knew
your tongue. I. I. I the stillborn.

Ismael. I wish you were alive, I wish, I wish, so I could hate you
and get on with it.

CHARLES EDWARD EATON was born in Winston-Salem, North Carolina. A graduate of the University of North Carolina, he has studied Philosophy at Princeton and taught English in Puerto Rico, returning to this country to take his M.A. degree at Harvard, where he studied with Robert Frost. He has taught Creative Writing at the University of Missouri and at the University of North Carolina, and has served as Vice Consul at the American Embassy in Rio de Janeiro. Mr. Eaton has published five volumes of poetry, the third of which, *The Greenhouse in the Garden,* was a final nominee for the National Book Award in 1957. His short stories have been anthologized in *The Best American Short Stories* and other collections. His second volume of short stories, *The Girl from Ipanema,* and a first short novel, *A Lady of Pleasure,* will be published in 1972. He divides his time between Woodbury, Connecticut, and Chapel Hill, North Carolina.

THE CASE OF THE MISSING PHOTOGRAPHS

THE EXPERIENCE of feeling like a punching bag is endemic to cocktail parties. People pass by, take a well-aimed jab just to show who the competition is, and leave you swinging wildly back and forth only too aware of what hit you but unable to do anything very decisive about it. Marjorie and I often come away with a sense of having been knocked about by champions or left to hang unnoticed in a corner of the social gymnasium.

Thus it can hardly be described as anything less than a "beautiful event" when someone turns the metaphor, surrounding us like a pleasant summer breeze where we are suspended, available and unthreatening, like those Chinese chimes that used to hang on old-fashioned porches. The pendent pieces of glass painted with flowers or little figures reminiscent of ideograms were at once transparent and appealingly exotic. There is nothing more congenial than equating one's feelings with such an image which can be approached, and is receptive, from all angles, responding with light-hearted music.

The day we were going to the Cowdens I was determined to maintain just such an affirmative mood. Lying in my bath, pleasantly relaxed, I initiated my usual ritual with Marjorie. Going over the list of our friends, several of whom I thought would be there, I planted in her mind the notion that we might meet someone new. We did not know the Cowdens all that well, and they must have a portfolio of at least ten or twelve people who were good prospects. Marjorie is patient with me in my bath, as though she understands what it is to be a supine male in his late thirties, subject to her intrusions from the dressing room where she carefully selects and applies just the right armor a Connecticut woman should wear in a given situation. I think, too, she rather enjoys the ritual of preparation, as if it might, indeed, exert some kind of mystical control over coming events, and, as I towel off, she looks at me as if *there* were a man who should be able to ring anybody's bells. Thank God, Marjorie and I are on very musical terms with each other, and I have no qualms about being "viewed in the nude" by a woman who long ago surrounded me like a summer breeze.

When we arrived at the Cowdens, Marjorie looked and smelled as fresh as one of the peonies which bloomed along the walk, and I might say that we could have been taken for a pair of champions if you only glanced at us. The party was in the garden, the light a filtered radiance of the sort one feels has been earned by the purification of the long winter, and the voices rose like a confessional of bees. But underneath the canopy of sound, more melodious than it would ever have been indoors, the reality of the situation set in. To whom were we going to talk—Mrs. Arlington Smith who had the longest nose and the oldest house in Meadowmount, the Laynes whose minimal art matched their personalities, the Daleys who pushed the collecting of old maps, the Irvings who seemed to breathe a cloud of geographical halitosis as they expatiated on their travels? Instead we soon found ourselves talking to each other. Marjorie began to look like a damp peony dipped in some social fountain of dismay, and I rocked back and forth on my feet, reflecting that an impasse of this sort can do sad and irreparable damage to a lovely Connecticut afternoon.

Janice and Nat Cowden looked utterly punch-drunk from their efforts to bring people together, but Janice finally got wind of the fact that all was not well in our corner of the garden, and snatched a couple from under the long nose of Mrs. Arlington Smith, applying them as a tourniquet to our ebbing spirits.

It was a brilliant decision to match us with Claire and David Steadman, for we prospered the moment we accepted the transfusion of their company. I am a literary critic, writing fairly successfully for the quality journals, and Claire, it turned out, had read one of my books, which in itself is always a summer breeze. David, an Englishman, applied just the right touch of gallantry to the damp peony which gladly entrusted itself to his subtle, grooming hand. While I was allowing myself to be praised, standing in a scented wind that dried up all my nervous perspiration, I discovered that I found the praiser physically attractive as well, not so much as Marjorie, but then a man's imagination must have its harem of second bests. Claire was tall and slender, but one could have wished for a bit less plain and a bit more promontory. She had gray-green eyes and hair of a rusted strawberry color tending in the direction of gold. Though her two front teeth were slightly pushed together in the point of a V as if her face had at one time meant to be broader, freer, then had contracted and crowded the oral cavity, it was not unattractive, suggesting the quality of a child who has yet to have her teeth straightened.

When we switched partners, David let me do most of the talking, perhaps in gracious acknowledgement of how attentively I had listened to his wife. But no one seemed stanched or repressed. We were brimming cups as our mutual interests bubbled up and over—books, music, painting, theatre, swimming, walking in the woods. David, who brimmed the least, nevertheless nodded frequently, looked wise, and, though he was not tall, his fresh English complexion, regular features, and imperturbable manners created a solid impression that provided weighty periods for his wife's ecstatic sentences. All of us went home happily assuaged as though four people had been making love in public. The garden had rung with our laughter, and Janice Cowden, tired as a sheared sheep, beamed gratefully at us when we left.

Claire was first to call and invite us to dinner the following weekend. They entertained, she explained, only on Saturday, since David, an English master at Choton, was always busy with extra-curricular activities during the week. Her directions were precise, and we found their house without difficulty, a charming old salt-box, huddled in a larkspurish and snapdragon sort of garden. There were two other couples, a young poet and his wife from Choton, and a doctor whose wife Claire had known in art school. Claire introduced us with just the right amount of pride in her voice as Evan and Marjorie Harrington, and managed to give us the impression that the party had been built around us.

As it grew cooler, we went inside for dinner, finding the tasteful interior one would expect from Claire, country-house Connecticut without any corny, pseudo-colonial effects, though we were surprised to find that they occupied only the first floor. Claire alluded to the fact when there was a loud scuffling above by saying that "our mice have big feet," but I noticed that her wit had an element of strain in it.

This was the first indication that she was not as much at ease in her own environment as she might have been. She served a delicious but complicated curry which was later to have such disastrous effect on our digestions that we were ready to answer Ruskin's famous question, "What do you have to say to India?", entirely in the negative.

It was pleasantly obvious, however, that Claire felt particularly drawn to me since she arranged for us to sit together both during and after dinner, and I had the foolish, though not ungratifying, feeling that she looked to me for some almost extrasensory communication not afforded by the others. Though everyone else

called me Ev, she always addressed me as Evan, but the formal
approach did not always harmonize with her ardent, almost hectic,
desire to get her thoughts across. Consequently, she tended to
enter a serious conversation without preliminaries, rather as one
might split a melon.

Noticing that I was glancing through a book on modern painting, she came over, put down her coffee, and observed, "I think
Vlaminck was right when he said Picasso was the perverter of
modern art, don't you?"

"Well, perhaps," I hedged. "If you mean he was obsessively
devoted to change."

"*Après* Picasso, *le déluge*," she persisted. "Nothing but a run-
away river of change. Nothing but fads and fashions. Abstract
expressionism, Pop Art, Op Art, Minimal Art. The works." She
picked up another book which had a painting of a large, unsavory
hot dog and bun on the cover and handed it to me.

"What about the Blue and Rose Periods?" I asked lamely, returning the book to the coffee table. "Paintings like *Femmes au
Bar* and *Les Saltimbanques?*"

"They were done by another man. Vlaminck wasn't talking
about them."

And that was that. No compromises. No concessions. Only the
high, thin laughter that floated around us when I looked too troubled. I sensed that in some way I was not satisfying her, but, for
the life of me, I could not discover what was lacking. When
she turned to talk to her other guests, there was an aura of psychological excitation about her which made me feel vaguely guilty
as if I caused her to react in a manner that was not altogether
good for her.

But the evening, nevertheless, was a "beautiful event" as far as
we were concerned, and we let only a respectable three weeks
pass so as not to seem pushing before we returned their invitation.
Marjorie keeps a sharp lookout for what she calls "the drama of
the garden", and tries not to invite anyone over between the acts.
For the Steadmans, the jeweled scepters of the phlox were in
bloom, and, in another part of the garden, the mounds of pink

and red rambler roses seemed to cover the barrows of ancient
kings. Our house is also old, but we have made less effort than
the Steadmans to remain true to the period, mixing old and new,
preferring to let it live its life in the present century as well.
Hoping to make them feel at home, we invited their poet friend
and his wife from Choton, inarticulate as we had found them to
be, and Maisie Freemantle, an English artist in her sixties, who
looked rather like a cocker spaniel fed all year on plum pudding.

We did not give them the tour of house and garden we sometimes inflict on champions for want of a better way of getting the
occasion off the ground, but Claire visited each flower bed like
a butterfly until Maisie, entirely unaware of the floppy canine
image she aroused, stood in her way before a final one as if to
say you have seen all the flowers in the world except the rarest:
"Smell me. Admire me. You don't know what you've been missing." But Claire soon sought me out, turning Maisie over to David,
and, taciturn though he was, I saw him occasionally open and
shut his mouth like a pair of shears as if even he were tempted
to cut the stem of her garrulity.

Again I noticed this ectoplasm of nervous irritability which surrounded Claire whenever she came to grips with me. I pass for
good-looking and have some reputation in the literary world, but
I have never thought of myself as either a lady-killer or a Sainte-
Beuve. But was I, without meaning to be, some kind of eidolon
to Claire? Was it that I had the qualities she associated only with
artists and yet had a comfortable and agreeable background, a
combination that might annoy a strict moralist such as I deemed
her to be?

Several times while we were having cocktails, when I flirted a
little or took her less than seriously, she made me feel I sat too
casually on the rock of my insouciance, a happy, sunny, but way-
ward toad who overlooked the lily pond where the mysterious,
disk-like leaves of her thought let down roots into the opaque
water. No one wants to be thought of as an ornamental toad, no
matter how gleaming and glistening with life, and I suppose I
went out of my way to illustrate that frogs were the equal of lily

pads. But none of this helped. I began to sense that the first, fine, careless rapture was over and that she wanted to take me down a peg or two.

During dinner this became awkwardly evident when, unable to keep the conversation light after compliments on Marjorie's excellent food went around the group, Claire introduced the notion of genius and asked whether an artist ever really *knew* when he was one. Various theories were proposed more or less idly by the rest of us who were at the moment more devoted to the first half of that maxim "Dine with the rich, and talk with the wise," when Claire turned abruptly to me and asked, "Evan, do you think you are a genius?"

With my mouth full of deviled crab, I laughed and said, "Of course, can't you see what a big head I've got. Geniuses always have big heads. Look at Churchill, Paderevski."

"Maybe some of it was hair in Paderevski's case," Claire went on with dogged seriousness.

Maisie, uneasy that this curious conversation might redound to my advantage after all, swallowed an enormous mouthful of food in one gulp.

"Talk about big heads. Have you ever seen one larger than mine?" she asked, and put her hands to her great cowl of brown hair as if it were a large rock of genius.

Ignoring her, Claire stumbled on, addressing me as though no one else were there. "So you *really* do think so?"

"Think what?" I said, slightly annoyed by now.

"That you are a genius."

The poet dropped his fork, and Marjorie broke in with her warmest smile, "Ev has no doubt whatsoever about his abilities, but he doesn't overrate them either. I find it restful. So few people have the courage to be realistic about themsleves. Have some more aspic, Claire, dear?"

"Thank you, Marjorie, my love," I said with a wink. "All that's necessary to have a happy life is to delude one other person. Whom have you deluded, Claire?" I continued, turning to her without a trace of apparent rancor, congratulating myself on how beautifully Marjorie and I worked together.

"Me, of course," David answered as he watched a deep blush spread over Claire's face like a contagion from her hair. "I agree with Marjorie though. I respect self-confidence. Do you remember E. M. Forster saying somewhere that he admired most the people who acted as if they were immortal and society eternal?"

Good old silent, watchful Dave, I thought. He had saved the day, diffusing the tension into something literary and general. He was my man from that moment on.

"You're so right, Mr. Steadman," said Maisie among whose many rôles was the ultimate one of peacemaker. "We can all be geniuses in that way, can't we?"

Suddenly, as if someone had just slain the dragon, we found ourselves admiring Marjorie's Bavarian cream molded into a white castle-like tower, and Maisie was able to go home thinking that she had made the party.

But, in spite of Claire's penchant for recognition scenes which dress the drabbest ego in the motley of bruised self-esteem, we saw a lot of the Steadmans and were determined to like them. I became more adept in sidestepping the conflict between Claire and myself, whatever it was, and, if the going got rough, Marjorie would advance like Salome and distract us with the beautiful veils of her wit and grace, and David was our philosopher.

Nevertheless, when Christmas came along with its round of parties, the Harringtons and the Steadmans were exposed to each other in circumstances that could not always be so delicately maneuvered. Maisie Freemantle went into her yearly deep mourning at the approach of the birth of Our Savior as if no man, mortal or immortal, should be given that much attention, and Marjorie and I joked about the "Christmas syndrome" when we noticed Claire growing paler and more staccato as the social pace quickened.

Someone had told us that she had a very beautiful sister who was the family favorite. Another suggested that she had brooded over the fact that she could not have children. In a psychologically oriented world, these little facts about each other seep out and seem to explain our actions as well perhaps, and as superficially, as the ancient humours did. We began to feel a little sorry for Claire, and, if she were not going to provide a summer breeze for us, our kindness and understanding might help to keep some of the winter chill from her heart.

This attitude still prevailed when we saw her on Christmas Eve at the Weavers', a charming couple who always try to give their parties an original twist. That evening it was to be the passing of a Christmas Box from which each couple would take a slip of folded paper, and whoever had the winning number would win a series of photographs of one person in the family. The prize had been donated by Jacques Rimbaud, a rather unsavory character and sometime photographer whose wife Maureen (née Rafferty) ostensibly ran an art gallery but actually specialized in acting out episodes from Krafft-Ebing.

I who never win anything drew the winning number, and I suppose there were others who thought "Them that has, gets," but everyone was perfectly agreeable about it. Only Claire spoke out in a loud voice. "Well, I hope you are going to let Marjorie have *her* picture taken."

Perhaps it was the word *let* that did it, but I had a nice Christmasy desire to slap her.

This time Marjorie was considerably quicker than I. "Claire, dear," she said, "you make it sound as if Ev keeps me in a dark room."

"Darkroom," one of the more potted guests snickered. "Isn't that where all the developments take place?"

Claire let the rest of the group move back to the punch bowl, and said again, "You *are* going to let her have her picture taken, aren't you?"

I could not think of any answer that did not have a four-letter word in it. But Marjorie once more came forward. "I think it's a family affair, don't you, Claire, dear? But since you insist, I think you ought to know I have already decided it is Evan's turn. He has a new book coming out in the spring."

Claire blushed like the little girl who peed in class, her eyes misted over, and I could have sworn she did not herself entirely know why she had persisted. I got a little drunk that night because I, too, did not know why I roused such infantile animosity in someone I basically admired. It was as though somewhere in the darkness of the soul Claire and I were children together, and I had been given something for Christmas which she wanted and of which I was unaware. No doubt for some people Christmas, in this sense, is the only day of the year.

After the holidays, there was no direct confrontation between Claire and myself, partly because the ties that bind were no longer so blessed, and we had begun gently to loosen them. Even so, whenever we did run into the Steadmans, Claire made some reference to "those photographs". If Marjorie had swerved one inch from her persistent marital decorum, I think Claire would have been all over her with protectiveness and solicitude. One sensed that her desire to ferret out some difficulty between us was overwhelming and that it had taken this bizarre outlet.

Meanwhile, posed as we were off and on before the camera of her obsession, we did nothing at all about the photographs themselves, admitting that we had developed a slight complex. We felt as though some bad luck would be hidden in a photograph which had become such a strange idol to someone we had so much wanted to like. It seemed to shuttle us foolishly back and forth between appearance and reality that we could be judged by the mere taking of a picture. If either of us decided to have the photograph taken, we would be yielding to Claire, who would read something into an act which was totally superficial in its implications for us.

Another disturbing aspect of the whole thing was that if this sort of febrile myth-making could go on in the mind of a friend, what caricatures of ourselves must exist in the thoughts of casual acquaintances. It suggested to us in our less sanguine moods that people simply projected others as they went along, posing them as subjects of a private pathology. Claire wanted a mug shot of me, and was determined to have it at the cost of a more pleasant "reality" I had been trying to present to her.

Nevertheless, at the end of February, when we received an invitation to an exhibition of Claire's paintings in the tiny gallery of the local bookstore, we accepted. It was one of those bleak winter days when the radiant Connecticut I so much love shows the sorrows of her soul, and the vivid colors of the paintings with their welcome warmth seemed like so many heaters of various sizes embedded in the walls. But the little room itself turned out to be crowded and stuffy, the paintings, at second glance, were considerably less than first-rate, and one had the uneasy feeling that that was where the work would always remain. Mostly of beautiful young women, conceived one felt in too precious an idealism, they revealed a certain interesting documentation of longing. I could not help thinking of Claire's sister.

Maisie Freemantle, dressed in a purple dress which made her bosom look stuffed with a bushel of mashed plums, was the first one to vocalize her feelings.

Pushing heavily against me, plums and all, she whispered loudly, "Aren't they awful? Hasn't she got a nerve giving herself an exhibition?"

The poet from Choton, thin and pale as a paper straw, was poking himself nearsightedly into a strawberry-colored painting as though stirring a soda. Suddenly I was touched with the pathos of it all. This was Claire's collection of friends, about each of whom no doubt she suppurated some "photograph", better or worse than the subject warranted. They were the real exhibit in all their weird vitality and variety, most of them totally unwilling to be developed in the darkroom of her temperament.

Astringent, fastidious Claire was beaded with sweat, her high laughter puffing out of her like steam, and she looked martyred with bewilderment. Not a single painting was sold, and the nonexistent profits were consumed at the large punch bowl. I knew I had to make a special effort and that, in this case, it would not be the "truth that set us free".

As we were leaving, I kissed her, tasting the cosmetic flavor of her damp cheek, and said, "Claire, what a handsome showing of pictures. We do want to come and see them again. Congratulations!"

She looked at me as though she thought I were lying and closed abruptly that hiatus of cordiality and good manners, sincere in its insincerity, in which we reveal and discover those representations which mediate between the world as it is and as we would like it to be.

"What about those photographs? Have you had them taken yet?" she asked, her face whitening. I was too confused by the harsh geography of the closing gap to do anything but smile, bow, and back away with my receding half of a friendship.

So the photographs that meant so much to Claire never got taken. I half-heartedly tried to persuade Marjorie to call Jacques Rimbaud and make an appointment with him to come over, but she said again she loathed the man and that he would merely use the sitting as an excuse visually to undress her. He did not pursue the matter either, and I had every reason to believe that the fact that I worked at home would have inconvenienced his philandering instincts. We agreed, however, that we would not let Claire know one way or the other. We felt we owed ourselves at least the vengeance of keeping the photographs forever in the files of missing persons.

Why didn't it end there? Why do human beings keep toying with each other past the point of reason and civilized endurance? Loneliness provides part of the answer, but I think one must look elsewhere into some basic lust for human encounter, some fascination with what's difficult in the face of the absurdities of human coexistence. Claire could not let go of us, and we would not let go of her as long as the unknown still had any potent charge left in it.

Maisie Freemantle's birthday came up in April, "the cruellest month". Maisie claimed to have known T. S. Eliot, and one of the local wags said that he had no doubt penned that line after encountering her on her birthday. Next to Christmas, it was the hardest day of the year for her to get through, and Claire decided to cheer her up with a "surprise" dinner party of some of her closer friends. We accepted but, the situation being what it was, Marjorie warned me to watch the drinks and steer clear of "the darkroom", the expression we had come to use about anything relating to my difficulties with Claire. I agreed and tried to put on the suit of *bienaise* I had first worn to the Steadmans', now stiffened, it seemed to me, beyond all style or comfort.

Maisie was to arrive late, but we found already assembled the Weavers, the poet from Choton, to whom Maisie had taken quite a shine since he said almost nothing and all of it complimentary of her, his wife, and the usual odd couple who would presumably provide the spice for the occasion.

By that evening, however, Maisie had worked herself into one of her moods, claiming that a storm which had passed through the evening before had upset her "vibrations". Maisie's perceptions extended to the ends of the earth, and a volcanic eruption in Japan produced a tremor in her. Consequently, she was not amused by the surprise party, for she had hoped to come over to the Steadmans', drown the knowledge of the passing years in alcohol, and "cozy off", as she would say of an evening which presented an unbroken aspect of adulation and acquiescence.

Downing a drink, she said to me, "Why didn't she say this was going to be a party for me? I would have worn something else. I don't like surprises. I think they are aggressive. They mean to throw you off balance. How did she know it was my birthday anyway?"

I couldn't resist saying, "Why, Maisie, she probably looked you up in *Who's Who*."

She blanched as if I had produced a birth certificate and promptly called for another drink. I mentioned to Marjorie that Maisie was seriously in need of some expert "cherishing", and managed to escape and spend a silent, restful cocktail hour with the poet from Choton.

It turned out that I needed it. Claire had gone all-out for the occasion, and was an incandescent bundle of nerves, particularly after she sensed Maisie's ingratitude. The dinner was delicious but promised for me a long and fiery trip down the alimentary canal. It was topped off by one of Claire's spectaculars which consisted of little clay flowerpots filled with chocolate ice cream like earth into which at the last minute she inserted an iris from the florist. It represented such a striving for effect I felt like eating the iris as I am told Einstein did in the case of an orchid a fancy hostess had put on his service plate. Maisie, overcome in spite of herself, wiped hers clean and stuck it in between her bosoms where it seemed to take root in the richest of soils.

After dinner I sat on the love seat with a generous glass of brandy as compensation for the fact I had had only two drinks, hoping that the poet's wife would settle down with me for some discreet politicking in behalf of her husband's career. But Claire, the grand effort of the dinner over, beat her to the draw. I stiffened perceptibly, and we sat there looking out into the room like two people in a daguerreotype, capable of only the most mechanical small-talk.

But it was destined momentarily to be a modern color photograph after all, for Claire soon began touching up our study in black and white with little caustic personal remarks. I instructed my diencephalon to hold its fire, but I am afraid it listened to the brandy instead, and the moment perhaps both of us needed arrived like a late, paltry, but nevertheless irresistible impulse from a Greek drama.

"Oh, Evan," Claire said, her face as feverish as Phaedra's. "You never did tell me whether Marjorie had those photographs taken."

"No, I never did," I said impassively, but my brain stem, having folded the gracious umbrella of its cortex, throbbed with mayhem.

"But you did let her have them taken, didn't you?" she continued, giving me her self-righteous Pallas Athena look which I so much loathed.

"God damn it, Claire," I said with a relief that had a curiously vital sensation in it. "Why don't you mind your own business? You've been hounding me about those photographs for months.

What's your angle?" I had at long last torn up the likeness of myself I had tried to maintain and given her the pieces.

Claire promptly burst into tears and left the room as if I had assaulted her. Barbaric little flakes of a relationship I had apparently exploded seemed to float down around me like fallout.

Too late now to do any good, the poet's wife came over to me, and I think I may have been fairly rude to her as well. David, who never rushed, did so this time to see to Claire, and Maisie gargled some foolish remark to the effect that Claire too must still be feeling the proximity of that awful storm, so hard on "us sensitives".

I knew I should have held on, but I simply couldn't. I wanted to pour corrosive developing fluid all over Claire as well as myself—See, this is what you are, Claire. This is what I am. Two can play at this game of photographs.

A rueful David reappeared after a while, looking like "a verray, parfit gentil knyght" who nevertheless had a serious woman-problem on his hands. Maisie, warm-hearted at her best, rose to the occasion, said all the appropriate things as she gathered up her birthday loot, let me nuzzle her iris in its very special place, and managed to make David think the party had been a success.

But that evening closed the darkroom forever, or so it seemed. Our friendship with the Steadmans had lasted less than a year, and, since it had every possible affinity to insure its viability, the loss was all the more regretted. The incident was gossiped about in Meadowmount for a while, and then nobody cared. In August we heard that David had given up his job at Choton and that they were living in New York where Claire could pursue her art studies. Later we were told they had gone to live in England, then Europe, and finally we lost track of them altogether.

Perhaps three or four years later, on a beautiful day in July, Marjorie and I went to a large cocktail party at Grandview, a club thickly sewn with the seed of champions. We were in a lucid, confident mood, and our skill at giving as well as taking the briskly delivered social punch was better than usual. But since

I can never be a wholehearted competitor, I withdrew after a while to smoke a cigarette and enjoy a moment of psychic distance so necessary to anyone who feels that most of his life is spent shadow-boxing with elusive ideas and images. Marjorie, beautiful as a marigold in yellow silk, relaxed and released from having delivered her share of uppercuts, was dutifully embrocating Maisie, who looked bruised and loose all over, a punching bag gone to seed. As I was on the point of joining them to add my adhesive touch, I felt a gentle tap on my shoulder, turned, and saw Claire Steadman, not looking a day older in a lovely green dress, but somehow more muted and insubstantial, like an image that had blown in from outer space.

One hoped to see David moving slowly through the crowd but sensed with desolating certainty that he was now inoperative in Claire's life. Perhaps it was this intuition that contributed to her insubstantiality—the look of a woman without a man, as if she mattered less to others because she mattered less to herself. It was horrifying, as I was later to think, that dear, kindhearted David had been the most expendable of any of us, so soon to have become a hardened, crusted memory, like a suit of armor from which the meat of a man had been extracted.

Though Claire kissed me lightly on the cheek, and I responded with an earthier vigor, something was missing. I realized that it was the cloud of intense nervous excitement that had always surrounded us. There was nothing obsessive in the air, but there was nothing else milling around either—no suffocating martyrdoms, no tortured mythologies. She told me she was now living in Philadelphia and working at the Museum, coming back to Meadowmount for occasional weekends.

I kept waiting for the question, which now seemed age-old, "Evan, what about those photographs?", but it never came. In the slow, suffering chemistry of her emotions, Claire had finally "developed" me. It was probably not the image I wanted to give her and certainly not the one she offered me, but it was a photograph we could both accept. Marjorie and Maisie came up to be kissed and to receive Claire's final version of their likenesses, and we talked together like perfectly normal human beings for half an hour.

None of us gave in to our latent feelings that it was "too late" in the cohesive sense of nows and tomorrows bound together. What might have been in its full, generous entirety would remain forever in the files of missing persons. But it was still time in that Claire had come back if only for a moment to meet us in that hiatus of representations where we suspend the opposing cliffs of personalities like the terrible, frozen music of avalanches which might crush beyond all recognition those fragile surrogates with which we mainly communicate with each other.

When Marjorie and I left Grandview without a noticeable bruise upon us, still looking like champions, Claire was already oddly mystical, even recessive, but it was, no doubt, all for the best that we had not stood too long under opposite eaves, neighborly though they appeared on the surface. The unknown constantly recharges itself, incubating its challenges and rebuffs, and Claire and I, perhaps, were not meant to endure together its struggles and depredations more than once. In retrospect, the mood for everybody concerned had been sensible and civilized: "Let's leave it at that." But when we remember, as we frequently do, how Claire "came back", a visitant to an enigma, Marjorie and I feel our hearts, like the futurists they insist on being, respond to their fond old dream of summer breezes and Chinese chimes.

MARGERY FINN BROWN lives in San Francisco. Her recent work has been published in *McCall's*. The story here was given a Special Award by the Mystery Writers of America.

IN THE FORESTS OF RIGA THE BEASTS
ARE VERY WILD INDEED

TAKE it on faith, make it a handclasp between friends: I am an ordinary woman, unmemorable in looks and endeavors. No one ever followed me home. I never won a prize in a raffle. Once, when I was riding by an open window on a bus, an apple core flew in and gave me a black eye. Later I married, had four children, lived in twenty houses around the earth, gave parties, seamed curtains, dreamed, encountered God, respected beauty, and one Thanksgiving, with my left hand in a splint, cooked dinner for thirty people.

My life has been "usual, simple, and therefore most terrible." Tolstoi? Dostoevski? No matter. What does matter is that since a massive cardiac eight months ago, I am obliged to take quarazine. You say it bluntly: the zine rhymes with *"cousine,"* a word that comes to mind because *Rosenkavalier* is spinning on the record player down the hall, and Ochs is importuning *"ma cousine."* Every note, every hemidemisemiquaver is etched on crystal. None of it matters.

Until eight months ago, music was an integral part of my life. So were books, as necessary to me as breathing in and breathing out. Now when I look at the rows and rows lining the hall— great books, mediocre books, poets, spellbinders, historians, windbags, *flâneurs,* friends—I feel a terrible sadness. This morning I tried again to read Yeats. "What shall I do for beauty, now my old bawd is dead?" The words march valiantly across the page. The meaning sputters through my head like a damp firecracker.

So, you may say. So you cannot enjoy music or read Yeats. So you walk with an obscene white cane and your dreams are stained with the echoes of cigarette smoke. So what? Bear with me, please. We have just left the runway, seat belts are still fastened. To get back to quarazine, its basic ingredient is warfarin. (Warfarin, oddly enough, is the basic ingredient in rat killers.) Quarazine is an anticoagulant. The thinner the mixture, the easier it is for blood to pump up and down the arteries, in and out of the main firehouse, thus lessening the possibility of a "recurring incident," to quote Doctor Chiclets.

How much quarazine do I take? It varies. Every Wednesday I go to Chiclets' office on Sutter Street and have a blood test, to determine the coagulating rate. Every Thursday between one and three, Miss—an old miss—Franklin telephones and says, "Mrs. George Manning? Katherine Manning? Your new dosage until next Wednesday is eleven. Repeat after me, Mrs. Manning, eleven milligrams." Eleven, I say. Eleven, incise it on your heart. Eleven, scrawl it on the Cinderella wallpaper in the bathroom.

I keep quarazine in two phials inside the mirrored medicine chest. The lavender pills are two milligrams. The peach are five milligrams. Eleven is two peach and one half lavender. After I take the quarazine, I close the medicine chest, regard the face in the mirror, and speak to it. I say, "You in there, old tomodachi, you with the sags and the bags and the puffy saucers under the eyes, you have taken your quarazine today. Do not repeat. Repeat, do not repeat today."

Why the ritual?

Thin blood can drown you. It drowns rats.

Stretched out on the mauve-taffeta bed in my room, I am waiting now for Miss Franklin to call. The headboard is a tortured rococo from Venice. The Boulle chest I paid too much for at Butterfield's auction. On top of it are a lamp made from a Water-ford candlestick, a princess telephone, and a book bandaged in blue, Yeats.

Yesterday, Wednesday, I went to the doctor's. I am not obliged to remember what happened yesterday. I am not a stone, a lizard. I have free will. I will think how beautiful the light was last night at dusk, the light made Hiroshige blue stripes on the water. I said, "Have you ever seen a more beautiful sunset? My head feels strange."

Before I closed my eyes, I saw my husband and my son exchange a look of utter boredom. (They are not mean, mind you, they don't know how to be mean.) I'm bored with me, too. There is not a damn thing I can do about it while I'm taking quarazine. It has dissolved the inside of my head. There's a forest in there now. It's thick and black. Nothing stirs in the forest. The sun never shines. The growth still grows, chokes. You know the painting by Rousseau, the one where the lion is eating the leopard head-first? Rousseau's trees and leaves and branches are shiny-green enamel. Ungloss them. Smudge them black, the lion has finished eating the leopard, the stillness is eternal . . . that is my head.

I am ashamed to tell anyone about the forest. It *is*. I am positive of it. The knowledge comes straight from the "zero bone." Emily Dickinson? Whitman? The zero bone tells you when you have had an encounter. A glance can be an encounter, or a word, a body's spontaneous gesture, the shape of a cloud, autumn leaves burning. You never forget encounters, nor do you search for them; they leap at you, unannounced. An encounter can be like a sunburn. Off peels a layer of skin, exposing a tender red hurting surface that toughens gradually. An encounter can mystify, enlighten, or terrorize. What it can never be is superficial.

Is it true for you? Has your life, like mine, bulged with people? Yet I have had few encounters, fewer still related to joy. A blistering night in Santiago, so long ago air conditioning had not been invented. My back burned with prickly heat. The woman in the next labor room screamed with every breath, *"Madre de Dios, Madre de Dios."* My doctor did not believe in anesthesia, so my first child was born *au naturel*. It took two days.

When I first saw Jamey, he was upside down, a tiny fish, shimmering under a waxy overcoat. The doctor said, "Mrs. Manning, you have been an excellent patient. I am going to give you a whiff of something before I sew you up." I told him to keep it. I didn't want to miss one second of this encounter—an upside-down baby with a pirate's grin and with an impudent gleam in his eye.

Another hot night, years later in Rome, an Embassy reception for R., a famous soprano. I had heard her sing, but never met her before. She wore a chrome-yellow Balenciaga, hoops of perspiration under her arms. Unlike her arrogantly assured stage stance, she looked shy, a please-like-me little girl at her first party. Everyone in Rome had turned out to meet her. Directly ahead of us in line was the British commercial attaché. I remember his guardsman's mustache and rabbity teeth. "In the foddist of Rrrrriga," he said, apropos of something, "the beasts are very wild indeed."

When I was introduced to R., I said good-evening. She looked me right in the eye. "Pray for me," she said. Startled, I said lightly, "Any special time?" There was no answering smile. "All the time," she said, "starting now."

Warrenton, Virginia. A shabby farmhouse with splintery floors and tribes of field mice. I lived there with the children for a year until we could join my husband in Djakarta.

A year is twelve months. He did not write for nine weeks. I found I could function without sleep for two days. Third night, my room would swarm with people, and the people would speak, and my own voice answered, shrilling through the empty dark. One night, I encountered God. He said four words. Did I imagine him? Did He imagine me? The words still live.

So fly a pennant for Warrenton, mute the strings in Djakarta. A mammoth blood-red moon, a hunter's moon, my husband said. The bamboo swayed, swivel-hipped under the window. I cannot even remember the girl's name. All that comes back is the smell of DDT. (Do you know about the parrot Paderewski trained to perch on the piano and say, "You're the greatest, you're the greatest, the greatest"?)

After that night in Djakarta with the hunter's moon, George would never again imitate Paderewski's parrot, and I would never again be his hatchet woman, chopping down his adversaries, making his life free of rent or wrinkle. Which makes neither of us superior. It merely removed one of the hundred reasons we took each other in marriage and bedhood. Vigor, in any event, is a marginal virtue in a woman. If I could create a new façade, I would be lazy and lovely and amiable as the trumpet vine lacing the house where I was born.

Durham, New Hampshire, a brown, shingled house rimmed in Gothic-green. Emmett, my stepbrother—his father married my mother—gets violent every ten years or so. He would never hurt me. We were close as twins. I taught him to ride a bicycle. He paid for my first permanent, caddying. When Father died, the house went to Emmett. I came home to Durham to help him dispose of the incunabula of eighty-some years.

The two of us alone, the night after the funeral, walking down the cellar steps.

"You know how Father hated taxes," Emmett said. "One night last winter he hauled me out of bed and made me bury a wad of treasury notes in the wine cellar. Then I had to cement over it. You're coming with me while I dig it up. I need a witness."

The back of my neck was ice. I kept walking down the steps, too frightened to turn back. "We will have to find Father's ax, won't we, Kate? You wouldn't know where he kept it, would you? I stayed in Durham. I took his crap year in, year out while you roamed, here, there, everywhere. . . . We're going to find that ax if it takes all night, aren't we, Kate?"

Encounters remembered. Deeds done. Words said. Tracer bullets lobbing over the forest. I was named Kate for my Irish grandmother. She dyed her hair with tea leaves and thumped the floor with her blackthorn if the service was poor or people didn't do as she liked. Stay fierce, she used to say, stay lean, Kate, take no man's guff.

Lardy, defanged, I exist in a mauve bedroom, waiting for the phone to ring. If only I didn't have to take quarazine. "If only" is a greased pole to nowhere. All there is is what is. Me. This minute. My left hand. How can I describe my left hand? It has gnawed cuticles, a wedding ring grown too large, grave freckles, wormy blue veins, a medic-alert bracelet on the wrist, a scar on the forefinger where I broke a dish of pickled beets twenty years ago. The framework consists of five fan-shape bones covered with skin the color of cheese. The bones are cut into five uneven strips, each strip ending in an oval cellophane window. Once, looking down from the loft of a stable, I thought, That's not a horse's back, that's a cello.

Listen: this is quarazine. I am frightened.

Listen: my mother-in-law's lobster claw clamped around your wrist so you would not leave before she finished one of her interminably long, pointless stories. My mother-in-law, a muscled, all-dark-meat woman. Squeaky dentures, lipstick bleeding into the pleats around her mouth, nicotined fingers worked to the bone. She adored George, "my only child, my son, the diplomat." George was ashamed of her. "God's sake, Ma, if you have to label me, just say I'm with the State Department."

Every summer she visited us. The pipes rumbled as she bathed, five o'clock in the morning. The ironing was all finished when we returned at night from a party. No, she wouldn't come, no, she wouldn't "fit in. Besides, I'm allergic to Mexican food." That, George said, was a lot of bushwa. So she went with us to the Troups' in Mexico City. She ate tortillas and drank sangría until she was sick, o, o, *con fuoco* all over the Troups' bathroom.

In the middle of the night, I awoke. The guest-room door had blown open, and I heard her trying quietly to light a match. (Lord, I thought, someday I'll be old and visiting one of my married children, and they'll be whispering in bed, "When is she going home? Lord, I can't stand this much longer.") It wasn't love or pity that impelled me to walk into the guest room. I needed a talisman to ward off my own future. "Mrs. Manning," I said, "can I get you something?" A phlegmy, raspy laugh. Out came the lobster claw. "Listen," she said, "I know I'm a damn nuisance, but I can't seem to help it." The next morning at breakfast, she was the same, lipstick seeping, calliope laugh, trying to woo her son, her only child, the diplomat. The same and never the same again. Martin Buber would say the I-It relationship had changed to an I-Thou. Alan Watts would say the she-ness of she encountered the me-ness of me.

What do I say?

I say our journey is almost over, we're coming in over the air-port, the landing gear is down and locked. Yesterday I went to the doctor's. I call him Chiclets for short and for spite. Why do I despise him? Fear, what else? He has wind-colored eyes, furry knuckles, and when he touches you, his hands are deft and con-temptuous, like a butcher handling meat. Why should a man so lacking in empathy become a doctor? Geld, more than likely, and status. God is his peer group. Pay homage to the doctor, oh yes, but forget the frank, insult, and mirth. His voice starts out in the lower abdomen, big and scornful, but after winding through fatty detours and truck routes, comes out of his rosebud mouth, mi-nuscule, unvaliant, ridiculous somehow, like a tricycle batting it down the freeway.

"Ah, you have not started smoking again," he says, blowing smoke in my face. "Ah, you have courage." (Not enough, I wanted to say, not enough, you two-bit twot. I heard you browbeating that incontinent old wreck in the hospital.) "As I have said before, Mrs. Manning, quarazine is a powerful drug and your coagulating rate is at best erratic, but never in all my experience have I en-countered a reaction such as yours." (Come off it, summer camper, sophomore in life, they should send you back to the worm, you're a waste of love and lust.) "My technician is getting married today, I will draw your blood, make a fist please." (How childish I was when my blood spurted on his shirt, so childishly delighted I found the nerve to ask that bitter-bile question.)

"Mrs. Manning, you may have to take quarazine all your life. It is more than likely, I should say, so you must resign yourself to that probability."

Resigned?

I ride down the elevator of the Medical Arts Building. The

blind pencil vendor recognizes my footsteps. "Your feet tapping weak today, Mrs. Manning." I say, "No, Mr. Holliday, I'm fine. How's the world treating you?" "Terrible. . . . No sense knocking it, is they?" Resigned, I can never be. Dead before I am docile. My neck aches from holding up the forest. I am dispersed. I have nightmares. I am frightened. Things frighten and attract me simultaneously.

The traffic island in front of me. I must cross the street to get a cab home. In the middle of the intersection, there's a pedestrian haven, a small raised triangle. When I'm lucky, I make it across the street without having the light change. Today I cannot walk fast enough. I stand on the traffic island, watching the cars arrel-bassing by, the trucks puffing smug and smog, wild-eyed buses so close they eat the breath from my mouth. I look down on my black alligator shoe. Put your little foot right there. Silly jingle. Right there, one inch, and it will all be over, Kate.

Stop pushing. Whoever is pushing me in the small of the back, *stop it*. No need to turn around. I know I am alone on the traffic island. I have no assurance that it would be quick, final, or painless. I could live all chewed up, fresh from the gristmill. Wouldn't that be loverly? When the light changes, I limp across to the cab stand. Be patient, patient. Be valid, invalid. Chop down the forest, but do not make me wait.

I've been waiting all afternoon. Look at the time, ten after three. The neighborhood children are coming home from school, sweater arms lashed around their waists. Elijah, a dilapidated coach dog, crawls out from under the hedge and gives a halfhearted hello.

"Hi, Elijah." I recognize the voice. The new little girl. Can't be five, wears mesh panty hose, and has the whole block in thrall. "Lijah, you know what?"

I pick up the phone before the second ring. It *is* Miss Franklin. I listen, repeat the new dosage, say thank you, hang up.

Lijah, you know what? I have to start taking twenty-two milligrams. *Madre de Dios*. In the hospital it was four milligrams. Then six, nine, eleven, fourteen, fifteen, eighteen. Twenty-two. I'll dissolve. I'll be in fragments.

Leaning on the white tree-stump cane, I walk into the bathroom. The wallpaper I've been meaning to change for years. It cloys—Cinderellas in hoopskirts stepping out of pumpkin coaches. I open the mirrored chest. Twenty-two. That's six peach. Six times five is twenty. One lavender is two. Twenty and two make twenty-two. I fill a cup from the dispenser with water. The pills go down smoothly. I close the medicine chest. Look, I say to the mirror, look old friend, you with the sags and bags, you've taken your quarazine today, so do not repeat. Repeat, do not repeat.

I say it.

There is no face in the mirror.

I can see the collar of a faded-blue robe. I can see a corded neck. Above the neck? Nothing. Air. Where the face should be, a square of Cinderella wallpaper.

An optical illusion?

I turn on the light switch. I can hear that humming prelude fluorescent lights always make. I can hear the last trio from *Rosenkavalier* wisping down the hall. My tongue is wet. We have nice water, it's tart and tastes of fresh mermaids. The porcelain sink feels like a porcelain sink—cold, and eternal.

Alles in ordnung.

I look again in the mirror. The robe, the neck, the air, the wallpaper. I lean over, shaking. I grip my arms tight around my stomach. My heart roars like surf in my ears. Quarazine turned my head into a forest, now it has dissolved my face. Persona means mask. It melted my personal mask. The head, then the face, what comes next? The heart? The zero bone that registers encounters, that labels true feelings and looks ahead and wonders. How will I get through the rest of my days?

The house is cold. I should turn up the thermostat. Feeling the pull of the rug under my slippers, I back into my bedroom, my little mauve vegetable bin. When feelings go, I'll be a vegetable. Carrots, broccoli, o garland me with parsley. The worst has happened, I encountered me. There was no one there.

Memory nags, pulls on my sleeve. A ravenously rough trip to the Aran Islands, all of us strangers, so sopped by the rain we clung together in the snuggery while cows groaned and thudded in the hold. The Guinness flowed like buttermilk. A little runty Dubliner with a tweed cap and yard-arm jaw apologized the first time the ship lurched and a wave of Guinness slipped from his glass into my lap. More lurches, more Guinness. There was no place to move to, nor did I show any sign of dismay. Each time his apology was curter, less gracious, till in a fit of exasperation, he growled, "Madame, ye've got to adjist to the whims of nature."

So I must. Nature never rejoices, mourns, never applauds, never condemns. Nature continues. I haven't the energy to cry. I sigh instead, a breathy sigh that nudges the walls like an airy puffball. Somehow it helps, when you are alone and no one can hear you, to sigh deeply, to say, "O dear. Dear me."

Dear me?

Dear nobody.

J. D. MC CLATCHY was raised in Philadelphia. He graduated in 1967 from Georgetown University (*summa cum laude,* Phi Beta Kappa) and continued graduate study in English at Yale University on a Woodrow Wilson Fellowship. For the past three years he has been teaching English at La Salle College in Philadelphia, from which he is currently on leave to complete his Ph.D. at Yale. His poems and essays have appeared in several journals and he is at work on a novel.

ALLONYM

"Disappointing." There was the word that particularly annoyed Adrian Holland. Disappointing. What did he mean—this, this Edward Newton Crofton—by "disappointing"? How could he, with so much swagger and so little style, proclaim that *A Waste of Shame* appears to be "less an achievement than we have come to expect from a man whose first three novels justly earned him an honored place among the true masters of modern French literature." That smug verdict was typical of the lefthanded manner the whole *Times* review displayed, and of which "disappointing" was the keynote.

And yet, curiously, this same Crofton had said earlier in the same article—where was it now?—that the new work surpassed its predecessors with its "typically—and admirably—French philosophical precision," and with its "vivid accumulation of sensory detail" (James had put it better and more briefly in "long-waisted," Holland remembered). Three paragraphs of praise described the "ingenious plotting," "the brilliantly lighted contours of physical and psychological landscapes," and the "virtuosic portrayal of the nameless, crippled author through whose tortured consciousness pass the events of his generation." And so on. Until that point in any review when genius is summarized, competition dismissed, and laurels awarded. But at that point the fellow suddenly becomes "uneasy" and diagnoses his "disappointment."

Then comes the condescending fuss—prefaced, in cowardly fashion, with a meek "one suspects"—about "a noticeable absence of genuine feeling . . . this disturbing, almost aggressive disinterest in his author-hero . . . and the reader is finally chilled by the lack of that larger vision he anticipated from one of the few men capable of projecting it." Holland considered that sort of vague objection oddly unsophisticated for a man whose dreadful prose revealed him—the editor's note merely confirmed it—as one of those many young, clever, untenured associates in upstate university Language Departments. One of those, no doubt, whose overcrowded classes were required to read Holland's definitive Pascal and paperback Mallarmé and had never heard of René Philippe Marineau, "a true master of modern French literature" or whatever it was now, this man at whose expense their anxious teacher sought to advance his name and career by the notoriety of this review.

Sipping again at his cooling coffee, Holland mildly reprimanded himself for angering at what he knew was just nonsense, though he could not help wondering if others that morning had come casually to the same conclusion. He began to speculate on the reactions of Elizabeth and Sam and Malcolm. And Jollie, what was Jollie thinking now? Perhaps he should call her—a witty comment right now would calm him back to the day's routine. He started to fold up the paper when his eye caught once more, impulsively, that one sentence—or a variation of it—he was long accustomed to: "Marineau is again fortunate in his translator (one might almost say, his collaborator). Adrian Holland's work is, as usual, impeccable: both literal and literate." Collaborator, was it? That fit in neatly with Crofton's betrayed sensibilities.

Yes, he *would* call Jollie, even at ten in the morning; he was too upset to do anything else. He tossed the paper onto the coffee-table and started toward the telephone in his study, smiling, remembering Jollie's comment at Orly last March, on their way to Rhodes it was, after they had been chatted at by Claude Batique, who was then making new-wave splashes in Paris and on his way to Rome to be awarded for them. "A witless life and a titless wife" was Jollie's reaction after two martinis in the airport lounge, and he was certain Batique heard it, and after paying for the drinks at that!

He dialed her number, as he often did, so quickly that his finger slipped on the last digit—a bothersome nine—and slowly he called again. Listening for the ring, he absently studied the portrait on the panelled wall ahead of him—a line-drawing by Matisse of the head of Apollonaire. That poet's scribbled stare seemed, in turn, to gaze toward the tall draped window beyond which stretched the moral wilderness of Manhattan and beneath which lay the sullen Park where Holland walked for half an hour each morning to his taxi on Fifth Avenue. Yet it was not of those worn rocks and branchless trees he thought now, impatient for an answer, but of Jollie in the spring, in the morning, with coffee on their small roof-garden at Lindos, spying with those silly pearl opera-glasses across the coved, metallic bay on the early tourists, in their plaid shorts and sunglasses and straw hats, climbing on drugged donkeys the steep dirt path toward the ancient ruined acropolis, and of his climbing one morning the narrow white stone steps with cool melon slices, and Jollie turning in surprise to say . . .

"Hello?" Damn, it was only the housekeeper; she was probably not up yet.

"Good morning, Margaret, it's Mr. Holland. Is Mrs. Rodgers up yet by any chance?"

"Oh yes, Mr. Holland, good morning to you, sir. Yes, Mrs. Rodgers is up and gone two hours ago. No, over two hours by this time. Gone to the Colliers in Philadelphia for the long week-end, you know."

"Yes, yes, that's right, I must have forgotten." Collier, Collier, Clark Collier, banking bore, orchestra patron. He was certain

Jollie had never mentioned this trip, and he had dined with her on Tuesday night, only three days before.

"I can give you the number there, Mr. Holland."

"No, no, thank you anyway, Margaret, I won't bother her. Just tell her I called, that's all."

He replaced the receiver deliberately, puzzled, even worried, by Jollie's silence. Was it spite, or had he just forgotten how independent she needed to feel? As he tried to determine a difference between the two, the other pressures of the day made it difficult to focus a decision. Sam would settle that. Sam would settle it all; he had to. Holland went over to the window and drew the drapes on long lines of silent, stalled traffic. He watched in the glass as he squared his jacket and straightened his tie, its silk threads scratching on his callus, which even the most elegant pen could not help but harden. Then suddenly turning back to the desk, he gathered up his papers into an initialed briefcase and hurried out of his apartment without an overcoat on what he had heard was not only the first of April, but the first warm day of the new year.

The elevator's annoyingly efficient hum, for some reason, forced Holland to admit to himself that the real cause of his muted anger this morning was having seen Elizabeth last night, after almost two years. He thought back on Jollie's divorce proceedings, on their tearful, absurd operatics, on her convulsing the judge by remarking with a smirk that her husband complained she "made love like an eager, clumsy cellist." How different with Elizabeth and him. There was no divorce, no need for one since neither would marry again; and certainly no lonely spasms of regret by either—or at least by him. The eight years of their marriage—five of love and three more of loyalty—had simply run out one day. For too long their surprises had been used up and they had had to begin to make promises to one another, until six years ago they had just let go of each other. For a while, at parties with unsuspecting and later embarrassed hosts, he had seen her and spoken and smiled. But he had his work to do, and until last night felt he had forgiven her too often. And then last night, last night, alone in the theater at a dull play and duller lobby, he glimpsed again that pale, withdrawn beauty of the sort Botticelli might have borrowed, there, in her eyes and hair where it had always been and had not yet paled, and he realized then that it was Elizabeth in *Sonata No. 3,* and it was Elizabeth who was the Algerienne giving him trouble in *Still Life.*

A slight jolt made Holland look up through the opening metal layers of the elevator and nod to the doorman. He crossed quickly into the Park, then slowed on its path to a steadier pace. It was even warmer out than had been predicted, reminding him that it was time again to leave the city, to escape the rounds and concentrate on *Still Life*—Marineau's *La Nature Morte.* Perugia, Cannes, Palma, Tangier, Rhodes last year and perhaps again. In each of those others, he had been able to watch his hands perspire as he wrote, hoping in turn that the effects of energy could cause it to occur. But in Rhodes it had been so hot he had cut out pieces of blotter and put them on his elbows with rubberbands to keep his pages dry. Rhodes was good; it was hot and it hurt and he had finished *A Waste of Shame* and knew it was good despite that damn reviewer.

An ugly, red child crying on top of a rock caught Holland's attention, but its swift and unnecessary rescue shifted his interest and eye lower, to a daffodil's green, bulbous spears hoisting leaves, matted and black with winter, like banners in some monotonous triumph. The coming of spring never surprised him, unlike most who, at least, let themselves be surprised, or hoped to be. It was like the news of a friend's death, which he always felt he had somehow vaguely anticipated for that very moment all along. It was like his success. It was like his secret.

He kept walking, and tried to remember if that was the word Elizabeth had used the night they returned late from the ballet and he asked how she had enjoyed the evening. Was it "disappointing"? *Décevoir. Une soirée décevante.* But perhaps it was another word, or just a tone, a silence even, something to prompt his joke about her not appreciating Balanchine's angular, athletic ballerinas. She hadn't laughed or spoken, sitting there on his bed's edge, brush-

ing the curled grace from her hair, stroking into it nervous lines
of light from his reading lamp: damp amber leaves sighted in beige
shadows. He had walked over—or had he been lying there watching her?—but when he touched her shoulder, it shivered slightly
as though for an insect.

"You know, Adrian," she said evenly, "sometimes you're so
goddam sensitive, you make me sick. Really. Sick. Just too sick
to leave, I suppose."

"Now what brought that on?" he asked in a few seconds, trying to make his voice sound more upset than it was.

She went on without listening to him. "That's what is disappointing." Now she turned to accuse his forced concern. "That's
not the right word. *You* could tell me what I *should* be saying,
couldn't you? If you knew what I *wanted* to say. It's you. It's *you*."

He looked up in surprise, having emerged suddenly from the
Park at Fifth Avenue, shielding his eyes from the glare to spot a
cab. But one was waiting by the curb twenty feet ahead of him,
as if by appointment.

He had difficulty opening the back door, and felt foolish yank-
ing at the stuck hinge. The driver, he noticed, never even looked
around. When the door loosened enough for Holland to wedge
through, he pushed his briefcase in first and edged himself toward the middle of the cracked leatherette. The taxi smelled of
smoked fish and urine. It was too late, he supposed, to switch
cabs, so he resigned himself to it as he had to so much. And as
he looked up to give the driver's head his instructions, his face,
lightly scarred by adolescence and more deeply by time, looked
annoyed and perspiring in the speckled mirror. The stiff, almost
grey hair seemed too long to suit the face, and he was uncertain
whether its length was a concession to current fashion or to the
paresse he had felt recently, but he resolved to have it trimmed
next week, perhaps before he left.

"Purnell's, 47th and Madison," he said, leaning forward. The
driver turned his head slightly, whether to hear or acknowledge,
and Holland tried not to look at the dark, dirty hole in the side
of the man's head where his ear should have been. Just beneath

it was an uneven cluster of discolored skin rimmed with old scab, and the frame of his glasses was held near the hole by a small strip of once-white adhesive tape. There's just the touch for Witold: clean up nature's wounds a bit, replace the scab with a silk patch, perhaps have the Algerienne flick her tongue around the absence of an ear. Except the banker, it might be more effective on the banker. Well, it would be easy enough to work it in somewhere. He would make a note of it at the office. But now, as the taxi moved uneasily through the heavy mid-morning Manhattan traffic, Holland felt as though he were in a thick liquid of heat and stench. He closed his eyes tightly, held his breath as best he could, and slouched to lean his head back. He felt very tired and his stomach was tightening. Sam would take care of that.

The brakes slammed him awake as much as did the surprise of having fallen asleep. He glanced quickly out the window and saw, above the oversized glass doors, the graceful gilt etched in sand stone: *John Purnell & Sons, Inc. * Publishers of Fine Books * Est. 1897.* Last night had apparently bled its own plea and, over *Fine Books,* had sprayed in outraged red: PEACE NOW. The meter showed a quarter less than the usual fare, and Holland debated whether to give it to the driver. Like compliments, he rarely gave tips, not because he felt they were rarely deserved, but because he felt neither the gratitude nor the fear that force most into giving more than they should, often more than they can. He reached into his breast pocket where he always kept two dollar bills for his taxi, and handed them up over his seat, studying more carefully this time the details of wax and dirt and scab. When the driver turned to take his fare, he suddenly gave Holland an incredibly gentle smile, as though of understanding, even of forgiveness, unnerving him into forgetting to ask for change as he had intended. Peace. Now: he grabbed the handle and shoved his shoulder against the door, which this time opened easily, as he realized he should have expected, given the morning's small ironies.

Well, at least he hadn't talked of the weather or the mayor or

the Mets, hadn't said "Thanksmac," or pulled rudely off before
he had shut the door. In fact, as Holland maneuvered across the
crowded sidewalk toward the entrance, he looked back to see the
taxi still at the curb, its silent driver still smiling at him in
the strangest way. He put it all out of his mind, however, when he
pushed through the glass into the familiar artificial atrium, with its
live geraniums and bamboo and powerized waterfalls, its elaborate
display of the firm's recent best-sellers, and its very live receptionist, herself a best-seller he guessed. Good morning, Miss Tu-
multy. Sorry: Gail (no, Gayle). He put his head down and, as
though by force, made his way to the small door behind some
bushed cupid which led to the gray, echoic stairway. His office
was only two flights up.

The position of Consulting Foreign Editor for Purnell's gave
Holland virtual control of its business with translations, and occupied the three or four hours of his day when he wished to get
away from his study and himself. His office was just next to the
stairwell and, though not as small, it was almost as severe as the
cell of some medieval monk. When he opened the door and
switched on the soft fluorescent ceiling, he had to narrow his eyes
against the light which made the walls ordinarily the color of new
cheese, seem as white as title pages.

He put his briefcase down on one of the two low bookcases
to the right and fingered through the day's mail neatly piled on
his drawerless desk. Nothing of note, except a new novel from
Paris by an author whose last book he had advised against. *Il
faut que le roman reconte,* and his hadn't. There was also a manuscript translation (from Henry, on the coast) whose margins were
already smudged with comments. Who read these things before
they came to his desk he had never learned and did not specially
care since he knew that, with Sam, he had final word in farming
out, supervising and approving the published translations. And it
was he who had to write those letters of recommendation or re-
monstrance or regret, all usually so cynical they sounded sincere.
He sat down with the typescript and thought proudly of the care
with which he chose a translator, avoiding the hack who'd find a

hasty substitute from a cheap dictionary for the last syllable of recorded time, as well as that free soul who for the spirit of the passage missed the flesh of the word. No, he would allow only the man who, like himself, was willing to submit to the discipline of discovery, to the patient search for a word's history and image, to the precision of phrase and feeling. And who, like himself, thought of translating as a real and important art in itself. After all, what had begun for Holland as an exercise for his nerves had become through the years a necessity, a compulsion even. For having established the classics and explored his contemporaries, he felt he had not only set new standards for his art but had found the secret for his own work as well. It was English that had kept his efforts mismatched with his intention—not the language itself but the knowledge of it. And so he had found—had had to find—Marineau's French in order to refind what had always been his but had been obscured in the genius of others. Now the alien clarity of Marineau's prose made words themselves like the events or ideas or emotions they sought to express, events imagined by memory or remembered by imagination, abstracted from the annotation of detail, isolated from their time into beauty, and set with exact freedom as emblems of the truest experience of his art. It all came back to translation.

For a third time he reread Henry's opening paragraph unable to concentrate on its practiced accuracies, and finally he put it down, leaving it for next week. Would he have time then? Was he letting too much go? He was becoming more anxious to talk with Sam and checked his watch. It was too early for lunch, but by the time he had done a little deskwork, gathered up Sam and walked the three blocks through dusty, gaseous sunlight, had his custom martini with two drops of Black Label, ordered and settled, by then it would be time for lunch, though he doubted he would be at all hungry. For this half hour or so, he called the airlines and his travel agent, who questioned his choice of Rhodes again but assured him of a booking and said he would try for rooms in Paris from the end of next week but he couldn't promise anything. Who could? Uncertain but satisfied, Holland buzzed for a secretary from the pool and dictated a few perfunctory letters, one to Henry to say he was halfway through his manuscript and would be back to him soon. To this, he added a cryptic postscript, reminding Henry of Zola's comment on writing: *"C'est un triste métier."* There is less self-pity in that evaluation than one expects, Holland was thinking when the girl interrupted to ask the spelling of that last word, the one in French. He told her just to leave out the whole thing and with a grin left the office, turned slowly into the dusky stairwell down a flight to the carpeted silence of executive suits.

Beyond the enameled information (*q.v.s. samuelson/president*) on the glass partition, Holland could see Sam in the outer office, gesturing with speechless determination to a man whose face was too small for his head—off-center and bunched above a fleshy, chinless neck. If, as they said, Sam and himself could easily pass for brothers, Holland speculated, then he must, decidedly be the elder version of his crisp younger self there, with its tapered pinstripe and tanned face, creased with confidence. He liked Sam, he always had, and their friendship had been strengthened by their business dealings, usually the topic of these weekly Friday lunches. Except when manuscripts or contracts were to be discussed, Sam tried to invite, for their mutual amusement, a "character" to join them. Holland reminisced, as he waited without intruding, on the anecdotal editors and enthusiastic anthologists he had put up with. Or those dark-eyed, sleepless Italian counts who drank too much (all Italians struck Sam and Holland both as elegant psychotics). A literary M.P., an occasional Parisian, or that mid-Western sports writer—Sam spotted him now and held up a helpless, one-minute finger—that sports writer whose radical opinions on basketball, he boasted out of the side of his mouth, were as popular in Nebraska as pigs in Palestine. For every Malraux or Simenon they had quietly enjoyed, there had been some unendurable freak like the Bolivian poet with an Irish name who composed only in numbers and whose latest epical work added up to 360,330— he'd never forgotten that number—which coincided with and was meant to celebrate, the man said proudly, the population of LaPaz.

The door opened now on Sam leading his man whose awkward face seemed angry but out of place, and obviously impatient with the soft declensions of courtesy Sam was escorting him with down the corridor. When he returned, Holland put on a tortured look and asked, "Is *he* this week's punishment."

"Lord, no. How are you, Adrian?" Sam answered loudly. Without waiting for Holland's shrug, he explained with a wink, "That, I'll have you know, was the esteemed president of the printers' union. But now that you mention it, he may be just the man."

"Come on, let's go," Holland pleaded, grabbing Sam's arm with a smile. "The last thing I need today is a harangue on workers' rights from someone in a clip-on tie!"

Sam smiled. "You win. Where to?" he called over his shoulder as he went back into his office. "I want to let Mrs. Lauffer know where we'll be."

"I don't really care. How about Amstel's?" They both liked Dutch food.

"Fine. I'll be with you in a minute."

Holland caught himself clenching his teeth and could see in the glass the bone bulging the tips of his jaw. Should he rehearse himself? No, he decided against any preparation, since his mind was made up and he had purposely kept from thinking about it all morning, hoping perhaps to upset himself with what he knew would jolt Sam. He merely hoped it would come out straight, reversing the order of the need as it had been occurring to him.

"All set?" Sam was suddenly there.

"All set."

On the elevator they joked about their third for lunch last month —a Polish philosopher who spoke only what seemed to be a very poor German, but who never stopped talking and ordered chicken salad for dessert.

"How do I *know?*" His face grew stern with sympathy. "How do you *think* I know after all these years? You just snapped at that waiter for being late with your drink, that's one. And for another, you've been quieter than usual and louder when you have spoken. No games now, Adrian, what is it? That *Times* review?"

Cautious and now even somewhat catty, Holland only stared at his glass with what Sam took to be a pout, and this confirmed his suspicions. "Good Lord, Adrian, you know you're the only man alive who could find anything at all upsetting in that piece. He loved it. And besides, sales are fine. You know that."

"I know that he said it was 'disappointing'."

Sam shook that off with a cliché. "So what do you care what *he* says?"

"I don't really, or at least I'm not supposed to," Holland said slowly, bringing his eyes up to Sam. "But all that praise was just so much throat-clearing to get to his vicious little attack." Sam turned his palms up to protest again—a publisher's duty—but Holland cut him off. "No, let's not go into that. That's not what I want to talk to you about anyway."

"All right, let's have it then."

How could he put it, or how to begin? Best just to let it be said for him. Try to make it sound reasonable and determined. And each word came out as distinct as a syllable.

"I want out."

Sam's eyes puckered. "Out?" he asked. "What do you mean, out?"

He knows exactly what I mean, Holland thought. Why isn't that enough? "You know exactly what I mean. Our arrangement. I want things set straight. Publicly."

In a tone of voice Holland found unexpectedly calm, Sam asked, "And how would you suggest I go about that?"

"I don't know. Could you call in some decent journalist—say, Briskin, or Hallowell in London even, he could handle it tastefully— and tell him the real situation? And wait till I'm gone, next week or so? Of course, I realize matters will have to be arranged in France." Better stop there for a minute to gauge Sam's reaction. The hardest part was out and over. He hadn't done it neatly, but he had done it and his throat felt thick with anticipation.

Evidently Sam's calm was wearing off into sarcasm. "Let me go over this once more. You want me to . . . well, in effect, to plant the literary bombshell of the decade. To make it known that there is no such author as René Philippe Marineau, that he is just a hired front for Adrian Holland, who poses as the translator but is actually the author of the most distinguished series of novels written in the last six years. The fact is, gentlemen," he addressed his imaginary stunned audience in a hoarse whisper, "the fact is that Mr. Holland not only prefers to write French and English versions of his books simultaneously in order to, to—well, you can ask him that yourself. *But*—that is the least of it—he has also insisted that they can be published only if an allonym is used, which has put our mutual firm under enormous pressures that have taxed . . ."

As if on cue, a waiter had come up and asked if you gentlemen would care for another drink, even while looking at their glasses which the conversation had kept almost untouched. Holland and Sam shared an awkward, anxious stare which hardened the eyes of both until Holland shook his head without looking up and Sam declined with a more gracious smile which the waiter returned and left.

The pause, fortunately, seemed to have relaxed the tension, and Sam shifted in his seat, perhaps to accommodate his uneasiness, but his voice grew intimate.

"All right, I'm sorry to sound off at you, Adrian, but I must admit your request caught me off guard." Holland began to hear a professional condescension in Sam's survey of his reaction. "Besides, I asked you the wrong question. Logically, the first question ought to be 'why?' Why this? Why *now?*"

"*Raison de coeur, cher ami*. No explanations necessary." He had tried to make that sound natural, but Sam's sudden, almost angry answer made him realize how foolish he had been to hope it would succeed. But what else *could* he say?

"Good God, Adrian, you don't seriously expect me to accept that, do you? After all it was you who initiated the whole thing, you who insisted on the arrangements. I went along because you were—because you *are*—my friend, and your novel was so damn good." He groped to give his accuracy its effect. " 'The security of secrecy': that was your phrase as I recall. And if that was what allowed you to work well, and those were the only conditions under which you'd allow us to proceed, then you didn't give me much choice. But you know as well as I do all the planning and expense that went into this fraud—hiring and maintaining a 'recluse author' in France, and the rest. Too many deals have been made for you to back out this late and this suddenly."

Sam sat back in his chair, the last touch to the finality of his assessment and it provoked Holland to a plea more grim than he had meant. "Yes, that was the only way I could work then, the only way that made sense and peace. But it doesn't work anymore, or at least I don't want it to work anymore. I don't know why. Honestly. You'll have to do something, though. If not, I'll do it myself."

"Without the firm behind you, I doubt you'd accomplish anything more than making yourself appear very silly," he said, leaning forward. "Besides, you were never one for publicity or acclaim. You've never minded being thought of as just a translator. Is there someone behind this? Jollie perhaps?"

Holland smiled into the martini he was about to drink and shook his head.

"Well she's the only one other than myself and Cohn in Paris—and Marineau, of course—who is in on this. Elizabeth doesn't know, does she?"

Again he shook his head, but this time he hadn't smiled and must have hesitated long enough for Sam to ask again: "It's Elizabeth behind all this, isn't it?"

Of course it was Elizabeth who was behind all this. Then why the reluctance, the refusal to admit it earlier to himself?

"Well, is it?"

"Maybe. Partly. I'm not sure yet." He was stumbling now, unconvincing but convinced. "She doesn't know, so far as I can tell. But I want her to."

"Then why not just phone and tell her. Or write. I'll tell her. Anything." His common sense missed the point, and Holland was beginning to feel as he had in the taxi: closed in yet desperately distanced.

"No, I want her to read about it. She'll realize from that that I'm tired of translating. Or I will." There, that was it, as exact as he could say it, and as inadequate.

"That sounds pretty childish, if you ask me."

"Look, Sam, I assure you this is no casual *crise d'identité*. I am tired."

"Well, I tell you what. Let's talk about it after your trip," he said expansively. "Right now my hands are tied, Adrian. There are so many publishing and financial arrangements, it would take a good while to untangle them. It's not as simple as you make it sound. In fact, it's a lot easier to set up something like this than it is to upset it, so to speak. And by that time you may even regret having done it."

With an uncanny sense of dramatic timing, the same waiter approached their table and told Mr. Samuelson that his secretary was calling and the phone is in the lobby if you'll follow me. "Thank you," Sam said and turned to explain he was expecting a call from the coast and had told Mrs. Lauffer to contact him here when it came through.

"I'll be right back," he said, visibly relieved for the interruption. In his hurry to leave, he even knocked against the table enough to rustle the service and jolt the glasses.

As he sat watching his gin spin lower, settling toward the center, Holland doubted he had the courage, perhaps even the interest, to resume his request, and he knew Sam would be grateful if he didn't. What had seemed, at first, an eager frustration, an obstructed escape, now seemed more like resignation, a comfortable inability, an easy unwillingness. Rhodes would probably restore his discipline: permit him to ignore what he needed and to concentrate on what he could use.

He finished off his drink and held it up to signal for another. These things calmed his stomach and his nerves and his conscience. After all, there was no reason for Elizabeth to know. Chances were she wouldn't guess his meaning; she never had. He remembered now how many things he had had to explain to her, how often he had wondered how she could fail to notice what seemed to him so obvious or unusual. Yes, he had always managed better on his own, had been better in secret—and never better than since his separation. What was that Rimbaud said? *"Je est un autre."* That was it.

HERBERT GOLD has written eight novels, including *The Man Who Was Not With It, Fathers,* and *The Great American Jackpot;* his most recent book, *The Magic Will,* is a linked collection of stories and essays which includes *A Death on the East Side.* Mr. Gold lives in San Francisco.

A DEATH ON THE EAST SIDE

"WHAT we like, my friend, is give away a lot of money so we can catch a little of the overflow for tax savings in line with—oh, well, the federal and state provisions." A boyish forty-nine-year-old man was winking at me. He was also engaged in instruction. "We find that money tends to stick in the nets, a little for everyone, nice like that. Not that you should bother your insides about it. You, sir, are beyond such distractions. You are an artist, head in the clouds, aren't you?"

I would have appreciated his ceasing the flirty winking, and at last, when I looked up from the oysters he was buying me at the Algonquin, he did. He was momentarily busy with his own little-necks—lemon, sauce, salt and wine—or perhaps he was just checking out his next move.

". . . the strength of oysters and the delicacy of clams," he was saying. "For spiritual sorts. The Baroness Blixen lived to nearly eighty on oysters and champagne." He rolled the last clam to its reward. "Isak Dinesen," he said. "We wanted to give her a year to write her final memoirs, but she said she couldn't spare the time. She said she was dying, and she was. Pity."

Philip Grove had served as vice president of various networks, he had been poetically handsome in his youth, he was a delight in middle age (luxuriant gray hair, ironic smiles); he had enjoyed

twenty-five years of faithful drinking and seventeen years of psycho-
analysis, both of them continuing nicely when we met. Two wives
and three marriages confused matters; he had married one of the
girls twice, numbers one and three—the oil lady from Tulsa had
leapfrogged the chanteuse from Copenhagen and Cleveland. He
was now redivorced from this first/third wife and paying her
double indemnity, suicide, revenge, menopause, got-the-midnight-
horrors alimony. Her wells had run dry. She was a three A.M.
telephoner and even incited their daughter, Carol, to make trouble.
"That hurts a bit," he said. "A lot."

A frequent refuge for Philip in times of stress was to enter
public service. Now he was director of one of America's greatest
second-rate foundations. They couldn't compete with Ford, Rocke-
feller, or Guggenheim, and that's how I came in: to help set up a
program for catching the artistic fish and eels that the bigger endowments let slip through their valves.

Lunches at the Century Club, dinner at the Four Seasons.
He wanted to get a positive result in whatever he did—even instructing me in how to live. I was flattered. We were both recently
divorced, both trying out as gray-flecked Manhattan boys again.
He had read my novels and thoughtfully quoted from me in conversation with me. That man knew how to make joy at small
expense. (The person writing this story is no longer the person
telling it.) I loved breathing the happy air. "Well, sir," he said
with the courtly manner of a slightly older man who is signing
all the checks, "I was probably paid more for reading your books
than you were for writing them."

Somehow this made me feel important, though there was surely
an edge to the compliment.

And advice on how to give money to artists? Now, there was
a dreamy, restful deal. So I just let my mind expand, a few folds
at a time. I suggested a program of special vacations for novelists,
story writers, and poets. The idea was to waste and live well for
a few weeks, to refresh the spirit with excess. A large sum of
money would be handed out with the provision that it be squandered in less than a month. I invoked some traditional models—

Dionysius, Bacchus, and C. Wright Mills (Philip expected nothing less from me). How would we check against the possibility of practical distortions—prudent mid-century poets laying on station wagons, laundry equipment, convertible preferreds for the children's education? Well, we could always go for receipts from Bahamian hotels and chorus girls freaked out on diet pills. Naturally, I preferred the honor system. I preferred to go that way.

Philip said he loved the idea, just loved it. As this meant he seemed to like it pretty well, I was sure the foundation would accept it, since he made all the important decisions. It was a brilliant day in the history of philanthropy. I was responsible for a great leap forward from the single flower of Puritanism into the thousand flowers of affluence and ecstasy. "Hmm," said Philip, "a keen article there for Gratefully Yours, the *Journal of Applied Philanthropy*. 'Affluence & Ecstasy: Expanding the Frontiers of Exemption . . .'" I was a mandarin ideologue in my first J. Press suit. Gongs, zithers, wine, silks and dancing girls for the contributors to the *Hudson Review*.

At the next regular meeting of the governing board my idea was rejected.

Ah, so. Another miscalculation. Another case of too much enthusiasm and trust on life's way. Again a deep brainstormer had misplaced his faith in the ability of others to understand innovations in quantum money dispersal. Well, no matter.

Our friendship survived this reverse. I expected a small check labeled "honorarium" for drafting the idea, typing it, too; but evidently the high-level decision was to pay me in lunches, dinners, oral quotation from my work, continuing instruction, and the companionship of Philip Grove. Well, some things are worth more than money, though perhaps a plate of oysters at the Algonquin is not one of them. I put away my mandarin dreams.

Nevertheless, taking a consistent pro-oyster position, one evening I accepted another session of charge-a-plate seafood. Philip wanted to explain. He was tender in his own heart, too. "I know what you think, I'm smart enough," he said, "but the fact is I really want to do something good every time I get into these—oh, complexities. The problem is making it happen. I don't mean gimmicks, I mean the clout, the thrust, the—" He smiled winningly. "The gimmick. I really hate it that you have reason not to respect me, pal. I *know* about respect and self-respect. Those are two of my fields."

It occurred to me, and I should have thought of it sooner, that he really wanted to commit fine acts, read beautiful words, think powerful thoughts, go to bed with sweet ladies.

"Ah-ah." He wagged a warning finger. "I have insights. I stay in touch."

"Sorry," I said. "I really like you, Philip."

"Not really," he said, "but you'll learn. However, I've called this little group together for another purpose." He hinted that he was looking about and planning to leave public service once more. It was not quite—well, take my delicious project, for example. A terrible loss, a personal embarrassment. How the bureaucracy of endowment misunderstands the creative temperament, both administrative and laboring in those lonely rooms which Sherwood Anderson of Elyria, Ohio, described so eloquently in his collected letters.

His large, dark, intense eyes bored into mine to see if I had caught his thought on the wing even before he had filed it along with the request for accrued vacation time.

Yes.

In my turn I hinted that I was nearing the end of the first draft of a new novel. Ah. New phases for both of us. We both sighed. We would digest all this news and return to it in the fullness of time.

We then settled down comfortably to discussing our mistreatment at the hands of women. We did not exactly wallow in our miseries, but we inoculated ourselves against cholesterol and useless fret by not keeping the secret. Although I had entered real life again, chasing limber ladies through the canyons and rushing gorges of Manhattan, I still took pleasure in these restful evenings of commentary and philosophy. Philip, ten years older, claimed to admire my energy, but liked to go at things a little more slowly.

Bring them to him by taxi, for example, or by limou when one was available. The permanent truths—friendship, accomplishment, good taste—were what interested him. His daughter, Carol (a "teenie," as he described her), had let him down. "Patience and cunning," he said, "that's what a man needs. But no exile, it's impossible, the whole world is Manhattan now."

"I suppose."

"What good are victories?" he asked me. "What good is the hunt?"

"Are you asking me a question? I feel you're making a statement."

"Well, take Carol for openers. She is bad news for some old man, pal. If not for her dad, for some other chap."

In quest of permanent truth, he left the foundation and went to work for a buccaneer millionaire who had reached the stage in his development where he needed to finance art movies. On the day he told me about his new job I confessed to him that he looked a bit like a leading man. He was tall, slender, handsome, with suave weariness worn like a halo. That's a neat style. In his youth he had played polo. In his youth, he confessed in turn, he had wanted to be an actor, but: "I had too much—oh, premature afterthought you can call it. The lines they gave actors in those days—couldn't say 'em." His eyes were dark, soft and tender as he explained why he chose not to be a star of stage and screen. Producer—well, that's all the difference in the world. Because I had begun to weary of his dramatic cynicism, I redoubled my efforts to express friendship. After all, he had been good to me. But I began to suspect he was wearing eye liner to accentuate that dark, soft, and tender gaze.

Oh, it couldn't be.

I denied it to myself. He wasn't that sort. I put it out of mind. I looked for the telltale smear.

In an agony of difficult friendship we exchanged gifts like shy romancers. He put me up for his club as if to tell me I should now consider myself middle-aged. I gave him a copy of *Shakespeare's Bawdy* as if to tell him he could still have boyish intellectual fun.

He asked to meet girls. I asked to meet interesting people. He was bored with the girls I introduced him to, and looked wan and bored. I was bored with the social people he introduced me to, and once escaped a party on Long Island through the library window. I hitchhiked back to Manhattan, frantic and drunk. We didn't see each other for a week, but then had a laugh over it and he wanted to take me to Southampton again so I could repeat my famous vanishing act. The cream that made me vanish was oil of small talk. He thought he might sell it along with excursions to Europe on Icelandic Airlines.

Ever since the peculiar thought about his wearing eye liner, I tried to conduct our meetings along with the company of ladies. Foursomes strolling Greenwich Village, four on weekends to Westport, that was my new idea. The old male intimacy dimmed a bit in our new occupations. He was irritated by my increasing implication in the temptations of Manhattan, as if only he had kept our interludes of talk pure, free of money and sex and ambition, just two friends sharing a flight through middle space.

One night, over the final brandy, he asked, "What's it all about? We are paper men, air men, we float and glide over this abstract town. Who are we? We are what we are—nobodies."

"I wish you'd speak for yourself, Philip."

He gazed mournfully into my eyes. Maybe he didn't wear eye liner, after all. It would be a sin to suspect him wrongly. He had hard, clear, bluish whites, he had a fixity of gaze. "I suppose I should only speak for myself," he said. "It's part of the disease—abstraction. I want to take everybody my own way, as if a crowd of paper figures could make one man of flesh and soul. I apologize. Nothing personal." He waited for me to reply. "My daughter is breaking my heart."

I had nothing to say. I was tired after the long evening—a divorced Wellesley girl and her best friend—and the abrupt moment of King Lear found me unprepared. We had been amusing the ladies and it left my philosophic skills a bit threadbare. After so much laughter, nudging, and tickling, here came Carol. I must have looked distracted.

"Take the service elevator out," he said. "It's faster after one. Wait, I'll show you."

I found other friends. Philip joined a Unitarian group. We were both in search. He thought up a TV special to promote, something about the revival of irrational religion. He asked me if I liked his working title for it: "The Now! Churches." Rational and irrational, he said; but in quest of some sort of purity. Ninety minutes of stomping and glossolalia, plus Erich Fromm and maybe Norman O. Brown—what did I think?

"Terrific, Philip."

"Sensational," he said, "*and* educational."

Also, as a remedy for that after-five feeling, that void, that anomie, that angst, those mid-century whatchamacallits, he fell in love.

In fact, despite the slow and stately stride of maturity, Philip the Pure was in love with the whole chorus line in the revived version of *West Side Story*. He had a friend whose skinny wife was a featured player and he would stand in her dressing room and look at the girls—High School of Performing Arts, Actors Studio, Merce Cunningham, readers of Buber and Frantz Fanon and *Variety*—through a crack in her half-shut door. They undressed with miraculous calm. Naked but for their eyelashes, long-limbed, cute, oh cute, they primped and jiggled and waited for the Big Chance near massed banks of hot white bare bulbs. Gradually he narrowed his devotion to just one, Sandy Grasset, and gradually she came to understand that he wanted her for his very own.

Okay, one Sunday morning after an ecumenical mass at a Now! church, she gave herself to Philip for his very own. A man deserves a Big Chance, too. But then it wasn't enough. He wanted to marry her, to keep and cherish her. "Will you be my widow?" he demanded, dropping to his knees and mumbling, "George Bernard Shaw, an early play, I have total recall."

"*Wha?*"

"I was quoting. Shouldn't joke at a time like this. Total visual, not oral. Marry me."

She laughed and laughed, though not at the touching whimsy he intended, and he coolly noted that one thin tape of eyelash was coming unstuck. But he only loved her the more for this single blemish on her perfection of greedy little showgirl.

"Naw," she said. "I have my career, and my afternoons I go to the New School." Her evenings, of course, belonged to the Theater. She also studied creative writing, mime (*meem*), and existential psychodrama for a time of crisis.

He stared, hair thick and white, body thumped and worked at the New York Athletic Club. "I need you," he said.

"I like you," she said. "Isn't it obvious, really clear?"

"I would hope it all means something."

"Does, *does,* sweetie. I wouldn't do . . . *that*"—and she made a pretty little moufie, as if to say dirty-dirty. "I wouldn't do that for just anybody. Not even to get a job I wouldn't. I don't have to, besides. I'm well known for not doing it unless—"

"Unless you really like a fellow?"

"Well, you could put it." She got the point a second later. "Okay, then, you be sarcastic and see if it encourages an I-thou relationship between us."

"I'm sorry," he cooed, miserable.

"Aw, come on," she said, wrapping him in her skinny arms.

But she dawdled about marrying him. He worked out a miracle plan: me. I should persuade her, me, with my inspired pleading of his case. *Who?* It was like filling out a recommendation for a foundation grant. It was not like that, but he had his peculiar notion that I could help and he arranged for me to meet her alone at her apartment one afternoon (all of us supposed to be there, Philip delayed, last-minute telephone call, a carefully orchestrated plan). By means of straight talk, full of depth charges there in the shadow of Lincoln Center, I was supposed to win him his third/fourth wife.

I felt a bit wooden and pasted together. I said, "Um, he really cares for you. He wants you badly. I think you would do well."

"Icky," she said. "He's not icky, but he is too old. Hey, how's about I make us some coffee?"

"You said yourself he's not icky," I said, "and with vitamin pills and the new statistics from the insurance companies, he's got many carefree years ahead of him. How long do you think you can dance, Sandy?"

"Three wives. Icky."

"But you're different. And it wasn't really three. And he's a boy at heart."

"Plus he tole me I remind him of his *daughter!* I wanna stay in show business."

"True, he'd like you to be a helpmeet, entertain, spend his money." I hoped she was listening. I'd hate to have to repeat that.

"Hey, he's really loaded?"

"Then you won't?"

She fixed me with her violet eyes in that starved, bony dancer's face. Cheekbones and eyes in the context of violet and good definition always make a fellow think profound. "How much—how much you *bet?*" she asked. First she grinned with elfin humor. Then a hilarious peel of jeering laughter as the implications began to deal with her. Blacch, another natural screamer, I thought. She looks so physical, so much body and dance, but she's like an actress, a nice suburban girl, a nice normal hysteric. Abruptly she stopped laughing. "Maybe I will," she said. "You think the kid, uh—"

"Carol."

"—'ll bug us a lot?"

"No."

"Cause I hate kids like that—the selfish age."

"No, the kid is grown up, nearly your age."

That was three fifths of a faux pas, but she didn't seem to mind. She was twitching with thought, tongue working in corner of mouth, Kleenex at eye, knees jiggling. Perhaps she was just practicing her new role of charming hostess, for she said, "Ooh, ick, the coffee's boiling over. Philip has a Chemex, doesn't he?"

On their honeymoon in Paris he suffered a ruptured blood vessel in one eye and had to go to the American Hospital. Too much drinking or love-making, an expatriate doctor commented, but I never heard that one before. That was one for Neuilly. Personally

I thought he got some dirt in it and rubbed. And that's one for
Sheridan Square.

They came back and it took a long time before they invited me
over to their new apartment (condominium, East Sixties, excellent view of the write-off). Of course, they were busy fixing it up,
but other friends got invited two, three times. I was out, it seemed.
I had been too close to the premarital examinations, but I still saw
Philip occasionally for lunch. He was keeping in touch and I'd be
patient. His eye was red for months afterward, as if he had just
been crying. Well, let him adjust to conjugal life again. It took
some pressure off me, too. Our friendship would find its natural
level.

One of the matters we shared was a friend, Baron Clausen, a
Danish money pirate with castles in Austria, ranchos in Mexico,
and ambitions to keep his tax-exempt fingers in all available tax-
free pies. His nineteen-year-old wife (he was sixty) distracted him
for a few hours each day, but then there were the sleepless nights
and days of Manhattan. He liked Philip for the reasons of Philip's
charm and savvy; he liked to discuss himself with me. Philip telephoned me one day at an odd early hour to say, "Clausen—you've
been talking to him."

"Of course, sometimes, when he lets me."

"Too much, pal. He's been spreading the gossip about you."

"Clausen? What gossip?"

Philip reminded me of an incident involving—oh, a silly trouble
about a party and a wife and her husband. I was irritated with
Philip for reminding me of it. I was infuriated with my smiling
Danish enemy. As soon as he next proposed one of his damn
smørrebrød-and-cigar lunches, I'd give him some honest American lip. Senseless malice: why should he do that to me? I was
shaking with the bachelor's dammed-up anger. I fretted, I sulked.
I wouldn't deign to reach Clausen.

He never telephoned.

In a few days it dawned on me. Somehow Philip must have
made him angry with me, too. What had I said of him? That he
was too old for his young bride? That he was hanging about the

artists to drink their blood? Well, I might have speculated along those lines—who doesn't speculate?

I should have had an explanation with Clausen, but the whole thing was a nasty bore. Foolish and foolishness. I let it pass. I forgot it. I fell in love. I let them pass, both of them, Clausen and Philip, and moved into another of the many worlds of Manhattan.

Only gradually, reluctant to admit the loss of friendship, did I guess that Philip was getting rid of me this way. He spread gossip about me among our mutual acquaintances because, well, he needed a bit of a change and he was in the business of opinion and that's how he did things. No matter. Another day, he must have decided from long experience, if I need him, I'll just come with my offer. He'll jump. There's no fun and profit in remembering history, which is mostly a series of grudges. He had once assured me that to his certain knowledge, people operate almost entirely in the light of their present interests. "Not principles or paranoia, friend, but what seems to be in the cards right now. I've found this to be true. It's tough, but it's nice to have confidence in the future, where you get what you want by talking about what's happening this afternoon. Say, listen, it's better that way."

Wine, oysters, talk, and the dangled carrot. Also a continual earnest labor at completing my education. Corrupt and corruption, I thought; no matter. I had other business in life. I felt like Dick Whittington come to conquer the great city. Although Philip had the knack of making his business seem important, more important than anything anyone else wanted to do, I found new routes through skyscraper and across plaza, up subway and into conference room.

Sometimes the crazy orbits of Manhattan intersect or collide. We remained acquaintances, but the old clubby exchanges were finished. We would continue toward new careers, wives, hopes and troubles on divergent paths.

I had a friend, J. Willis, a long-time Village writer, with three stories and a poem to his credit after twenty years and four grants, who turned out to be dating Philip's daughter, Carol. There's a crossed path for you. Willis had presided over his self-contempt for

so long that it had become a friend to him—a deadly enemy to the
ladies he sucked dry. Carol was a pretty thing with long blond
bangs that tickled her eyes as if she had no interest in where she
was going. Willis took his exercise on such girls and thought he
was a man. If I had been Philip with a daughter . . . but I was
not Philip with that daughter.

Baron Clausen started a foundation, incidentally, and made
Philip the president of it. Philip may have suspected me of wanting
to push into the foundation business.

Sandy was an odder girl than she appeared—girl making out
okay in Manhattan. Dancing seemed to have trained the upturned
corners of her mouth, but there were also secret down-turning
depths. She had been supported for several years by Rico diRico,
the Jukebox King, who had known the joy of seeing his picture in
Life, not in connection with his Wurlitzer musical activities, but
because he was a friend of friends of folks with complex police
and FBI records. Rico preserved his friendship with Sandy after
her marriage, and also with Philip. It seemed a sporty connection
for that elegant veteran of Washington conferences on the arts and
network efforts to upgrade popular culture. (*From Shlock to
Kitsch,* an autobiography by Philip Grove. That was his idea. Sub-
title? "Through Darkest Camera with Grant and Program.") Philip
didn't fear for reputation, since most of Rico's arrests had not
resulted in convictions.

There is a reason, or a season, or at least a cause for everything,
as Ecclesiastes almost says. Philip wanted to produce his first
movie, based on a forgotten novel about the Depression. There
were many curious elements in the equation. The book was written
by a man, now rather elderly and a senior editor of *Reader's Digest,* who at one time had been an iron-willed literary Marxist
("The land is the people! The people is the land!" was the last
paragraph and hiccup of the novel). The original story aimed to
show (a) the American working and peasant classes oppressed by
county banks and agents of Wall Street in jodhpurs, then (b)
their gallant uprising at the iron will of the novelist; the movie

script aimed to show the warmth and humanity of immigrant racketeers, who managed by means of tenderness and vigor to crash through staid class lines, thereby getting the grateful girl in the end. The suspense for her was terrific. She would have to wait ninety minutes, eighty if cut for drive-ins, to discover she was worth more to the hero than land, people, or his mama's hand-stuffed lasagna. Much more; a symbol of the transcendence of Norman O. Brown's polymorphous perverse eros over economic determinism; a really modern scam, actual, contemporary, today, existential, and within the limits set by the concept of redeeming social importance, dirty.

Sandy played a small part, mostly leaning against a white piano in a speakeasy, looking fearful, as if the chandelier might fall. The financing came from Rico diRico, who may have been crooked but who was not necessarily clever. The film lost money, even with a syndicated sale to TV. The Bonnie & Clyde epoch was not yet upon us. But was it real coin-operated money? Probably the lonely toy money of drugs and gambling that sought warmth and companionship in the real world of tax losses.

Anyway, it made sense for Philip to keep good connections with diRico. Perhaps he could count on cultural impetus in the future, too. I used to run into the three of them, Philip, Sandy, and diRico, at those steamy steak palaces on Third Avenue where you also find popular priests, daytime game-show emcees, and out-of-town buyers working hard at their expense-account cholesterol. Once I sat with them through dessert (I was meeting an option holder from the Coast, who was late). Philip, I noticed, played with his food. He looked pale, and the broken vein in his eye had never quite mended, so that it always seemed as if he were recovering from a recent crying jag or had spent too much time with his accountant. He was hoping to do his second film, maybe this time with Sandy as the star. DiRico was considering it.

Then one morning I got a call from Philip's secretary. Mr. Grove wanted to see me at his office. As soon as possible. Very important. Of course, like all writers, I seek any possible opportunity to avoid work. I was showered, shaved, and in a cab within half an hour. Manhattan traffic jams being what they are, I needed a shower by the time I arrived and wished I had taken a subway, but my shave was still intact.

I carried it through an honor guard of new receptionists and secretaries, Itkin décor, wormwood paneling—the diRico touch. Philip began right off: "What do you do with people, chap?"

"Who people? What people?"

"The public. My daughter."

That pretty girl with the regulation straight blond hair, wan little face, dropout credentials from Sarah Lawrence, and those eye-tickling bangs. She had left J. Willis, my Charles Street pal. She had been moving pretty fast.

"I want to tell somebody," he said, "and then I want to forget it. I'm going to tell you." It sounded like a threat. Before I could say *Oh no you don't,* or *What about your analyst?,* he was on the way and all the way there: she had died of hepatitis in San Francisco.

He looked at me with his peculiar courteous attention. I was frozen with misery and confusion. He waited until he decided I was okay.

"She was taking methedrine sulfate, I think they call it. Speed. Dio-metha-something, I don't know. Affected her mind—memory, reasoning power, she was a skinny thing, not the pretty girl you met. But it wasn't speed that killed her. It was a dirty needle."

"Philip, I'm sorry."

"She was always careless with her things. Her mother used to complain, but what could I do? I wasn't responsible—could I be? That woman really cut me off from her, so how could I?"

"Philip, where is she?"

He looked at me through his one red eye, his two eye-lined eyes. "Ah, she was buried out there yesterday. What's the good?" He shook his head. "I wanted someone to know. Pass it on. Communicate." I realized he was slightly drunk. "I suppose it's better," he said.

"What's better?"

"Hey, fella, let's go to P.J.'s. You can have a hamburger and I can have a freshener."

"No, I can't, Philip."

"Okay, a small salad. I need it. I need to sit with you—someone."

"Okay, Philip."

He smiled, stood up, shrugged his shoulders in that handsome, boyish, stylish way. "What did she have to live for? Her life was a mess. Man, I know about the problems with *my* oedipal hangups. I tried as much as I could, I worried about her, fella. But that rusty needle probably just saved a lot of trouble, agony, and expense."

The secretary came in and he waved her away. "Please. I'm taking an early lunch." He waited until she closed the door. He turned to get his coat and said to me, "Life—what is it? Let's not frighten ourselves with that question, but we got to ask it. China. India. It's time for some perspective. Carol. It's pathetic. But when you've had as much therapy as I have, eighteen years and a small fortune, one thing you learn is admit your secret feelings. Expense and worry and what good is it?"

I was out of that office in a few seconds. I noticed I was gone when the elevator door showed me lobby and street. It wasn't grief that made me flee, or not only grief.

But it wasn't as if I could shake him so easily. That conversation about Carol had gone past the end for him, too. After I left the office, he waited a few weeks and then summoned me about what he called a "reasonable" project—miscalled. "Let's just discuss," he said, "with no obligations on either side. I always find you have an interesting mind." Which meant: I'm sure you'll want to do what I want you to do. He hired me to work on a film script he was "developing." That means, speculating in. First he told me it was to be based on a story of mine, but it turned out to be based on a story by the network computer which told him what he could (a) get into the nabes and then (b) presell to television. Rico was putting up the front money and Sandy had a slightly smaller part —one scene where we would all presumably share the curve of her dancer's thighs through the magic communion of the cinema art. While I wrote, she became pregnant; no connection. "I'll be an instant grandfather," Philip announced with his shyest smile that invited you to think whatever you liked about his feelings.

However, he didn't look well. His skin had become blue and his body slow and spectral. He should have seen a doctor. He said he was on to what they were selling. His nose bled. He sweated at night and Sandy slept in another room because he felt icky in bed. He refused to go to his doctor. I suppose he knew what he was doing, and buying.

One afternoon we had a meeting about the script. He suddenly closed his eyes as if thinking, as if sleeping. He lay at an odd angle, like a stick in his chair, and I caught him before he fell. He quickly came out of the faint, blinking and smiling, but his secretary called the doctor and we got him to a little private hospital nearby, in the East Sixties. No problem with the heart. Weakness, general weakness. The doctor ran blood tests to confirm what he already suspected.

There was an abnormal increase of white blood cells originating in a disease of the bone marrow. They gave him transfusions to increase his strength for the time being, temporarily. They do that to provide a breathing space. Leukemia.

Philip got the news early. He conned the doctor into telling him everything. Calm and elegant, he heard him out and asked intelligent questions and it seemed the doctor was flattered by the patient's interest. He might live as little as six months. He might last from three to five years. The suppressant drugs have variable results. When one wears out, or starts to wear out the body—the side effects are often very disagreeable—the doctors shift to another drug.

"And of course," Philip said, "by the time you finish rotating the known drugs, they may have some new ones."

"Or a cure," said Dr. Berman.

"Or even a cure," Philip said, smiling and nodding. "Thank you very much."

I suppose there is no normal routine for handling the friends

and relatives. Philip told me, his wife, Rico; he told the poodle
and his newborn son; he told the people with whom he did business and cab drivers and stopped just short of writing letters to
the editor stating that he had six months left to live. He set up a
means for sharing the experience, irony in him, horror in others.
He seemed pleased and proud. I wondered if he was taking mood
drugs, and perhaps he was, but the euphoria seemed genuine,
rooted in the vain and frantic blood. He would call me in the
middle of the night to discuss "our" script, and then his illness. He
wanted to get the script finished and shot before he "went." He
dwelled in an ecstasy of energy and good will, popping into the
hospital for tranfusions and then flying off to do rapid business
with banks and studios and networks. It made story conferences
difficult.

"I can't write that girl as man-eater," I would say. "She's sad,
but she's not mean."

"Look," he replied gently, "let's cut the crap. I may have only
six months left and I see her for what she is: a bitch-whore-
destroyer."

The only-six-months argument won his way about character,
style, money, whatever the day brought into his office. As some
people are name-droppers, he would sit in Sardi's East and death-
drop his own death to get one up on me. He was doing it all
around, with agents, creditors, secretaries, and even with his wife.
Ever since these two events had come to complicate her time—the
birth of her child, the announced death of her husband—she had
grown quieter and the silliness had disappeared. She had discovered something outside herself. She was interested, frightened,
appalled. It was all happening at once. I believe she even stopped
seeing Rico, though that may have been his doing, a superstitious
fear. She had the eye-liner look which seemed to run in Philip's
family—his daughter, too—but it gave her a bit of staring style. He
may have succeeded in instructing her to care for him. For sure
Sandy was going through the miseries.

Philip's production staff accommodated his various television and film projects. He used to charm them into working long hours, bending to his will; now he bullied them.

"What are you complaining for?" he would ask a secretary who needed something, such as time off, which he didn't want to give her. "After all, you have your whole life ahead of you."

She blushed.

"So do I, of course."

He got his way. Midtown Manhattan knows how to be nervous and even how to suffer, but this was one boss, handsome Philip, that a secretary couldn't handle.

"What do you mean, you don't like the project. It's changing into, okay, so kitsch. Never mind, listen, now is the time to communicate—gut level. There will come a day," he told me, "when this will be the last project I can close. I won't be able to come to the office." He smiled. "It'll be *me* closing. I'll turn into a vegetable," he said affably, "except it'll hurt a lot, fella."

I was learning to hate him.

"That's for openers and up front," he said.

And yet I couldn't pull out at this stage, could I? Just because he was slurring and jiving and bullying, and using his own death as a marketing and production tool, was that any reason to give him more trouble than usual?

The job became more complicated than most jobs. Rico and Sandy had me talking to doctors; Sandy because she was broken-hearted, Rico because he couldn't believe the happy-boy partner would really let him down at some point in their business together. Philip was piling ahead, grandiose and furious, with the energy of a pink-cheeked young producer despite his bluish skin and his death's-head eyes.

The doctor said, "Remission. Like a lot of them . . ." He added cautiously, "Mr. Grove—Philip—seemed almost disappointed when I told him his place on the curve may be rather late. It won't be another six-month deal. He might well have five years, and then what? We don't know any more."

Disappointed?

"You'll see that sometimes—disappointed."

It was a hard campaign to live up to. It was a whirlwind campaign, intended for a six-month promotion; Philip wasn't programmed for a five-year plan. Nobody could put up with his dying for five whole years ahead. Speaking as an associate, it would kill us all. Or at least give migraine headaches, anxious nightmares, Manhattan boredom assaults, creeping paralysis. "They're out to get us," one secretary kept muttering. She meant the leukocytes. We became experts on the disease, as if it were an un-American conspiracy, like Communism or Swedish art films.

He was killing friendship by falsity.

Let me be fair: he was also killing enmity by creating an eerie contempt for his suffering. He made his own suffering unreal by using it as a public relations trick. He was trivializing his own and everyone else's feeling about the primary fact. He was barring his own recognition of death the friend, death the enemy.

Bravado: manipulating his own emotion.

Worse, a public relations bravado: manipulating the emotions of others and calling them his own.

Which?

Both. I wanted to say: China, India, what is life? Your daughter dies. You die. Everybody dies; big deal. Phony trouble. But where then is the real trouble?

I tried to see through the strategy of management to the terror beneath, but felt myself failing beneath my own spite. I began to have nightmares about the emptiness within myself that made me want to destroy this man, or to take relish in his self-destruction; no, not nightmares, black insomnias full of shooting dreams like meteors and murky under-earth movements. Because I found myself hating him and hating myself, I was tied to him by a pity suspiciously like self-pity. What in the past gave him such energy and resolution? How could the mask fit so seamlessly, and leave him so malignant and joyous? He was a mystery to me, and a fearful one.

I visited him whenever I could. I let him work his will upon me. Submissively I awaited new indignities. Confusion. To live with the confusion made the life of New York seem avid, arid, abstract, and horrible. We spent our workday lives in those radiant East Side glass tombs. It was as if I had some wasting disease.

I entered his office one lunch hour—the secretary was out—and found him crooning over a photograph of Carol. He was bowing and rocking and his face was broken. When he saw me, he brightened up immediately. "I didn't hear you come in!" he cried happily.

He had not heard me come in. It was the truth. I had found him alone, entirely alone with his grief and regret.

And it was double the pleasure, double the fun, when he realized that this scene had just come naturally, it was a happy accident, it gave the touch of life and truth to his act, it was sincere. He profited handsomely from his own incontestable sincerity. The incident was proof positive. The secretary had gone to lunch and left him unprotected. I had walked in with no appointment. Who could find a flaw in the deep feeling which I had discovered despite the deep feeler's intent to keep it absolutely mum?

During this same sincere period in his life, Philip was using the opportunity to "speak frankly"—to bad-mouth friends, to encourage confidences and then to betray them, immune to reproach. He stalked like the white death in our midst, swaddled in graveclothes, clutching at our sleeves and murmuring, "Hey, I'm dying." We wanted to shake him off like those midtown alcoholics who beg for sympathy in the lounges. But he was not dying on time. The months passed. His friends wanted to say to the sleeve-clutcher, "Aw, go away, will you?"

One day I said to him, *"Don't."*

"Don't what?"

He was spreading silly rumors—oh, silliness—such as something, well, on the order of being mean to my former wife. In fact, that was it. Exactly. Mean to stepwife. Now, what a stupid story! Who would ever do a thing like that? But that was what he said—mean (me?) to that dark lady of my miserable twenties.

Of course, I'd have liked to be meaner than I was. As mean as I managed to be, it barely saved my skin. But he tried to tell people I wasn't nice. And you know what? They believed him.

People are funny about believing what they are told, especially
when the delicious news is coming from someone as credible, as
mortally ill as Philip; and especially if there are some really nasty
tidbits.

"Don't what?" he repeated with great earnest concern.

"Don't voice your opinions as if you know. Don't tell people
you think I'm this and that and wait to have them pick up on it
and then tell me what they say and then tell them how I react—
just *don't,* Philip. Okay, gossip if you have to, but I'd rather you
wouldn't."

"I have no time for small talk, buddy."

"That's not what I'm asking you."

"Wait. You cut the crap at a time like this." He put his hand
on my arm and squeezed it gently. He made my gaze meet his. He
gave me a long look from dark, sad, beautiful, almost girlish
eyes. He squinted them slightly and looked deep into mine. "You
fail to appreciate how this changes a man's life," he said, retreating,
hurt, leaving me to meditate on his soft turning away of my irrita-
tion. He had become a master of the pronoun *this,* a word with
a subject and predicate, a dense clause of unspoken explanations
and commands.

"Okay, Philip," I said, "I don't suppose I should try to educate
you."

"I just try to call the shots how they are," he said. "I've said
and done things in the past, things I regret. Carol. Well, you know.
Now, with what's left to me, *this,* I'm just trying to be as straight
as I know how."

"Okay, Philip, you've explained."

"I want you to understand me, pal, you above all. I've opened
up to you. You've seen the worst. I don't even mean I intended it
that way, that's just how it worked out. You're someone I really
trust and count on."

That's a hard one to answer if it's only the eve of battle, but
when it's leukemia time on old Madison Avenue, this country boy
from Cleveland, Ohio, found he was losing the argument.

"Thank you, fella," he said, "for understanding where I live."

At first it only seemed like giving him his way on script changes because of *this,* but now it was letting him get away with undoing the little world in which we all moved. Digs, jabs, pryings, and do everything he wanted. Finally one six o'clock after a long session of mixed work and philosophy, I yelled at him, "Goddammit, don't! I don't care! I don't care what's happening to you."

"You don't want to say that," he remarked serenely, coming back into his office to hear me out.

"You have no right!"

He pulled the drapes and stood staring into the swollen orange-gray light of the late-afternoon Manhattan sky. Then he turned back to me, huge and spectral in the altered glow of our glass section of the glass tomb.

"Let's discuss a moment," he said happily. "You've brought this up before. I know I've changed, even as to manner. I feel I have a special emergency built in, a sense of crisis, and it gives me an intensity, a certain clarity and directness—"

I walked out.

I didn't see him for several days. Everyone brings confusion for everyone else. He brought too much of it. He left messages for me, but I took off for Easthampton.

Then Sandy called and got through to me. Her voice gave a correct but incorrect message. "He's in the hospital," she said.

"A relapse? What's up?"

"He may die."

"So soon."

Again the confusion. He had crept close in my life, and lent me moments of power. What right had I to judge him?

"Pills," she said. "They pumped his stomach, but I'm not sure . . ."

He recovered. They gave him blood, they kept him in the hospital for a few days, and then they released him, as good and as bad as ever. He had only taken six or seven Seconals. He apologized to everyone individually, including me. It was just an impulse, he said, a silly one, to spare us all the trouble.

"I'm a little foolish and desperate," he said. "I'm sure I'm being a little, ah, extreme, but who is to say what is proper behavior at a time like this?"

"Philip."

"Please forgive me—please? For the sake of old friendship? You once had a good feeling about me. Will you hold on to it, friend? I know I've done some bad things. We were friends. Try to remember, okay? Please?"

Despite all this busy play, it was finally about to happen. Philip's body began its mortal closing down. The rhythm of trips to the hospital, ameliorations, remissions, transfusions, new techniques, interventions, failures, hopes, desperations, was now a familiar matter. Accelerations did not change the pattern. Hope and despair provided a kind of vividness; then the vividness, like an amphetamine, wore out its host. Sandy became a stilled, sick child with a grin like the beginning of tears and a strangled voice reading the packaging of Philip's old habits: "Hiya, fella." She had learned other things from him, too. "I think he's a little better today. You're going in to see him, aren't you?" She uttered her grief and made his demands for him and slid through the day stricken by the smiling horrors.

Their son was invisible. He had disappeared almost as completely as Carol. Well, this was no time for a baby.

For every man there is a last trip to his office. Philip made that final visit, knowing it was final, and walked out without taking his briefcase. He left his appointment book open, three lunches scheduled for next week. He walked with the stiff gait of a sick man under tight control. He told his secretary he would be back after the weekend; she knew he would not be back. He had drawn into his diminished body. The writer would miss his oysters at the Algonquin; the agent would miss his *scampi* at Fontana di Trevi; the expense account had drawn to its end.

I wonder if many men in business put an exact close to the work by which they think to define themselves. Well, nothing is eternal, not even a great tax gimmick, not even a good East Side address. But Philip made no plans for his uncompleted projects.

He left no provisions. He walked out. It was dead to him—the public relations, the TV series, the movie. Someone else could do it; someone else could not do it. He felt nothing for it. Rico might move someone in to try to hatch the eggs, but Philip ceased to fret about it. It was as dead as Carol, and about this retreat from work he was as dry and cold as, it seemed, he hoped to be about his own death. It was no longer what he used to call a plus factor in the daily round.

I came to see him. He was propped in a hospital bed with a lever sticking like a key out of his back. No, there was a thin mattress behind his back, and then the crank. His eyes were burning out of the bluish skin. "They shave me," he said. "I can still shave myself, but this way I have strength left over to waste." He grinned. "I got to figure out what to do with the strength left over from not having to shave myself."

"How are you feeling, Philip?"

"How do you feel when you know the end is near?"

"I don't know," I said.

"You will someday, I trust, fella." As if to soften the malice, he quickly added, "I try to get Sandy to take the towels home from this place. You know what it's costing my estate?"

"I can imagine."

"Oh, boy. Imagine on through."

A nurse was standing in the doorway. "It's time," she said.

"A treat or a treatment?"

"Mr. Grove, it's time now."

He grinned at me and said, "You mind waiting? I'd like to talk to someone when I get back."

"What are they going to do to you?"

"Stick needles. In the veins, that's okay. In the bone to get at the marrow, that hurts. Would you wait? Do you mind waiting?"

The attendants wheeled him out. I waited. He didn't go far. There was an adjacent laboratory. I could hear a distant creaking through the walls, Philip howling with pain, and then abruptly nothing. I was soaked in my clothes when he returned. He looked stunned and goofy. His pajama top was unbuttoned. His chest was covered with unhealed needle marks—deep scars and lesions. He was panting, but quiet. He tried to button one button of his pajamas, but his hand fell away, exhausted. I thought maybe he wanted to sleep.

"No, don't go."

I waited.

He said, "What do you do when you *know?*"

I couldn't answer yet.

"They keep making experiments, I think. Pieces of marrow they drag out. I don't heal any more, either—the skin—not that it matters. All for sweet research. I'm happy to stop healing."

I had nothing to say.

"Relax and enjoy it, I guess," he said.

The nurse came in with two pills. She held them to his mouth, a glass of water in her other hand. She was a black girl with good country looks, a prim intelligent face, an opulent intelligent body in the rustling uniform. He shook his head to the pills and took them in his hand. "My friend'll give me the water," he said. I took the glass. His hand closed tightly over the pills. "Stay and talk . . ." He meant me. "No, you can go, nurse. Thank you."

I had nothing to say, but I said it: "That must be painful."

"I'm sorry if it bothers you, pal. I found these tears in a test tube. The doctor gave me the sample, and I sprinkle them everywhere. It's convenient. Too bad I didn't have them when Carol died." He closed his eyes. "You're right," he said at last, "relax and enjoy it."

"I didn't say it. You said it."

"I thought you said it."

"*You* said it."

"Am I getting confused? Now, there's a nasty."

He was stretching and wiggling, and the sweat kept starting on his upper lip. He wiped it with his sleeve. I stifled my panic. "Can't they give you something for the pain?"

"Yes, of course, they did."

"Why are you suffering so?"

He opened his fist. The pills were soggy and crumbled. "I didn't want to get dopey. I wanted to talk to you first, before I take them."

"Take them!" I said.

He shrugged and put them in his mouth. I held the glass to his lips. He drank.

Yes, I wanted to turn away. It's not so easy! I wanted to take all the opportunities he gave me to trim the recognition of decay and death with disgust at a performance. I assured myself that his refusal to complain of pain, to confess his mortal fear, was just another matter of style; he knew it would capture me; it was the unspoken in art, the hidden dream of time in a melody, an esthetic trick like his other tricks. But no, his discretion was real, I think —the foundation of style and comeliness within all his cunning chic. He tried not to frighten me with his body so that he could teach me something with his soul. His selfishness may have been very deep, as his style was most pervasive. But his intention was also to make me learn from him. I could complain and strike back. I couldn't follow my itch to flee. I couldn't be honest and impulsive that way. I couldn't simply walk out on him. How nice it would be to withdraw to criticism. He gave me grounds. I had to follow my yearning in another way.

"Thank you very much," Philip said.

"For what?" I saw the bottle of sedatives by his bed and remembered what the doctor had said: "I give them the pills and let them make the choice. I warn them: 'Too many and you sleep forever.' But they just wait, usually until they have no choice. Stubborn—most men are stubborn."

"For entertaining Sandy, I mean taking her to the movies, talking to her—I mean everything, friend."

"Nonsense."

"Please try to be a little more gracious when I'm being grateful, pal."

My own history with him is not very pretty—a history of falling in with his schemes, taking his money (never as much as I expected), letting the con give me coffee nerves, and then walking out with cold parting shots and angry resolutions. Well, I couldn't just walk out on him any more. He was in the thick of battle. He—not his words, not even his deeds, but Philip himself, the person hidden beyond all tricks—was telling a part of the truth, like all men, and more of the truth than many. Good-bye to the con. He was suffering. I learned some sour facts about myself from him; that's familiar enough in these days of prideful self-examination and self-laceration; but what was more common, traditional, and yet surprising, I was learning something about him. He struggled for control; he sought to master himself. He no longer thought of killing himself. The rest of life was precious to him, and not merely something he could use. He smiled handsomely, histrionically, and yet he was truly brave in his way.

The disease was marching through his body, consolidating its gains around his organs, receding, sending out marauding scouts, voraciously living off the country, blood, lymph, liver, spleen. First he felt weakness and dizziness, like a rapid elevator to earth, then seasickness and landsickness; remissions, illusions; then pain to breathe, pain around the heart, his body poisoning itself, drowning in its own fluids. This animal suffering he did not include in his public performance. He did not know how to use it; yet he was suffering atrociously. The horror of inexorable, irreversible pain is a great incitement to drama. He refused it. He suffered and left the suffering apart, as if it were the last holy object in his life.

His lungs filled with fluids. The doctors were making taps, inserting drains. They strapped him up like a sick tree and drew interesting substances from the trunk. "Did I tell you I was raised in Vermont?" he asked me. "Maple-syrup time again. Listen, we learned to say very little in Brattleboro, we learned to hide, and when I got garrulous those years in New York—"

"New York'll do that to you."

"I know. That's what I wanted. I never got good enough at it, was what I'm getting at . . ."

He was in torment, and reconciled to the fact that this time he could not pass it on as gossip or conniving. Could there have been some joy in giving up the mission of promoter, of user? No, but relief at defining the area of no copout. Something. Anything. There must have been, I pray there was, some brain flash of discovery and relief. This was not borrowed pain, picked up on the free-lance market. It was his own, his personal creation, he had world rights to it. Once, or sometimes, or steadily through the new and terrible routines of his nights and days, he must have received the message, he must have gotten through to himself. Oh, surely he would have agreed to do without in return for ease, but it was offered anyway—that brain flash, that ebb of sea over the meshed debris of depths, that withdrawal, clarity, and renewed confusion. An accurate, silent, perfect recognition of himself! And still rich in confusions.

He had stopped leaving his room. The transfusions were no longer perking him up; his body said no to the cortisone and mustard and cell suppressants; the organs, the whole system was disoriented.

Now what? How long?

Last week propped lightly in a chair with book and glasses; sometimes shaving himself, sometimes dressed.

Now wearing pajamas and shaved by his wife or a nurse, saving the strength for sitting and talk. It was too much trouble to turn face and lift chin. He should let the gray-mottled beard grow.

"I'm going to sleep," he said. "Wait. Wait a sec." He was working something out, his lips moving, racing the pills in his blood. He smiled as if it were a game. He nodded. He had found what he was looking for. "I'm carrying it by myself for the rest of the way— ah, that's nonsense. Forget it. I'm sorry."

"For what? It's unnecessary."

Behind drugs and coming in after drugs and without drugs at all, in the spaces wrought by disaster, he was finally exploring a territory which was his alone, bordered entirely by Philip, traversed solely by Philip, private beyond any despair or consolation.

"It's soon now," he said.

"Might be."

"First I'll sleep."

"That's fine."

"I'm finished promoting my last asset," he said.

"Shush, Philip."

The panic had left me. I too was calmed, as if for the first time Philip was present in the room with me. The games were done and there was no more advantage.

"There was something I wanted to say before I got confused by one thing or another, but that wasn't it—the romance of my little situation. Not that. Oh, not that, buddy."

"No hurry, Philip."

"Yes, hurry, pal." He winked. "Didn't I do some bad things to you? I seem to remember. I can't remember."

At the last minute, I was thinking, death might come to him as the friend he had always sought, or another enemy, or as an ecstasy of distraction; or merely as a new campaign and project— there was no reason to expect more of death than of life.

"Didn't I?" he asked anxiously. "Bad-mouth you one time? Put you on?"

"Never mind, Philip."

No, none of these. It would slip over him as it slips over animals and men—a diminution, a withdrawal and an acceptance. He would be here like other men and then he would be gone.

"It was someone else then."

"Forget it."

"No, it was you *and* someone else. Plus a lot of others."

"I said forget it."

He shut his eyes. "Next year at this time I'll be a better person," he said. "You wait. This same time next year." There was an almost girlish, peaceful look on his face—eyes closed and mouth in a sensual, smiling pout.

I sat there, watching him, trying for my own sake to try to carry something away with me; and for his sake, too. Despite the drugs and vanity, the money and power and the cleverness, the common paraphernalia of hospitals and the special vaults of Philip's character, his body and soul were falling from him just as other men's do, and I had to meet my own abiding distrust of him in coming to see that he had a soul like other men's, like mine; and he did the best he could for his daughter and his wife, and if it wasn't enough to suit me, it was still all he could do; and finally he held the monster close, as every man one day must.

He seemed to be asleep. I tiptoed out.

"Bye-bye," he said. "Take care, fella."

I looked back, but his eyes were shut and I suppose he was sleeping.

DONALD BARTHELME was born in Philadelphia in 1931, raised in Texas and now lives in New York City. His books include *Come Back, Dr. Caligari; Snow White; Unspeakable Practices, Unnatural Acts,* and *City Life.*

SUBPOENA

AND now in the mail a small white Subpoena from the Bureau of Compliance, Citizen Bergman there, he wants me to comply. *We command you that, all business and excuses being laid aside, you and each of you appear and attend . . .* The "We command you" in boldface, and a shiny red seal in the lower left corner. To get my attention.

I thought I had complied. I comply every year, sometimes oftener than necessary. Look at the record. Spotless list of compliances dating back to '48, when I was a pup. What can he mean, this Bergman, finding a freckle on my clean sheet?

I appeared and attended. Attempted to be reasonable. "Look here Bergman what is this business." Read him an essay I'd written about how the State should not muck about in the affairs of its vassals overmuch. Citizen Bergman unamused.

"It appears that you are the owner or proprietor perhaps of a monster going under the name of Charles Evans Hughes?"

"Yes but what has that to do with—"

"Said monster inhabiting quarters at 12 Tryst Lane?"

"That is correct."

"This monster being of humanoid appearance and characteristics, including ability to locomote, production of speech of a kind, ingestion of viands, and traffic with other beings?"

"Well, 'traffic' is hardly the word. Simple commands he can cope with. Nothing fancy. Sit. Eat. Speak. Roll over. Beg. That sort of thing."

"This monster being employed by you in the capacity, friend?"

"Well, employed is not quite right."

"He is remunerated is he not?"

"The odd bit of pocket money."

"On a regular basis."

"See here Bergman it's an allowance. For little things he needs. Cigarettes and handkerchiefs and the like. Nose drops."

"He is nevertheless in receipt of sums of money from you on a regular basis?"

"*He is forty-four per cent metal, Officer.*"

"The metal content of said monster does not interest the Bureau. What we are interested in is compliance."

"Wherein have I failed to comply?"

"You have not submitted Form 244 which governs paid companionship, including liaisons with prostitutes and pushing of wheelchairs by hired orderlies not provided by the Bureau of Perpetual Help. You have also failed to remit the Paid Companionship Tax which amounts to one hundred twenty-two per cent of all moneys changing hands in any direction."

"One hundred twenty-two per cent!"

"That is the figure. There is also a penalty for noncompliance. The penalty is two hundred twelve per cent of one hundred twenty-two per cent of five dollars a week figured over five years, which I believe is the period at issue."

"What about depreciation?"

"Depreciation is not figurable in the case of monsters."

I went home feeling less than sunny.

He had a knowing look that I'd painted myself. One corner of the mouth curled upward and the other downward, when he smiled. There was no grave-robbing or anything of that sort. Plastic and metal did very nicely. You can get the most amazing things in drugstores. Fingernails and eyelashes and such. The actual construction was a matter of weeks. I considered sending the plans to *Popular Mechanics*. So everyone could have one.

He was calm—calm as a hat. Whereas I was nervous as a strobe light, had the shakes, Valium in the morning and J & B beginning at two o'clock in the afternoon.

Everything was all right with him.

"Crushed in an elevator at the welfare hotel!" someone would say.

"It's a very serious problem," Charles would answer.

When I opened the door, he was sitting in the rocking chair reading *Life*.

"Charles," I said, "they've found out."

"Seventy-seven per cent of American high-school students declare that religion is important to them, according to a recent Louis Harris poll," Charles said, rocking gently.

"Charles," I said, "they want money. The Paid Companionship Tax. It's two hundred twelve per cent of one hundred twenty-two per cent of five dollars a week figured over five years, plus of course the basic one hundred twenty-two per cent."

"That's a lot of money," Charles said, smiling. "A pretty penny."

"I can't pay," I said. "It's too much."

"Well," he said, both smiling and rocking, "fine. What are you going to do?"

"Disassemble," I said.

"Interesting," he said, hitching his chair closer to mine, to demonstrate interest. "Where will you begin?"

"With the head, I suppose."

"Wonderful," Charles said. "You'll need the screwdriver, the pliers, and the Skil saw. I'll fetch them."

He got up to go to the basement. A thought struck him. "Who will take out the garbage?" he asked.

"Me. I'll take it out myself."

He smiled. One corner of his mouth turned upward and the other downward. "Well," he said, "right on."

I called him my friend and thought of him as my friend. In fact I kept him to instruct me in complacency. He sat there, the perfect noncombatant. He ate and drank and slept and awoke and did not change the world. Looking at him I said to myself, "See, it is possible to live in the world and not change the world." He read the newspapers and watched television and heard in the night screams under windows thank God not ours but down the block a bit, and did nothing. Without Charles, without his example, his exemplary quietude, I run the risk of acting, the risk of risk. I must leave the house and walk about.

MAGAZINES CONSULTED

Ann Arbor Review—115 Allen Drive, Ann Arbor, Mich. 48103

Antioch Review—212 Xenia Avenue, Yellow Springs, Ohio 45387

Aphra—Box 3551, Springtown, Penn. 18081

Aphrax—4 Jones Street, New York, N.Y. 10014

Ararat—Armenian General Benevolent Union of America, 109 East 40th Street, New York, N.Y. 10016

Arizona Quarterly—University of Arizona, Tucson, Ariz. 85721

Arx—12109 Bell Ave., Austin, Texas 78759

The Atlantic Monthly—8 Arlington Street, Boston, Mass. 02116

Audience—241½ 32 St., New York, N.Y. 10016

Ave Maria—National Catholic Weekly, Congregation of Holy Cross, Notre Dame, Ind. 46556

Carleton Miscellany—Carleton College, Northfield, Minn. 55057

Carolina Quarterly—Box 1117, Chapel Hill, N.C. 27515

Chelsea—Box 242, Old Chelsea Station, New York, N.Y. 10011

Chicago Review—University of Chicago, Chicago, Ill. 60637

Colorado Quarterly—Hellums 118, University of Colorado, Boulder, Colo. 80304

The Colorado State Review—360 Liberal Arts, Colorado State University, Fort Collins, Colo. 80521

Commentary—165 East 56th Street, New York, N.Y. 10022

Cosmopolitan—1775 Broadway, New York, N.Y. 10019

The Critic—180 N. Wabash Avenue, Chicago, Ill. 60601

December—P.O. Box 274, Western Springs, Ill. 60558

The Denver Quarterly—Denver, Colo. 80210

Descant—Dept. of English, TCU Station, Fort Worth, Tex. 76129

Epoch—159 Goldwin Smith Hall, Cornell University, Ithaca, N.Y. 14850

Esprit—University of Scranton, Scranton, Pa. 18510

Esquire—488 Madison Avenue, New York, N.Y. 10022

Evergreen Review—64 University Place, New York, N.Y. 10003

Fantasy and Science Fiction—347 East 53rd Street, New York, N.Y. 10022

The Fiddlehead—Dept. of English, Univ. of New Brunswick, Fredericton, N.B. Canada

Forum—University of Houston, Houston, Tex. 77004

Four Quarters—La Salle College, Philadelphia, Pa. 19141

Generation, the Inter-arts Magazine—University of Michigan, 420 Maynard, Ann Arbor, Mich. 48103

Georgia Review—University of Georgia, Athens, Ga. 30601

Good Housekeeping—959 Eighth Avenue, New York, N.Y. 10019

Green River Review—Box 594, Owensboro, Ky. 42301

The Greensboro Review—University of North Carolina, Greensboro, N.C. 27412

Harper's Bazaar—572 Madison Avenue, New York, N.Y. 10022

Harper's—2 Park Avenue, New York, N.Y. 10016

Hudson Review—65 East 55th Street, New York, N.Y. 10022

Intro—Bantam Books, Inc., 271 Madison Avenue, New York, N.Y. 10016

The Iowa Review—EPB 453, University of Iowa, Iowa City, Iowa 52240

Kansas Quarterly—Dept. of English, Kansas State University, Manhattan, Kans. 66502

Ladies' Home Journal—641 Lexington Avenue, New York, N.Y. 10022

Lamb Rags—English Dept., Wayne State University, Detroit, Michigan 48202

The Laurel Review—West Virginia Wesleyan College, Buckhannon, W. Va. 26201

Lillabulero—Krums Corners Rd., R.D. 3, Ithaca, N.Y. 14850

The Literary Review—Fairleigh Dickinson University, Teaneck, N.J. 07666

The Little Magazine—P.O. Box 207, Cathedral Station, New York, N.Y. 10025

Mademoiselle—420 Lexington Avenue, New York, N.Y. 10022

Malahat Review—University of Victoria, British Columbia, Canada

The Massachusetts Review—University of Massachusetts, Amherst, Mass. 01003

McCall's—230 Park Avenue, New York, N.Y. 10017

Midstream—515 Park Avenue, New York, N.Y. 10022

The Minnesota Review—Box 4068, University Station, Minneapolis, Minn. 55455

Mundus Artium—Dept. of English, Ellis Hall, Box 89, Ohio University, Athens, Ohio 45701

New American Review—Simon & Schuster, 630 Fifth Ave., New York, N.Y. 10026

The New Mexico Quarterly—University of New Mexico Press, Marron Hall, Albuquerque, N. Mex. 87106

The New Renaissance—9 Heath Road, Arlington, Mass. 02174

The New Yorker—25 West 43rd Street, New York, N.Y. 10036

North American Review—University of Northern Iowa, Cedar Falls, Iowa 50613

Northwest Review—129 French Hall, University of Oregon, Eugene, Ore. 97403

Panache—153 East 84th Street, New York, N.Y. 10028

The Paris Review—45-39, 171 Place, Flushing, N.Y. 11358

Partisan Review—Rutgers University, New Brunswick, N.J. 08903

Perspective—Washington University, St. Louis, Mo. 63105

Phylon—223 Chestnut Street, S.W., Atlanta, Ga. 30314

Playboy—232 East Ohio Street, Chicago, Ill. 60611

Prairie Schooner—Andrews Hall, University of Nebraska, Lincoln, Nebr. 68508

Quarterly Review of Literature—26 Haslet Avenue, Princeton, N.J. 08540

Quartet—186 Ridge Road, Utica, N.Y. 13501

Ramparts—1182 Chestnut Street, Menlo Park, Calif. 94027

Redbook—230 Park Avenue, New York, N.Y. 10017

Red Clay Reader—6366 Sharon Hills Road, Charlotte, N.C. 28210

Shenandoah—Box 722, Lexington, Va. 24450

The Sewanee Review—University of the South, Sewanee, Tenn. 37375

The South Carolina Review—Dept. of English, Box 28661, Furman University, Greenville, S.C. 29613

The South Dakota Review—University of South Dakota, Vermilion, S.D. 57069

Southern Review—Drawer D, University Station, Baton Rouge, La. 70803

Southwest Review—Southern Methodist University Press, Dallas, Tex. 75222

The Tamarack Review—Box 159, Postal Station K, Toronto, Ontario, Canada

The Texas Quarterly—Box 7527, University of Texas, Austin, Tex. 78712

Trace—P.O. Box 1068, Hollywood, Calif. 90028 (Discontinued)

Transatlantic Review—Box 3348, Grand Central P.O., New York, N.Y. 10017

Tri-Quarterly—University Hall 101, Northwestern University, Evanston, Ill. 60201

The University Review—University of Kansas City, 51 Street & Rockhill Road, Kansas City, Mo. 64110

Vagabond—66 Dorland (roof), San Francisco, Calif. 94110

The Virginia Quarterly Review—University of Virginia, 1 West Range, Charlottesville, Va. 22903

Vogue—420 Lexington Avenue, New York, N.Y. 10017

Washington Square Review—New York University, 737 East Bldg., New York, N.Y. 10003

Western Humanities Review—Bldg. 41, University of Utah, Salt Lake City, Utah 84112

Woman's Day—67 West 44th Street, New York, N.Y. 10036

Yale Review—26 Hillhouse Avenue, New Haven, Conn. 06520